Cemetery Cove

old skipjack

Sandbar

"The Island"

Mr. Russell's Boatyard

Town Ramp

Leo's Place

Lapshok Dock

The Country Club

Miss Ginny's Boatyard

The Ferry

Walking Path

Mr. Paul

Edison Garden

Garbage Alley

Mr. Tawes

Miss Ginny's Empty Lot

Edison's Shed

The Wharf

Old Inn

Miss Hattie's

Kate's House

Customs House

Yacht Club

Tessie's House

Sunset Beach

Old Inn

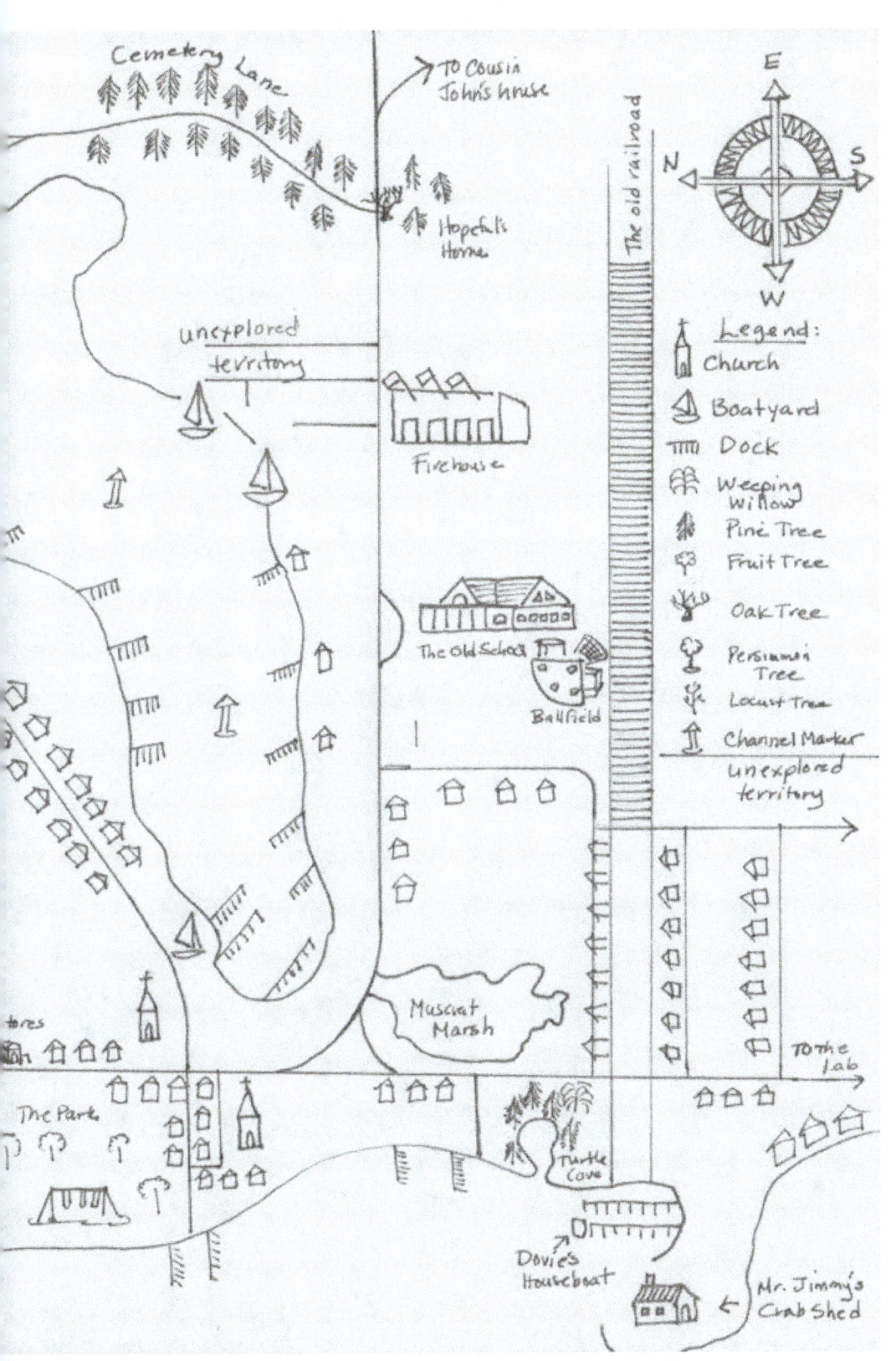

Anchors

ISBN 978-1-62806-462-9 (print | paperback)
ISBN 978-1-62806-463-6 (print | hardback)
ISBN 978-1-62806-464-3 (ebook)

Library of Congress Control Number 2025916846

Published by Salt Water Media
29 Broad Street, Suite 104
Berlin, MD 21811
www.saltwatermedia.com

Cover artwork by Patti Lucas Hopkins

Interior pencil illustrations by Shelby Clendaniel
Illustration of box turtle by Peter Hanks

Anchors

Cathy Schmidt

To the angels of old Oxford.
I love you all.

Contents

Chapter I

— Freedom —

It seemed just minutes prior that spring had arrived. Kate's feet, guarded by woolen socks and sturdy shoes for half the year, welcomed the warm sun. Feet, tender at the onset of summer weather and waters, hardened with each warm day. Now that the river had lost its winter sting and the oysters could rest, the brackish air beckoned children away from their schoolbooks. Summer wind whispering in ears, calls and calls and calls; relentless as it is haunting, no one was able to ignore the lure, the calling of a river awakening.

The salty river air filled every corner of the classroom, pushing school out of Kate's mind. Gazing out the window she let out a deep mournful sigh. Summer had arrived and Kate could hardly resist the pull. As such she slid, twitched and itched in her school chair.

"Kate!" her teacher centered upon her. "Sit still!"

"Can't," she replied, although to the teacher it seemed flippant, she didn't intend it to be; she simply couldn't contain the season's gravitational pull.

"Can't?" The teacher walked closer to Kate, challenging her answer with hands on hips, lips pursed, and eyes focused intently on the wiggly child.

"I'm sorry, Miss Smith, but I can't help it."

"And why is that?"

"Summer's calling, and it's out there." She pointed to the open window. "And I'm in here."

Miss Smith was stern, well respected, and on occasion, known to have a heart. She looked around at the other students whose eyes seemed wider and more innocent than normal. She closed her eyes and breathed deeply. The briny essence that permeated the classroom transported her back to her own childhood. Acutely aware that all her students were focused on her, she let out a big sigh and opened her eyes. Knowing it was the last day of school, she abruptly announced that there would be outdoor recess until the end of the day. The schoolroom erupted in rapturous cheers.

"Line up!" Miss Smith ordered.

Quickly, they filed in line, and she set them free to run. As the afternoon wore on, nothing could tame their energy. When school finally let out, and all the desks had been emptied into backpacks and satchels, Miss Smith collapsed in her desk chair, leaned back, and stared at the ceiling. She was perfectly exhausted by fifth-grade energy. After a few minutes, she found herself caught up in uncontrollable giddiness. The boisterousness of the day had challenged her prim composure. Once she settled herself into a relaxed smile, she began thinking about her own summer plans.

⚓ ⚓ ⚓

KATE'S BUS RIDE WAS SHORT. The bus took the students from the new school and dropped them at the old dilapidated school that had been closed a few years back. One bus easily held all the water town kids with just a little room to spare. The young riders were overflowing with irrepressible joy, and had begun their infectious summer melee. The driver, well seasoned, knew she needed to change her temperament to survive the ride home.

Miss Barbara generally ran a tight ship, but today she ignored everything she saw in her rearview mirror. When the bus pulled into the circular driveway and stopped, she stood up and turned towards her passengers and wished them the most adventurous of summers. Then, as anticipated, she popped open a large cooler filled with ice and sodas. This was a tradition, and everyone, thirsty to the core, thanked and hugged Miss Barbara. They thoughtfully picked their pleasure from the cooler as they left the bus. Kate gave Miss Barbara a side hug and reached for a root beer. The boy behind her took an orange soda and shook Miss Barbara's hand.

"Thank you, Miss Barbara, and you have a nice summer too!" he said reverently.

Miss Barbara blushed and patted him on the back as he skipped down the steps. When the last child had cheerfully departed, Miss Barbara collapsed into her seat and gazed at the old school she had attended. Showing its age with cracked windows and peeling paint, it looked lonely and forgotten. The new school was a much bigger building, one that could hold the children from two towns instead of one. The county called it progress, but Miss Barbara thought it a shame the town school had closed. After a few minutes of quiet, she leaned forward and picked up an ice-cold can of 7-Up. Sipping and smiling she turned the key for the ride back.

⚓ ⚓ ⚓

THE WALK HOME WAS A talkative one while they sipped on their sodas. Kimmy and Angel, sisters who lived just a few streets away from Kate, walked together with her every day to and from the bus stop. When they reached Truman's Store, Kate reached into her pocket and pulled out fifteen cents.

"You guys want something?"

Angel and Kimmy laughed at her even posing the question as they opened the door. It was busy today with it being the first day of summer and the line to the counter was long. The girls chatted while they waited for Miss Mabel to take care of the kids in front.

"What are you guys doing this summer?" Kate asked the sisters.

"Don't know," replied Kimmy. "Odd jobs in the neighborhood, I guess."

"I don't know what I'm doing at all," said Kate.

When they reached the counter, Kate got an Atomic Fireball, Angel got a Tootsie Roll, and Kimmy, a Mary Jane. They thanked Kate with their mouths full and Kate waved goodbye as the sisters turned right towards their home a block away. Kate's house was not very far from Truman's Store. She lived on Main Street, but sometimes it was called Front Street; it just depended upon who you talked to. She kept straight on Main Street.

⚓ ⚓ ⚓

UNPRETENTIOUS THEY STOOD, HOUSES LARGELY indistinct from each other, save for the inhabitants and apparitions inside. Intermittently of the pervasive whitewash, a dull yellow or shallow grey covered the wooden siding. Either way, the town seemed to have missed the Victorian age altogether, as its homes looked to be built before and after but certainly nothing with any frippery in between.

The absence of flourish might have marked a downturn in economy except that the surge of construction in the late 1800s had little to show for the garish style of the times. In an age where one might distinguish themselves on the block with finials and ornate gables, it appeared no one had the means to oblige the conventions of that time. Instead practicality, simplicity, and economy guided construction.

Situated on very long lean lots, many properties stretched all the way to the river with room for vegetable gardens, sheds, and shoeless children to play. In low-lying areas, rivulets would visit twice a day, beginning with a slow trickle and quietly swelling in size to form small streams for crabs and minnows to visit the land. These wisps of water retreated as quickly as they arrived and took the sea creatures with them. On nights of the fullest moons, tiny minnows would shine and shimmy up the wide ditches as if talking to the lightning bugs. Flashes back and forth, back and forth the glimmers, a code between friends.

Kate's house stood nondescript in the center of town and blended with the landscape so well as to be unnoticeable. The fence was just like any other made of white cedar boards with flaking white paint, veined with moss. Boxwoods had overtaken the front yard, so plentiful that only a small path wove through them, worn away by 100 years of family dogs' daily routine. Within these walls lived a grandmother, a mother, a father, two children, and most recently, a wayward cousin named Lowell. All the women bore the last or middle name of Seth; with this tradition, the females could carry the family name on in some way. Known by townsfolk as the "Seth House," the house that was built by Kate's great-great uncles, had only ever known one family. As such, a few friendly "ancestors" stuck around to look after the newer generations.

Surrounded by plain houses, it was in Kate's estimation that the only thing that made one person different from another in town were their skills and disposition and perhaps their gardens; everything else felt parallel. One might be distinguished by their occupation, the trees on their properties or their kindness much more than their Front Street facade.

With no street numbers and many street names not permanently fixed with a sign, people and places were described as "…you know, the artist that lives in the house with all the blue hydrangeas." Or, "… Miss Gale's place, the house on the corner with the lilacs that smell so good; she finds homes for stray cats. Her husband, Mr. Jimmy, works the water." More commonly, the description of a person had nothing to do with the individual themselves, but instead lineage was used as a descriptor. Mind you, lineage had nothing to do with status but was more the pride of knowing the genealogy. Such as: "Miss Alma, the deaf seamstress is your great grandfather's brother's child." (or another cousin).

This working man's town nestled on the Chesapeake Bay peninsula was filled with people who went day by day immersed in honest work. They dealt with their troubles as they came up as best they could in the ways they knew how. Generational inhabitants had learned their coping mechanisms from their parents, grandparents, and great-grandparents. And truly, these social coping devices absorbed throughout the generations had helped the inhabitants weather the ever-shifting winds of life.

Work harder, pray more, love thy neighbor, and at the same time, an eye for an eye. If recompense was due, assuredly, the parties involved would know. These social strictures that played out amongst the adults were done so with few words. A shift of an eye or a turn of the head communicated enough. Unspoken language said more than words ever could. The tacit undercurrent was strong, and the youngest learned quickly how to mark an ebb or flood tide.

Kate lifted the gate latch that had been fashioned by Poppy out of an old brass scale beam. Poppy, Kate's great-grandfather, long since passed, had left his marks of cleverness throughout the house and yard. Kate was instantly greeted by River, the family's lovable mutt, and she dropped her backpack and rubbed the dog all over. He was still losing his winter coat and his brown and white fur floated up into the air.

"Hey boy, what's happening? You know I can play with you more now that it's summer!" He wagged his tail as if he knew exactly what she was saying. She lugged her backpack through the door and tossed it in the corner by the front steps. The rest of the day she spent basking in the glow of that just out-of-school freedom that excites the hearts of all children when summer is brand new…

⚓ ⚓ ⚓

ON HER FIRST FULL DAY of summer, Kate was joined at breakfast on the screened back porch by her mother, Mary, and Mary alone. When she jumped out of bed for breakfast, she had been enthusiastic about her prospects, but now she sensed that perhaps a dreadful conversation was about to happen. Meals in the Seth house were group events as it was customary for family to work together on projects, eat together, play together, and pray together. To be singled out by a parent was to surely be reprimanded or informed of something very important. So when Kate was joined at the breakfast table on the back porch by her mother while everyone else had scattered, she did not eat her breakfast with her usual zeal. Kate waited cautiously, lingering over her buttered grits. Mary slid onto the opposite bench with a cup of tea in hand. Kate put her spoon down and readied herself.

"Kate, I want to talk to you about the town," she said matter of factly. "There are some things you should know."

Kate looked up from her grits. This wasn't a reprimand; this was something else altogether.

"Most people in town are good folks, but there are a few people you may come across this summer that I want you to be aware of."

Kate was attentive as her mother spoke, scarcely taking a breath.

"First off, don't mind Beezy. I know you've seen him around; he talks to himself and telephone poles, but he's harmless. He doesn't notice people too much, but sometimes he'll say a word or two. He's been this way since he was a young man, when his drinking got ahold of him. Now he is an old man and never harmed anyone."

"Secondly, the men at the Country Club are drinkers and like to heckle people. Just wave and keep on your way, and that will be fine."

"Thirdly, and most importantly, you must know about the Tuffin boy. His family lives at the other end of town, on the corner near Miss Alma, the seamstress. The yard is littered with trash, and there are holes in the siding. He is deaf in one ear because his father beat him in the head when he was four. The whole family is bad news. The Tuffin boy is your age and you are not to play with him or go near his house. He's near about the only redhead in town; that's how you'll know him."

"Do you have any questions?"

Kate was trying to process all the information and paused a moment before she said, "I don't think so…"

"Okay then, it is settled." Mary got up and headed back into the kitchen.

Kate wondered why she was told all of this, shrugged her shoulders and finished her lukewarm grits. Placing her empty bowl into the kitchen sink, Kate headed through the porch and out the back door to see what her father was up to. Mother had hung the laundry out early on the weathered clothesline that stretched from the corner post of the back porch all the way to the corner of Edison's shed. The strong morning sun and light breezes would make the clothes dry by noon; meaning two washes could be hung today.

Stepping off the back porch was like being at the beginning of a maze. She navigated it well and the grassy path she chose eventually took her to Edison's outdoor workbench. Kate stood by the rough workhorses made from old pine and topped with two wide, thick oak boards. They were decorated by stain, paint, and varnish, the under shelves piled with sawdust and mixed with scatters of assorted nails and screws. She peered into Edison's shed.

The knots in the long boards bled a dark stain through the weathered white paint as if announcing they would not go unnoticed. His slanted shanty anchored the far right corner of the yard. Edison said it tilted under the weight of all his tools.

He was busy looking for something, so she thought it best to leave him alone. She skipped over to the sunken claw-foot bathtub that made for a small but deep goldfish pond that everyone had fallen into at some point. Behind her, piles of wood in all different shapes and sizes, "sure to be made useful for something," lay in neat stacks against the fence. Poppy was the one who had dropped the cast iron claw foot bathtub into 2-foot hole it sat in. Kate perched herself on the edge and looked around for the goldfish.

Kate's father finally came out of the woodshed with a handsaw and started cutting a board. Edison was what he was called, but his birth name was Edward. A carpenter, general Mr. Fix It, and tinkerer, Kate's father grew up in the next town over and started dating Mary at 19. They met at a tractor pull near the ice cream truck and married at 21. The only thing Edison brought to his marriage was a cigarette habit and a beat-up brown Chevy pickup. The bed was just a few rainfalls from rusting through, so a warped piece of raggedy-edged plywood lined it. The rust and the paint blended together to make the truck a color that would never need washing.

Edison's father was an abusive drunk. Edison grew up rough, poor, and longing for a better life. Not only did he love Mary, but deferred to her on almost all matters of consequence. She changed his trajectory and without saying so - in joining Mary's family, he could easily let go of his own.

Quiet and resourceful, he was not very social. Although he was always "around" he was often in his own space, figuring out a better way to make or fix something. His sudden moody spells were usually followed by a kind gesture like picking Mary flowers; what he couldn't say with words, he said with actions. Although good with numbers, it was Mary who kept the books as he was too occupied with work to have the patience for it. With being one of a half dozen independent carpenters in town, work kept him busy as all the other handymen were generally employed by one of the boatyards or worked the water.

Perched beside the little pond, Kate had named all the goldfish and the resident frog. Herman, a common green frog, liked to hide under an old broken clay pot nearby that Kate had repurposed for him. He jumped in for swims often to lay in wait just under the surface for mosquitoes, water striders, and dragonflies. Fat and happy, the banjo sounds he plucked made Kate giggle.

"Herman, how are you today?"

He answered with a plop, and then a few seconds later, his tiny eyes appeared under the edge of a lily pad. Kate noticed the bud heads were rising through the muck and it would be just a few days before the yellow Lily flowers would bloom. They were right on time. Excited by this, she jumped up, flinging her arms in the air and proclaimed, "It's summer!"

"Yes," said Edison, standing at his workhorses, turning his head towards her. "What are your plans?"

Kate hadn't really thought much about it. She wanted to run, she wanted to ride her bike, she wanted to play down by the river, she wanted to crab and fish and swim and see her friends and pick vegetables from the garden. Overwhelmed by the question, she went over to the matriarchal dogwood tree across from her father's work area and crawled under the weathered wooden sailboat that sat upside down on two rickety saw horses.

"Kate? What are you doing under there?" Edison asked.

"Making plans," she replied, but that was a falsehood. She was just catching her breath. Overcome with the prospects of summer, she felt electrified and affected. So there she sat for a time, counting all the dandelions she could see from under the boat until she could breathe normally again.

Just then, along came Tansy on her bike, fast breaking just inches before hitting the fence, and grazing her elbow on its gaps, some paint flakes falling to the ground. "Hi Mr. Edison, where's Kate?"

Kate heard her and crawled out from under the boat renewed. She threw up her arms, "Right here!"

"Kate, let's go to the docks and feed the ducks."

"I'll ask Mother," Kate said as she headed towards the house.

"Hold up," said Edison, "Did Mother talk to you this morning about what to look out for in town?"

Kate thought back to her conversation over the buttery grits. "Yes…"

"Then you may go. Just be back by supper, by that, are we clear?" Kate was halfway to her bicycle under the lean-to when he finished his sentence. "Kate, look at me."

She turned towards her father. "By the six o'clock church bells."

She faced him straight on, "Yes, Father." With that, she and Tansy were off to the docks.

⚓ ⚓ ⚓

A PLASTIC BREAD SLEEVE WITH several butt ends of stale bread and a dried-out corn muffin was tied to Tansy's handlebars. It was high enough not to bump against the spokes of her tires. They turned left at the end of the back street and right again onto Main at the corner where Miss Hattie's shop was. Her storefront, shaded by a tin roof stretching over the wide sidewalk, made a shady place to display her wares. The wide wrought iron 10-gallon pot in the center of the sidewalk was always filled with deep red geraniums in season. T-shirts, pants, brooms, and iron wares hung from the rungs of her metal roof frame; the pants fluttered in the breeze. Her well-worn captain's chair sat outside the ornate French doors with peeling paint. Like decor from a play that ended 50 years ago, these items for sale were advertisements for the real adventure that lay inside.

Kate waved at Cousin Tessie, who had a straw hat adorning her head and a bright red outfit as she pulled weeds. The girls glimpsed at the water; no white caps today. The wharf was a busy place; there was almost always a casual crabber on the pier, and when the tide came in the oldest men in town would appear with rod and tackle in one hand and an aluminum lawn chair in the other. It was rarely quiet at the wharf.

The ferry boat that carried workers and tourists back and forth to the opposite shore was always on the move. It visited the wharf dozens of times a day. Since the early settlers made it a port, it was rebuilt again and again. If any of the original rough-cut oaken planks or pilings had remained, they would have told stories about the English ships offloading cargo and the years of economic decline that put the town on the edge of desolation. The pilings would have told stories about the 1800's oyster boom and the skipjacks laden with bushels of oysters, the steamboats tied to its piers, and floating theaters that brought entertainment. Now, spectators watched regattas from its weathered planks and water skiers and recreational boaters tied up for a walk uptown. The activity adjusted to the times but never fully stopped, and neither did the ferry.

Forever omnipresent in the lives of the townspeople, the wharf lay at the bottom of the only hill in town. Kate took her feet off the pedals and put them on the crossbar as she flew down the hill in a fever. The wind in her hair and the smell of the briny river widened her eyes, and a wild spirit stirred inside her. The thrill of the ride came to an abrupt end as she slammed on the brakes and skidded to a sand-flying stop at the water's edge. Tansy was by her side the whole time, bag of bread hitting her knee and matching Kate's skill. It was a well-rehearsed motion.

Kickstands down, and before Tansy untied the bread, the girls instantly noticed that the ducks were gone. In that moment they were acutely disappointed; the fizzle was sharp like a child's first balloon popping.

"Maybe they will be back this afternoon," Kate offered up as their plans collapsed.

Tansy's disappointment didn't last very long. She became distracted by movement near a grassy area nearby. "Look Kate!" As they walked closer to the flutterings in the tall grass, a baby duck emerged in a panic, squawking at them. The size of a child's fist, the baby duck had much fight in its fluff, even with its injured foot.

"Aww," Kate melted; her wild spirit was tamed with deep compassion as she knelt down to look closer.

"It lost its mother," said Tansy.

"She needs help," Kate replied.

"How do you know it's a she?"

"I don't know I just feel like it is." Kate said, "And I know just who can help her."

Kate knelt down, picked up the small baby, and gently held it in her hand. "Come on Tansy, let's go see Miss Pat."

⚓ ⚓ ⚓

LEAVING THE BIKES BEHIND, THEY started the untrustworthy journey along the rock-strewn waterfront pathway all the way to the eastern edge of town with their patient. Their feet flitted from one stone to another as they thoughtfully picked the flat ones that had no slippery moss. It was tricky to balance oneself with hands occupied, but Kate persevered by jockeying elbows and knees. There was no way she was going to trip with the lading held in her cupped hands. Along the way they commented on the flickers of light shimmering off of rat's eyes deep within the stone bank and the slithering of snakes in and amongst the gaps.

"We really rescued it," Tansy beamed. "If a water snake didn't get it, a rat would've." Kate agreed and swelled with pride of their rescue. The wildlife they encountered along the way had no shock value. The rats and snakes were a part of the waterfront, it was expected. That's not to say they didn't keep vital watch of their footing as to not tempt a challenge, but this dance had been done before. As long as their eyes were keen and footsteps confident, there was little worry. The closer they got to Mr. Russell's boatyard, the static noise announced its propriety.

A varnish perfume perpetually lingered in the boatyard air in the warm season, dissipating only when it was too cold to lacquer. No sign marked the yard; there was no need; all one had to do was follow the sounds and smells. Inside the hidden entrance, various boats of different rigs, colors, and lengths rose above the sand and gravel on high metal stilts.

Their attention was drawn instantly to the foreman, Mr. Russell, who was barking orders at the men. He was broad and burley, worn and weathered, hardy and harsh on a good day. His wife, Miss Pat, seemed to be the only one who could tame his fury and she stayed close by, working the docks and the desk in what was considered an office but looked nothing of the sort.

Miss Pat was often found in the first shed, not more than 10 x10. It distinguished itself from the other structures by what little charm a woman could bring to a man's yard. Years ago, she painted the door's wooden exterior a warm red with an Arcadian mermaid. The colors were now noticeably scaly from many years of wind and rain.

A stoic character, Miss Pat had a soft heart for animals. Not being able to have children herself, she mothered every stray dog or lost duckling that came in her path. Her constant companion, Sam, a dog she rescued out of the river on a cold winter day, was loyal and protective and knew who belonged in the boatyard and who did not. Still, he understood Miss Pat's need to help his fellow animals and became a guardian of all the animals she nurtured back to health with the savage protection of a mother. No one in Sam's accepted sphere could find a more loyal protector.

With only a path to her desk, under the heavy walnut table was always a soft, warm blanket for Sam, cotton in the summer and woolen in the winter. Close at Miss Pat's feet is where Sam liked to be. When Pat walked the docks to check the boats or tie up or move a boat from one slip to another, Sam sat on the dock patiently watching, never in the way and astutely observing her delicate touch with the wheel of all the vessels. Large or small, sail or power, Miss Pat could maneuver each boat with precision and handling of the gentlest feel. No one could dock or tie up a craft better with definitive ease and confidence. The docks were in good hands.

On these trips to the piers she would often stop and talk to the men about their life at home. She knew everyone's birthday, who had a baby on the way, who was going through a difficult time, and who was blessed with good news. An integral part of the inner workings of the yard, her talent for figures and role as confidant were paramount to keep the contented dispositions of the men. She was also key for sanding the oak edges of Mr. Russell.

The girls drew their attention away from the thundering Mr.

Russell to check Miss Pat's office. When first entering "Miss Pat's Shack," one would notice that there was little room for more than themselves. All four corners were flanked by tall stacks of boxes that held records of the boatyard's business; years and years of work with one match could disappear in minutes. Centered in the shed were two wide black walnut planks dovetailed together as a table supported by aged bald cypress stumps. Varnish on it was layered so thick, it reflected light against the walls when the sun shone through the east window in the morning.

A captain's chair with a tattered corduroy cushion was where she propped herself to answer the phone, figure the bills, and order supplies. The rusty filing cabinets could hold no more, yet she always found a way to jam one more paper in. It took very little time for her to produce records asked for by a customer or yard worker for reference. To the casual observer, it looked as though the shack had been abandoned years ago, but it was very much in service, and even though its haphazard appearance suggested otherwise, no one dare disturb her antiquated system.

Peeking inside the girls saw it was empty and turned their heads to peruse the yard. By now Kate's hands were very sweaty, and the baby was working itself up into a dither.

Timeworn wooden step ladders marred by gouges from hard use and metal ladders of varying lengths littered the landscape. Cans of seaworthy paint colors full to empty and everywhere in between were strewn about as the men rhythmically dodged the debris. Faithfully shuffling back and forth between the many dilapidated workshops and the vessels in various stages of restoration, the men worked with a tide-like rhythm they made their own. From sun up to sundown, the cutting, grinding, and drilling machines sent out a pitch barely tolerable to the ears of passersby. It was simply white noise to the men in the yard. Loud hammering broke out on occasion, penetrating the air like an arrow and dwarfing the shop machines. When fired up, the caustic sounds of the travel lift won out over all the buzz on the grounds. The racket echoed throughout the town; it was the sound of hard labor.

Miss Pat suddenly stood before them, Sam at her side - they never saw her approach. She was drawn in by the fluffy lump in Kate's hands, trying to break free.

"Girls! You have come to the right place! Let me look at the baby!"

Kate opened her hands just enough for Miss Pat to see it was a baby duckling. "Bring it inside," Pat said with an excitable confidence that rubbed off on the girls.

"It's a she!" Kate blurted out. "I'm sure of it."

Once inside Miss Pat's office, Kate gently put the baby down on Sam's soft bed. They all crouched under the table side by side, knee to knee, shoulder to shoulder, while Sam guarded the door. Miss Pat saw the small cut on its foot webbing and expressed some concern. "With a little antibiotic cream, bandaging and luck it should heal," she commented. "The baby also needs food and water."

"I have my stale bread on my bike, but it's back at the docks," Tansy offered.

"No need," said Miss Pat. She was always on the ready for such occasions and had on her desk a small jar of cracked corn. She grabbed a teaspoon full and put it on the blanket. The baby gobbled it up.

"Go get some water from the house, girls - here's a jar to put it in."

Without delay they scurried out of the office to Pat's house. In the short time they were gone, Miss Pat had already set up camp for the little duck. A large wooden crate sat just outside her office door, with a soft blanket inside and a small water dish ready to be filled. She had bandaged the foot and laid more food on the pine bottom of the crate. Kate and Tansy were in awe of the routine and ease with which the little sanctuary was erected. Tansy poured the water into the dish, and the little duck went right to it, anxious with thirst.

Kate looked up at Miss Pat, "Do you think she will live?"

"I think this duckling has a very good chance," Miss Pat said with confidence.

"We should name it!" Tansy burst out.

Kate interjected, "How about "Squawk?" And then retracted it, "It doesn't sound like a girl's name though."

"Kate, we won't know if it is a boy or a girl until it's true feathers come in," said Miss Pat.

"I like the name Squawk," interjected Tansy.

"Squawk it is," said Miss Pat. "Now I need you girls to do me a favor; do you know where Mr. Paul lives?"

"Yes," Kate replied. "My mother visits him often, he lives right across from father's garden."

"Edison does have a fine garden," Miss Pat complimented. "O.K., he makes his own beer. Please tell him Miss Pat needs some brewer's yeast."

The girls were perplexed but said they would carry the message to Mr. Paul.

"Bring it with you when you visit Squawk tomorrow." Pat smiled at the little duck. "Ducks like company."

They agreed and felt good about Squawk's living arrangements.

Saying goodbye to Miss Pat, they walked out of the yard waving, with Sam faithfully standing guard. By now they were both hungry and ran back to their bikes, never looking up from the waterfront stones. No one ever forgets about the rats and snakes unless you're a tourist.

Tansy said her grandmother was home, and they could fix sandwiches there. In agreement, they walked their bikes up the hill, jumped on their seats, and headed to Tansy's house. It was just a few doors down from Kate's, and its cottage-like appearance made it a smaller version of the other houses on Main. The baby blue hydrangeas out front added color to an all-white house. When they arrived, a tremendously fat white cat was stretched out on the grey porch swing, lounging happily. They dropped their bikes in the front yard, not bothering with kickstands as hunger had taken hold and all they could think about was lunch. "Gram!" Tansy yelled as she opened the screen door. There was no answer, indicating she was probably in her upstairs studio, in her own world, painting. In the kitchen they found a jar of peanut butter, fig jam, and bread. They made sandwiches thick with peanut butter and hearty with jam. The contents bled out the sides and licking the knives and spoons, they placed them in the sink and wrapped their sandwiches in a paper towel. Kate held their lunch while Tansy grabbed two glasses from the cabinet and filled them with water from the tap.

A screened-in porch connected the kitchen to the backyard. Two wooden steps led them outside to a brick patio with a white wrought iron table and three chairs to match. As Kate sat down, her hair grazed an oyster shell wind chime that hung from a large branch of the mature dogwood that shaded the patio. Remnants of the last May blooms still lingered on a few branches, but almost all had fallen and lay in various stages of decay on the bricks and surrounding grass. They set their glasses down and ravenously took large bites of their sandwiches, leaving peanut butter and fig jam to stick to their faces and fall on their paper towels. They talked about Squawk and made plans to visit her tomorrow. Mid-conversation, they heard the upstairs back window jiggle and they looked up to see Gram opening it up wide.

"Girls come up and visit me!" she yelled.

"O.K. Gram!" they yelled in unison.

Known to the girls as Gram, in the neighborhood she was Miss Lucille, the artist.

She painted, made pottery, collected sea glass, and crafted oyster shell wind chimes. Walking up her curved staircase to the second floor was like walking through an art exhibit. From bottom to the very top, oil paintings of the town covered the old plastered walls. Kate always walked up the staircase slowly to peruse the town scapes, finding something new to look at each time. She tripped once from lack of attention, catching herself with the banister.

At the top of the stairs was a dark wooden threshold worn in the middle from 100 years of use. They crossed a small hallway and passed a majestic looking claw foot tub that sat in the tiny gray bathroom on the right. Two steps into Gram's studio, Kate smacked her head on the entrance.

"Ouch," said Kate while holding the right side of her head.

"Kate, you've been up here enough times to know better," Miss Lucille said in a surprised tone.

"I know," Kate replied while rubbing her head. "I wasn't thinking."

The studio was quaint and surprisingly cool. The slanted ceiling gave it an attic feel. Small open rectangular robin's egg blue colored glass windows on opposite sides of the room let the breeze whip through.

"What have you been up to girls?" she asked, while cocking her neck up and blowing out a long drag from her brown cigarette, as not to let it hit her canvas.

"We rescued a baby duck!" Tansy burst forth.

"A duckling? My word, no mother?"

"No mother AND a hurt foot," Kate offered.

"Where is it now?" Gram inquired. Tansy laid out the whole story in much detail.

"Well, good deeds today, girls, good deeds."

"What are you painting?" asked Kate. Gram turned the easel towards the girls and it was an oil on canvas waterfront scene of the area they had just walked.

"I've decided it will be one of three paintings as the entire waterfront street is just too big to fit all details into one. The left painting will be a hint of the boatyard with silver masts in the distance, the middle the stone path with houses behind it - the right painting will be the crescendo - the ferry," she announced while picking up a brush and continuing her craft.

Kate and Tansy settled in to watch quietly, sitting with legs crossed on the gray-painted floor. Gram mixed the paints on her palette and brushed them on. It was soothing to watch, almost mesmerizing. After some time passed Kate and Tansy slipped away downstairs, Gram too engrossed to notice their departure.

⚓ ⚓ ⚓

THEY DECIDED TO PLAY CROQUET. The day had been splendid so far as to risk a game they usually fought over. Good temperament was essential before a game of croquet was even considered. Rivals since they were six, if Kate and Tansy were going to fight, it would definitely be over a game of croquet. Kate set the stakes with her mallet and Tansy the wickets. Out of the shade of the dogwood, the air was warm, and the sky was bright. A robin flew over to the fence and watched the girls set up, its head flitting side to side.

"Do you think he's criticizing our setup, Tansy?" Kate joked.

"Probably, if he didn't, we would," laughed Tansy.

Kate was in such an elevated mood, she made a gesture. "Tansy, you go first."

"Is that because you think I'm not as good as you?"

"I was trying to be nice, Tansy; I mean I did win the last game."

"Be quiet!" she scoffed. "I'll start."

The tension grew steadily. Tansy won the first game, so Kate suggested two out of three. By the end of the second game, they were tied and suddenly much more serious. Kate's first hit went through the double wickets and struck Tansy's ball. Instead of taking her two shots, she put her ball against Tansy's and whacked it all the way under the fig bush on the opposite side of the yard. Tansy said nothing when she crawled under the fig bush. Distracted by early summer fruit, she broke the tension.

"Hey, the early crop is on!"

Kate ran over and pulled a ripe fig off the branch, broke it in

half to check for wasps, and ate it. Tansy did the same. They picked a few more, and Kate proclaimed they weren't as sweet as the August crop.

"Yes, they are!" Tansy said.

With her head back in the game, Tansy hit her ball so hard it went backward through the center wicket and into the cucumber vines.

"Ha!" yelled Kate, irritating Tansy.

Kate played flawlessly for her next few turns while Tansy could barely get out of the cucumbers. Kate was on the home stretch when she realized what Tansy was up to. She wasn't struggling with the cucumber vines; she was just wasting turns so she would be in the perfect position to get Kate back on her way to the finish.

"Bam!" yelled Tansy as her ball cracked into Kate's.

Dancing around, she used her mallet as a cane and put on a show that Kate did not appreciate. With Kate's ball now stuck under the backside of the fig, Tansy proceeded to clear wicket after wicket, much to her own delight.

"You faked bad turns!" Kate yelled from behind the fig bush.

"So what if I did?"

Mad by Tansy's tricks, Kate hit the ball as hard as she could down the fence line towards the birdbath and struck it so hard that the top wobbled and bobbled, water sloshed, and it slid right off into the yard. Panicked, she ran over to see if it had broken. It hadn't. Tansy fell on the lawn laughing so hard that Kate couldn't stand it.

"Tansy! I'm going home!" Kate stormed off, slammed the back gate, and stomped down the street to her house, leaving her bike behind and Tansy rolling around on the lawn laughing.

Chapter II

— Beets and Bi-Planes —

The heat of the afternoon had grabbed hold, and Kate became quite thirsty. Opening the back gate, she noticed no one was in the yard except River who came running up wagging his tail, glad to see someone.

"Where is everybody, boy?" Kate asked as she approached the screen door.

Three tall glass pitchers of sun tea sat on the wide redwood porch windowsills, brewing in the afternoon sun. She went to the cabinets, grabbed a glass, filled it to the top with tap water, and drank two inches off the top in one gulp. Then she opened the freezer door and put her dirty hand into the ice cube box, and plopped a few cubes in her glass. She noticed River's bowl was almost empty, so she filled it. Glass in hand, she wandered the house in hopes there was someone to talk to, anyone but Tansy.

She stepped into the dining room, which was small but of fine decoration. The well-adorned room had a mahogany dining table, with a deep shiny finish and two heavy silver candlesticks thoughtfully placed in the center. A simple but elegant light fixture centered the room.

Her eyes settled upon the antique free-standing buffet cabinet. Hand-embossed linens from a time when ladies did such needlework lay on top. They had just been ironed and stacked neatly, ready and waiting for the next ladies event. Not the slightest bit interested in sewing, Kate could not imagine a more fastidious project than the designs sewn on the dainty linens, but she did find them a lovely rest for the eyes.

She touched the silver iced tea spoons that lay on top, also ready for the next gathering of ladies. Beneath, the drawers held silverware, serving utensils, and platters for very special occasions. The prettiest of all chests of drawers was shadowed by the simple elegance of a tea service. A wedding gift to Jammy and Walton, Kate's grandparents, Jammy often commented on it being the last thing she would have ever sold.

Past the dining room was a long hall out to the front door. A bathroom stood on the right that at one time had been a pantry when shelves were filled with colorful canned vegetables and fruits from local gardens and wild hedgerows. Above the door still remained a dimpled blue-green glass window, the color of the river, that could be propped open to air out the pantry and keep its contents cool.

As she sauntered through the hallway, she heard, "Miss Kate, is that you?"

"Yep!" Kate smiled as she turned left into two elegant living rooms divided by a sliding parlor door. Jammy was sitting in the corner of the front parlor in her favorite chair by the breeze of the front window, reading a book.

"What have you been up to, Miss Kate?" she asked, closing her book.

Still irritated about the croquet game, Kate shrugged her shoulders.

"Croquet with Tansy?" Jammy inquired.

"How did you know?"

"I think the whole neighborhood heard you," Jammy laughed. "You have a competitive spirit, Miss Kate, and that is good, but you should not walk away from a game when you are losing, it's bad form. You must see it through. It's easy to start something but not always easy to finish it, especially when it is not going your way. It's that way in sports and in life."

Jammy had a way of answering a question Kate didn't even

know she had and turning it into a life lesson. She would then change the subject before Kate had time to fuss at her.

"Shall we play some cards?" That question transformed Kate's mood, and she settled into a game of rummy. Playing cards with Jammy was an exercise in concentration; a competitor herself, she didn't let her grandchildren win. Quietly they played, concentrating on the other's hands, trying to guess each other's next moves and anticipating what the next card would be. Two hours passed quickly, softly as a feather dropping from a telephone wire.

Mary called from the kitchen, "I have dinner jobs!"

She had snuck in the back door after an afternoon of visiting with Miss Pearl, a dear friend who lived at the other end of town. Many an afternoon they spent together, and although Kate didn't know what they talked about, it seemed they had an awful lot to say. Mary could be gone for the whole afternoon if she was with Pearl, but she always returned in a better mood than when she left.

Jammy and Kate headed to the kitchen. "Go to Father's garden, Kate, and pick us some beets for dinner. And don't dawdle, I stayed way too long at Miss Pearl's."

Jammy inquired, "Did you solve all the problems of the world?"

"Near 'bout," Mary said with a smile.

Kate already had a quarter in her pocket she had plucked out of the spare change jar and was jogging towards the back gate. With a wheelbarrow ready for the journey, she headed to Edison's garden, by way of a paper street, whose path once traveled every day by old rusty pickup trucks full of trash, was now overgrown for lack of use. The town refuse pile, which had long ago been moved outside of town, was still in use in the deteriorating mind of Mr. Tawes. He was the former dumping fee collector whose backyard butted up to the old path. Troubling those who happened by for payment as he did years ago, was taken in stride by those who had known him when he worked for the town. Often, passersby would hand him a quarter for old time's sake, to which he would thank them kindly for their payment to the town. Well into his nineties, it was Mr. Tawes' wife, Miss Virginia, who kept him well-fed and generally out of trouble throughout his cloudy years.

Kate walked a dozen yards up the street and made a soft right turn onto the old, weedy dirt path, where she saw Mr. Tawes, anchored to his rickety lawn chair, whittling on a stick with his pen knife. She set her wheelbarrow down, and Mr. Tawes assessed her empty load.

"I'd say, cost you 'bout a quarter."

Kate reached into her pocket and pulled out her fare, placing it in his outstretched hand. Kate marveled at the length of his slender fingers and wondered if he ever played the piano."Mr. Tawes, do you know how to play the piano?"

"No time for it, what with working for the town and all."

"So you used to?" she inquired. He ignored her, thanked her for her prompt payment, and then, without pause or additional conversation, picked up his whittling stick and carried on with his craft.

The Seth family had owned the old dumping ground for generations, and during that time, the petite property had succumbed to two fires. Half a century ago, it held a modest-sized two-story building that dueled as a barbershop and a men's service club, known as the "Knights of the Pythius of North America." After an evening meeting of the members, the wooden framed structure went up like parched kindling and burned to the ground. The fire was later determined to have been ignited by one of the men's cigars that had been left burning after a night of poker, disguised as a late-night service meeting.

Following the fire, the town was in need of a dump, so Poppy let the town use the space until one smoldering August day the trash pile caught on fire. It was extinguished quickly, but being so close to other houses, the town determined it best the dump be relocated to the outskirts of town.

Edison, spent the next decade cleaning up the property, removing broken bottles, cracked bricks, oyster shells, and many tin cans. All the stuff that didn't burn up in the fire was eventually removed. He then added a truckload of dirt to clean sections once a year until it was fit to grow vegetables. Edison always claimed the number of years it took to clean it up was equal to the number of years it held the town's refuse. He was probably right, but no one kept track.

Kate followed the rubble-lined path dotted with black-eyed Susans popping out of the many crevices and crannies to her father's garden. She stopped to grab a switch below a formidable grandmother willow and whisk it back and forth through the air as if fighting off an invisible enemy. The property behind the old willow always grabbed her curiosity. Its lonely persimmon tree called to her in a way that would have her set down the handles of the wheelbarrow and lean upon the property fence, gazing at its solitary nature.

In a powerful yet devious way, it distracted her and pushed everything out of her mind so that she could focus intently on the tree. Every spring, mockingbirds nested there aggressively protecting their brood from their vocal cousins, the cat birds. Kate thought it must have been comforting to the mockingbird knowing that in the fall they could visit the tree and feast on the orange flesh of the wild fruit.

Kate soon became aware that it was quiet in the neighborhood as most families were eating dinner, and realizing this lateness made her pluck the beets quickly and push the wheelbarrow home as if she were in a race. Blood-colored beets bounced about along the rutty, ragged alley to their own Vaudeville tune, knocking the big chunks of dirt away. The wheel hit the pavement, and for the rest of the jaunt, smaller pieces of dirt fell to the bottom of the wheelbarrow, leaving it so the beets merely needed a rinse. Entering the kitchen, holding a handful of beets by the green and red veined tops, Kate set to work rinsing them off.

"No one likes a vegetable that's crunchy because of sand," reminded Jammy who had grabbed an apron and began making biscuits. After the beets were clean, Mary placed them in a pressure

cooker and then gave Kate a bowl of fresh green beans. She went outside and sat in the grass near Jammy's garden because she hated the sound of the pressure cooker. So did River, who followed her out and kept her company.

When she snapped the bean ends, she transferred them from the glass bowl to the colander to be washed, leaving the ends in the grass for River to eat, although he acted like he was not fond of them. While sitting cross-legged she looked closely at the herbs and tried to remember the names of each one. The tall, thin ones that tasted like onions were chives; the parsley she knew well because Mary used it often, but she couldn't remember the other two. She would ask Jammy later. The penetrating noises of the pressure cooker made her instinctively place her hands over her ears as tightly as she could. She never liked the sound, and she never would, she was sure of that.

Edison and Johnny came in the back gate.

"We must be having beets," said Johnny. "Kate's doing the ear thing."

"Well, I don't like it!" Kate projected Johnny's way.

Her brother had seen this before, laughed, and went into the shed with Edison. The noise stopped and Kate brought the beans inside for round two of the pressure cooker. She went back outside to the garden and looked for butterflies. It was too early for butterflies, but the hunt distracted her from the noise. Johnny and Edison shuffled around in the shed until Mary leaned out the back door and yelled, "Dish up!"

The six o'clock bells chimed right on schedule. It was one of Mary's favorite hymns, "Faith of our Fathers," and Mary hummed while everyone washed up and grabbed a plate. In the summer, basket plates were preferred over china. The flat basket held a thin paper plate on top, making it sturdy and easy to clean up. Summer was Mary's favorite time of year, and she didn't want to waste it doing too many dishes.

Also humming to the tune of the church bells, Jammy placed her hot-out-of-the oven biscuits on the table with butter and fig jam. Kate put some fried chicken on her plate, potato salad, beets, beans and biscuits. She was awfully hungry. Mary dumped ice into the warm brewed tea and placed the pitchers on the table. Edison poured a glass for everyone, and Johnny handed out napkins. As the bells ended, Mary grabbed those hands closest and started grace. "Lord, we thank you for this beautiful day, a chance to be with friends and family, a chance to work, and a moment to pray.

Thank you for the food you have put before us, and bless those less fortunate. May they be twice blessed in the near future. Amen."

"Amen!"

Kate asked where Cousin Lowell was. "Not fit to sit at this table," said Jammy sternly.

Mary changed the subject. "So what did everyone do today?"

Johnny piped up. "I made thirty-seven dollars in tips today working breakfast and lunch at the restaurant and another five dollars cutting Miss Ginny's lawn."

"That's good," was a solid response from Edison. Johnny smiled.

Kate all of a sudden remembered Squawk. "Me and Tansy, we saved a baby duck!"

"I heard," said Edison. "One of the fellers uptown told me, right good deed, Kate."

"We need to check on her tomorrow."

"Well done," Mary smiled.

Jammy reached under the table, patted Kate on the knee twice, and whispered in her ear, "That's my girl."

Kate finished the last of her plate, grabbed another biscuit, and slathered it with butter and figs. Edison stood up and refilled all the empty glasses with more sun tea. Edison was chatty tonight, which was unusual. He was a man of few words so when he spoke at dinner, all were obliged to listen.

"The corner of the roof is rotten up at the market, so I need to get on that. I went to measure today so I could gather all the materials I need to fix it. I hear rain the end of the week, so gotta get it done soon for Truman. Johnny, do you have any days off at the restaurant?" "Tomorrow," Johnny replied.

"Then it's settled," which meant Johnny would work all day with his father.

The dishes were done, but the sun had not touched the trees across the river shore. Mary and Edison went for their usual evening walk. Jammy went to sit on the front porch, and Johnny went straight to his room. Kate curiously followed. Messy, unkept, malodorous even with the windows open, his bed covers were halfway on the floor and hadn't been changed in more than a month. His minimal regard for hygiene permeated the air. The only thing clean was the top of his desk, where he was meticulously constructing a balsa wood bi-plane by hand. Posters of rocket ships and the moon landing hung from his walls; he wanted to be an astronaut.

Kate stood at the door. "What are you doing?"

"Making a super light bi-plane. I just finished." He said as he turned towards Kate with plane in hand. It was framed in balsa, but its body and wings were covered with a thin white tissue paper. Anxious to see it fly, he went past Kate and around the corner to Jammy's room. Carefully setting it on her bureau, he pushed her back window open more.

"Come on, let's see if it flies."

Jammy's window opened to a long but narrow roof that covered the back porch. Johnny removed the screen, climbed through and Kate handed him the plane, following right behind. They cautiously stepped around the small Jon boat stored upside down on the roof. A hurricane had completely flooded the town in Mary's youth and she forevermore wanted to be prepared. Days without electricity or fresh water and roads only navigable by boat had left an impression on her, so much that the Jon boat stayed on the roof on the ready when it was not in use for fishing.

Johnny crouched on the edge of the roof while Kate watched from behind; he aimed his aircraft at the old wooden boat in the back corner of the yard and let it go. It flew above the old boat, and then a light breeze that funneled around the house from the west lifted it up over the back gate; it veered to the south and disappeared behind Edison's shed. They scrambled through Jammy's window, forgetting the screen, ran down the steps, and blasted outside. River sensed the excitement and stayed close. At first glance over the backyard gate, they did not see the flyer, but once they opened the gate, they saw it on the road, still in one piece as if it had made a perfect landing.

Excited by his test run, Johnny went into Edison's shed and came out with a bottle rocket. Unsure and yet eager to witness what he was up to, Kate followed along happily. Stopping in the kitchen, he rummaged through the pantry and came out with an old glass vase and some matches. "This is going to be great," he projected, wildly enthusiastic about his plan.

Back on the roof, the bottle rocket had been gingerly taped to the bottom of the bi-plane, and the vase angle pointed over the roof line of Edison's shop, towards the open field beyond it. He concluded that if the plane made it as far as the street with just a throw, with more energy to it, the bi-plane could at least fly to the field or perhaps Miss Ginny's boatyard or beyond that. Lighting the match, he touched the wick, and sparks flew instantly catching the tissue paper on fire as it shot from the vase. Its body was engulfed in flames as quickly as the Hindenburg, and in a wild blaze, it landed in the open door of Edison's shop.

Frenzied beyond reason, Johnny launched himself back through Jammy's window, down the steps to the kitchen, and grabbed a full iced tea pitcher left over from dinner. Tearing a streak to the shed, he dumped the tea on the burning remnants of his bi-plane. Kate followed not far behind, looking all around and eyeing neighbor's windows for faces to see if anyone had witnessed the unfortunate event. The area looked clear of watchers and she told him so as he stood overtop of the puddle of tea and a few bits of charred balsa.

"I'm sorry your plane is wrecked," she offered.

"Are you kidding?" he countered. "That was amazing!"

With some old rags they cleaned the entranceway of any evidence and put the few bits left of charred wet residue in the trash can.

Now below the trees, the sun made the western sky a creamsicle orange. The day was almost done, and Kate was tired—not just any kind of tired but dog-tired. The kind of tired where you could

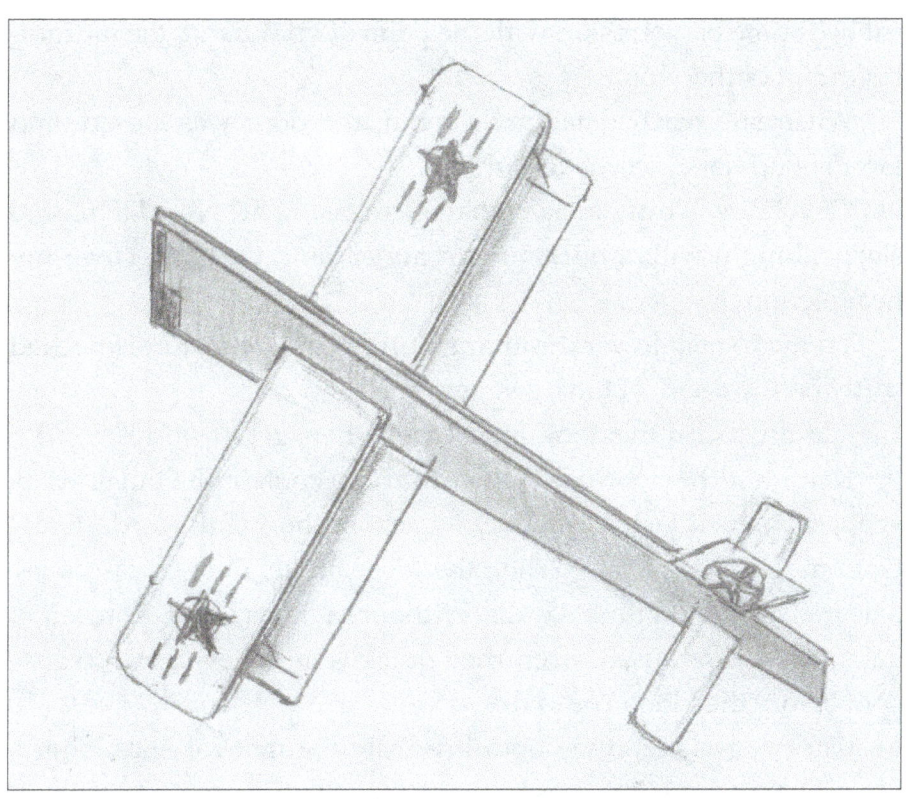

curl up right where you were and find it comfortable even if it was a cold and lumpy patch of dirt and be out in seconds. Staring at the glowing western sky, her trance was interrupted by Jammy yelling out her window.

"My room is full of mosquitoes! What were you two doing on the roof?" Johnny and Kate looked at each other anxiously.

Johnny yelled, "We'll come fix the screen right away!"

Jammy countered, "Well, you better bring a handful of swatters, too, because I'm not sleeping in this swarm!"

Johnny headed up the back steps, skipping every other step, and Kate followed behind with a handful of swatters and a Mason jar of Jammy's homemade mosquito repellant. Kate had watched her make it several times and knew the ingredients by heart: two cups witch hazel, several drops each of lemon balm oil, lavender, and tea tree oil, and a tablespoon of apple cider vinegar. When you rubbed some on your skin with the palm of your hand, the mosquitos didn't bother you.

When she reached Jammy's room, the door was closed, and Jammy had harsh words for Johnny.

"You know we are lucky to have screens, right? Now I'll have to sleep all night with a humming in my ear and the sheets over my head, Johnny!"

Trying to help lower the temperature in the room, Kate knocked softly on the door. " I have swatters and your oil…"

Jammy thrust the door open. "Well, then, get to work!"

Kate shut the door behind her to try to contain the bugs. Snap, snap, snap, their task was wild with action, short with words. Snap! Got one! Snap! Got one! When the fever broke, little carcasses lay smeared all over Jammy's walls. Without saying a word, Kate left to get some damp rags. She returned quickly, and they cleaned every spot before the blood could dry.

Once completed, they both inwardly thought for sure Jammy would be pleased. She was not and sent them on their way, commenting that tomorrow was a new day, but this day, she could not get the bitter taste out of her mouth. Kate left the repellent and swatters in her room, and she and Johnny quietly crept down the front steps, saying nothing.

Sitting on the front porch, they could hear Jammy through the upstairs window swatting at the mosquitoes, followed by a very loud "Dammit!" Not long after Kate and Johnny had settled on the front porch, Mary and Edison returned from their evening walk.

They came up the front brick steps onto the gray floorboards of the porch, opened the door to the screened-in area and sat down.

"See much?" asked Johnny.

"They're catching spot at the wharf," Edison reported. "Haven't had one of those for breakfast in a while," he hinted. "I do love a good fish breakfast, and full tide should roll in tomorrow morning about eight or so…"

Kate broke the silence and said she had been thinking she might want to go fishing in the morning.

"That so?" said Edison. "Well then, it's settled. Kate will fish in the morning."

Kate really hadn't planned to fish the next day, but she hadn't planned to do anything else either, and she liked to fish. Besides, if she caught something for Father's breakfast it might give her some favor in case he found out about the Hindenburg incident.

Snap! "Dammit!" Mary and Edison looked oddly toward the noise.

Johnny jumped in, "So pop, what' ya think about starting early with work tomorrow, I'd like to get a jump on it."

Kate admired his cleverness as he distracted them from the upstairs dance.

They turned back towards Johnny. "Look at that Edison, he's got a taste for work," chimed Mary.

Edison stared him down sharply for an uncomfortable amount of time, then succumbed. "Then it's settled, 6 a.m. it is." Johnny let out a retrained moan.

Kate and Johnny both found reasons to head up to bed. Johnny dressed for bed in his room while chasing mosquitos around with a dish towel but wasn't fast enough to kill any. Kate got dressed in the bathroom and then met Johnny in the hall in front of Jammy's room. They plotted how Jammy might let them use some fly swatters and oil on their arms and faces before bed. Johnny took a deep breath as he leaned to knock on her door, but Kate reached out quickly and grabbed his hand.

"Wait!" Kate whispered, "Look!"

Outside her door was the mason jar of oil and two swatters. They looked at each other and smiled. She knew just what they needed before they asked - Jammy had forgiven them in her own way. They each took turns rubbing the oil on their faces and arms, anything that would be exposed from a bed covering. The swats faded away as the sky tempered itself towards a deep evening summer blue. It was finally night, and Kate eased in under the bedsheet, pulling it up to her eyeballs.

The air was a familiar kind of heavy, but it was an oddly comforting embrace. The yearly cicadas droned outside her window with a deep penetrating noise, only interrupted by the rhythmically faint squeaking of her rusty electric fan, issued to her at the beginning of the warm season. The cicadas came every year, some more than others, but always by July. They were early this year.

A wild Hackberry tree limb brushed up against her screen and in the moonlight she could see it already had a few galls on its leaves but no drupes yet. The waxing three quarter moon was bright enough to light up a clear sky. She remembered seeing the sickle moon just about 10 days earlier signaling the beginning of early summer; she knew it to be true as the corn was sprouting in the nearby fields.

The street out front was quiet, broken occasionally by a slow wandering car headed home from one of the bars or an occasional night walker, wearing themselves out to sleep without pause. She put her hand upon her screen demonstrating an assured confidence of its protection from the night bugs striking it from time to time; drawn to her window undoubtedly by her faint but protective nightlight. Not everyone in town had screens. She was grateful she did.

She adjusted her pillow and crooked her neck to look upward at the bright dots that speckled the cloudless sky in a most unpredictable pattern. To try to make sense of them was to examine until she could look no more. Her eyes would soon shut only to be wakened briefly in the wee hours by the low hum of the fleet of workboats headed out the creek. She rolled over and looked at the rusty, rickety old fan waving back and forth, back and forth, and then it was morning.

Chapter III

— Gardens —

There were no roosters in town, but instead, an elderly neighbor calling her cats in a shrill morning drawl. "Maisy! Everham! Breakfast!" Her pitch quieted the cicadas, and made Kate sit up and look out her front window. A bright sky bore an electric blue. A few people passed by the house on their way up town for coffee and a newspaper.

Kate sprung out of bed, her bare feet surprising the old pine floorboards with their enthusiasm and they flexed and crackled when she landed, leaned over, and turned off the metal fan. A clean tee shirt, stretched from drying on the clothesline, slid easily over her head; leaving the rest to chance, she concluded yesterday's shorts couldn't be that dirty, and with a clean top her mom might not notice the rest.

Down the hall she scurried, stomach first, past Johnny and Jammy's empty rooms, down three steps, through her parents room to the back staircase that butted up to Lowell's door that was shut. The smell of fried scrapple traveled up the steps, settled deep within and it was all she could think about. Steep and narrow, the steps let out an aged groan when she charged the top of the flight. That first step was a signal, and mother expected her. When Kate spun around the corner to the kitchen Mary was just sliding the scrapple out of the skillet onto a paper towel.

"Good Morning, Kate," she said with a smile.

Kate smiled back, "Morning, Mom."

River was there to greet her, and also to escort the scrapple to the table. He prided himself on keeping the floors clean for the family.

"Where's Johnny?" Kate asked.

"He and your father left early to fix the roof on Truman's store."

"Where's Uncle Lowell?"

"Sleeping in."

"Where's Jammy?"

"Weeding her garden, and I am not your daily newspaper. If you want to know what's going on, then get up earlier."

"O.K." Kate replied less enthusiastically.

"I'm going fishing after breakfast," she announced.

"I remember from last night," Mary said, adding, "you might have slept past the high tide."

Not wanting to disappoint Edison, she ate her scrapple and eggs double-time and ran out the back door to look for worms. She could hear Jammy digging up weeds around the corner, and before she could say anything, she heard Jammy offer:

"You know there are plenty of worms in my garden."

"How'd you know I needed worms?" Kate looked at her perplexed.

"You have the determination of a fisherman who is late to the river."

Her observation was accurate, so Kate headed over to Jammy, paused, and then asked,

"The mosquitos keep you awake?"

"I killed a few more and then settled into a good sleep. Today is a new day, Kate." Relieved by Jammy's words, Kate smiled. Jammy reached for Kate's hand and put six dirty but lively worms in it.

"Thanks!" Kate ran off towards Edison's shed waving goodbye.

Edison always had extra stuff she might need in his shed, and wanting something to put the worms in, Kate knocked around a bit, stubbing her toe on an anchor, looking for just the right container. She found an old glass mayonnaise jar on one of his many cluttered shelves. She put the worms in it, added a little more dirt, and held the metal lid steady on his workbench with one hand while she punched five holes in it with an old nail using the flat end of Edison's ball peen hammer. The tapping scared a wren out of the shed and made her jump. She screwed the jar top on and put it in the bottom of a 5-gallon bucket, then grabbed her rod and tackle box.

Trying to balance everything on her bike was not easy, but she had been practicing for a few years now and had a system. Tackle box and fishing rod on the left handlebar and bucket on the right gave her just enough room to also hold the handle bars. The reel rested in her lap so all she had to do was place her index finger around a thinner part of the rod.

Getting started was shaky but once on her way she did not risk stopping as to avoid a clumsy restart. The waterfront smells grew stronger as she approached the river, briny and brackish, it lacked the smell of low tide. She reached the top of the hill quickly. With equipment to balance, she rode the brakes down, having learned her lesson last summer not to go full tilt down the hill with fishing gear; the scar on her knee reminded her.

Parking her bike off the road, she looked over at a full wharf. The sun was reflecting so severely off the water, it was only then she realized she had forgotten her sunglasses. Squinting, she took notice of a half dozen very active fishermen. Peeking into their buckets as she walked by, she ascertained most were half full of spot and some nice-sized white perch. With only a few open places left to throw a line, she settled into a spot on the east corner so she could wave at cousin Will next time he docked the ferry.

Due to her regular appearance and the fact that her family had lived in town for many generations, she knew most of the men at the dock but spoke very little to them when the "fish were on." Fishing was very serious business when they were biting, and one should not wreck the opportunity for success with idle chit-chat. Laying down her gear, the first thing she did was pick the fattest worm and spear it with the hook. She pulled the bale back, held the line with

her finger, flipped the rod behind her and thrust forward with an easy yet definitive motion.

The first bump came within 30 seconds of her cast. She let the fish play with it a little and then, when the timing was right, yanked her rod suddenly to the right. The end tipped down towards the water and didn't bounce back up. She had caught one; she could feel the pull. She let it take some line and then rhythmically pulled the rod close to her and reeled. She repeated this motion again and again until she saw flashes of silver in the water. One last big reel brought the fish in.

She liked to take the fish off the hook in the bucket as she had lost many a catch overboard taking it off over the dock. Laying the rod thoughtfully on the worn wood planks, she reached into the bucket and put her right hand over the fish, starting with the head, and instinctively moving her hand carefully over the fins, grasping it in a way so that the barbs would not stab her. She held tight while her left hand grabbed the top of the hook and slid it out of the fish's mouth. Her rod was free, and she moved it to the side, taking a closer look at her fish. It was a good size. Using a ruler from the tackle box, its length of 11 inches made her smile. It wasn't a record holder for a perch, but it was a fine fish and it was fat too. Her father would be so pleased.

She noticed some feet standing near the bucket and looked up to see Mr. Brown, a dear friend of the family.

"Fine fish, little lady."

"Yeah, it is!" She blurted out.

"I have a half bucket full, but none of mine are as fat as that one."

Kate twinkled with pride but remembered her manners and complimented him right back.

"I bet you caught a lot of good breakfasts, Mr. Brown."

"Indeed, I have been here since sun-up. Wind's laying out now, and tides about to change. You might of caught the last one of this round."

Kate's smile faded as she looked around the dock and noticed some of the fishermen packing up.

"I'm going to try for another," she told him and got busy skewering her next worm. "Good luck," he said as he went back to his spot and gathered his things.

Kate cast again, saw the ferry approaching, and reeled in her line some so it wouldn't get caught in the propellers. She held her rod with one hand and waved to Cousin Will with the other. The whitewater churned with the force of the propellers when the captain put her in full reverse to slow for docking. She knew the reverse engine sound well; sometimes she even heard it in bed in the early mornings before she got up. She optimistically stuck around for a few more casts, but nothing was biting. The fish were gone.

As she gathered her gear, she saw Tansy skipping up the dock.

"What cha got?" she asked, smiling.

Kate tilted her bucket just a little so she could see. Tansy stretched her neck just enough to see the prize.

"Oh, Kate, that's a real nice one!"

"I know, I got really lucky. What are you doing here?"

Tansy reminded Kate they promised to visit Squawk and they had to stop at Mr. Paul's to get the brewer's yeast.

"I got to take the fish home and then we can go," said Kate, walking off the dock with all her stuff.

Tansy offered to lighten her load, and Kate gave her the tackle box, which made the ride home much less treacherous. They parked at the back fence and after putting the tackle box and fishing rod away, they stopped to see Jammy still tending to her garden just as busily as when Kate had left. Kate handed her the jar of worms.

"Jammy, I only used two, here's the rest back for your garden."

Jammy was happy she remembered to return the unused bait. "Ah, you even added some dirt so they are still cool."

She pushed some soil aside and dumped them in under the cover of her parsley.

"You look awfully pleased." Then she inquired, "What's in the bucket?"

Kate tipped it just enough to get her attention.

"Oh My! What a fine fish! Edison will love it!"

Kate left Tansy with Jammy and took the fish inside. Mary was in the kitchen and also admired the catch.

"Put it in the fridge now and you can clean it this afternoon."

Kate complied, rinsed out her bucket and took it back outside.

Jammy was tending to her memory garden. To her, a garden always had something to teach and she told the story behind each flower as they bloomed in the summer. Each year, it was a pinch different with hints of continuity and tradition throughout. Although hollyhocks are biennials, they were so established they returned annually to flank the white fence behind them in varying blushes of pinks, creamy whites, and buttery yellows. Year after year they returned and year after year Jammy reminded the family they were there to call attention to where the outhouse used to be and how lucky they were to have indoor plumbing.

Another repeat was the Chesapeake chicory, wild and leggy with stems as wiry as a coat hanger, its robin egg blue color was so distinct it could not be lost in memory. One year Jammy uprooted some of the plants to make a coffee drink. The family watched the process throughout the day as she plucked them up, washed and dried the roots thoroughly, and placed them in a metal pie tin. They roasted slowly at a low temperature in the oven for part of a day. Then they were placed on a cooling rack. The chicory's roots were tempered when they could be snapped, and then she put them in her hand-crank coffee grinder and ground them fine. She mixed the chicory half and half with coffee grinds, and the family was well pleased with the flavor of the hot drink.

A large lavender bush centered the garden and its dried blossoms were gathered for tea in the late summer, and lemon balm for tummy aches grew unrestrained in the yard so prolifically, that when Johnny cut what little grass there was, a lemon effervescence lingered in the air. Red Poppies recalled a time when Jammy's father-in-law sold poppies to a local florist as a side hobby, thus gaining him the nickname of "Poppy." Bright blue bachelor buttons mixed in with the poppies and Jammy tapped into a personal sadness in their color. She would say they were the blue of her love, Walton's eyes. At times, you might see her graze the tops with her hand and look off into the distance.

Peonies along the back fence were also a love of Poppy's and remained stalwart and predictable every May, with a penetrating spring smell to awaken even the less attuned individual. Pink and proud, they called attention by sight and smell to all who glimpsed them.

One couldn't look upon Jammy's garden without breathing deeply, exhaling, and smiling. It was in a way a visual narcotic for the senses, demanding one's gaze in the subtlest way. A tactile representation of magic, it made the yard radiant, and in a glance could make one forget all their troubles for those brief initial seconds of discovery.

Separate from her flower garden, Jammy added her touches throughout the yard. Money plants grew prolifically under the dogwood she planted in the corner of the yard. A purple lilac marking a past family baptism partially hid the kerosene tank from the street view, and morning glories of all colors fanned out in heavy layers over the rest of the tank to disguise it from even the most observant. Next to Edison's shed was Mary's love, a fig bush that Jammy also tended to.

Tansy, captivated by Jammy's stories behind the flowers, was drawn away by Kate on their mission to see Mr. Paul. He lived across the street from Edison's garden. His house was so weather-worn, his roof looked like a patchwork quilt. His foundation was on a slight tilt, and so was he. The windows had no screens, and in the back right corner of his yard was a loosely organized pile of scrap metal in an old wooden loafing shed that hadn't seen a chicken in years. Townspeople would stop by now and then and pay him for a piece of stainless steel, a scrap of tin, chicken wire, metal flashing, or whatever was needed to complete a project. If you needed a piece of metal, Mr. Paul's place was where to go.

A widower just two years ago, his loss was obvious to his neighbors. Not only was the yard not as well kept when Miss Anna was alive, but the touches of a woman had all but disappeared. There was never any laundry on the line nor petunias planted in the front of the house. No smell of food cooking in his kitchen, and he rarely waved when people walked by. The two of them, Anna and Paul, had spent much time sitting in their lawn chairs just outside the kitchen door. After Miss Anna died, Mr. Paul kept the chairs just as they were, side by side, summer or winter, rain or shine, snow or gale; the chairs kept each other company.

Kate and Tansy pulled up on their bikes and put their kick stands down. A gate in the same disposition as his house, no longer latched, nor held much paint, swung open with just a little push. Mr. Paul's back was turned digging with a shovel so the girls announced themselves and halfway turning around, he nodded his head for them to come over.

"Working on my little garden, girls. What do you think?"

Two tomato plants looked healthy, with strong metal cages around them. His sugar snaps had already climbed the strings he had strung for them and were loaded with juicy pods. The beets were up and squash plants had a few flowers on them.

"Mr. Paul," Tansy exclaimed, "it looks very healthy, especially those broccoli plants!"

His broccoli was just as full as could be.

"Here, girls, help yourselves to some sugar snaps."

Kate and Tansy reached for the peas and each picked a handful, eating them, pod and all. "These are some of my favorites," said Kate while crunching away.

Distracted by his tiny but bountiful garden, they had almost forgotten the reason for their visit.

"So, what are you girls up to today?"

"Oh," said Kate, "we almost forgot, do you have any brewer's yeast?"

"Yes, but what do you girls want with brewer's yeast?"

"Well, we don't rightly know," said Tansy, "but Miss Pat from the boatyard sent us to ask for some."

"So she's got a baby duck, does she?"

"Yeah, how do you know?" Kate inquired.

"There's something special a duckling needs from the yeast. I don't know what it is but I'm happy to help out Miss Pat. She's always sending one of the yard men down to buy my metal. Good lady, that Miss Pat. You know I had a good lady, too."

He looked down at his garden.

"When Miss Anna was alive we would plant all the vegetables together, we had a garden three times this size…but still not as big as Edison's, Kate."

Sensing his vulnerability, Kate offered up a kind word.

"Well we sure do miss her, too. She made real good brownies."

"Yeah," said Tansy, "... and she was real nice."

Mr. Paul got very quiet, turned and walked up two stairs and onto his screened-in porch where he brewed his beer. He put a scoop full of yeast into a brown liquor bag and walked back out and handed it to Tansy.

"Thanks, Mr. Paul," they said in unison.

Jumping on their bikes, they rode along happily munching on their sugar snaps. However, forward laughter and the raw noise of loud men grew stronger, and Kate suddenly remembered the proximity of the Country Club and slowed her bike. To call it a "Country Club" in the true sense of the word was a misnomer.

The weather had not been kind to the mustard yellow dilapidated abandoned shack. What was left of the front porch roof leaned to the right, precariously supported by rotting posts as if one more gale would surely bring it down. Brambles and vines where flowers once bloomed decorated the exterior and competed with the English ivy for the prize of covering the crumbling chimney. Even the trees closest to the shack were in ill health.

The front yard, never mowed but worn to the dirt by the activity of its members, displayed a half dozen or so rusty lawn chairs loosely placed in a semi-circle. A club sign hung by one nail on an angle next to the rotted-out front door. Black lettering on a dirty white painted plywood board read: "The Country Club."

The "members" passed around a bottle wrapped in an old brown liquor sack, laughing themselves silly by tales they elaborated on with each sip they took. Chairs would fall and grown men would roll. This debauchery sometimes began before noon, especially on hot days.

Sensing Kate's caution, Tansy slowed her bike too and looked at Kate.

"Don't mind them, Tansy, just smile and wave."

And that's just what they did when one of the illustrious

members stood up and waved back, tripping over his own shoe-string and falling flat on his face. The howling was so loud, everyone in a two-block radius would have curiously paused at the sound. Kate and Tansy sped up, turned the corner onto a shiny oyster shell road, peddled along the fenced side of the boatyard, and then turned right and glided into the busy yard.

Sam was there to greet them and assure them that Squawk was being well looked after. She was nestled into her blanket, but ran to the edge of the box towards them putting her feet right into her water bowl when she saw the girls. The water bowl tipped over and made her corn turn to mush.

"Aww, Squawk, you're making a mess!" Tansy said fondly.

Miss Pat came out of her office. "There you girls are, did you bring me the yeast?"

Tansy proudly handed it to her.

"Wonderful!" she said with a smile as she turned and went back into her office.

Kate poked her head in the door, "What's it for?"

"I add it to the corn for nutrition," she said, "and I have jobs for you girls."

She mixed two tablespoons into a cup of cracked corn and came back outside.

"Girls, raising a baby duck is hard work, and I'm going to count on you for some help. Squawk needs to forage in the grass by the beach for bugs and go in the river for a little while. Let her splash, but don't stay too long, baby ducks get cold even in the summer. When she's eaten enough bugs and played a bit, wrap her in this towel and bring her back."

The girls nodded their heads in agreement, feeling quite privileged that Miss Pat trusted them with the duckling. After all, she didn't let just anyone help with her babies. Tansy picked up the baby gently and Kate carried the towel.

They loved watching Squawk poke around in the grass for bugs and tried to encourage her to go down to the river. She waddled right up to the river's edge but when a small wave came in she ran away from it, back up the bank to Tansy and Kate squawking. This happened over and over again; Squawk would try to brave the river and then turn tailfeather and run for the girls, who couldn't stop giggling over the duck that was afraid of the water. After a while, the tired baby duck climbed into Kate's lap and she wrapped her in a towel. When they returned, Squawk's cage had been cleaned and had a dry blanket, food and a full water dish. Kate carefully laid her on the blanket.

Miss Pat poked her head out of the office, "Did she eat some bugs?"

"Yeah, lots of them," said Kate, "but she was afraid of the water."

"No worries about that, she'll take to it in time," Miss Pat assured them.

"Now Kate, I need you to bring me a fresh bunch of greens from your father's garden sometime soon."

"Okay," she said. "My dad has lots of greens!"

The baby duck fell asleep in her blanket and with Sam standing watch, they decided to leave.

Miss Pat sensed they were hungry. "Girls, you've been a big help; I'm sure you're hungry being it's already afternoon; go in the back door, and there's some ham in the fridge for sandwiches."

"Thanks Miss Pat," they said smiling, and ran over to her house, which was on the boatyard property, and slipped in the back door. Her kitchen was small but very neat and clean. Kate opened the fridge and saw the ham roast and grabbed some mayonnaise. Tansy saw the bread on the counter and got a knife. Together they constructed ham sandwiches to tame their hunger, and poured two glasses of water. They even made one for Miss Pat, wrapped it in a napkin and put it on her desk before they left. She was already back in the yard tying up boats; she never seemed to sit still for very long.

Heading back the way they came, the rambunctious sounds of the Country Club grew stronger and cautiously they slowed down.

"Remember," said Kate, "just smile and wave."

Tansy grabbed Kate's arm, stopped her bike and put her fingers to her lips. Kate stopped too and they quietly stepped off thier bikes. Kate followed along as they crept up behind Miss Clara's prized rosebushes.

"What is it?" Kate questioned.

That's my neighbor, and he's drunk again," said Tansy.

Kate took her nose out of a blossom and peeked through the foliage. "Wait," she whispered, "that's my cousin… and my dad!"

Both girls became quiet.

"Listen you S.O.B, you better clean yourself up or you won't have a bed in our house anymore," Edison yelled at Lowell.

Lowell, staggering, swung at Edison who dodged it.

"You don't have to worry about fighting me Lowell, it's the Seth women and your wife Sally you should worry 'bout. Your stoking the fire with your drinking and hell hath no fury like that crew." Edison pulled himself together and looked at Lowell. "I've said my piece."

Edison then walked off leaving Lowell to fall backwards against one of the half-rotten trees, where he passed out. During all of this, the men at the Country Club watched and sipped, watched and sipped. When it was all over, the conversation started up as if nothing had happened.

Tansy and Kate looked at each other wide-eyed and speechless.

"Oh yeah," Tansy whispered, "I heard he was staying at your house. How's that going?" Kate shrugged her shoulders, "He's never home."

When they deemed the path clear and rounded the corner, Mr. Paul surprised them. They were so focused on Edison and Lowell that they hadn't seen him. He jumped out of his chair, brown bag in his hand, staggered forward and stretched out his hand towards them, but couldn't get his words out, he was so drunk. Without even contemplating what she saw, Kate waved "hello" to him but kept her peddles turning. Tansy waved without words.

Once they were past, Kate rode straight to her father's garden, hopped off her bike and stood for a minute staring across the street at Mr. Paul's empty house. Mr. Paul's behavior was a drastic change from their earlier visit. Tansy pulled up beside her, also silent. Kate quickly diverted their thoughts to something more pleasurable.

"I think there might be a few strawberries left in Father's garden," Kate said.

When Edison wasn't working, he was gardening. While Jammy favored native flowers and French herbs, Edison was more practical in his approach and enjoyed the pleasures and disappointments of growing fruits and vegetables. Between the two gardens on a blessed night the family could have a well-seasoned bounty on their plates and flowers on the table, too. Mary nicknamed this a "moon and stars" meal.

When driving or riding past Edison's garden, one might not notice it was there at all. Blocking its beauty was an old greenhouse that was used by Dr. Emmitt, a chemist who performed experiments on plants. Upon entering the greenhouse, a chemical smell beset all senses. The most interesting plants grew all over his many wooden shelves, but no one could ever stand to visit very long for holding their breath.

Behind the wooden and glass structure and the lingering smells that escaped its walls, visitors were greeted by a grapevine entrance to Edison's garden. An old wooden ladder propped up on each side by 4x4 posts provided the height for the Steuben grapevine to run riot so vigorously that it had run several lengths of the ladder back upon itself, as Edison had trained it to do. Laden fruit dropped below the arbor and along the posts in its own natural proclivity. This portal made everyone who entered feel as though they were destined for a rare experience exclusive to their own prejudices on the definition of beauty. There was a benevolence to the space, where breadth and width became illusive.

The garden was of simple design, a brick walkway in the center carved the area in two. To the west, the wild blackberries suffocated the border fence; and in between lay a patch of Ambrosia cantaloupes, Crenshaw melons, Sugar Baby watermelons, and sweet honeydews. To cross over top of the melons and through to the berries a tall stump path was created, and to challenge the obstacle course without error was to claim victory with berries in hand as a trophy. A fall was always blamed on the invisible but sprightly garden nymphs.

The east side of the garden was split in two: the northern side and southern side with the bordering east fence supporting an ever spreading native honeysuckle vine, its red trumpets calling loudly to the hummingbirds in the warm season. Edison always planted row crops from north to south for maximum sun exposure. Running parallel, the southern quadrant had rows of carrots, beets, Swiss chard, kale and collards, broccoli, green and wax beans, leeks and sweet onions. In the northern quarter lay sweet potatoes, yellow crooknecks, zucchini, patty pans, eggplants, and cherry tomatoes. The raised beds flanking the entrance boasted Edison's prized heirloom tomatoes, and, until the middle of June, juicy strawberries. There were no contests in town, but neighbors and happy recipients of his large and healthy tomatoes saw them as a prize and named them such. If there had been a tomato challenge, Edison would have definitively won a blue ribbon.

At the far South end of the property, a compost heap lay between airy walls constructed of old wooden pallets. A rusted pitchfork remained at the ready, leaning upon the rickety structure. Behind it, the lonely persimmon tree Kate had gazed at the night before called to her; every time she saw it she sensed sadness. With its companion tree at the neighbors, on occasion she felt compelled to jump the fence to have a chat with it, but not today. On either side of the compost pallets, against an old rusted wire fence, more blackberries grew prolifically, their glossy black shine rarely broken by an occasional golden raspberry cluster. Rhubarb grew untamed at its base, having been faithfully divided every few years for decades. It now grew like a wild, untamed animal expanding its territory to beyond the wire fence and into the main thoroughfare of garbage alley.

At one time, the space between the blackberry fence and Edison's garden was street width, but over the years, the width had been encroached upon not only by the rhubarb, but also by a hundred year old fig bush that had been left unpruned, as well as the grandmother willow she visited the night before. Her branches hung so low they scraped the ground creating a peaceful and shady hiding spot.

The number of visible weeds between rows was an indicator of just how busy Edison was with his carpentry work. A weedy garden meant he was busy as ever, an immaculate one, while pretty, was foreboding. Somewhere between weedy and tidy rows lay a happy medium for Edison and the family he supported. The Seth family ate well out of the garden all summer long. In fact, Mary bought just a few things outside of town. Mary froze much of the produce Edison grew. Beyond what the family could eat, and the family freezer could handle, was graciously given away to family, friends, and neighbors. Proudly, there was often much to share. Edison's pride of abundance was a healthy kind of pride and well received by others.

Kate and Tansy stood by the strawberries and leaned head first over the short lattice wall that kept the rabbits out. Peeking out amongst the expanse of green strawberry leaves were slivers of red - clues that more strawberries were hiding, and ripe for the picking. They got to work picking and eating, picking and eating, until they were full.

"Sometimes they have a crunch to them," said Tansy.

"That's the sand in the dirt, strawberries like sand," said Kate.

Wiping their mouths by stretching their shirt fronts up to their faces they walked though the grape arbor.

"Looks like the grapes are not ready, they're hard and small," Tansy observed while squeezing one.

"Yeah," replied Kate, "grapes come on later in the summer." Walking the brick aisle perusing the plants, they discussed what was almost ripe, and what had weeks to go.

"What's been picked there?" Tansy pointed out the empty, slightly weedy row near the greens.

"I think it's the broccoli." said Kate, "We're probably having it for dinner or mother is blanching it to freeze. Dad will probably plant some more beans there in the next few days. They have a short season."

Kate noticed the weeds were only of moderate concern and she smiled. Kate looked right towards the cut through path lined with black-eyed Susans for a yellow shop building that butted up to the ally. That's where Mr. Tawes sat, his empty aluminum lawn chair had more rust than shine but still reflected enough sun that the light bounced off of Kate's eyes and made her squint.

"Hey, you want to get some greens for Miss Pat?" asked Tansy.

"I need to ask first," said Kate. "Father always shares but he most definitely has to be asked first."

When they had finished their garden sojourn, they walked out through the arbor and jumped back on their bikes.

Chapter IV

— Poaching and Poetry —

"Let's go check the docks for crabs," said Kate. "Come on, I have nets at my house."

Tansy agreed and they headed to Kate's, parked their bikes out back, and looked under the lean-to for the nets. They jumped on their bikes, and each balanced their own net while riding to the docks. When they arrived, the wharf was quiet, and there were no crabbers. The ducks had returned, waddling on the beach next to the ferry, talking up and down with each other like townspeople.

They walked out onto the wharf. Instinctively, Tansy looked on the pilings off one side and Kate on the other.

"I see one!" yelled Tansy. Kate ran over in time to see Tansy scoop up a jimmy and a peeler.

"A doubler! We should have brought a bucket," Kate lamented.

Then she remembered a trick that Mr. Brown had taught her when she went fishing one day and forgot a bucket.

"Keep them both," she said and headed over to the beach and rocks. Many times, wooden bushels would float ashore and come to rest on the rocks. Sure enough, she saw one not far from the ducks. As she walked through the chatting Mallards, they scattered little as they were used to humans, their company, and bread bits.

"I have nothing to give you today, guys," Kate apologized as she walked ever closer to the basket. Her pace slowed as she approached, looking for flashes of eyes or brown slithering movements. All looked still around it. Leaving no chance for an up-close surprise, she used the pole end of her net to slip through one of the handles and raised it up above the rocks. A water snake slithered quickly back into the rock pile as she pulled the basket closer. Upon close inspection the basket was in decent shape, not too much algae had gathered, and it had not been shipwrecked long enough for barnacles to grow. One handle was missing, but it was a usable find.

She ran back to Tansy with her net in one hand, basket in the other. Tansy dropped the crabs into the basket, and Kate used an old t-shirt someone left on the dock to cover the top and shade the crabs. It seemed as though every other piling had a crab and Kate scooped a doubler just swimming by. They basked in their afternoon lottery with high fives and laughter and an unexpected bounty. By late afternoon their basket held four peelers and 12 jimmy's. Wanting to surprise their families, they headed back home with the crabs. Kate managed the basket with the one good handle and rested it on her right knee while she steered with her left hand. Tansy took both nets, stacked them together, and slung them over her left shoulder.

First stop was Kate's house. No one was home so she put her half dozen jimmy's in a bucket in the shade out back. At Tansy's house Miss Lucille was so pleased with their surprise she hugged them both and went to ready a pot from her kitchen.

"We'll cook them when you get back from selling your peelers, Tansy," Miss Lucille said with a tickled look on her face.

The girls were off again with one last delivery. At the other end of town, next to a restaurant, was Jimmy's Crab Shed. This is where he bought peelers to shed in his tanks into soft crabs. Kate and Tansy arrived just as he was getting into his truck.

"Mr. Jimmy!" they yelled and Kate stopped her bicycle and held the basket up over her head to get his attention. He smiled, stopped, and put his truck in park. Just behind his truck his business sign read: "Jimmy's Jimmys."

"What you girls got for me?"

"We got four peelers!" Tansy blurted out.

"Four? That's pretty good luck for just working the wharf! I suppose it helps that we are racing towards a full moon. Well, let me take a look at them. Bring them over to the shed."

The girls skipped over with their prize catch to Mr. Jimmy. He reached in the basket, and held the first by the backfin, then the second, third, and fourth.

"Well girls, three of these peelers are green on the fiddler, but one is pink 'bout to turn red. I need all I can get tomorrow, so how's about I give you a quarter each for the green ones and 75 cents for the red? She'll be shedding tomorrow; the others have several days." The girls nodded as he handed them $1.50 in quarters, which they split evenly. Saying goodbye to Mr. Jimmy they sped off, each anxious to get home.

As Kate rolled her bike in the back gate, Edison turned her way but said nothing.

She ran to where she had left the crabs, but they were gone.

She turned to Edison, "Where are the crabs?"

He ignored her again, and so she went in the back porch door and found Mother boiling water and adding vinegar to it.

"You found them!" Kate said joyfully.

"Yes!" replied Mary. "What a wonderful surprise! Did you catch them all at the wharf?" Kate repeated the story in great detail, and Jammy showed up in time to hear about the 75 cents Kate had jingling in her pocket.

"They will go great with the fish you caught this morning," Jammy pointed out. Kate had completely forgotten about the white perch and pulled open the refrigerator door.

"It still needs to be cleaned," Mary interjected.

Kate grabbed the fish, a filet knife and a cutting board. First she scaled it, washed the scales off under the sink then gutted it, trimmed the fins, and then turned to Mary.

"Should I filet it or leave it whole?"

"Filet it, then it will be easy to split up for everyone."

"I thought it was for Father's breakfast?" Kate questioned.

"Maybe the next fish; I'm making this part of supper." Kate shrugged her shoulders and started working from the tail end to filet.

"You know your father starts at the other end," Mary interjected.

"I know," Kate said, flipping the fish around and cutting off its head.

By now, the crabs were steaming, and the Swiss chard was getting tossed into boiling water. Mary pulled deviled eggs out of the icebox. With the hot oil sparking in the skillet, Jammy, with apron on and ready, dusted the fish with cornmeal and a little Old Bay seasoning mixed in, and placed it in the fry pan.

Mary walked over to the screen door and yelled to Edison, "Dish up!"

Then she yelled up the back steps to Johnny, "Dish up!"

Johnny flew down the steps fresh from the shower, in clean clothes. Jammy looked him up and down.

"Plans?" she quizzed.

"I have a date!" he announced proudly. "With Lizzie Parks."

The questions flying out of the females of the house were rapid and intense.

"When did this happen?" asked Mary.

"Where are you going?" asked Kate.

"You must meet the parents first!" Jammy insisted.

Overwhelmed with questions, Johnny backed up took a breath and said, "I saw her today at Truman's store, and we got to talking, and I wondered if she'd like to go for ice cream tonight after dinner, and she said yes. So I'm picking her up at her house at seven. Good enough?"

Mary and Kate nodded yes in approval.

But Jammy added, "You will shake Mr. Parks' hand, of course."

"Yes, Jammy, I will shake her father's hand."

With the parameters of Johnny's date satisfied, everyone carried something to the table. One perch and half dozen crabs were hardly enough to feed a family of four, more than a taste of each, so Mary had also warmed the leftover fried chicken from the night before. Edison walked in and sat down. He didn't pour the tea as usual, so Johnny stood up and took on the duty. Kate noticed that Lowell was absent but thought it best not to mention it. Mary led the grace, and then Kate, helping herself to some Swiss chard, wondered why they weren't eating broccoli, which reminded her of her visit with Mr. Paul.

"Edison, Kate caught the perch and the crabs for dinner tonight." Mary seemed to be attempting to lighten Edison's mood.

Edison mumbled something under his breath. Clearly, he was occupied by thoughts other than dinner. Kate sensed the mood and pitched into the effort to engage Edison.

"Tansy and I saw Mr. Paul today," she offered. "His garden is looking real good even without Miss Anna. He gave us sugar snaps, and they were real sweet."

Jammy was interested. "What else did he have growing?"

"He's got two real nice tomato plants in strong cages, some squash plants, beets, and a whole row of broccoli that looks ready to pick."

"That's it!" Edison slammed his fist on the table, "That son of a bitch, poached my broccoli!"

Edison stood up, gave the hinges on the screen door a workout, and stormed through the backyard and out the back gate. Kate instantly got a lump in her throat. Mr. Paul had stolen her father's broccoli plants and replanted them in his garden.

Worried for Mr. Paul, Kate rose slowly from her seat asking, "What's father going to do?"

Mary grabbed her arm softly and gently pulled her back into her seat.

"There will be words and a resolution," said Mary, "but do not worry Kate, Edison is not a violent man. He developed a distaste for violence at a young age."

Kate, overwhelmed with worry, stared at her dinner, no longer hungry. Jammy put a deviled egg on her plate. "All will be well, Kate. Have a deviled egg; they are one of your favorites."

Kate became quiet as she often did when troubling thoughts overwhelmed her. She took one bite of the egg and then put it down.

Dinner clean up was routine as Kate kept quiet and her worries close. She dutifully washed some utensils, wiped the counters, and dried the pots and pans. Johnny skipped out of cleanup to preen before his date, and soon after, he was out the door. Jammy went upstairs to work on her poetry, and Mary kept busy sweeping the floor and fussing about tidying the kitchen.

Kate was confused; she felt like she was the only one in the family on high alert. In her uneasiness, she went out the back door and looked for River. He wasn't in the backyard, so she walked the side yard, observant of the dainty ferns that cozied up to the brick and the moss that grew underneath them. Ferns hid the brick foundation with a beautiful precision that only nature could craft. Their softness called to her, and she paused, instinctively running her hands through the delicate feathery fronds. Normally, she would call River's name, but quiet felt better. She wandered silently taking in her surroundings.

The neighbors on the north side of the house weren't often there, making it their weekend home. A concept many in town had a hard time grasping, that someone could have a weekend home. When neighbors were there, Mary and Edison had pleasant conversations over the fence during the day, and at night, they were a source of drunken entertainment for those sitting on the front porch.

River was resting in the dirt under the shade of an old boxwood and came running as soon as he spotted Kate. They sat together on the lawn, Kate petting him and he soaking it up. She heard the back gate click and walked to the corner of the house. Peeking from behind the morning glory-covered kerosene tank, she saw Edison had returned, and Mary, who had seemed so calm earlier, was running out to see him.

Hidden from view behind the fragrant purple lilac, she listened.

"Edison, what did you do?"

"I yelled at the son of a bitch, of course. Told him I'd always shared with him and all he has to do is ask. I would've given him some broccoli, just not the whole damn row. Heck, I bring him stuff all the time without him asking! Crazy old drunk."

Mary paused in relief. "How did you leave it?"

"Shit, Mary, he's planting the broccoli back in my garden. Which makes no damn sense; it's started to wither from the first time he pulled it up." Edison put his hands on his hips and huffed.

"I guess we'll have broccoli for dinner tomorrow, and I'll blanch and freeze the rest," Mary offered.

Edison huffed again, paused, and thanked Mary.

"I'll visit Mr. Paul tomorrow; he'll want to talk," Mary stated.

"He's too embarrassed to be saved tomorrow, Mary."

"I know!" she retorted and huffed too.

Kate was well relieved that this altercation was settled. Mr. Paul was a curiosity to her. How could he have been so honest about missing Miss Anna during her visit, all the while knowing he had stolen her father's broccoli plants? How could he be engaged in conversation in the morning and be a slobbering drunk by the afternoon? It seemed as though when Miss Anna died, he lost his anchor.

She threw the ball to River a few times and filled his water dish. The sun was down, and the mosquitos were coming out, so she decided to go inside and see what Jammy was up to. As she walked up the front hall closer to the porch, she could hear the porch slider rolling back and forth. The sound made her tired. She poked her head through the window, and there was Jammy all by herself, rocking back and forth, back and forth. Edison and Mary had gone on their evening walk.

"Come, sit next to me, Kate." Jammy motioned with a pat on the seat next to her.

Kate nestled in next to her and looked out at the lamplights. The rhythm of the slider and the drone of the cicadas made her eyelids heavy. She reached down and scratched a mosquito bite.

"Jammy, I'm goin' upstairs."

"Goodnight dear; see you in the morning."

Kate crawled through the window and climbed the stairs as if she had lead weights tied to her ankles. She went to pull her sheets down, and on her pillow was a handwritten note. Her eyes widened. It was Jammy's latest poem. It read:

Mosquito

Who is it works while others sleep
His nightly tete a tete to keep?
Who knows no word as privacy
As boudoir usually means to me.
Mosquito.

Who is it hovers 'round my bed
And makes me cover up my head?
Who sings his plaintive lullaby
While stars are twinning in the sky?
Mosquito.

Who is it finds the tender spots
On grown up folks and tiny tots?
Who is it feasts his evening meal
On some poor soul's uncovered heel?
Mosquito.

Who is there in the universe
Can free us of this awful curse?
Who'll take away this dreadful pest,
The robber of our beauty rest?
Mosquito.

She giggled, fell into her soft pillow, and disappeared into night dreams.

Chapter V

— Mary, Mother, Methodism, and the Metaphysical —

One by one, almost simultaneously, front doors all over town were shut, keys were turned, and residents stayed home to watch their penny jars. Of course, Kate didn't know this; their house was flanked on one side by occasional weekenders and on the other by Miss Charlotte, who kept to herself, never advertising whether or not she was home. Tucking oneself away as Miss Charlotte did was unlike most residents. Most left front doors wide open and screened doors unlatched in anticipation of welcoming company. Unaware of the impending intelligence report, Kate sat thoughtfully by the goldfish pond this morning, discussing her latest adventures with Herman.

Mary had been out riding her bike about town, during which the most disturbing news had been shared with her. The scuttlebutt breezed through town like a squall catching everyone by surprise — the Gypsies had arrived. Riding home swiftly to share the news, Mary approached the back fence of the Seth house, took her feet off the pedals, and glided like an arrow to the back gate. Edison, witnessing the focus in Mary's eyes, was brought to full attention. Mary whispered over the fence to him.

"Where's the key?"

"I don't know; how about the living room drawer?"

"I'll try there first...Gypsies," she said as she opened the back gate.

"I figured," replied Edison, saying, "I'll stay in the backyard and keep an eye out."

Mary strode quickly through the backyard labyrinth, barely noticing Kate, who had left the pond to admire Jammy's garden.

Kate became instantly attuned to her mother's hurried pace and curiously followed. By the time Kate had entered the kitchen, Mary was coming out of the living room and headed towards the pantry.

"What's going on?" Kate asked.

"I'll tell you after I find the key." She exited the pantry and started up the back steps. "Mother! You up there?" Mary called.

Jammy came out of her room as Kate had climbed the back steps and worked her way to the short set of three steps that connected her parents' room to the upstairs front hall. From here, she sat curiously watching the exchange.

"I can't find the key."

"Oh dear," Jammy said in a worried tone.

They stared at each other with pause and then looked at the ceiling in reflection. Kate was quickly shushed when she started to ask more questions. Quietly, they stood there, mother and daughter, as granddaughter Kate watched patiently. What seemed like an eternity of silence was broken by Jammy.

"You've already checked the living room drawer and the pantry jar," she said in a statement rather than a question. This was followed by additional pause and reflection. Jammy's abrupt wave of her hand broke the concentration.

"Come, I am remembering something," she said, and Mary, relieved by her epiphany, followed at her heels into her bedroom. Kate tip-toed behind with deliberately soft footsteps. Standing behind the two matriarchs, Kate watched her grandmother pull a small book with a brittle brown leather binding off her shelf. Underneath it laid a tarnished old-fashioned metal key. It was large compared to car keys, about three inches long, and made of brass. It was similar to other keys Kate had seen around the house, but what made this one so special?

"Mother! You've found it!" Mary exclaimed. "Of course, I remember we decided to keep it in your care."

"Gypsies?" Jammy questioned.

"Yes. Just outside of town, they've hit the Anderson Farm. Mrs. A is so distraught over the departure of her oriental rugs."

"Of course she is," Jammy agreed.

Mary left to lock the front door.

"Jammy?" was all Kate had to say for a full explanation.

"Miss Kate, every few years, the Gypsies come to town to steal rugs and coins. They are not dangerous, but they are very crafty thieves as they don't ever seem to get caught. I say they are not dangerous because as long as your door is locked, they will leave your property alone. If you leave your door open, it is seen as a sign that they are welcome to enter. They are so sneaky that only one person in town has actually seen one."

"Who was that?" Kate's eyes widened.

"Miss Ginny, up the street. She walked in on a Gypsy who had Ginny's change crock in her hand. Upon the sight of Miss Ginny, the Gypsy dropped the crock, it shattered, and she ran straight out the front door. Miss Ginny followed her to the middle of the street and looked in all directions, but the gypsy had vanished. It was a rare sighting since most folks only know they have been hit after their rugs and coins are gone. I believe the last time we locked the front door was when they were in town a few years back…"

Kate was mostly satisfied with the answer. "But Jammy, what do they look like? How will I know if I see one?"

"Miss Ginny described the Gypsy that visited her home as very beautiful with long dark wavy hair, glowing skin, and dark shimmering deep brown eyes; but at the same time, gaunt with hunger." Jammy added, "As they travel from place to place, they have no home; they have no anchor. Kate, they are a people that blow in the wind."

With that, Jammy headed down the front steps to join Mary and spread the word.

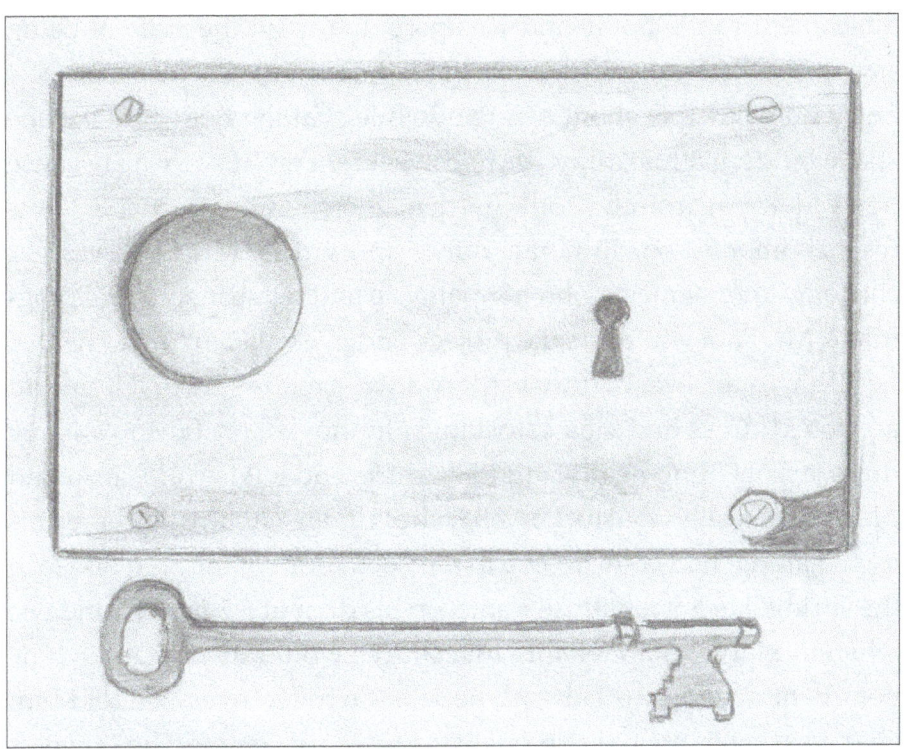

Kate felt safe now that the door was locked. She hadn't ever really thought about the fact that the door was never locked until now. The more she thought about it, the more she wondered why no one seemed to lock their door in town…which she easily answered herself with the Seventh Commandment: "Thou shalt not steal." Kate had learned the Ten Commandments from all her "churching." Mary and Edison wanted their children to know the ways of Christ and so church was a paramount force within the family and also the community at large.

A woman of strong Methodist values, Mary divided the people in her life into two categories: drinkers and non-drinkers. Drinkers would either be judged at the gates or on the edge of saving on earth, and which category they fell into was a blurry line, and her reasons weren't always understood. Some were considered wayward souls, and others recalcitrant.

Her Cousin Lowell, who was a wayward soul, had an unhealthy

attachment to the bottle and was perpetually on the edge of being saved. Yet Mr. Paul, who lived around the corner, was "a lost cause." She would say this about Mr. Paul while shaking her head, yet she still would visit and pray for him weekly. Perhaps it was because he lived across from Edison's garden, and she was practicing "love thy neighbor." Poor in home, mind, and virtue, Mr. Paul was her challenge, her nemesis, and her patience and persistence were pragmatic. Mr. Paul was quite the project, and everyone in town knew it.

Up at 6 a.m. every Sunday, Mary always made sure that Kate had an ironed dress and clean stockings. Johnny's and Edison's Navy dress jackets hung neatly and their shirts and kakis were clean and pressed as well. Cousin Lowell, who, under circumstances of his own making, had come to live in the back room of the Seth house in the spring. He got a faithful knock on his door at 8 a.m. on Sundays, wherein Mary would tell him that church would do him good. If he got up, her eyes sparkled with hope, if he rolled over, she told him God was watching. On a recent Sunday, Mary, angered by Lowell's debauchery the night before, yelled for the whole house to hear: "Lowell, you have two children that need you and church would do you good!"

Although she had no formal musical training, it never showed. Mary was an excellent organist and piano player, playing only by ear as she could not read notes; she knew all the favorite church hymns by rote. For her part-time job, she received $7.50 per church service and the same for funerals and birthday parties, but $10 for a wedding.

Mary and her mother were an integral part of the ladies' church circle. This group of devout women met every Wednesday morning to discuss church and community needs, plan bake sales, and organize church suppers. Jammy sang soprano in the chorus, so each Sunday, Mary and her mother walked up together, and the rest of the family joined in the pews later.

As a product of the Depression, Jammy's early married life was

in a time when ingenuity and cleverness were often a replacement for money. A fervent saver of tinfoil, a holdover habit from the war effort in the forties, the woman was one of the wisest in the neighborhood. She was also a woman of quiet distinction as her father was a lawyer, and in her youth and early twenties, she was exposed to higher education and finer things.

After the stock market crash of 1929, she yielded to the loss of some family finery and, a little more than a decade later, the devastating loss of her love in the war, Mary's father, Walton. War-torn and battle-ready, she would get her hands and knees dirty in the garden and, on the same day wash up and put on white gloves to attend a formal party, not that there were many formal parties in a working town. But Jammy had these interesting connections from the past that would pop up now and then and she would be off to visit in her best dress in the next town over where she grew up.

A petite woman of slight build, she had the perception of a prophet, the manners of a queen, and the determination of an Olympian! Her energy was comparable to that of dynamite. With all these powers at her disposal, the one thing she could not do was hold her liquor. So she imposed on herself a strict one scotch limit for social occasions. And even that, at times, seemed to overwhelm her constitution, as for one to assume she had been with drink all night. Known for the first 50 years of her life as Miss Katherine, Johnny, her first grandchild, bestowed upon her the name of Jammy, his 2-year-old version of Grammy. From then on, the townspeople called her Jammy. But in the town where she grew up, she was still elegantly called "Miss Katherine."

A card-playing, scotch drinking Methodist, she did not assume the typical behaviors of a true Methodist church woman. Nonetheless she was devout in her own way, never gambled and put a chain on the scotch. Usually, scotch was only drunk outside the house but oddly both Mary and her mother kept a bottle of dark Jamaican rum and a bottle of Kentucky bourbon under the steps for "special occasion" cakes.

The step that lifted up always fascinated Kate when she was younger. It was the last step of the bottom flight of back steps, and it had hinges on it. When Kate was smaller Edison sent her on a mission to go under the steps to fish an electrical wire through. At five, she was skinny enough to shimmy her way through the opening. Once through, Edison handed her a flashlight. The flashlight revealed about a dozen Clark bar wrappers, the skeleton of a dead mouse, sawdust, and some odd nails, most likely from when the house was built. Thinking she had found something of consequence, Kate yelled, "There's Clark bar wrappers under here!"

Brother Johnny who was watching the event, started to turn away as if he was going outside when Mary said, "Johnny!" She turned towards him with raised brow and focused one eye on him. He froze and looked at the floor.

"I told you to lay off the candy!" Mary bellowed.

He remained focused on the floor. 'Sorry, Mom."

"You should be," Mary snapped back. "You've got three cavities so far; I do not want to pay for another one!"

Edison turned the focus back to the task of the moment.

"Kate, I'm going to run a wire from under the kitchen cabinet to you, and you need to thread it through to the opposite hole on the wall." Kate fished it through quickly and exited; she had discovered a family of spiders just above her head. She wondered if they were Methodist, too.

This hidden step, where Mary and her mother hid the cake booze, was joined by a bottle of elderberry wine in case of flu. In 1918, when the Spanish pandemic hit, Jammy's mother was given a large bottle of elderberry wine from a folk medicine lady named Imogene. Everyone in her family, even the children, had a glass of wine, which caused them all to throw up violently. However, none of them became sick with fever. After watching her elderly neighbors succumb to the flu while her relations were spared, she put great stock into the practice of herbal medicine and dabbled in it herself.

Mary and her mother had been through much together, and so they learned to lean on each other and the Lord. When Mary's father died young, his parents, Jammy's in-laws, and young Mary stayed together in the house. When Ma and Poppy became ill, the family home was entrusted to Jammy and then in turn to Mary. They treated it as a responsibility and an honor.

Ma and Poppy, Mary's grandparents, still visited after their deaths to check in from time to time. In times of stress, one could hear their anxious pacing in the upstairs hall and the opening and closing of doors as they made the rounds. If one did not become accustomed to these apparitions early in life, they might have been scared. But contrary to the bad publicity of ghosts, Ma and Poppy meant no harm, only goodwill. Their love for family was unbreakable and it was of comfort to know there were interested parties keeping watch over the Seth household.

Great Uncle Will, who built the house, also checked in on occasion and favored visiting with Johnny, whose middle name was his namesake, and would inquire as to what was happening in the household. Great Uncle Will, if alive, might have been considered a bit of a gossip, as his first question to Johnny every time he visited was, "What's going on?" He also timed his visits when the family was under stress, and on such occasions, Johnny was dutiful in his reports.

Kate could hear Johnny and Great Uncle Will talking in Johnny's room, which was situated next to hers. She found this amusing and would often ask Johnny if he had told Will everything. If he didn't, Great Uncle Will would surely be back, not that Kate or Johnny minded the visits, but Kate thought it only fair that Great Uncle Will have all the details. Johnny wasn't always as thorough as Kate thought he should be. While the Seth women could converse with the ancestors, Johnny was the only one bestowed the gift of being able to actually see them.

When daily life was hard, or they were puzzled by family history, Mary and her mother would often quiz Ma and Poppy by talking to the ceiling or simply staring upwards. Sometimes this was in vain, and other times, the answer would pop into their heads like a spark. It amused Kate to watch Mary, Jammy, and the ceiling interact with each other. She took it all in without pause, and these encounters nestled deep inside her, an early formation of ethereal awareness.

The Seth house was not the only house in town that housed apparitional phenomenons. Throughout town, ancestral beings that clung to their earthen dwellings were not uncommon. These transparent inhabitants were spoken of in whispers. Over time and repeated experience, these whispers gathered validity amongst those who, despite their attempt to disavow their presence, could not deny what they saw, heard, felt, and experienced through all the senses given to them at birth.

Just next door, at Miss Charlotte's house, Miss Eliza Sheffield, who had long since passed, called Johnny over for cards once a summer at twilight. He was fascinated by the stories she told him of her husband's adventures as a ship's captain before he perished at sea. Johnny and Miss Eliza would play cards as she sipped English tea he had brought her on his last voyage. As darkness descended, she faded into the evening in search of her lost love. How odd it must have looked to out-of-towners who saw Johnny on the front porch of Miss Charlotte's house pretending to sip tea and be in conversation with himself.

Johnny had a standing invitation to visit Miss Charlotte's front porch. Miss Charlotte had also experienced Miss Eliza wandering the backyard from time to time in a mournful mood, but her worries seemed to abate for a few weeks after a visit on the front porch with Johnny. Mrs. Sheffield liked to "Bounce about on the third floor," Miss Charlotte would say, sometimes keeping her up at night until she would climb the attic stairs to tell her house ghost to "go to bed!"

It was intimately understood amongst extended family that the presence of ethereal beings made them nothing less than angels, a gift from God, a guide from above. How solid one can feel when they know a faithful presence is keeping watch. At its core, the Seths could not deny the existence of the watchful ancestors in their house. They were firmly entrenched in their psyche and felt in their hearts. The family's modern existence had been shaped by generations of life schooling, love, loss, and learning that had inexplicably reformed and improved their habits with each generation. As such,

God's work and angels' conveyance was omnipresent in their daily lives.

Methodism seeped out of the groundwater and trickled out of the faucets. It was the high tide, timely and dependable. It was the beacon of light that the moon shone onto the land, and it was in the sparkle of the sun reflecting off the water. It inserted itself into one's being in a way that daily life itself was a consistent practice of faith in word and deed. A Methodist's life became inherently centered around God without shouting his name. Deeds were as good as words and often preferred over conversation. God formed an active presence in the lives of the young before they realized the divine was at work within them. Do good, do no harm, believe in the love of God and his forgiveness of sins, love thy neighbor, practice faith by serving God and in turn serving others.

Despite the drinking, gambling, and other more subtle differences, the Episcopalians also had a hold of a few souls in town. The Quakers, too, kept many in their light and fit in well with the Methodist mentality that permeated the entire Eastern Shore. Protestants had the monopoly on religious activities. However, there were always a few outliers. For those with the firmest roots in faith, outliers were accepted as a challenge and loved as any neighbor should be. A jar of fresh strawberry jam given over the fence went a long way for building neighborly relations, and perhaps encouragement enough to visit church. These exchanges and friendly conversations begot trust, and where it went from there was entirely up to the parties involved.

God does not turn his back on you, but you have free will to turn your back on him. This was always understood. The core of this free will kept the community strong, and the townspeople's uniformity of reciprocity made for congenial relations.

Outsiders, while cordially invited, were held at arm's length from the core of neighborly interaction. While treated with jovial spirit, outsiders were not wholly accepted into the undercurrent of town business and daily interactions until they had been time-tested. Casual visitors were treated with the same kindness that kept well hidden an underlying skepticism.

This skepticism was well justified in the case of Gypsies and also city folk, who amongst other visitors, were classified as "out-of-towners." This moniker was tough to be relieved of. Very few had transitioned from "out-of-towner" to "local" as it was a cultural challenge for all involved. Take, for instance, the couple that moved from the city to a place on the creek near Miss Ginny's boatyard. Word had it that they complained at the town office of all the clanging and banging in the boatyard. They were answered with: "Well, then why did you move here? The boatyard isn't going out of business for you." If they were trying to escape the noise of the city, they had chosen poorly.

The clanging and banging that annoyed the "come here's" was the town's lullaby that in childhood soothed the "born here's" to sleep. The metal halyards hitting the masts as the wind gusted through the night assuaged many a nightmare. When traveling out of town, adults would report back they did not sleep well away from the river; it didn't feel right, and they became restless and homesick.

Customs and countenance were as natural as the weather, and Sunday habits were especially methodic, in a way that comforted all who participated in a day of praise for the Lord and time with family. There was unexplainable assurance and inner peace in knowing what to expect when so many life events are unexpected, and so it was on Sunday, dressed and pressed, the Seth family attended church with Jammy singing soprano in the choir and Mary's fingers dancing across the organ keys.

The mingling beforehand amongst different groups was predictable. The eldest congregated towards the back of the church, while the families waited outside until the last minute so their children could "get their run out" in the park adjacent to the church. A call to worship by a familiar tune was the signal to take to the pews and without marking territory, every family seemed to have a particular spot. The Seth family and their many relatives took up the last three rows of the left side of the church, with cousin Tessie always sitting in this section on the last pew at the end closest to the door.

Being the wife of the ferry captain and, above all, a lady of great kindness and an excellent cook, Tessie was a self-imposed greeter to the congregation. No one slipped into the church without tapping Miss Tessie's shoulder, giving her a hug, shaking her hand, or giving her a wave. Mr. Tommy, a local funnybone, always blew her a kiss, which made her giggle. Despite her happy mannerly greeting, Miss Tessie would softly cry throughout the service. If you didn't know this you might wonder what was wrong. She cried for all that were lost at sea, the hurt, the starving, the sick, poor and decrepit. She cried for all the unfortunate souls in the world. She cried with a vulnerable compassion, and her selfless exposure made her one of the most respected parishioners in the church. Those nearby would hand her a tissue from time to time, and when the sermon drew to a close, she wiped her tears and dried her face, took a deep breath, smiled, and was thankful for her church and family.

This particular Sunday happened to be a double blessing: Cousin Lowell joined the family, and it was potluck supper, which was held once a month to encourage conversation amongst the congregation. Held in the basement, Kate looked forward to these dinners if not for the conversation, but for the food. In a town of country cooks, everyone had a special dish and they were all divine.

Not a fan of itchy stockings, Kate was often the first down the steps after the benediction. All she had to hear was, "May the lord bless you and keep you…" and that was her cue to be the first to the bathroom. The basement had a mustiness to it that was oddly homey. Perhaps Kate associated the familiar smell with church suppers, but either way, it wasn't unpleasant. Once in the bathroom, Kate would pull off her stockings, find her mother's purse, and stuff them in it. They were so binding and itchy that she hated stockings. The only good thing about the July and August heat was that Kate didn't have to wear stockings.

A few ladies took turns putting out the dishes that had been dropped off just before church service. The meat always came out of the oven hot, along with the rolls or biscuits—whatever some-one had decided to share. Before anyone went through the line, all bowed their heads, and Pastor George led a grace. Having just sat through church, he kept it very short.

"Dear Lord, we give thanks for your daily presence in our lives. We ask for continued guidance in all that we do. Bless this food so that we may use it in thy service and make us ever mindful of the needs of others. Amen."

The children lined up first, the older children helping the young-er as was custom. Baked ham slathered with apricot sauce, scalloped potatoes, Under the Sea Jello Mold, macaroni and cheese, deviled eggs of all varieties, buttered corn, green beans, pickled beets, fried chicken, baked pineapple, beaten biscuits, hot dinner rolls with but-ter and homemade jams graced the table at one end. Homemade pies and desserts blessed the other with Miss Tessie's apple cake, coconut cake, lemon meringue pie, chocolate chip cookies, oatmeal butterscotch cookies, brownies, and chess pie. Johnny went through the line close behind Lizzie Parks, and they sat together with her family. Mary had one eye on them and one on Cousin Lowell. It's a wonder her fork hit her mouth without incident.

Cousin Lowell was a new addition to the Seth household after he was thrown out of his own house by his wife, Miss Sally. God helps those who help themselves, but Lowell hadn't done much to help himself by drinking away what little savings he had for boat repairs, so when his boat sank at the dock he didn't have the money to haul it up. Frustrated with his inability to put food on the table and his deplorable drinking habits, Miss Sally locked him out in early April and took a job at the local town grocer to pay the bills.

Being that Lowell was Jammy's nephew, there was a desire to help in some way. What that meant was, he could stay in the Seth house but not indefinitely and he had to sober up. Although no time frame was given for his transformation to a reliable father and working man, patience was wearing thin as the heat of the summer came on.

He was told at the beginning of his boarding three things: one, there would be no rent as all his money should be given to his family. Two, his stay was not indefinite. And three, if he came to the dinner table drunk, that was the last dinner he would eat with his extended family. Understanding the concrete terms of his tentative stay, he in no way tried to push his limits with Mary and Jammy, and so he never drank in the house as that would lead to immediate expulsion; instead, he spent his evenings at one of the town bars. His love affair with gin went uninterrupted for two months after Miss Sally kicked him out until he couldn't pay his bar tab.

As soon as the crabs came on, he went to work as a boat hand with Mr. Jimmy. If he didn't show up rested and sober, Mr. Jimmy wouldn't let him work. Without a word, Mr. Jimmy assessed his condition when he arrived at the dock in the early morning darkness. If his condition was unsavory, Mr. Jimmy would shake his head and leave the dock without him. This wordless reprimand had an effect on Lowell. He didn't like being left at the dock; it embarrassed him. And so lately, he was showing up in shape to work, but that didn't mean he had stopped drinking—because he still wasn't showing up to family dinners. He was just imbibing less, but that was a start.

Miss Sally brought their children, Anna and Justin, to church where they could see their father under the watchful eye of the church folks. His children didn't see him slip into the pew for church, but when they caught a glimpse of him in the basement, they ran into his arms. His attendance at church did not go unnoticed, and comments in the most positive light were made directly to Lowell by many of the women parishioners:

"Lowell, we are so glad you are here." "Lowell, the Lord has blessed you with two beautiful children, hasn't he?" "Lowell, Sally looks especially nice today, don't you think?"

The men acknowledged him by saying his name and nodding their heads yes, which was all that was needed to let him know he had their support. To add to his positive review, several parishioners witnessed him giving Sally some money for the bills. His spiritual restoration was only beginning as patience and persistence were the Methodist path, and he had just stepped onto it. It was time for Lowell to reset his anchor, and the Methodists were watching.

Chapter VI

— The Park —

"Empty lots were made to play on." At least that's what Miss Ginny always said. After spending Sunday afternoon playing baseball on Miss Ginny's back lot with Angel, Kimmy, and neighborhood friends, then kick-the-can and ghost in the graveyard well into the evening, sleep passed as quickly as River leaped for frisbees.

If the world had disappeared overnight, Kate wouldn't have known in a slumber so deep as to rival hibernating bears; not even the roar of the waterman's diesels in the morning darkness woke her.

Finally, late into the morning, she opened her eyes and rubbed the thick grit away with the back of her hand. She gazed sleepily out the window as cars rode past, dodging bicycles. The day had begun without her, and she felt a little upset it had. She wondered what she missed in these first few hours, surely something interesting.

Just then, she noticed a mustard colored van riding by, sputtering smoke. She sat up straight and leaned into the window screen. There was a dark brown wavy-haired boy with shimmering deep brown eyes looking out the window at Kate's house. Kate's eyes widened as she followed the van past her window view. The last thing she noticed was a rug tied to the top of the roof. It motivated her enough to dress quickly and head downstairs. On her way down she remembered she needed to bring Squawk some greens. She hoped Edison was in a better mood.

Johnny and Jammy were not in their rooms, and the kitchen was clean and empty. She looked out the back screen door and saw

River sitting and watching Edison intently while he carried tools from his shop to his truck. Anxious he may depart before she could ask about the greens, she ran outside and caught him just as he was leaving.

"Can I pick some greens for Squawk?" she asked as he turned the key.

"Sure," he said quickly and then drove off to Truman's store to finish up his project. He left so quickly, that Kate didn't have the chance to tell him about her possible Gypsy sighting. But she was relieved she caught him in time. Her stomach, empty since dinner, gnarled in anger. Returning to the kitchen, she discovered fresh zucchini bread under a tea towel and she cut a thick slice to tame the pain. Then she poured a large glass of sun tea, and she went out onto the back porch, plopped into the soft cushion of an old wicker chair, her leg hanging casually over one of the arms, and ate the bread with wild ferocity.

Laundry had been hung early, and she could tell just by watching it flutter in a light breeze that it was almost dry. She watched the oyster wind chimes adorning the porch that Miss Lucille had given Mary. Each oyster was a trace different from the next, muted by their similarities. Kate wondered if anyone ever noticed the unique subtleties of the shells: the button-sized mark in the middle was blue-gray or purple or silvery or all three but never exactly the same.

Mary pulled up out back on her bike, and smiled and waved at Kate. After she put her bike away she joined Kate by flouncing on the opposite wicker chair.

"You really slept in today! I'm so glad you are rested because we are having a picnic in the park and swimming this afternoon."

Kate laughed with excitement. "When are we meeting everybody?"

"At noon, you can help me pack the picnic."

Excited for an afternoon at the park, Kate nodded and smiled. They went into the kitchen together and discussed what to take for lunch. Kate opened the refrigerator to discover an enormous amount of broccoli. Jammy had made some ham salad early in the morning, and when she saw it, she quizzed, "Where's Jammy?"

"She's off with an old friend today having lunch."

Satisfied with the answer, Kate pulled the ham salad and the last of the deviled eggs out of the fridge and Mary cut two thick slices of zucchini bread. A thermos was filled with sun tea, using up the last of it. They prepared three more glass pitchers for dinner and put them out on the porch in the sun.

Grabbing a big canvas bag, they filled it with an old blanket, two large beach towels, and the thermos. Kate ran upstairs to put on her swimsuit. With all that they had to carry, they left the bikes behind. Mary carried the bag and Kate the cooler; the park was an easy two blocks away.

The park was a popular spot in the summer to swim as a sizable jellyfish net was set just off the beach to protect swimmers. Anchored by a single piling, metal stakes marked its awkward octagonal shape as it encircled the beachfront. Families from out of town would come to cool off, as evidenced by many cars parked up and down Main Street. A vast cooling canopy of grandmother oaks, silver maples, tulip poplars, and sweet gums cast their shadows across the soft grassy expanse of the park and accommodated a sprawl of colorful picnic blankets scattered eight rows deep. Through the eyes of a creative child, it looked like an enormous patchwork quilt.

The locals had their favorite spots and, with territorial pride, made it known in the kindest words that they favored a certain stretch of shade under the only locust tree nearest to the water. On most days, this accommodation was made, but occasionally, a new family might test the boundaries of park manners and lay blankets only to move them when whispered it was a "reserved area." With thoughtful contemplation, most acknowledged this was fair compensation for descending on an otherwise quiet small town.

Encumbered by their necessaries, they weaved a crooked walk to the locust tree. Friends were waiting under its protective arms, smiling and waving as Mary and Kate got closer. Miss Lucille and Tansy were already there, along with Miss Dovie and her two girls, Carolyn and Bridget, Miss Margie with Junior, Dempsey, Goldie and Nancy, and Miss Pearl with Molly. Molly was the oldest of all the kids, having just turned 16. Her shapely figure and long blonde hair had captured the attention of nearly every boy in town. However, Molly was too occupied with varied pursuits of waitressing, growing flowers, and babysitting to notice. This must have been her day off as she worked at the same restaurant as Johnny.

Mary and Kate laid their blanket next to Miss Pearl's. The oldest and wisest of all the town mothers, Miss Pearl was the high school nurse. Everyone kept her close and her knowledge saved many a family from expensive hospital bills over the years. Her other children were grown and married, Molly was her youngest.

Miss Margie had a "bundle," that is four children in a succession of five years. She always seemed tired but hid it with a strained cheerfulness. Miss Dovie lived on a boathouse at the other end of town. With no yard of her own, Mary often visited and brought her vegetables from Edison's garden.

"Where's Johnny?" they asked.

"He's working the breakfast and lunch shift at the restaurant," Mary explained. "I hope he'll join us later; I left a note on his bed."

Unsatisfied from breakfast, Kate quickly ate two deviled eggs, washed them down with sun tea and ran down to the beach with the other children. A sandcastle was in the making, and she joined Tansy, who was absorbed with the construction.

Sandcastle formation is serious work. Tansy had already created a general structure, and the fun part was in the details. It was close enough to the water's edge to fashion a moat, and Kate began to dig a trench with the wide end of an oyster shell. Tansy's turrets on the corners were decorated with sea glass, and she wandered off looking for cattails to pierce the middles.

To her back, a commotion in the river caught Kate's attention.

She heard, "Room! Room!" She turned around to see two small sail-boats close together, rounding an orange mark. They were part of a bigger fleet sailing just off the park. About a dozen sailboats darted back and forth in all directions as a formidable lady with a whistle in a Whaler yelled to them. Kate, puzzled as to what the boats were doing, looked at them squinty-eyed as if she would gain some divine wisdom for doing so.

Tansy returned with cattails and drew her attention back to the castle. The moat was nearly complete. A back door to a garden was inspired by the small square piece of driftwood that floated ashore within eyeshot. Seaweed stretched out in rows formed the garden and oyster shells lined the path to it. Dried reeds gave the garden definition and fencing. Tansy proclaimed it a masterpiece. Sweaty from the fever of sand art, they stood up and stood back pleased with their creation. The river beckoned.

The afternoon played out in its usual fashion. One of Miss Margie's bundle cut their foot on an oyster shell; Miss Pearl tended to it. Then, her two boys got into a fistfight over nothing of consequence. One sat on Mary's blanket, the other on Miss Margie's with backs to each other on an extended timeout. The sandcastle was destroyed by a motorboat wave and the girls never tired of making upside-down hair-dos in the river.

A jellyfish snuck through the netting and stung Kate. Christened early in life by the burn of a nettle, she had been taught the local trick of rubbing wet sand on the insult quickly; relief was instantaneous. An evening redness would remind her of the perils of river swimming, but for now, she shrugged it off. The drama of such an event was much more pronounced for the "out-of-towners."

The river breeze had a cool, playful feel, and despite the antics of the afternoon, happy laughter won out. As the afternoon wore on, coolers became empty, and children's noises were eventually tamed by physical and artistic exhaustion. By late afternoon, many lounged on their towels, facing the sky, cloud watching.

Kate turned on her side towards the river. "It really is beautiful, isn't it Tansy?"

"What is?"

"The river, of course," Kate replied.

"Oh, I thought you meant the mama duck with all the babies following behind."

Kate sat up. "Where?"

Tansy pointed, and Kate jumped to her feet. "Tansy!" she said with sharp recollection, "We forgot to take greens to Miss Pat!"

Tansy jumped too, and they turned to Mary and Lucille, frantically explaining the situation.

Released from the park, they ran back home to get their bikes and met at Edison's garden. They skidded into a wild arrival, and bumped into the outside of the greenhouse. As they approached the grapevine arbor, Edison stood up and turned around. He had finished his job at Truman's Store early, and that left some time for him to tend to his garden. He tossed a handful of weeds into the compost pile.

"Running around in your bathing suits today, girls?"

Kate interjected quickly, "We forgot to get greens for Squawk."

"The chard and collards are thick; how about a handful of each?"

The girls smiled and walked down the rows of the vigorous, deep green foliage. Tansy's hands followed the vibrant colored stems of the Swiss chard to the base and then she snapped leaves off one by one until she had a big handful. Kate did the same with the white veins of the collards.

Hands too full to wave, they smiled and nodded at the men at the Country Club who, by late afternoon, were so inebriated their boisterous jubilations were now only quiet mumbles. The girls rounded the corners swiftly and darted into the boatyard just as Miss Pat was coming out of her shed. She stopped and put her hand on her hips.

"I'd 'bout given up on you girls today, but here you are."

Squawk saw them and ran to the closest corner of her crate to talk to them.

"I've been too busy to take her out today, so she needs all your attention."

Kate responded, "Sorry, Miss Pat, we were at the park."

"I can tell from your bathing suits."

Just then her office phone rang, and she went back into her shed. Squawk was very excited to see them. She ran back and forth in her crate, talking away and making a terrible mess. They took her straight away to the grassy patch and watched her hunt for bugs. She was very quick to lunge when she saw something move; her fondness for grasshoppers was immediately made evident by her choices.

Next, they went to the beach and were surprised when she headed straight to the river for a drink. Placing her bill all the way under the water, she then looked upwards to wash the water down. She did this in succession many times until she was satiated. Her hurt foot had almost healed in just a few days and she ventured into her wild river just two steps and then turned and looked at Tansy and Kate.

"I wonder what she is thinking?" Tansy asked.

"I think she is thankful for us," said Kate.

"I love that little duck." Tansy giggled as Squawk, still not ready for the water, turned her tail towards it, ran to Tansy full speed, and hopped in her lap, talking away.

None of the parties involved seemed to tire of the games they played or the mess they made as they created a miniature pond next to the water's edge for Squawk to splash in. Their games would've continued indefinitely had it not been for the suddenness of the six o'clock church bells that broke the spell. Panicked by the reminder of time, Kate picked up Squawk and jogged back to the boatyard. Tansy ran into Pat's shed to let her know Squawk was back in her crate, and Kate handed Miss Pat the greens. They raced back past the Country Club, now empty as the men had staggered home, past Edison's garden and Mr. Paul's house, rounded the corner to the back street, and waved goodbye as they aimed for the fences of their respective houses.

Kate entered the back gate as the last of the church tunes played out, and by the time silence had expanded its grip on her, she burst through the back screen door with a gasp. One eyebrow raised, Mary looked at her from the dinner table and there was an uncomfortable quietness that hung in the air like wet dew.

All eyes locked and expectant, Mary broke the tension with, "Just in time Kate, grab a plate."

A collective sigh initiated the start of dinner and everyone held hands to pray, even Cousin Lowell.

Prayers complete, Edison poignantly looked at Lowell.

"Tell us about the crabs so far this season, Lowell. Are they strong?"

"Yes, they are; we've been doin' well on the water," he said, with a mouthful of coleslaw.

"One of these days when you have a good day, I'd like some for our dinner."

"I'd be much obliged to bring some for dinner soon."

"Then it's settled."

Edison smiled and looked at Kate. "We haven't had much from the river this season except for what Miss Kate caught the other day at the wharf. The perch she caught was very tasty."

Kate smiled, tickled that he noticed. The conversation turned to Johnny's recent outings about town with Lizzie Parks.

"What have you and Lizzie been up to, Johnny?" asked Mary.

Kate giggled, but Jammy stared her down, and Kate immediately looked down at her food.

"We're going to get ice cream again tonight, but tomorrow, we're going on a bike ride across the river. We'll take the ferry over and back. I don't have to work until the dinner shift. I'd also like to take her out in the boat sometime soon if that's ok."

Mary nodded her head in approval.

After clean up, Mary asked Kate if she would walk up to the park to retrieve the Thermos she had left behind. Happy to return to the park, Kate made a stop at Tansy's to ask her along. Miss Ginny lived next to Tansy's house and her grandson Davey was visiting for a week. Over the years, he had become an expected summer playmate and he hopped off his front porch when he saw Kate coming.

"Hiya girls!" Kate and Tansy waved and smiled, and he joined right in like he had been invited all along. "Both of you, your hair is longer than last summer," he said observantly.

"So is yours!" Tansy quipped back. Kate giggled.

Davy's hair was always unkempt, and the longer it got the wilder it was. It pointed in every direction but down on his head.

"Grandma says I don't have to cut it in the summer; none of the boys in town do, so I don't have to either."

Tansy saw an opportunity. "So by end of summer you'll look like a girl?"

Davey smacked Tansy on the arm and everyone laughed. To someone outside their triangle, it might seem as if they were fighting, but far from it. Their realism and revelry were a summertime tradition.

All the sidewalks in town were made of local brick, bumpy from tree roots below worming their way through the ground. They were tricky to manage for even the soberest of individuals. A few of the deep red bricks were stamped by their maker with a letter or word etched on their face. Tourists may or may not have observed these symbols but the locals knew the code as to where each marked brick was crafted. Scattered about the journey to the park, they jumped from brick to brick, yelling their codes as they jumped, giggling when they missed or tripped. The "B" bricks were the most common, and Mr. Charley chuckled and shook his head when the jumping triangle passed by his front porch, yelling, "B Brick! B Brick! B Brick!"

The park was not their first destination. With Tansy and Kate's pockets jingling from their catch at the wharf, they stopped at

Truman's Store for ice cream. Truman's was a store completely in the present, but it looked, smelled, and felt like a step back in time. There was no sign out front that said "Truman's," there was no need. As the old wooden painted screen door swung open, the oiled floorboards, a quarter inch thinner at the entrance, had a cushioned feel under your feet as if you were crossing the threshold into the most comfortable place in town. Worn from decades of local patronage, the thin strips of old oiled oak had greeted everyone in town a thousand times over.

The cigar smoke that hung on the patron's clothes was firmly entrenched in the store, mixed with the smell of Italian meats and cheeses, pickles in a barrel, and black coffee. The olfactory effect was that of contentment; the store felt like home and was kept in that fashion. They carried a little of this and some of that, odd items that might be found in your junk drawer at home, but when needed, were absolutely necessary.

Truman's mother, Mabel, could just about pull anything out of the cabinets behind the counter, and all you had to do was ask. Paint brushes, ribbons, safety pins, masking tape, lightbulbs, ladies' stockings, pens, notebooks...batteries, scrub brushes, Easter egg dye. The store itself acted as a grocer with fresh bananas, eggs, bread, milk, Tastykakes from Philadelphia, canned goods and laundry soap, but what was hidden throughout was treasure and Miss Mabel had the map in her head.

The candy counter was just inside the door to the right with a glass top with wooden edges, varnished and inviting. Many a child had rubbed the edges smooth to the bare wood while making very weighty choices. For those with only glass bottle deposit money to spend, there were jars of 5-cent candies: Mary Janes, Tootsie rolls, Gobstoppers, Atomic Fireballs, root beer barrels, Now & Laters, and bubblegum. For those with more jingle, candy bars of all kinds: Lifesavers, licorice, and peppermint sticks held the young folks' attention.

This counter also sold lottery tickets that Mr. Paul liked to buy, and cigarettes and cigars. It was a busy spot. Deeper into the store lay the soda fountain whose faux marble counter with metal edges was laden with a jar of pink pickled eggs, pigs feet, Lance crackers, Slim Jim's and in the late mornings, sandwiches for the working men lay under a cloth tea towel ready for the lunch crowd.

This counter is where the trio stood that evening, reading the flavor choices that were posted on a "Joy" ice cream cup sign just above Truman's head.

"What'll it be?" Truman asked. "I've got dipper's elbow, so go easy on me - no quadruple scoops tonight, OK?"

They giggled because Truman always had dipper's elbow from dipping ice cream; it was an occupational hazard. The children genuinely worried about his suffering from the affliction so much so that they would often inquire about this malady and how he was managing. He gave a full report to anyone who inquired as to the status of his elbow, and after a laborious elaboration of his affliction, he would finish his exquisitely detailed narrative with, "Don't worry about me, I'll be alright. It gets rest on Sunday."

Predictable as last summer, Davey ordered a scoop of chocolate.

"You haven't changed at all from last year, have you?" Tansy joked. "Always chocolate. Don't you want to try anything new?"

"Nope," he said as he climbed upon the spinning stool at the counter. He kicked his foot off the bar wall and spun around on his knees.

"I like getting chocolate because it fusses you." He stopped the stool just in time to grab the ice cream cone from Mr. Truman. "Thanks!" he said. He grabbed his cone and hopped down to the floor, reached into his pocket, and slapped 35 cents on the counter.

Tansy was still speechless from Davey's remark so Kate piped up and ordered a scoop of coffee on a sugar cone. Tansy then ordered fresh strawberry. Truman knew exactly what she meant when she called it "pussy cat pink" ice cream.

They left their coins on the counter, waved goodbye to Mr.

Truman and headed outside to cross the street to the park. Just before the screened door, Kate stopped and remembered something else she was going to buy and walked over to the candy counter.

"Miss Mabel!"

Miss Mabel walked slowly towards the counter, shuffling her feet as if they had slippers on them. Everyone knew she slowed down at the end of the day, but even so, it seemed like her pace was slower than usual as she rested her forearms on the glass top and let out a sigh.

"What'll it be, Kate?"

"I'd like some Lucky Lights, please," she said, laughing.

"Well, better Lucky Lights than Lucky Strikes," Miss Mabel responded while handing her a pack.

Kate handed her two dimes and headed out the door to meet Davey and Tansy.

The brightness of the sun melted like ice cream into a long, thin, deep orange puddle above the trees, dripping through the web of leaves in bursts of sparkles. Their cones half eaten by the time they reached the river's edge, they all sat down on the shallow bank side by side, hip to hip, and gazed out at the river. Wind laid out, and breezes only whispered. Faces to the sun and eyes closed, they took in the last weathered warmth of the day, the last solar energy before the day washed off the surface of the river, and it disappeared into oblivion.

They sat silently until their ice cream was finished. Kate pulled out her pack of Lucky Lights and placed one in each hand, stretched out in request. The three held the cigarettes close to their lips.

"Okay, one, two, three!" Kate said, and all at once they put the candy cigarettes to their lips and blew. Dust from the powdered sugar that lined the bubble gum shot out at once, and a plume of fake smoke lingered in front of them. They unwrapped their cigarettes and shoved the bubble gum in their mouths. Davey was the first to the swings followed by Tansy, then Kate. No matter how

hard they tried, they could not swing a 360 around the top pole. Johnny once told them it was physics, but they didn't believe him.

"I love the long swings where all you see is your feet in the sky," yelled Tansy, "…the kind of swing that if you jumped and the world was flat, you would be jumping off the edge into outer space!"

Kate suddenly remembered her reason for coming to the park in the first place, jumped off the swing, and headed over to the locust tree to look for her mother's thermos. Now that the sun was nestled behind the horizon, the swatting started and home seemed the best course of action. The thermos's red and black plaid pattern made it easy to spot. Kate grabbed it and joined the others as they jogged back home, slapping their arms and legs every third step or so.

It was twilight when Kate opened the gate to the Seth house with thermos in hand. River greeted her by licking tiny drops of ice cream that had unnoticeably fallen on her feet.

"How was the park?" came a voice from the front porch.

In the twilight, Kate couldn't see who it was; the voice was not that of anyone living in the house, but it was very familiar.

"What ya say, Kate?" Mr. Brown had stopped by for a visit.

Wise beyond his years, his stories captivated, his voice was deep and centered her. His advice was flawless. He and Jammy were friends and spoke the language of the war generation that wasn't entirely out of Kate's sphere. However, there seemed to be an agreement between the two that Kate's generation sure did have it easy. Occasionally, there were colloquialisms that eluded Kate, which, of course, always made Jammy and Mr. Brown chuckle and wink at each other.

Both widow and widower, one might have thought these two contemporaries might get together, but that would never happen. Jammy had been widowed for decades and Mr. Brown about eight years, but keeping with the societal framework of their generation, they, like many others, subscribed to never even conceive of marrying again. That didn't mean they didn't appreciate company, and so Mr. Brown stopped by about once a week or so to chat. These were the best nights to swing on the porch.

Kate opened the screen door and closed it very quickly behind her, much to the disappointment of the night bugs. She handed Mary the thermos and sat down on the last chair left.

"Oh, Mr. Brown! I'm tired." Kate let out a sigh.

"I hear you've been enjoying your freedom around town and saved a baby duck."

"Oh yes," Kate piped up. "Her name is Squawk, and Miss Pat at the boatyard is showing us how to do it right."

"I am so glad you are interested in animals," he paused, "because I was hoping you might be able to save this box turtle I found on the road."

The twilight casts many shadows and all along a turtle had been in a small shoebox sitting next to Mr. Brown's chair.

"I found him on the road out of town where the forest meets the macadam."

With a new energy Kate popped back up and leaned over to look into the box that Mr. Brown was now holding.

"Ohhh… I see," Kate said in a low, sad voice. The box turtle had been hit by a car, and the right corner of its back shell had been broken. All its arms and legs were intact and able to move. He poked his head out of his shell and looked at Kate. She looked back at him and looked at his wound. It was bleeding ever so slightly and it worried Kate. She felt like the turtle might really be hurting.

"I'm not sure how to fix the shell, do you know, Mr. Brown?"

"I may know a lot of things, Miss Kate, but fixing turtles is not one of them. I suspect Miss Pat may know something."

"Good idea!" Kate felt relieved she could ask someone else to advise in this grave situation.

As Mr. Brown handed the patient over to Kate, he said, "Don't be upset if this turtle doesn't make it. You are trying to help, and that's all you can do."

Jammy piped in, "He's right, Kate, just do what you can."

Mr. Brown put his hand on hers. "Here's an old saying I believe in: 'We don't find turtles, turtles find us.'"

Both buoyed and reminded of the reality of the situation; Kate immediately went out back to Edison's shop to look for a larger box and an old blanket. Once his new home was fixed, she placed him in her room so she could keep an eye on him through the night. Kate put a bowl of water, some lettuce, and a handful of fresh blueberries in the box. In the morning, she would look for pill bugs; that's what turtles like best. At least that's what Edison told her. She washed her hands, brushed her teeth, and then peeked into Johnny's room. He must have been out with Lizzie because his room was empty. Kate crawled onto her bed and turned onto her side, facing the turtle.

"What shall I name you?" she asked the injured creature.

"Hopeful" popped in her head. Hmm, she thought, I do hope he lives. I'll call him "Hopeful."

"Hopeful, good night, I'll see you in the morning." Kate rolled over. The moon looked blurry tonight; she couldn't focus on it. It must be cloudy, she thought, but the stars winked at her anyway, and the noise of the adults on the front porch telling stories and laughing faded away into nothingness. Sleep came easy; even the redness from the jellyfish sting could not demand her attention. Slumber bubbled up within her, a mighty tonic that permeated her veins and was insuppressible.

Chapter VII

— Ditches, Dandelions, and the Dead —

When morning broke, something inside of Kate sang. It was a feeling of joy and it grew stronger as she opened her eyes and turned to look out her window. A rabbit hopped through the yard and disappeared under a boxwood, the mourning doves were cooing, the cicadas were humming, and the ferry was in full reverse at the dock. These sights and sounds brought Kate a tremendous feeling of comfort. A deep warmth at her core for her surroundings was a contentment that could not be put into words. The sky was bright, and so was her mood as she turned to look at Hopeful, the box turtle. He was munching on lettuce.

"You're alive! I knew it!" she proclaimed as she bounced out of bed. She picked up Hopeful's cardboard home and glided down the hallway.

The sizzle of the bacon grew louder the closer she got to the back steps.

"Save some for Kate!" Kate heard her mother yelling at Johnny.

She bounded down the steps and rounded the corner with a smile, Hopeful in her arms.

Mary smiled, "It's about time. I'm about to beat your brother off the bacon with this spatula."

Johnny rolled his eyes as he snitched one more piece and ran for the door.

"Johnny!" Mary yelled.

The bacon was already in his stomach, and he was halfway down the brick path to the bikes. Kate looked and saw two pieces left for her, which was just right for a breakfast sandwich. She pulled out a pan to fry an egg while Mary finished cleaning the breakfast dishes.

"Kate, I'm going to see Dovie and take her some vegetables from the garden this afternoon. Would you like to come along?"

"Sure!" Kate said in a lively tone. She loved visiting the houseboat.

"I need to take Hopeful to see Miss Pat this morning."

Mary peeked into the box. "So you've named the turtle Hopeful, good choice. I see he's still with us."

Kate's egg fried quickly on the pre-warmed burner, her toast popped and a breakfast sandwich was born. She placed Hopeful in a chair across from the table where Kate sat to eat her breakfast and perused the newspaper comics. She loved Charlie Brown. After breakfast she walked to the brick pile next to Edison's shed. Long ago, she learned from Edison that turning bricks over was the best way to find pill bugs. The bricks that stuck to the soil were the best hiding place for the little bugs that looked remarkably like minia-ture armadillos. She found about a dozen. Using the shoebox that Mr. Brown had brought Hopeful in, she put the pill bugs in the box. The shoebox was much more travel-friendly. She cut a hole in the lid and wrapped duct tape around it so Hopeful wouldn't bounce out.

She headed off to Miss Pat, holding Hopeful firmly in her right hand while steering with her left. She didn't petal with her usu-al energy but instead took a slower steadier pace for the sake of her patient. Upon arrival at the boatyard, she wondered if the loud noises would bother Hopeful. He surely didn't hear these noises in the woods. After putting her kickstand down, she walked over to Miss Pat's shed with the turtle but stopped along the way to visit with Squawk, who ran over to Kate as soon as she saw her.

"How you doing today Squawk? We have a new friend."

As Kate bent down to pet Squawk, Sam came running up to Kate and anxiously began sniffing the shoe box and wagging his tail.

"I'll show you in a minute, boy." The door creaked open, and Miss Pat smiled when she saw Kate.

Immediately intrigued, she asked, "What's in the shoebox, Kate?"

Kate unwound the duct tape and opened up the vessel. When the injured turtle was revealed, Sam stepped back slowly and laid down with a soft whimper. Miss Pat's reaction was of a serious nature as well.

"A cracked shell, it's a miracle he's still alive."

"I named him Hopeful," Kate interjected.

There was a pause from Miss Pat as she assessed the situation.

"Excellent choice of names," she said as she knelt down and took a closer look. Hopeful seemed somewhat lethargic, but lethargy is a hard diagnosis to make on a turtle.

"I have read about such injuries," said Miss Pat. "The first thing we should do is clean his wound, and then we can try to tape his shell together. Come, bring him inside my house."

They walked over to Miss Pat's place and went in through the kitchen door.

"I don't have turtle-saving supplies in my office, but I do have some hydrogen peroxide and cloth tape in here. You know Kate, their shell is like a bone. So Hopeful has a broken bone, he must be in terrific pain. I wish I knew what to give him to help his pain, but I am not a veterinarian, so we'll just have to do the best we can." Miss Pat picked him up carefully with both hands and looked him in the eyes.

At first he retreated into his shell but then quickly reemerged to see her.

"I wonder what he is thinking?" asked Kate.

"I think he is not too scared otherwise he would have stayed in his shell," replied Miss Pat. She then asked Kate to fill the sink with an inch or so of tepid water. Kate obliged and Miss Pat placed Hopeful in the water.

"Box turtles don't swim, so that's why we make the water

shallow. Now let's wash this cut off by taking handfuls of water and gently pouring it over him."

They did, and as they poured, bits of dirt and dried blood washed away from his shell and into the sink. Next, Miss Pat picked him up and laid him on a soft towel she had placed next to the sink. She dried him off gently and then drizzled some hydrogen peroxide over his wound; it fizzled and foamed and ran down the side of his shell onto the towel. She repeated this three times until she felt satisfied the wound was as clean as she could get it. Then she gently dried off his shell and asked Kate to hand her some cloth tape from a nearby cabinet. The tape was cut into two pieces and placed across the shell while Kate tried to gently push the two split pieces together.

Kate felt weepy. She knew this probably hurt Hopeful, but ultimately she was trying to help. She wanted to know she wasn't making Hopeful's pain worse, but in her gut she knew she was. It upended her. A tear flowed down her cheek and landed on the turtle's head. Miss Pat noticed her grief.

"All we can do, Kate, is our best, and then it's up to nature. Please know whatever happens, you did the right thing for Hopeful, especially in giving him the perfect name."

Kate wiped away her tears with the back of her hand. Miss Pat sensed a fragility in Kate she had not seen before.

"Kate, would you like to take him back home or leave him with me? I can watch him today if you would like." Kate wanted to take him back home, but she was also overcome with sadness. She could sense the turtle was losing his life energy and she feared the worst.

"Will you watch him for me, Miss Pat? I can check on him later. I have to go see Miss Dovie with Mom today, and he should always have someone with him. I don't want him to be alone."

Miss Pat gave Kate a hug and promised to keep an eye on him.

Kate felt drained. She stopped again to see Squawk and ran quickly back inside Miss Pat's house to fill Squawk's water bowl. After she filled the water dish, she shredded some of Edison's greens for her. She left the boatyard feeling gloomy.

To add to her distress, as she pedaled, her left foot hurt. Barefooted, it couldn't be a rock in her shoe. As she glided past the Country Club she didn't look up or wave, she just kept pedaling. Her thoughts were preoccupied with Hopeful's fate, but nature is the master distractor, and the wide and deep ditches on the right side of the road were shining. Minnows had found their way into the tidal trenches, and the shimmering schools caught her attention.

She brought her bike to a full stop next to the ditch and leaned over it, casting a shadow; the shimmers danced away to sunnier spots. She got off her bike, moved it off the road into the driveway, and put down the kickstand. The flood tide often brought visitors to the water town, and this was a bounty. In the three-foot-deep channel minnows swam with two small crabs, too young to be caught. Kate kneeled down and watched from the other side of the ditch, now aware of casting shadows.

She studied how the crabs swam side to side, claws tight to their

Queen Anne's Lace
© Shelly Claudaniel
11 January 2021

bodies, their fiddlers paddling them along the inclined walls of the narrow waterway. Water bugs jumped across the top of the surface and dragonflies and honey bees hovered around the water-loving wildflowers in bloom on the edge. Queen Anne's Lace, Beardtongue, Chicory, and Swamp Milkweed roots held onto the edge of the yard where river water trickled inland. As summer carried on, some flowers would die, and others would pop up in July, like Turtlehead, Golden Tickseed, and Rose Mallow, a favorite of the hummingbird.

An old blind couple lived in the dilapidated house on the property. Most days, they sat outside on their front porch, just listening to life around them. Kate looked over her shoulder, and they weren't on the porch today. She thought what a shame it was they could not see this pretty ditch every day and thought maybe one day she could describe it to them. When some in town tried to groom their ditches, she wondered if abandonment was the better course. This foray into nature lifted her spirits, and after a few more minutes of observation, she got back on her bike and rode home.

By the time she arrived at her fence, her foot was hurting, a hurt she hadn't experienced before. She waved to Jammy, who was sitting near her garden reading a book. She stowed her bike and walked gingerly up the path.

"What's with the foot, Miss Kate?"

"I dunno, Jammy, but it hurts when I walk on it."

"Go wash the dirt off your feet under the hose, and let me take a look at it."

Kate did so and returned, sitting down right next to her grandmother. Kate didn't think of her as a grandmother, but more of a second mother, and she was deeply attached. Jammy ran her fingers over Kate's foot.

"Aha! You have a plantar wart!"

"What's that?" Kate didn't like the sound of anything that implied it had a root in her foot, but that was exactly what it was.

Jammy picked a dandelion from the grass and broke open its stem, revealing a milky white substance. She squeezed the substance out of the stem onto her finger, and then she rubbed it on Kate's wart and began to blow on it until it dried. Kate hadn't seen Jammy do this before and wondered where she learned it.

"My mother taught it to me. Do this every day for one week. Each time you put new dandelion blood on, dry it by blowing on it and then cover it with a bandage and extra tape so it won't fall off. If this doesn't work well enough, we'll start on remedy number two - apple cider vinegar and duct tape."

"Thanks Jammy."

Jammy saw a teachable moment. "You know, Kate, somebody somewhere decided that dandelions were no good and invented all kinds of ways to get rid of them, but they aren't bad plants. Once you learn about them, they are really quite amazing. Remember, Kate, other people's opinions don't have to be your opinions."

"What do you mean by that?" Kate quizzed.

"Study the topic at hand before you form your own thoughts. It's easy to latch onto other's passions but much harder to form your own because that takes initiative. Not everyone has initiative. So don't judge a dandelion by what others believe it to be." She paused, "Some of the best discoveries in your life may seem like dandelions to others, but they may be orchids to you. Besides," she added, "not every flower is this much fun."

She picked one with a ball of fluffy seeds, blew on it and they watched the tiny seeds float high up into the June sky to be whisked off by the morning breeze. Kate smiled and looked at Jammy lovingly for a long time. It was her way of holding on tight to the moment.

"What are you reading?" Jammy turned the book over to show Kate the cover: Ovid's *Metamorphoses*. Jammy read the title to her.

"Sounds fancy," Kate replied curiously.

"Kate, I learned long ago that if you ever want to be a good poet, you have to read good poetry."

Kate took the book into her hands and attempted to read it.

"It's in another language?"

"Yes, it was written in Latin." Kate, puzzled, handed it back to Jammy.

"Well, what's it about?"

"Transformation, change, and the idea that the only constant in life is change."

"Well, everyone knows that," Kate said, "because every day is always different."

"I'd say you're right about that," agreed Jammy, "but sometimes big changes are scary."

"What do you mean?" Kate pressed.

"What if one day you woke up and everything around you was different? Maybe your home is no longer your home. I was never your grandmother, and you were never you?"

"Now that would be scary, Jammy. I don't want that to happen. I like this place the way it is."

"And so do I!" Jammy proclaimed. "There is a Latin phrase that I like, 'Mora Temporis,' which means to pause time. I think we are in a 'Mora Temporis' right now. A time delay, but it will not last forever because…" She looked into Kate's blue eyes for her answer.

"…because… the only constant in life is change?"

"That's my girl." Jammy smiled and patted her on the leg.

Kate looked into Jammy's hazel-colored eyes. Her right eye had a tiny speck of dark brown in it, the color of Mary's eyes, which were that of melted dark chocolate. Her mind sufficiently stretched, Kate changed the subject.

"Why are my eyes blue and yours are hazel?" Kate asked.

"That's because you have a bit of Edison in you."

Mary called Kate from the kitchen, interrupting the moment, and Kate jumped up and hopped inside.

"Yes, Mom?" she called while sitting in the inside porch chair looking at the bottom of her foot. Mary rounded the corner and saw Kate's problem.

"Wart, huh?"

"How did you know?"

"The white stuff." she replied, "Jammy did that for me, too, when I had a wart. Miss Ginny called and invited you and Tansy over to have lunch, but don't stay past one; we need to go see Miss Dovie."

"Okay!" Kate said excitedly as Miss Ginny made the best grilled cheese sandwiches. Once bandaged, she headed over to Davey's house. Tansy was waiting for Kate, and when Kate walked by, Tansy jumped off the porch and joined her in knocking on Miss Ginny's door.

"Come on in!" They heard her yell from the back of the house.

Her house was long and lean, just like Kate's, and her kitchen was also all the way in the back. Kate and Tansy entered the house and started calling for Davey.

"I'm helping Grandma in the kitchen!" he yelled back.

When they reached the kitchen, they were immediately thrown into a laughing fit. Davey was wearing his grandmother's pink apron and cooking grilled cheese.

"Don't laugh girls," said Miss Ginny, "he's doing a mighty fine job."

Tansy interjected, "It must be the magic in your apron, Miss Ginny."

"Very funny, Tansy, but he really is cooking quite well." True to Miss Ginny's word, he placed four nicely browned grilled cheeses onto individual plates by spatula and didn't drop one on the floor. Four glasses of milk were also poured by him neatly. He was very proud of his accomplishment, but he didn't brag as Miss Ginny told him he wasn't allowed to.

Lunchtime passed excitably. Stories of Mr. Arthur and Miss Ginny's boatyard fed the fever. The boatyard was situated behind the empty lot where they all played. This was also the boatyard where clanging halyards in heavy winds rocked Kate's neighborhood to sleep.

"Miss Kate, it's time for you to head home; I believe you and Mary have an afternoon planned?" reminded Miss Ginny.

Kate was glad someone had kept track of the time because she certainly hadn't. She said her thank you's and left hurriedly for home.

⚓ ⚓ ⚓

KATE AND MARY OPENED A large paper bag grabbed two sizable heads of broccoli from the refrigerator, and placed them in the bottom. The rest of the vegetables they would gather from Edison's garden. The bag, much too large to manage on a bike, was placed into the back of Mary's baby blue station wagon named "The Blue Goose." Like a winged bird on the ready for flight, she was the largest station wagon Ford ever built, and with her ample V8, she could really fly.

Mary kept her foot in check while cruising through town, but on the way out of town, the tires could really heat up the pavement. They rolled down to Edison's garden and filled up the rest of the bag with kale, beets, carrots, and collards. Edison always planted these crops early and babied them during the chilly spring nights by covering them with old, thinned sheets. By late May or early June, they were ready to be picked.

By the time Kate and Mary arrived at the houseboat, the sun was strong enough that the heat from the dock planks tested the early summer thickness of Kate's calluses. Mary carried the bag while Kate stopped to look at each piling for crabs on their way to the end of the pier.

"Thank you so much for coming by!" Dovie said cheerfully. "I am so grateful for these veggies, no gardens on a houseboat."

Mary carefully handed the bag of produce to Dovie from the dock and then stepped onto the boat. Kate followed behind, being careful to hold the piling with one arm to steady herself. The tide was low and the jump to the boat was tricky being she had shorter legs than Mary. The white fiberglass decking was a relief to her feet.

"Miss Dovie, are Bridget and Carolyn here?" Kate asked expectantly.

"I am sorry to disappoint you, Miss Kate, but Bridget is off to town with a friend. Carolyn is helping teach sailing part-time this year, but she should be back soon."

Kate, although disappointed, was not too put out as she could be completely entertained all by herself on a house boat. Exploring the inside fascinated Kate, and she marveled how anyone could fit an entire home into the width and length of a slip and also make it float, move, and steer, too.

"May I look around?"

"Have fun, Kate."

Dovie and Mary stayed on deck to soak up the sun and discuss town news. Dovie handed the bag of vegetables to Kate.

"Please put these in the galley on the table, Kate." Kate smiled and graciously put out her hands.

Dovie turned to Mary, "There must be at least enough vegetables for a week! Oh, I just can't say thank you enough!" Mary blushed, smiled, and they settled in for a two ice tea afternoon.

Kate gently placed the vegetable bag on the thickly varnished, shiny wood counter next to the gimbaled stove. The kitchen nook contained a small icebox refrigerator, a sink, racks for eight plates, a slot for paper towels, and a wooden rack for herbs and spices, all securely laid out with wooden slats to keep items from falling. There were cabinets and drawers with special brass latches to keep them from opening while underway.

"They thought of everything," she said to herself. "Even a can opener!" she said out loud when she saw it hanging by a thin rope from the long pantry door.

Towards the bow and just to the left of the kitchen nook were the steering wheel and navigation instruments. She put her hand on the captain's wheel, and it felt just right. The chrome-handled controls, compass, and gauges shined against the mahogany. Sun beamed through the front windshield and threw sparks of light throughout the cabin making Kate squint. As she turned her back to the sun and walked further in, a varnished wooden dining booth on the right revealed itself, and beyond that, the head, the girls' bunk beds and through another door, Miss Dovie and Mr. Sherman's bedroom.

Mr. Sherman was a lieutenant in the Navy and rarely home. Nicknamed "Tomcat" for the aircraft he worked on, he was stationed at a Naval Airbase across the Chesapeake. Miss Dovie was on her own many times for weeks on end, but she managed life well as she was very smart and resourceful, and so were her girls.

Kate slid onto the smooth bench of the dining booth and pulled back the curtain that partially hid a sliding window. The window faced the parking lot, and she saw Carolyn put her kickstand down and walk down the dock. Excited to see her, Kate slid out of the table and went back through the door and out onto the deck where Mary and Dovie were chatting away. As Carolyn rounded the finger pier and put one foot onto the boat, Kate waved and smiled.

"Hiya Kate, I've been teaching sailing!" Carolyn said with a smile.

She said her polite greetings to Mary and her mother and immediately went down into the galley for a cold drink. She pulled a cleverly designed iced tea pitcher out of the icebox and poured two glasses, offering Kate one. The pitcher was rectangular and had a rubber stopper at the top to prevent spills. Kate curiously played with it for a minute, amused by the design.

"You should take sailing lessons, Kate; it's really fun down there at the yacht club," Carolyn said. Kate shrugged her shoulders. Johnny had taken some lessons there for a few summers, and Jammy sometimes played cards there, but other than that, she didn't know much about it or sailing.

"Come on, I'll show you some knots."

They went back outside, and Carolyn found two ropes, one for each of them. Time whittled away as Kate learned a figure 8 knot and clove hitch. She liked the way the rope felt in her hands and the challenge of the knots. She wanted to learn more, but Carolyn said she had something special to show her.

"We're going to the inlet, Mom," said Carolyn as they disembarked the houseboat and walked away towards what Carolyn called "Turtle Cove."

After braving the warm planks on Carolyn's dock, the macadam sizzled under their feet for a few quick-paced steps. The outer drive of the marina consisted of crushed oyster shells, and it was much cooler than the blacktop but dangerous on newly calloused feet.

"Should've brought flops," said Kate. Carolyn agreed, but their dance on the white, jagged road was short, and they were soon rewarded with a lush green, yellow, and white-speckled meadow adjacent to the marina. The grass was soothing to Kate's feet, and relieved by it, she told the same to Carolyn as they walked closer to Turtle Cove.

"Shhh..." whispered Carolyn. Kate looked at her as she pulled back some phragmites hiding the water's edge to reveal a small inlet hidden by reeds, mosquito bushes, and cat-tails. Through the window that Carolyn created, Kate saw a thick line of turtles on the edges of the opposite bank and many turtles sunning themselves on fallen trees half exposed at the waterline. "All Diamondbacks," whispered Carolyn excitedly.

Dozens of Diamondbacks of all sizes relaxed at their leisure, untaxed by human activity just yards away. They could have watched for hours, if not for the unwanted interactions with the marsh mosquitos. Kate swatted one hard, and it splattered on her forearm.

"That one was extra big," she whispered.

"It must have come too far north. It looks like one of those southern county types," said Carolyn. "The kind that swoop down and carry off all the feral cats."

They both giggled, dodged, and danced their way through the meadow, back over the steaming parking lot, leaving behind the mosquito and turtle-crowded marshland.

Students of the marshland these young people were, whose bare feet muck about on warm and wet grasses, soft pine needles, slippery seaweed-blanketed stones, rounded sea glass, driftwood, pebble tide lines, burning driveways, and oyster-strewn roads. Unable to restrain an inner drive to explore, youth wanderings were essential to a budding spiritual existence. To play in ditches, smell wildflowers, to be an audience to the struggle of life and death along the sandy shores and deep in the woods was to awaken all human sensations. Immersion at the earliest opportunity into the nature of the peninsula would not be denied by the adults of the waterman's village. It was "essential education."

At birth, the tidelands became the playground, and the taste of the brackish river water baptized an unbridled reverence in the young for all of God's creations and plans. Wholly christened at their first gasp of the river air, exploration was a destiny they could not deny.

Ripe with news of their discovery, Carolyn and Kate returned to the houseboat with tales of turtles as far up the cove as they could see. Their enthusiasm was so brazen with imagination that one might have thought they would've sworn the creatures had become layered two, three, and four deep. The young people felt and saw things that adults, with exposure over time, became accustomed to. For adults, nature is real; for children, it is surreal. This moment in time was as surreal for Kate as it was for Carolyn when she discovered it a few days earlier.

"Mr. Tim knows all about the turtles but says he doesn't tell anyone so they will be left alone," Carolyn said as she sensed Kate's fondness for the creatures.

"Mr. Tim is wise," Kate agreed.

Mr. Tim had run the marina for years and was known to have a personality that would leave well enough alone.

"Kate, it's time we head out," Mary said as she rose from her deck chair. They said their farewells and drove home in Mary's car. Kate suddenly felt a pang in her chest. Her senses jumped, and she turned to Mary.

"I need to check on Hopeful."

"Of course," said Mary.

As soon as she parked the car, Kate put shoes and socks on her burdened feet and headed off on her bicycle for the boatyard. She peddled at a brisk pace, feeling frantic inside. When she arrived, she rounded the corner to see Miss Pat sitting on a chair next to Squawk, talking to her. She looked up as soon as she saw Kate as if she was waiting for her. Kate's periphery turned black, and all she could do was focus on Miss Pat, who did not say a word. The look on her face told Kate everything she needed to know. Hopeful did not make it. Kate's throat felt tight, her constitution exhausted.

"Oh, Miss Pat," Kate said softly, "he didn't make it, did he?"

"You are right, Miss Kate. We lost him about 15 minutes ago. I knew you'd be by soon to pay your respects."

Kate hung her head.

"I have a nice spot picked out for him on my lawn," Miss Pat offered. "Will that suit you?"

"Yes," Kate whispered. Squawk piped up to try to get Kate's attention, but Kate was too consumed to notice. Miss Pat had already placed Hopeful back in his shoebox, ready for burial.

"Would you like to see him one last time?" Pat offered.

Kate lifted the lid ever so slightly, took a peek and closed it. They walked over to "Miss Pat's Cemetery for God's Beloved Creations." The sign had been painted a pale blue like the sky with the lettering in stenciled white. It was a lovely little plot laid out in her side yard that currently held the earthly bodies of three dogs, four cats, a snake, two ducks, a squirrel, and a bullfrog.

Miss Pat grabbed a shovel and started to dig a hole when Kate announced, "He should have a stone."

"You are right, Miss Kate. Will an old brick do?"

Kate nodded in approval and went over to a pile of bricks that lay next to Miss Pat's house. She picked one out and took an oyster shell, and used it to write Hopeful's name on it. "There," she said. "This is more proper, don't you think?"

"Of course, I think it's a lovely idea."

As Miss Pat patted the dirt down over the box with a shovel, Kate diligently affixed the brick where a headstone belonged. They both stood back and sighed, looked up to heaven, and wiped away tears.

"Miss Pat, should we put flowers at his grave?"

"Oh Kate, not to worry about that; dandelions always grow where graves are bare."

Kate hugged Miss Pat, walked to her bicycle, and rode straight out of town. Just outside of town, the corn flanked the road on both the north and south fields in summer and geese peppered the open ground in winter, scavenging corn left behind by the combines. Just a few miles out, the field was rudely interrupted by a small woodland, daring enough to grow right up to the edge of the road.

The loblolly pines, maples, and hackberry trees challenged the road as closely as they could. Resting her bicycle on the south side of one of the swamp oaks that had rooted many yards off the road, she set out to wander for a time in a place that had been reclaimed by the forest. The ground was cushioned by pine needles and dead brown leaves that had layered themselves on the floor. Occasionally, a muffled "crack" was heard underfoot as her weight broke an old twig hidden by the leaf carpet. These were the brittle bones of the forest, and this snapping noise reminded Kate of how fragile life can be.

Water bubbled up in many spots, perhaps an indication of an underground stream. If a turtle were to be found, this is where it would be - near the tiny pools littered with fallen acorns, sprouting ferns, odd-looking mushrooms, rotten leaves and woodsy mud. The kind of mud that smells of clay and rot. The kind of smell that sticks to you and holds on.

Hesitant walking was practiced in the woods as if she was breaking and entering into someone else's home. She did not want to intrude, but yet she did. Kate didn't belong but wanted to. So she proceeded with caution while taking note of all that surrounded her. Her gaze fixated on a wolf spider's web strung between two maple saplings and was drawn away by the cawing up in the trees, higher than she could possibly climb. That's where the crows would be watching her - an invader. She felt guilty for intruding but had to walk deeper in; it felt necessary.

Soon, she found a familiar grove, a persimmon, a locust, and an oak, almost in a perfect triangle with a small pond in between. The moss had covered the north side of the old oak, and it looked like it was wrapped in a velvety cloak, a queen of the woods. Hugging the old friend, her hands did not touch; its girth was a testament to its strength.

At the fringe of the pool, she knelt, waited, and watched. After many minutes of utter stillness, squirrels resumed their bustling, and nuthatches pin-balled from tree to tree. Ripples appeared on the pond, and a red slider poked its head up from the water. Kate wanted to talk to the turtle but choked it down. She was invisible and liked it that way. There were so many things she wanted to say to the turtle, how sorry she was about Hopeful, but she didn't. Kate just stared into his eyes and let her tears flow quietly down her cheek.

Did the red slider feel her sadness? Did the forest? The coolness of the pond water seeped into her shoes, making her socks heavy. After sitting still for so long, a centipede strolled over her feet and went on its way, headed east. The musty, damp smell of the pond wrapped around her and begged her to stay, but she knew the woods would just as well have her gone. Mosquitos took notice, and the mantra of their circling hum grew louder. It was time to move, but she wasn't ready to leave. So deeper in Kate went.

Squishing along in waterlogged sneakers, she made more noise now, and even more when she stubbed her toe on the old railroad tie. It had been a long time since she had been this far. The woods had tolerated the railroad invasion long enough, and now, with its service long since discontinued, the woods were reclaiming its ground. If she hadn't injured her toe, she might have walked right over it altogether, but by standing between the ties and looking east to west, Kate could see where the forest was thinner, the trees were shorter, the old path was fading, but still a deep cut ran through the middle of the timber. A scar on the wooded land. A bruise trying to heal.

Kate's mother had once ridden on that train a long time ago. One car for passengers, many more for the oysters it carried. When there were no more oysters left to catch, the train stopped its daily laceration into the woods.

Kate could hear it whirring along, screeching with each turn, spewing a choking cloud gasping for more coal, while the animals scattered and the trees soaked up the suffocating stench. Cold tar black steel number 6510 was headed straight at Kate with no compromises. It was a heart-pounding, haunting vision and so she took her eyes off the path and stepped away from the tracks. Stepping away was to end the film.

Heavy air heaved within Kate, and the dark smoke made her cough. She looked to the ground, to the wet leaves, to the pill bugs, inhaled the dankness of the woods, and returned to the present. All was quiet; the birds and squirrels ceased their merriment, and so Kate turned north and headed back towards the road. She had stayed long enough. The sun was in its late afternoon stance, and she had to be home before the six o'clock church bells, or Mother would come looking.

Chapter VIII

— Boat Rides —

Drained from the death of Hopeful, Kate hung around home for several days, where she could be found watching Herman hunt for bugs in the pond, helping with Jammy and Edison's gardens, or assisting Mary in the kitchen. Tansy went home to her mother's for a few weeks, quieting the neighborhood. Kate had been faithfully tending to her wart with dandelion blood, and after a week, the wart did recede and disappear. She was relieved to be rid of it, as cleaning and bandaging her foot every day had become an inconvenient nuisance.

After just a few days at home, Kate began to feel guilty about not visiting Squawk, so one morning after breakfast she got on her bike and rode down to see her.

Squawk remembered her and ran right to her. Kate knelt down, grabbed some of her cracked corn out of her dish, and fed it to her in a cupped hand. She loved the way the duckling tickled her fingers as her bill scooped up the little bits of nourishment. She knew she had been selfish staying away and approached Miss Pat at her office by gingerly tapping on her partially open office door with her foot and peaking, one eye exposed around the doorway. Pat looked up and smiled.

"I thought I'd see you soon, Kate, and here you are!" Pat understood from her own experiences the sensitivity of rescuing wildlife and its unpredictable aftermath. To try to stave off death and lose is a formidable blow to one's optimism on life, especially for a child.

"I'm sorry I haven't been around," said Kate, her eyes fixated on the boatyard gravel. "Nonsense, Kate!" Pat stood up from behind the desk and pushed the thought away with a wave of her hand. "I am glad you are here. I want to show you something; bring Squawk."

Kate scooped Squawk up and, in doing so, she noticed that Squawk weighed significantly more than the last time she had carried her. She also noticed her soft baby down was shedding. When they got to Miss Pat's side yard, Kate put Squawk down in the grass, and the duckling went straight for the first grasshopper she saw, savagely grabbing it and swallowing it whole. Squawk's aggressiveness shocked Kate as she thought ducklings to be the gentlest of creatures.

"She's really getting good at grabbing bigger bugs," said Pat.

"I see that," said Kate, still in awe from the barbarity of it.

"Wild animals are just that, Kate, wild. They need to be aggressive, or they will starve. It may seem cruel when wild things die, but it is how God made them. Without you, Hopeful would have died, with you, he had a chance."

"A lot of good I did!" Kate said, voice cracking.

"You did a world of good, Kate. Because of you, Hopeful did not die on the hot asphalt alone. You made him comfortable, gave him food and water, cleaned his wounds, showed him mercy and caring. You did make a difference. You gave Hopeful care and hope."

Kate smiled; she had never thought of it like that before.

"As you have noticed," Miss Pat said, changing the subject back to Squawk, "she has outgrown her pine box cage, and it's time to give her more room to run. I have some fencing for you to put up, not necessarily to keep her in, but to keep any hungry foxes out. Here, run it around this tree."

Pat pointed at a medium-sized hickory tree in her yard. "I think I have about 20 feet or so here for a circumference, so plot the cage out that way. You can take any unpainted wood off the scrap pile to make it as you wish. And there are tools and nails you may need on my porch. I have to get back to the office, but I will check on you later."

Distracted by the project at hand, Kate put her full energy and attention into building a new area for Squawk. While Kate measured and staked the metal fence posts with her feet, Squawk wandered the yard feasting on bugs. Kate would ask her a question, and she would squawk back. Time glided like a sailboat reaching in a stiff breeze.

When Pat checked back in, Squawk was enjoying her new marine plywood lean-to shelter and a large grassy area to roam.

"Excellent work, Kate. You may have some of your father's talents; careful now or we'll put you to work."

Kate smiled. She felt better than she had in days. She gave Pat a hug and turned to go say goodbye to Hopeful, whose grave lay just around the corner. As she approached the bare square of dirt, she took notice of a large dandelion that had sprung up in the grass next to the brick marker. It seemed bigger and brighter than the others nearby and demanded her contemplation. Different than any other dandelion she had ever seen before, it glowed. She turned to ask Miss Pat if she saw it too, but she was gone, leaving Kate the only witness to what was surely a sign from above. Kate looked up at the cloudless sky and winked.

Feeling ready to take on the world, Kate left the boatyard and headed to the wharf. Along the waterfront beyond the shallows, little sailboats flitted about, turning their sails back and forth, back and forth like laundry on a breezy day. The wind was quiet inland, but beyond the flats the water pattern was something less than breakwater but more than glass. The wind ripples, small but steady, were fueling the tiny dancing boats. Their rhythm was hard to break away from, such that Kate stopped peddling and gazed out, enchanted by the scene.

The ferry was at port across the wet divide, so she decided to visit Cousin Tessie while she waited for its crossing. Jumping back on her bike, she rode past the wharf and turned the corner to see Cousin Tessie out weeding her garden. Having no aunts of her own,

Kate fondly called Tessie "Auntie," and Tess was honored to have this distinction.

Kate came to a full stop; Tessie looked up, saw Kate, and smiled at the impending visit.

"I was wondering when you would stop by, Miss Kate. I've seen you riding by many a time, very busy with your summer."

"There has been so much to do this summer, I can hardly catch my breath…"

Tessie laughed and gestured her right arm towards Kate, and she went in for a side hug.

"How is your garden, Auntie?" she asked as they walked alongside it.

"I'm glad you asked; my lettuce is withering in this June heat," she said, lifting her bright red gardening hat with its ample brim off her head and wiping the sweat off her brow with a handkerchief.

"I think I shall pick it all at once and give it away: will you take some home with you for the family?" she questioned Kate.

"Yes, thank you."

"My tomatoes are coming along nicely, as you can see."

Kate inspected the plants, heavy with green lobes and agreed. Tessie took Kate by the hand and led her behind the house.

"You must see the orchard!"

Kate, remembering the peaches from last year, got very excited.

"Are they ripe yet?"

"Not yet," replied Tessie, "but you will see they are on their way."

Behind Cousin Wilhelm's workshop and shed lay a small orchard with a dozen fruit trees. Ten peaches, two plums, and a fig bush that was most likely the largest in town. The peaches and plums were laden with many unripe fruits and the figs were showing a small first crop.

Kate smiled, "I will help you when it is time."

"I know I can count on you, Miss Kate, and I look forward to it; it won't be long now." Wandering closer to the matriarchal fig,

Kate reached in grabbed one of the inner branches, and pulled its springy wood towards her. The branch bent with her will, and she was able to pick a fig that had been clearly above her head. Plucking it from the branch, she found the hole at the bottom and broke it into two pieces to reveal the ripe flesh inside.

"No wasps," she said and handed half of it to Tess.

They each took a bite and, in unison, proclaimed it was not as tasty as the second crop would be in August. The predictably lean first crop was not fussed over too much, as the second was always sweeter and prolific. August bore the kind of crop you would want to make preserves with.

"Will you come in and have a bite?" asked Tessie.

"I am quite hungry..."

"Of course you are."

Tess was the best cook in town and loved to share with everyone.

Before they walked up the front steps together, Kate stopped to smell Tessie's roses. An old-fashioned climbing variety, Tessie called them "grapevine roses," their perfume unmatched by any garden around. At the other end of town, there were some gardeners who would confer with Tess as they, too, were passionate about their rose ancestry. Tessie believed hers to come from nursery stock almost 100 years old, but no one knew for sure.

Remembering her manners, Kate reached ahead and opened the screened door for Tess. The threshold cast a spell upon all who entered to gaze with mouth open up and down the walls. Tess walked past the mahogany banister towards the kitchen while Kate, same as many other visitors, strode forward to touch the newell post and hang to it while she looked up to where the ceiling met the walls. From top corners to the bottom trim, the heavy plaster walls were laden with pictures of Captain Wilhelm, or as Kate called him, Cousin Will, who should not be confused with Great Uncle Will who wandered the Seth house indefinitely.

There were photos, artist's renderings, postcards from all over the world, ship models, and newspaper articles all about Cousin Will. It was enough illustrated adventure to put any observer into a sea-faring trance. Just as one would feel stepping onto the dock after days at sea, the floor moved under Kate's feet, and she held onto the post tightly to balance her mind. Cousin Will was an erudite of the sea, well respected in town, and someone Kate very much admired.

"Come on in, Kate!" Tessie's voice called from the next room.

She had already laid out on the oak dining room table two china plates with egg salad sandwiches, pickled watermelon rind, lemon sponge cake, and sun tea. Kate was so hungry that when she saw it she grabbed a watermelon rind and shoved it into her mouth.

"Kate!" Tess said sternly. "Not before thanking the Lord!"

Kate apologized, and all was quickly forgiven as Kate led them in grace.

Next to the table lay a dress that Tess was sewing. It was a unique dress so Kate inquired.

"This is my colonial costume for when I serve as a docent at the Custom's House."

"Oh!" Kate knew all about the Custom's House as Jammy had taken her there. Kate's mind drifted off to a time when tobacco was as good as money and ships from England visited the port.

The red calico print of Tessie's dress trapped her eyes, and she snapped back to the present. Trimmed in thin lace and garnished with working wooden buttons, the sleeves had a lace "flare" to them, and Tessie was repairing one.

$$\downarrow \quad \downarrow \quad \downarrow$$

TESS AND KATE CAUGHT UP on family and town news. It had been a few weeks since they last talked and much can happen in just a few short weeks. Tess especially wanted to hear about Johnny's new girlfriend. When lunch was finished and gossip spent, they shared dish duty together and then walked out to the front porch where in just a short while Tessie's visitors had become stacked up. By the time Kate left for the ferry, Tessie was holding court on the porch. Still tasting the sponge cake and thinking about picking peaches, she licked her lips and the wind blew them dry as she headed down towards the ferry dock.

Avoiding the nettles so early in the season, the town boys swam every day at the wharf in the early summer. The first to jump into the river in May was the bravest, and on any June afternoon, one could find a gangly group of shirtless boys climbing to the tallest pilings and standing upon the hot tin-covered posts like kings. They would pronounce their superiority over all the other boys until pushed off into the plume of churning white water as the ferry departed. Then another lad would claim the throne until they succumbed to the next mutiny. As tradition would have it, insurrections happened all afternoon long on sunny days until the boys' stomachs and church bells pressed them home.

Johnny had only just been allowed to swim at the docks the last two summers, and Edison made him pass a test before he was allowed to partake in the unruly games. He took Johnny down to the wharf one late spring day, and while Johnny was taking his t-shirt off for a swim, Edison pushed him in. Tangled in his shirt, he managed to escape, pop back up to the surface, and climb up the barnacle-covered ladder barefooted without complaint. That night at dinner, Edison proclaimed him fit for the ferry docks.

Kate's shirt billowed and rippled off her back as her bike whizzed down the hill. She parked her bike down by the shallows under the shady willow where she and Tansy had found Squawk just a few weeks ago. Cars were filing off the ferry one by one, and a line of tourists looked anxious to embark on the ten-minute journey across the water to another oyster town, where many more of Kate's cousins lived.

That's what all these little towns were: oyster towns. Oysters were once so numerous that some village sections were constructed upon the mounds of discarded shells. Built up as fishing ports, they were discarded by the industry when the river bottoms were picked clean.

In many of these water towns the families that remained carried within them a quiet pride. Favored to have a life that was bent on the will of the river, many were "fishers of men," some were not, but the collaborative spirit of the community wove the tightest rope of brotherhood.

Collective grieving, healing, praying, dancing, working, and cooking was a built-in kind of therapy. This inherent congenial living held a kind of social capital that could never be bought or understood by someone outside the sphere of an oyster town's esoteric verve.

Kate watched the tourists file onto the ferry and she saw the town boys were as raucous as ever. Kate tried to ignore them but couldn't when she saw Johnny wave.

"Hiya Kate!" he yelled, arms in the air as he was pushed off the coveted king piling and splashed headfirst into the water about 20 feet from the ferry's churning white water. Kate waved at her brother as she walked closer. Cousin Will smiled when he saw Kate. She dutifully reached into her pocket to pull out her passage fare of a dime when Cousin Will, as anticipated, told her to "put it back in her pocket and save it for Truman's Store." Kate giggled. She loved this ritual with Cousin Will. She had never paid for a ferry ride, but staying true to Jammy and her Mother's teachings, she knew it was always polite to offer.

Kate shadowed Cousin Will as he reached above his head to pull the weighted barrier gate down by its hinges to block the way onto the ferry. Readying to disembark, he closed the gate and then placed beveled wooden chocks under the front tires of the lead cars, collected the fares, and uncleated the salt-weathered lines that held the boat at port.

Into the wheelhouse he slid; Kate followed quickly as he took

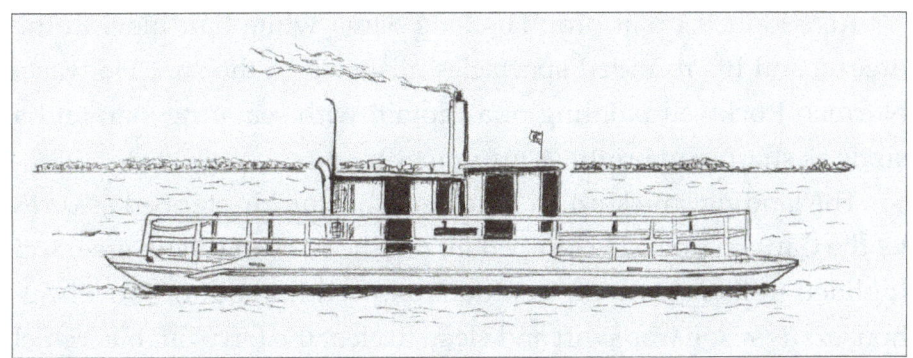

the wheel to depart from the wharf. The engine groaned as he put it in gear and true to tradition, the tallest boy, Harry, was pushed into the aft churning waters of the departing ferry. The boat glided quickly out of port and Harry, who knew Captain Will well, popped up and waved in the surf as the ferry gathered speed.

Once away from the landing, Captain Will asked Kate if she would like a turn at the wheel. Kate, always honored by the gesture, looked up and down river before taking the helm; the boat traffic was light today. The wooden wheel had been varnished many decades prior but still had a shine that made Kate's eyes sparkle. She loved its warm smoothness. It comforted her fingertips as she molded her hands around the amber wood. The places on the wheel that were touched most often were wrapped ever so precisely with an old, thin, braided rope for grip. She placed her hand on them and looked forward. The river looked very deep green today, and its color captured her.

"How is your summer going, Miss Kate?" Captain Will asked.

"It's been exciting!" Kate said proudly. "I have been visiting everyone; I just saw Auntie before coming down to see you."

"How is my Tessie doing today?"

"Very well, we had lunch together, and her lettuce needs to be picked."

"Yes," Will replied, aware of the lettuce situation. "Everyone in the neighborhood will be having salads and sandwiches for a week," he said smiling.

Kate looked up at him. His long Santa white hair blew in the breeze, and his rounded spectacles glistened in the sun. He was a Norman Rockwell painting of a captain with seafaring skin and a smile as sharp and bright as a summer moon on a velvet sky.

The landing snuck up on Kate, and she quickly stepped aside to let the Captain dock. He jumped in, put the ferry in full reverse, and it glided in like skates on ice. Kate followed him out of the wheel-house. His stride was swift and clean to cleat the ferry off. His vessel was his lady of the sea and he treated her as such with the respect and admiration a true lady deserved and required. The two worked in unison it seemed, man and vessel, and Kate thought no one could be attached to a boat more.

"Kate! Katie girl!" Kate turned to the right and, looking over the starboard side, she saw Mr. Brown in his Jon boat with a fish on a hook.

Kate waved wildly and yelled, cupping her hands around her mouth, "What kind of fish?"

"Hardheads are here… I can pick you up if you want to throw a line!" Kate turned sharply to look at Cousin Will.

"Who am I to stop you from fishing, Miss Kate? Next time, I'll put you to work to earn your ride…"

Kate had been wanting to hear those words for a while. She ran over to hug Captain Will, "Thank you, Cousin!" she said with great affection.

Then, she promptly ran off the boat to meet Mr. Brown dock-side. Kate had always wanted to tie up the ferry when it docked and had even practiced her cleats at home for just such an occasion. She would take Captain Will up on his offer next time, but since the fish were biting, that dream would have to wait.

The ferry dock on this side of the river was long and lean and ran the whole length of the shoreline. She ran down the aged planks with an eager cautiousness, intent on avoiding the rough, splintered wooden spots. At the end of the pier she turned to her right and ran the whole length of the dirt path, haphazardly lined with mosquito bushes, out to the jetty where many families were casting lines from their woven lawn chairs.

The mosquito bushes and young loblolly pines grew in place of what was once an expansive canning factory that fed both world wars. The buildings had long been torn down and now the ground at the water's edge, covered in oyster shells, fragmites and cattails, pretended the industry never existed. Kate knew of the factory from stories on the front porch.

Her Poppy, Walton's father, had managed the packing house workers who shucked and picked all day long. Long since a memory for the older folks in town, Kate had never seen this industry in its heyday, but in her imagination, it towered above the river, casting shadows on the shoreline of what once was the livelihood of many, until the river could give no more. Discarded skipjacks carved a new shoreline where Mr. Brown now fished, and they, too, had disappeared. Rotted away by river water, they were swallowed up by the same river they dredged. Everything on this side of the river, it seemed, had been reclaimed by the water and lost in time like it was a fever dream.

Kate's sprint left a trail of dust blown away by a gentle western land breeze. The aluminum frames of the folding chairs had brightly colored lattice backs, which made for a shiny tapestry by the waterside. Mr. Brown waved to Kate from the end of the jetty; his boat rocked back and forth in the ferry wake while he held the bulkhead with one hand. Kate swiftly found the straightest path and was soon climbing aboard Mr. Brown's Jon boat. Kate's new skipper settled back into his spot aft by the old Evinrude and grabbed the tiller to reverse away from the dock. They putt putted back to his original spot in the river, and he put the engine in neutral.

"Tide is slack, about to change," he said as Kate lowered the Danforth anchor down into the river.

She knew from other times she had fished the spot that they

were in five to six feet of water. She gave the anchor a tug as Mr. Brown reversed; as soon as she felt it catch the bottom, she let out another dozen feet of line and cleated it off. He turned the engine off. Grabbing the extra rod in the boat, she looked for the bait board. A few pieces of peeler had already been cut, and she grabbed a red claw as she always had good luck with them.

"How many you got so far?" The proud fisherman gently lifted the old t-shirt that covered a five-gallon bucket.

Kate peeked inside and then gasped. The bucket was three-quarters full of fat hardheads croaking away; there must have been at least a dozen or more. She immediately cast her line, and before she could congratulate Mr. Brown, a fish was on. The rod bent and Kate kept the tension as well as she could. As quick as it bit, it was in the boat, and she threw it into the bucket. Mr. Brown did the same with his quick catch. They repeated this three more times until the bucket was so full that the t-shirt covering the fish was moving from the flicking tails of the fresh catch.

"Miss Katie, I think we've caught our limit!" Mr. Brown announced loud enough for the folks standing on the jetty to hear.

"You've got dinner for a week!"

Many of them shouted back words of congratulation—the joy of a full bucket was contagious as all the fishermen on land had also filled their buckets. The air, electric with excitement, seemed to bubble up around them off of the river and pop with emotion. Kate laughed and laughed. Mr. Brown gave the lawn chair captains a thumbs up, opened up his small cooler, and offered Kate a cold root beer. She thanked him and took a swig.

"Miss Kate, I want you to know that if you have a Jon boat, you have everything."

"What do you mean?" replied Kate.

Mr. Brown elaborated: "A complete feeling of contentment is an illusive thing. But here on the river, I find that comfort. It may be the fish I've caught, or it could be a sunset I watch. To be able to escape the chains of the land and float about freely in the grandness of nature is an appeasement for the burdens of man."

Kate thought long and hard about what he said. "That makes sense since I'm always happy near the water."

"Yes, Miss Kate, you are drawn to it."

They stared contentedly at each other and smiled.

"Ready to head back to the other side, Miss Katie?"

"Yes!"

The old 2-stroke Evinrude 9.5 was nimble, and she started on the first pull. The plume of smoke she generated dissipated as the craft pushed forward and quickly got up on a plane. Kate loved the wind on her face and the way it blew her hair back. The bucket of fish rattled as the chop hit the aluminum underside. She kept one hand on the full fish bucket and the other on the gunwale. They came round the back side of the ferry and coasted into the shoreline near where Kate had left her bike. Wrapping six big fish up into the old t-shirt by rolling and tying them off, he handed them to Kate.

"Oh, thank you, Mr. Brown!"

"Kate, tell Jammy about our afternoon. I know she loves fresh caught croaker."

"I will!" Kate said as she tucked the package under her arm. She looked over to Mr. Brown to wave, but he was already headed out to the river, his back to the land. The fish were hard to hold so after pushing her bike up the hill with one hand and holding the fish with the other, she decided to see if Tessie had a bag or bucket with handles she could borrow.

⚓ ⚓ ⚓

KATE LEFT TESSIE'S WITH A bucket large enough to hold her fresh caught fish and a pile of garden lettuce wrapped carefully with a double tea towel on top. The ride home was an arduous journey. The fish were very heavy, and her knee banged into the bucket every time her foot pedaled 'round. At the corner of Miss Hattie's store she stopped to sure up her grip on the treasures, but her attention quickly shifted to the opposite corner of the street where Beezy, a tall, lean elderly man, was arguing with a telephone pole.

His right pant leg was held close to his calf by a tight rubber band to keep it off the chain of his bike. His bicycle, upright next to him was meticulously kept; his only ride in any weather. Repairing and shining the chrome on two-wheelers was often how he earned his money, in addition to selling honey from his beehives he tended outside of town. Surrounded by hollyhocks and stalwart to his insults, the pole just stood there, motionless and expressionless infuriating the man, leading him to resort to rude gestures of the middle finger. This unusual street corner animation played out while Kate stood tall, fish bucket in hand, watching.

Beezy stepped back, paused and folded his hands like he was listening to what the pole had to say for itself. He nodded no, he nodded yes, and then gave the pole a high-five slap. Once their argument was settled, his eyes wandered to Kate who was caught staring with her mouth hanging open. Embarrassed, she tried to get back on her bike, but her bike fell over. Beezy's long legs glided across the street, and with a brisk motion, he picked up her bicycle and held it upright, slapping the seat and motioning for her to get on. At first, she was hesitant, but remembering her mother's words, she thanked him for his help, hopped on, and took off. Looking back, she saw a little wave from Beezy.

When she arrived home, she proudly hauled her bucket into the kitchen, where Mary was making a pie.

"What kind?" Kate inquired.

"Blueberry, of course. Do you not know when your birthday is?"

Surprised by the news, she went right over to the calendar on the refrigerator. "My birthday is tomorrow!?!" she exclaimed.

"The older you get, the easier it is for them to sneak up on you," laughed Mary.

Kate smiled and handed her mother the bucket.

"What do we have here?" Mary inquired as she picked through it. "Wonderful, just wonderful!" she exclaimed, "We shall have it all for dinner tonight!"

Kate was relieved they were having it right away as she did enjoy the fresh fish but she did not want it for her birthday dinner. Her birthday dinner was a meal she looked forward to with great anticipation, and she asked for the same menu every year: fried chicken, potato salad with hard-boiled eggs, English peas, and blueberry pie. If the sweet corn, baby squash, or tomatoes were early she would ask for that too. She set to work scaling the fish and filleting them for Mary, which gave her time to put in a word for what she would like for her birthday dinner.

"I know, I know, I have it memorized by now," Mary smiled. "Is there anything you want for your birthday?"

Kate didn't have anything in mind. "I'm sure you'll think of something," Kate replied.

Mary shook her head and smiled as Kate, per usual, did not know of anything she was anxious to have, making gift-giving both easy and difficult. Birthdays in the Seth household were fairly low-key. It was the only time of the year when you could request what you wanted for dinner and dessert. The family gave small presents after dinner, sang Happy Birthday and that was as far as the fanfare went. Birthdays were treated as a happy but humble occasion, one to be noted but not overdone.

⚓ ⚓ ⚓

LOWELL JOINED THEM FOR DINNER, which pleased Mary very much. Kate took up most of meal time, relaying her events of the day and promising that Mr. Brown could back up her story that the bucket was completely full of hardheads. Fish stories ran rampant through town, so Kate needed to supply a means of proof, as if dinner wasn't proof enough.

Johnny was noticeably absent from his chair and it was announced that Johnny had taken Lizzie on a picnic dinner on the family boat. Jammy ate Johnny's share of hardhead and appreciatively noted Mr. Brown's generosity by announcing she would be making him some fresh biscuits as a means to return the favor.

The family boat was a 16-foot Thompson Lapstrake. Its pearly white sides and varnished bow made it an eye-catcher for those who appreciated a run about with style. Cousin John, who lived on the water just outside of town, had given it to the family in his aging years. No longer nimble enough to captain with his arthritis, he passed it along to Johnny specifically and the family at large. It was a tremendous gift as the family could have never afforded it on their own.

Luckily, a town slip had just opened up, so they were able to dock it nearby down Market Lane. The boat slip was one of the oldest of many town docks that were mostly inhabited by watermen's boats and a few townspeople's pleasure crafts.

The well-used Johnson 55 was a project engine, but Johnny and Edison stayed on top of it and kept it running despite its aging parts. She was a sweet little boat, and Johnny and his friends spent many free afternoons water skiing off it.

Kate was the third eye when he was short a person for skiing. The boat was fast and wild, and Kate loved when they turned circles in the river, and the skiers would fly off to the side and gather a burst of speed so they were almost even with the boat. Sometimes, Johnny let her drive. With towels on the seats to keep their legs from burning on the hot, varnished wood, they could pass an afternoon as fast as a hummingbird flies, only quitting when the gas was low, the church bells were imminent, or when the nettles were too thick.

Kate had tried water skiing a few times but never took to it, but Johnny was pretty good at skiing and saved up his tips for a slalom ski. She loved to drive, watch the skiers, jump overboard, and swim off the boat on hot summer days. Johnny had just finished varnishing the seats and the bow for the season a few days ago, so the Lapstrake was looking sharp and shiny for his date. Mary packed them some sandwiches, deviled eggs, and cookies, and Johnny filled up a jug of unsweetened tea. When Mary wasn't looking, he dumped a cup of sugar in it and shook it well to make it sweet for Lizzie.

After dinner, Kate played Kick the Can and Ghost in the Graveyard on Miss Ginny's lot with the neighborhood kids. Kimmy was not only one of her school bus chums but also a neighborhood friend and clever checkers adversary. She had the largest checkerboard mat Kate had ever seen. A square quilted blanket Kimmy's grandmother had made. When they rolled it out on the floor it took up all of Kimmy's living room. The squares were orange and bright blue, and the wooden checkers, made by her grandfather, were slices of an old cedar limb that had been sanded smooth. Half were varnished with the bark edges still attached, and the other half were painted a creamy soft white.

One of seven, her family was a lively bunch and always out and about town. Many summer afternoons she and her siblings could be found at the park or walking the streets looking for odd jobs, mostly helping old folks with little tasks for a quarter each and then pooling their money for sodas or treats from Truman's Store.

Kate ran and played until the mosquitos sent everyone home. Itchy and sweaty, she went straight upstairs to shower and went right to bed after saying good night to everyone on the front porch. She thought she would fall right asleep, but instead, she was restless. Knowing the next day she would turn eleven made her want the day to come quickly. She thought about the blueberry pie her mother had made and wondered how she might spend her day. Would she go swimming, take a boat ride, or crab off the wharf?

Looking through the screen, the evening sky had a brightness to it that seemed to display an endless ambivalence toward the struggling night sky. Soft blues and faintly feminine pinks fought each other until the blue grew deeper and pressed close to the landscape until only a sliver of pink held on tightly above the treetops. This stubborn pink was the color of Jammy's bath soap, and such as it was, Kate could almost smell the sunset. She heard Jammy's feet on the top of the stairs.

"Jammy," she called to her softly. "I can't sleep."

Kate slid over as Jammy sat on the edge of the bed. "Anxious for your birthday, are you?"

"Yes, I can't wait."

"Roll over, and I'll give you a back rub."

Kate loved Jammy's back rubs and quickly obliged. With her gnarled fingers, Jammy gently rubbed Kate's back.

Kate wondered, "Jammy, do your fingers ever hurt?"

"Sometimes," she replied, "but never when I rub your back."

Kate calmed quickly and soon she was sailing ships and catching turtles on a cloud in the sky.

⚓ ⚓ ⚓

SOMETIME IN THE MIDDLE OF the night, Kate became restless. Her dreams, fraught with fearful shadows and strange noises, made her thrash and twist her sheets. There was pacing, too, lots of anxious pacing in the hall; she could hear it in the background of her dreams. Struggling to wake herself, she had become attuned that some kind of madness was afoot. She reached her hand out to touch a doorknob, but it would not turn.

"What were the noises behind the door?" Her eyes opened wide and she sat up in bed, confident that something was very wrong in the Seth house. Strained voices trailed from the kitchen, and she heard Uncle Will knocking about in Johnny's room, but no words from Johnny. She peeked through the corner of her door to Johnny's and saw that the room was empty.

She walked past Jammy's room and saw it was also empty. Down the three steps and across her parent's empty bedroom, she cautiously walked towards the troubled voices in the kitchen and as she did, she noticed that even Lowell's room was empty. She pieced fragments of sentences together and surmised that someone in town had gone missing. Halfway through tip-toeing down the steps, there came an urgent pounding on the front door, and the kitchen inhabitants rushed to the front of the house with Edison leading the charge. Kate went back up the stairs and also headed quickly to the front of the house. She arrived at the hidden curved landing of the front steps when the door flung open, and a woman with all the vexation she could muster yelled: "Well, where the hell is she? You know he'll have to marry her now!"

Kate peeked around the corner. An exceedingly tall, stout, red-faced, red-haired woman stood in the Seth's front hall seething. Agitation and condemnation bubbled out of her pores. She glared at Edison evenly in the eye. Her imposing figure dared anyone to speak, and her hands stuck so tightly to her hips you could hang clothes hangers from her forearms.

"Step away from me, Mizz Parks!" Edison growled angrily as he spoke.

She was not used to anyone challenging her and the look on her face bore a perplexed squint as she took a step back.

"See here," Edison continued, voice raised and razzed, "We don't know what's happened; we don't even know if the kids are alright. Get your priorities straight, woman!"

For the duration of this confrontation, Mary's face showed true the weight of a mother's love and the toll it takes. Her face was pale and drawn, her eyes sunken and dark. One look at her mother's face was all Kate needed to piece the story together. Johnny and Lizzie had never come home from their picnic dinner on the Lapstrake. They were missing.

With this realization, everything in Kate's periphery magnified.

The upstairs pacing of the ancestors was so loud it became white noise to the grandfather clock. It chimed three o'clock so poignantly that everyone went quiet for a moment, and Mrs. Parks cautiously backed away from Edison further. Her expression changed from condemnation to panic. Even River, a dog of friendly disposition, became agitated and barked aggressively at the newest person to arrive at the Seth house.

Officer Duncan, the town policeman, who had been on the case since midnight when Mary had called him, stood at the front porch with River on his heels. Edison stepped forward, opened the screen door, and swatted River away from Officer Duncan's ankles. Named after his uncle, Duncan was the 24-hour policeman on a first-name basis with everyone in town. With roots embedded as deeply as a father oak, he knew everyone, their parents and grandparents, which house they inhabited, and their favorite ice cream flavor. Nothing happened in town that he didn't know about. He was the most trusted and respected man in town, after all the ministers, of course. Duncan stepped forward and handed an orange life jacket to Edison.

"This is what they found in Coon Creek, Edison. I know it doesn't look good, but we'll keep looking."

As Mary cupped her hands over her face to hide her desperation, Jammy excused herself to the front parlor to talk to the ceiling, and Lowell stepped forward to stand next to Edison and show his support.

"I'll get the waterman on it," Lowell said, then briskly turned, went out the back door, and headed straight for the docks.

Kate wanted to stay out of the fray but also felt drawn into it. Emotions ran high and Kate absorbed it all until she could take no more. She stepped forward, and halfway down the steps everyone turned to see the girl who had heard it all.

Kate, holding the banister with one hand and pointing with the other, said, "Our life jackets look different than that; we have black ties, and that one has white ties."

Mary exposed her face and motioned for Kate to come to her. Kate obliged, and Mary hugged her and kissed her forehead.

Kate whispered softly in Mary's ear, "Johnny's alright, I just know it."

Jammy came out of the living room and smiled at Kate. "I feel it too," she whispered for both generations to hear.

Mary made an announcement, "I'm going to sit on the back porch. Will you join us, Mildred?"

Mrs. Parks, looking rather embarrassed by her earlier behavior, kindly accepted the offer and asked to use the phone to call Mr. Parks.

The old wicker chairs made cracking noises as they all sat down, especially the one Mrs. Parks sat in. Duncan had left to get back to the search party on Coon Creek, and Edison had gone with him, leaving the women to themselves. Jammy put hot water on the stove for tea, and Mary offered sandwiches to be polite, but no one was hungry. If Kate could bet, she would've said they were all a little nauseous. So there they sat, the three Seth women and Mildred. The conversation was vapid.

The minister arrived. Pastor George had been relieved of sleep by someone in the community, and arriving at the back screened porch door, armed with his bible, he let himself in and sat in the last open wicker chair. Before any conversation or hearing the worries, doubts, and fears of the women, he put his hand up and said, "Let us pray. From the book of James 1:6 …But ask in faith. Never doubting, for one who doubts, is like the wave of the sea, driven and tossed by the wind. And from Isaiah 41:10, Do not fear, for I am with you. Do not be dismayed, for I am your God. I will strengthen you and help you: I will uphold you in my righteous right hand. Says the Lord." He closed the bible softly and then pronounced to the tiny congregation of four as they held hands in prayer, "Faith is an anchor in a sea of doubt."

This interjection of faith into the women's raging fear had a most calming effect. All were silent and reflective for several minutes. Mary, when she felt the time was right, broke the silence.

"Thank you, Pastor George. You are, of course, a welcome sight in this worrisome time." Everyone nodded in agreement.

Pastor George, then, in another act of kindness, provided additional relief with distraction. "Mary, I hear you have been checking in on our neighbor Paul. How is he fairing these days?"

Jammy interjected, "Mary has been very faithful about visiting him; he's surely missing his Anna."

Then Mary said, "Paul, of course, we all know, has taken to the bottle." Everyone shook their heads in agreement. "I have stopped by and prayed with him about twice a week, but Pastor George, I don't think I am helping him. He still goes to the Country Club in the afternoons."

Pastor George then interjected, "I will also pay him a visit soon. I hear he doesn't have any food. Is this true?"

"I'm afraid so," Mary confirmed. "I went to visit him at home one day last week, and he was eating cold peas out of a can. His garden is withering to brown from lack of attention. Edison brings him food from his garden every other day or so—as things ripen."

"That is very neighborly of you, Mary." said Pastor George.

She replied, "Well, it's the Christian thing, despite the broccoli incident."

"The broccoli incident?" Pastor George inquired.

"Oh, don't worry about that," said Mary, who flushed and then changed the subject by waving her hand. "I'm planning on taking him a chicken next week."

"God bless you, Mary. I will put him on our prayer and care list."

Not to be outdone, Mildred countered with," I'll take him some homemade bread tomorrow."

Again, Pastor George could not be more pleased with his flock. "Mildred, you are doing the Lord's work."

He opened up his bible. "Matthew 7:12, In everything, therefore, treat people the same way you want them to treat you, for this is the Law and the Prophets."

The time went much more quickly with Pastor George there, and the ladies, while surely not forgetting the reason they were up at what was now 4:30 in the morning, held their heads high as a show of faith in the Lord in front of their minister. They discussed additional church news, such as the Fourth of July hot dogs they sold in the park during the holiday. Mildred was in charge of that, and while she apologized for not having the figures at hand, she roughly voiced her numbers and plans for the small church fundraiser.

"Well, it sounds like you have it under control," he said, followed by a quick turn to Mary. "Are we straight for the wedding music in two weeks?"

"Yes, the bride and groom have given me their preferences, and I have already listened to the songs once.

"As always, you are on it, Mary." He turned to Jammy.

"How are you enjoying the choir, Jammy?"

She graciously replied, "Very much, Pastor George, it suits me."

Kate sensed the sky was hinting towards morning with its ashen blue hue; and with the sun rise, Kate thought, it might be easier to find Johnny and Lizzie.

"Ladies," Pastor George said with a noticeably deep-felt sincerity, "Our church is truly blessed to have you all in its service. And Kate, you too are an important part of the church."

"I am? How?"

"You, Kate, are our future, and I don't mean just the church; I mean the next generation to do goodwill towards men."

"What do you mean by that?" interjected Kate.

"From Psalm 91:4," said Pastor George without his bible even open. "The Lord will cover you with his feathers, and under his wings you will find refuge; his faithfulness will be your shield and rampart."

Kate stared at Pastor George with her tongue ever so slightly appearing as her lips began to fall with her jaw. She snapped it up, still staring and replied, "What do you mean, I am your future?"

Pastor George smiled sheepishly. "I meant the future of mankind!"

Kate thought long and hard and then countered with, "That's a lot of pressure, Pastor George."

Everyone's boisterous laughter was instantly silenced when the phone rang. Mary picked it up, "Yes?"

"It's me, Mom, I'm down at Leo's Place with Lizzie."

"PRAISE THE LORD! JOHNNY AND LIZZIE ARE BACK!!! AMEN!!!" Mary shouted with a two-block amplification.

Neighborhood house lights snapped on, women in hair curlers peeked through their bedroom curtains, and men in boxers found themselves peeking out their front doors. These were the folks that didn't work the water. For those families that did work the water, the celebration began when Johnny was spotted attempting to paddle across the main channel with one oar while being slowly pushed up the river by the flood tide and westerly breeze.

One CB announcement was made for all the watermen to hear—he and Lizzie had been found, and it wasn't in Coon Creek. Jimmy and Lowell were the ones lucky enough to spread the good news and tow them in.

When Mildred, Lizzie's father, Pastor George, Mary, Edison, Jammy, Kate, and Duncan arrived at the old packing house ramp, a ruckus of pride and celebration had broken out amongst the watermen, and beers popped and fizzed in union as they toasted to the rising sun in the east.

One voice rose above all others as Pastor George grabbed the attention of the town rabble and, laying quiet the morning crows, set a short yet poignant proclamation:

"Let us all take a brief moment to thank our Lord and Savior, Jesus Christ, he truly is the miracle worker. Through his guiding spirit, we had two watermen bring Lizzie and Johnny to safety. It was just an hour ago, I was telling the families of the lost that 'Faith is an anchor in a sea of doubt.'"

"From James 1:6: ...But ask in faith, never doubting, for the one who doubts is like the wave of the sea.' How true we see this message delivered to us before our very own eyes. In our Lord, we are blessed and thankful. Let us not forget to pray throughout the day to let our Lord and Savior know we are truly humble servants of his amazing powers. Do I have an Amen?"

"AAMMMEENNN!!' The crowd screamed with beers raised to a deep red-orange sun and to a new day on the river filled with promise.

Edison backed the trailer down the boat ramp to collect the Lapstrake. The algae growing on the ramp made it slippery under Kate's feet, causing her to catch herself on the side of the truck more than once. The tide was either halfway up or halfway down. Kate wasn't sure, but she knew it couldn't be high tide because the green algae, when submerged, floated about like hair blowing in the breeze, now lay exposed, desperately wanting protection from the strength of the morning sun. While vulnerable barnacles lay bare to the sun, gasping for breath, Kate watched intently as a crab shed floated by.

Even as early as it was, the cooks in the kitchen of Leo's place, a seafood restaurant next to the public boat ramp, were already breaking a sweat as they cut, sliced, chopped, and stirred up Leo's special recipes for lunch and dinner. Mind you, no recipes were written on paper; they resided in the minds and at the whimsy of the many cooks who kept the good food coming for those who could afford to eat out.

Exhausted from the ordeal, Lizzie and Johnny retired home with their families as the sun climbed higher in the sky. Once at home, they were questioned nose to nose by each father and they swore up and down nothing happened but engine failure. Lizzie's virtue was safe with Johnny. Mildred appeared several days later with a three-layer coconut cake for Edison, which he accepted graciously.

The sun may have been up but the Seth house was unusually quiet as each and every one took to their beds for a very long nap. Lost deep in a mountain pass with flickers of light guiding her to an ending, Kate dreamt of an adventure far away in a place she had never been. Noises echoed within the walls and the pass seemed so very long and dark. Kate kept focusing on the light and the moans and groans in the walls she blocked out until Johnny shook her awake.

"Kate, a squall is coming; we need to shut all the windows!"

As Kate jumped out of bed, she glanced out the front window. The sky had darkened, and it began to growl just like the noises in the mountain pass. She shut her two windows and ran from room to room with Johnny shutting all the windows as fast as they could.

Lowell's room was empty and each wondered silently if he was still out in the boat with Mr. Jimmy.

Chapter IX

— After the Squall —

Lowell did return in his wet slickers in the middle of the storm. His hair dripped on the kitchen floor as he stood in the doorway and proclaimed that all the boats were tied up safely at the docks. Some men were waiting it out hunkered down in their forward cabins, telling fish stories, drinking coffee, and smoking cigarettes, while others like Captain Jimmy and Lowell headed home in the mess, wanting desperately to be dry and fed.

The rain did not let up for hours, and the tin roof took a beating. It resounded like thunder throughout the house. Squalls usually passed quickly, but this one lingered until early afternoon when it let up and headed east to the next town, leaving a strong sun and gentle wind to dry out the foliage.

Kate ventured outside to walk the yard. Birdsong filled in the silence of the departing storm and danced in and out of Kate's ears as if she were listening to Beethoven. Toads came out from under frilly ferns for a breath of cool air. Kate breathed in the post-thunderstorm air, too, and it felt crisp. After a squall, air always felt cooler and lighter, as if the heaviness had been stripped away and all that was left was a freshness. She stood over the fish pond first, which nearly spilled over with rainwater. Herman was happily waiting for a late lunch under a lily pad.

With her back turned to the fence, she was startled with "Hello" from their neighbor. Miss Charlotte was out looking for her poor cats. They had been caught outside in the storm. Miss Charlotte, in her 70s, mostly kept to herself, but her concern for her cats made

her come out into the backyard. Kate turned around to meet her at the fence.

"Have you seen Everham and Maisy?" she inquired.

"I haven't, Miss Charlotte, but can I help you look?"

Miss Charlotte smiled, delighted with the offer.

"I'll bet they are hiding under your house; that's where all the animals go in the rain," said Kate loudly as she ran out her gate and skipped around to Miss Charlotte's yard.

"Everham! Maisy!" she called.

Kate bent down on her knees in the mud and peeked sideways under the house that was raised about 18 inches off the ground by brick pillars.

"Everham! Maisy!" Kate called. She saw two set of eyes flash in a quick moment and knew it was them.

"They're here!" she yelled happily to Miss Charlotte, who was walking the yard looking for them under old boxwoods and a large silky dogwood bush whose branches hung low with raindrops.

"They aren't coming out," Kate said, puzzled.

"They are probably scared out of their minds," said the neighbor. "I'll go and get them some food; that will surely work."

She went inside, leaving Kate to continue to coax them out.

"I know you are scared," said Kate to the cats, "but the storm is over."

Their eyes flashed repeatedly as if they were shaking their heads, "no." Kate giggled, thinking it rather funny, knowing cats don't shake their heads "no."

"Any luck, Kate?" the neighbor asked, returning quickly with a bowl of food.

"Not yet. I think they are still very scared."

"I think you are right. I will leave them some food in a dish right where you are and check on them later. They might just need some time."

"Okay," said Kate, standing up and wanting to brush off her knees, but seeing they were muddy and not dusty, she held off.

"Thank you so much for your help, and by the way, Happy Birthday!" Kate paused. In all the madness of Johnny missing, being up all night, and the storm, the intense distractions made her forget that a day had actually passed.

"Oh, thank you!"

"Kate!" Mary called.

Waving goodbye, Kate ran around the fence towards home. When she entered the kitchen doorway, Mary turned from the sink and let out a reserved sigh when she saw Kate's knees.

"I've invited some cousins for dinner to celebrate your birthday."

"Which ones?"

"Lowell's children Anna and Justin, and Lowell's wife Sally. Please go clean up, use a washcloth on those knees, and brush your hair."

Kate obliged and went into the bathroom. After cleaning her hands and knees, she looked in the mirror and noticed some dirt on her face. She splashed some water on it and wiped it off. Grabbing a brush, she started with the back of her head, and it became entangled right away.

"Mom!"

Mary came quickly. "Kate, this wouldn't happen if you brushed your hair at least every morning."

"I don't have the time," Kate replied, because in her mind she didn't. There were just too many other important things to do than to think about her hair. Mary dislodged the brush and wet it. Kate felt as if she had aged another whole year while Mary slowly and painfully worked out all the knots and tangles.

When she was finished, she said, "Now you're straight; no one will recognize you!"

Kate laughed because she knew this to be true. She never paid any attention to how she looked and rarely looked in a mirror. Mary hugged her.

"Happy Birthday, Kate."

Kate smiled. "I almost forgot it was my birthday."

"I know, that's O.K.," replied Mary. "Because I will never forget when you were born."

"Really?" Kate seemed surprised.

"Really," Mary countered. "I prayed and prayed for a girl, and God delivered."

Kate hugged her mother and bounced up the front steps to her room. Stopping halfway up, she looked down at the front hall and replayed the events of 3 a.m. A pang of worry briefly returned as she hashed out all that had happened in the last day. Relieved that Johnny was alright, she sighed and continued to the top step. She couldn't imagine life without her brother.

Jammy's door was shut and Johnny was in his room lounging in bed. Standing in the doorway she quietly got his attention and whispered, "I'm glad you're O.K."

Johnny turned towards her and smiled, " I am too."

"What happened?" Kate asked.

Johnny turned on his side, held his head up, and leaned on his elbow. "We decided the view of the sunset would be better over by Spring Cove than in Coon Creek, so we anchored there. When the sun went down, I tried to start the engine, and it wouldn't turn over."

"Lizzie's mom was mad at you! She thought the two of you had gone all the way." Kate said wide-eyed.

"Nah," Johnny said leisurely, we've only gone on a few dates."

Kate changed the subject, "We were all real worried, but I didn't show it. I knew deep down it would turn out O.K. But you know, sometimes doubt creeps in."

"I get that. I was worried, too. I knew I'd catch you know what for getting stuck out there." Johnny said wearily as he rolled over.

Kate skipped into her room, yawning.

Still worn from the night before, Kate succumbed to the power of suggestion and flopped onto her bed as well. Laying on her belly with her feet up in the air, she reached under her bed for a comic book and pulled out *Mighty Mouse*.

⚓ ⚓ ⚓

MEANWHILE, ALSO RENEWED BY THE thunderstorm abating, Mary felt compelled to check on Mr. Paul. She had a few moments before she had to start cooking dinner, so she left her apron and dish towel on the counter and took a quick jaunt to Mr. Paul's. When she arrived, the gate was loose and open as usual, and the house was shuttered and quiet as if no one lived there.

"Mr. Paul!" she called several times from the front yard as she walked towards the back yard through the tall, wet grass. She heard a shuffling of feet and the back screen door slam. "Paul?" Paul looked up as he held onto the porch rail to keep from falling. "I thought with the storm you might not venture to the Country Club today," said Mary to an obviously drunk man.

"I didn't," he replied, slurring, "I stayed right here all by myself with no one to talk to but this bottle." He held up his liquor like a trophy. Mary took a deep breath. Paul continued, "Heard your boy was missing?"

"Yes, he is safe and sound, praise the lord," Mary replied.

"Praise the lord! I'll drink to that!"

Paul gestured with the bottle and Mary reached out to catch him as he lost his balance and fell down the short flight. She embraced him mid-fall and tried to lean him back towards the steps to sit but he swerved sideways and landed in the grass. Edison, who had been watching this sad sketch from his garden, appeared alongside Mary.

"Let's get you up, Mr. Paul," Edison said as he lifted the heart-broken man and sat him on the steps.

"Come on, Mary, he's as drunk as a sailor; let's leave him to his stupor."

"Not without doing this first," Mary said as she poured out his liquor onto the grass.

Edison took her hand and led her out of the yard. As he did, she paused and turned back towards the lonely old man.

"I will pray for you, Mr. Paul."

She was stunned when he briefly sobered up and replied, "Please do, Miss Mary."

She lingered by the fence next to Edison, looking at the house and looking at the man, and wondered what God's plan was for him.

"He's pickling himself," she said under her breath to Edison, who lit a cigarette. He invited Mary into his garden, hoping its green would improve her outlook.

As she walked through Edison's arbor, her mood shift was instantaneous. In that moment of Mary's anxious uncertainty, the plants filled the void in her heart and stirred within her a swift transformation that only nature can instill. She smiled. With June's imminent departure and the impending arrival of July, the last of the lingering dandelions had faded away, and butterflies floated in.

Their wings, wet with rain, were heavy as the Clouded Sulfur butterflies skipped about sluggishly from blossom to blossom.

The tomatoes had begun to burden the vines that held them, which meant it was time for them to ripen. The fruits at the bottom of the cages always ripened first, and predictably, there was one with a slightly pink hue to it. Mary was pleased to know her Fourth of July might be graced with a taste of the season's first ripe tomato.

The squash blossoms that had closed in the darkness of the storm began to open and let the hungry honey bees inside. The baby yellow crooknecks were just the right size, and these tender yellows had the most flavor, so Mary picked a dozen and put them in Edison's wheelbarrow, along with two sweet onions she plucked from the ground.

Edison kept a long, thin pole handy for checking on the melons. With measured precision, he pushed back some of the foliage to see if there were any baby ones. There were many, and both Edison and Mary beamed at the sight of them. By the end of July, the garden would be overflowing with the sweetness of summer cantaloupe.

Late July was Edison's favorite time of year. A man of few words, he was a man of action. Friends, neighbors, and relatives could expect a ripe melon on their doorstep in late July, courtesy of Edison. It was his way of thanking the cherished people in his life. Predictable as the next tide, the ripening of Edison's melons was an event the whole neighborhood looked forward to each summer.

"Edison," Mary marveled, "your garden is really impressive this year."

He smiled at her as he picked up the handles of the wheelbarrow and headed back to the house via the shortcut through garbage alley. The burst of fresh rain had caused more of the black-eyed Susans to open, and that made them both smile as Edison set down his wheelbarrow to talk to Mr. Tawes.

"What'll it be today, Mr. Tawes?"

Mr. Tawes rose up from his lawn chair to assess the contents of the barrow. "I'd say 'bout fifty cents."

Edison countered, "Gettin' a little pricey, are we?"

Tawes thought long and hard while the couple stood patiently. "Yeah," he replied, "more like a quarter."

Edison reached into his pocket and gave him a quarter.

"How's the day been so far?" asked Mary.

"Very slow on account of the rain," he replied.

"Oh yes, of course," replied Mary. "Well, you have a good rest of your day and say 'hello' to Miss Virginia for us."

"Will do," said Mr. Tawes as he picked up his penknife and whittling stick.

By the time they arrived back home, Jammy had set the table and picked flowers from her garden, arranging them just so. She gingerly placed them in a vase of cut glass etched with tall ships. A creamy white hollyhock stalk cut to fit the vase centered the arrangement, and red poppies surrounded it. Lavender spikes made the eyes dance and were inserted throughout. Mary put on her apron to fry the chicken while Jammy peeled the squash.

"This is a nice addition to her birthday dinner," Jammy commented to Edison.

As preparations were underway, Lowell walked in with a baker's dozen ears of sweet corn grown just outside of town. Johnny went outside to shuck them as Anna and Justin arrived at the back gate—they eagerly joined in.

"I'll bet we find two worms," said Justin.

Anna wagered on three, and Johnny, wanting all the ears to be perfect for his sister's birthday, bet on there being none.

"It's too early for worms," Johnny said.

"No such thing," said Justin. "It's warm enough."

All but the last shucked ear were perfect, and Justin and Anna watched Johnny take a knife to the wormy end of it in the kitchen.

Lowell's wife Sally made herself useful by placing ice in glasses for the sun tea. When Lowell's loud feet hit the bottom back step, she turned to see his face tanned by the strong June sun, and their eyes locked. He smiled at her, and she flushed, thinking him looking very well put together at that moment.

"Let's go play fetch with River," he said to his children, and the group of three headed outside.

⚓ ⚓ ⚓

WHEN DINNER WAS READY, EVERYONE began to gather in the kitchen. Mary brought out a stack of her grandmother's finer china, reserved for birthdays and special occasions. She put the stack on the counter and announced there was simply too much food to put it all on the table. She called for everyone to dish up in the kitchen.

The kitchen chatter was broken when Johnny piped up above the hum, noticing Kate wasn't present for her own celebration. The family paused momentarily, followed by layers of laughter and chuckles and, in the case of Justin, an all out boisterous belly laugh.

Johnny ran upstairs and found Kate's head rooted to her pillow, resting in a pile of her own drool.

"Kate!" He shook her awake. Her eyes cracked open, and in that moment she was confused and thought it morning.

"Get up!" Johnny taunted. "You're sleeping through your birthday dinner. If you don't get up there'll be nothing left to eat!"

Groggily, she sat up, wiped the drool off her cheek with the back of her hand, and, while swaying a bit, gazed out her front window to the west. The sun, in its six o'clock stance, brightened her eyes, and the daylight and church bells brought her attention to full measure. Bouncing out of bed, she rushed with Johnny to the back steps, and when she poked her head out at the bottom of the flight, the kitchen crowd jeered affectionately.

"Glad you could make your own birthday," yelled Edison above the kerfuffle.

Plates were expediently filled with fried chicken, potato salad with eggs, English peas, yellow squash with sweet onions and butter, sweet corn, and Jammy's biscuits with fig preserves. Everyone's stomachs had finally settled after a raucous 24 hours, and following a very short grace, the dinner table became quiet, and the hunger was broken with only an occasional comment on how tasty the food was. First servings were followed by seconds, and when stomachs were satiated, the conversation picked up when Lowell announced he would be supplying a bushel of crabs for the family Fourth of July.

"A crab feast it is!" proclaimed Mary, who, in her enthusiasm, invited everyone at the table to return in just a few days. "By then," she surmised, "…we may have our first summer tomatoes. Edison's garden is very fine this year."

Kate felt warm. Not fever warm, but the kind of warm one feels when contented and happy. It was then that she noticed Jammy's flower arrangement.

"It's a moon and stars dinner!" she proclaimed loudly, and Jammy thanked her for noticing. She also noticed a small pile of presents stacked on a side table. Her heart skipped. Jammy and Sally started clearing plates while Mary grabbed the blueberry pie and some dessert plates. Mary nestled into her chair with the pie server and then paused.

"Kate, would you like to open your presents before or after dessert?"

Kate was torn. On the one hand, the pie looked especially good, and on the other, she was very curious about what was under the wrappings.

"Presents!" blurted out of her very suddenly as if she had no control over her choice. Anna and Justin were only too happy to bring her the presents.

"Open that one first," said Justin, putting his family's present in front of her.

Kate obliged and unwrapped a box of large colored chalks.

"For hopscotch out back!" Anna and Justin said in unison.

"Thank you," said Kate.

Next was a card from Lowell wishing her a happy birthday with $1 in it.

"Thank you, Cousin Lowell."

Sally was caught smiling at Lowell. Mary winked at Sally and kept it to herself. Johnny anxiously handed her his present, which was long and skinny. Kate knew what it was before she opened it because of its shape and Johnny's attraction to fire.

"Sparklers! Cool!" beamed Kate.

"We can use them on the Fourth of July," said Johnny.

A card from Tessie was next, wishing her a happy birthday with a $5 bill inside. Kate's eyes lit up. "Wow," she said, staring at it, her thoughts wandering to Truman's Store.

The biggest present was from Edison and Mary. When Kate went to open it, she noticed it was squishy and soft. Eagerly she opened it to discover an extra large beach towel with a picture of Snoopy and Charlie Brown making a sand castle. Kate hugged it.

"We figured it was time for you to have your own beach towel instead of one from the family pile of tattered ones," said Mary.

"I love it!" said Kate.

The last present was Jammy's. Kate also knew what this present was but held her thoughts as to not disappoint the crowd. The size gave it away, really.

"A new deck of cards with shiny sides!" Kate marveled at the blue sailboats on top and the silvery finish on the edges. These were elegant playing cards and much crisper than the soft, worn ones they usually played with.

"It is time you learned gin rummy," Jammy said.

Kate was so happy she almost forgot about pie until a piece was placed in front of her. Jammy started to sing "Happy Birthday," and everyone joined in. Kate dug into her pie as soon as the ritual was over.

"Oh, I forgot!" said Mary rather unexpectantly, and she ran to the pantry, returning with another present wrapped in brown paper with colorful splashes of paint on it. "This is from Tansy and Miss Lucille, and by the way, Tansy is coming back soon to visit again."

Kate was very happy to hear this and opened what was a very fine water coloring set. There were a lot of oohs and ahs, so she passed it around for everyone to see.

There were still a few hours of daylight left by the time they finished, and Kate, Johnny, and the cousins ran out back to make a hopscotch sketch with the new colorful chalks. Kimmy happened by, and they all entertained themselves with the game until dusk when Sally came out the back gate to say goodbye. Kate thanked them for coming as the three headed back up the street to their house. Kate yelled goodbye to Kimmy, who was swatting at mosquitos on her legs as she ran for home.

Putting her new chalks inside Edison's shed, she then stopped to talk to Herman and tell him what she had gotten for her birthday, but he wasn't around. Slightly concerned, she stood up and looked around in the grass and then shook her head. Well, she said to herself, he's gone missing before and then showed back up. She shrugged her shoulders and went into the house.

The kitchen was quiet and clean, and all that was left on the table was a small pile of Kate's presents. She carefully laid her sparklers, watercolors, deck of cards, and money on top of her new beach towel and wandered to the front of the house, where she heard quite a ruckus. Everyone was laughing on the porch, and it piqued her interest. She laid her gifts down at the bottom of the front steps and poked her head through the front parlor window to see what all the fuss was about.

"There's the birthday girl!" Mr. Brown said boisterously.

Kate waved, smiled, and sat in the last remaining chair.

"Mr. Brown was just telling us stories about growing up on his farm," said Mary.

"I'll bet that was so fun," said Kate.

"It was also a lot of hard work," he countered. With a sly smile, he then told the story of the time the cows got loose, and they had to chase them out of a neighbor's creek.

"I slept good that night!" Everyone laughed, especially at the part where he slipped in the creek, got wet from head to toe, and ripped his pants up the back seam.

"Good thing I had on underwear," he chuckled. "But, you know, we didn't realize how much fun we had until now, that is, my siblings that are left."

Kate, enthralled by the story, turned inwards when she sensed a sadness in his words. Mary asked when he would be fishing again, and the conversation carried on if only in the background of her awareness. She had always sensed Mr. Brown had a working childhood, and she wanted to know more.

"Mr. Brown," she asked when a gap appeared in the conversation. "What was in your garden growing up?" Mr. Brown beamed at the question and, looking upwards as if to access the recesses of his mind, he began:

"We grew all our own vegetables and canned them, like cabbage, potatoes, sweet potatoes, green peppers, onions, beets, beans, tomatoes, spinach, corn, and carrots."

He meticulously counted each crop on his fingers, wanting to leave nothing out. "We also foraged for wild winter cress, asparagus, and blackberries. Trees and shrubs from the woods on our property gave us gooseberries, mulberries, cherries, peaches, apples, and pears, and Mother spent her days cooking and canning for winter. Of course, pickled watermelon rind was my favorite, and I also loved fresh beets, and every kind of preserve you could imagine."

Everyone was silent, intent on the next words out of his mouth. He continued, "We really didn't buy much food from a store," he reminisced. "There were nine of us, but we ate well. We milked our own cows and raised a few hogs, chickens, geese and guinea hens, and some turkeys for Christmas time," he paused. "Although I never cared much for killing the chickens, but often enough, that was dinner. We hunted for pigeons, rabbits, squirrels, and muskrats. You know, deer were rare in these parts at that time, not plentiful at all like they are now. Of course, the river gave us oysters, crabs, and plenty of fish. We only went to a store to buy flour, cornmeal, molasses, and an occasional soda pop."

Overwhelmed with putting a visual to all this information, Kate began to paint a picture in her mind of Mr. Brown's farm days.

"Did you have electricity?" she wondered.

"No, Miss Kate, we didn't."

"Wow…." she replied, aghast.

With that question Mr. Brown decided it was time to stop holding court and announced, "That is a story for another time."

Johnny, who had been silent the whole time, stood up when Mr. Brown did and extended his hand to Mr. Brown.

"Can I shake your hand?"

Perplexed, Mr. Brown said, "Sure, but why?"

"I don't know," said Johnny. "It just feels like the right thing to do."

Mary was noticeably tickled with Johnny's gesture of respect. Mr. Brown exited the screen door, stopping just short of the front gate, and turned towards the porch.

"Forgive me, Miss Katherine, I did not thank you properly for the delicious biscuits you made me."

"You are very welcome," replied Jammy, smiling.

"Although, Miss Mary, I should think they would be better next time around if I had some fresh fig preserves to put on top," he said.

Mary countered, "You shall have a jar from my first batch this year."

He smiled and said, "I would be so pleased." He slipped out the gate and turned to his right towards home, a few streets over.

"I love his stories," said Kate.

"Yes," said Edison. "We can all learn much from Mr. Brown."

After Mr. Brown left, the conversation became intermittent and as the moonlight grew stronger, eyelids became heavier and one by one the Seth family left the porch and headed to bed until only Edison and Mary remained. They switched seats so they could sit side by side on the glider. Holding hands they sat for another hour in intermittent quiet conversation while the slider glided back and forth, back and forth.

Chapter X

— Holiday —

The wide beams that made the joists of the sturdy lumber shed were said to have come from an old sailing ship that had made its way to the shores of the oyster town over two centuries ago. The old English oak was strong and could support the weight of all the wood the boatyard stored. Raised about a foot off the ground and set on brick pillars, the men often joked the brick would crumble before the oak ever did. The brackish river air circulated underneath and kept it dry. On occasion, feral cats would find refuge under the old building but at present none had been seen since Sam kept watch. Then, one night in early July, a fox lay in hunt under the timber shed.

Kate's neighborhood was too far away to be in earshot of anything less than a boat falling off its stilts, but not quite close enough to hear the ear-shattering shrieking of a wild fox. The first time Kate had heard a fox in the night, she ran to her parent's room, certain that a small child was being murdered in the street. Edison and Mary jumped out of bed to listen but then, taking it all in and retrieving their own memories, soon defined the blood-curdling noise. Even so, it took Kate a while to return to her room, temporarily scarred from its vicious sound. She had only heard one other fox since and still didn't care for it one bit and pulled the covers over her ears.

A few foxes lived in town here and there, and most people thought that was a good thing; after all, foxes kept the rodents and rabbits in check. Without this natural order of things, the mice, rats, and bunnies quickly became problematic. There were always a few who didn't care to have a fox den nearby and would shoot them or fill the burrows with water and kill the kits. The townspeople who were quick to kill foxes were not taken too kindly in their manner of dealing with wildlife. Most felt, when left alone, every animal kept every other animal in check. Nature had a way of sorting things out.

However, there were instances when foxes got into hen houses, and ohhh the ruckus! A neighborhood could be disheveled for days by an angry chicken coop tender looking for the culprit that ate the next week's breakfast. In these cases, most neighbors turned their backs when the culprit was found and dealt with. An eye for an eye.

When Kate arrived at the boatyard entrance the next morning, she felt hesitant to enter. Miss Edna, who lived next to the entrance and kept mostly to herself, was in her rocker gazing out at the river.

She saw Kate lingering and said, "I suppose you heard it did you?"

"No, what are you talking about, Miss Edna?"

"That damn fox woke me up at 5 a.m. with all the carrying on."

"Fox?" Kate questioned.

"Yes, its hollering woke up the whole neighborhood. Thank goodness Miss Pat came out right away with her shot gun."

"Shotgun?" Kate questioned again.

Miss Edna, known for her sour replies, put up her hand and waved Kate off.

"Oh pshaw, Kate, you need to start drinking coffee; you are exhausting me. Go talk to Pat; she'll tell you the whole story."

Kate felt a delayed kind of panic that bubbles up slowly from your stomach until all of a sudden you want to vomit. She ran inside the entrance and turned right towards Pat's yard, but stopped cold when she saw Squawk in her pen with a few missing feathers. Miss Pat was on the back porch, and Sam lay next to her on the porch swing. His head was in her lap; the oiled porch floor strewn with bloodied bandages. Kate tried to take it all in. She wanted to burst into tears at that moment but instead let out a startled gasp when she saw a dead fox at the bottom of Miss Pat's steps. Kate's eyes welled up, and her throat tightened. She felt as if she had to struggle for air. She sat down right there in the grass and just pointed from disaster to disaster, wordless.

It felt like an eternity before Pat spoke.

"Sam saved Squawk, I saved Sam, I hope..." Her confidence was weak.

"Oh, Miss Pat," Kate struggled to talk; she felt sobs building up inside her.

"Kate, I am not a veterinarian, I've done all I can with what I know."

Kate gasped and put her hand over her mouth as if to suppress a scream as devilish as the fox's. At that moment, Mr. Russell pulled up alongside the yard in his pickup truck and got out.

"Bring him Pat, we'll take him to the Doc," he said as he threw the dead fox in the bed of the truck. "This damn fox will have to be tested for rabies."

Pat looked shocked, "...but the money..."

"Sam is family; bring him here—we need to get him help."

Pat smiled. Her natural buoyancy flickered in her eyes as she gingerly tried to lift him and keep him comfortable. Kate jumped to help and support Sam. She lifted his bloodied back legs while Pat glided him into the cab, resting his head on Mr. Russell's lap. Mr. Russell looked away when Sam whimpered; it seemed his oak edges had been sanded.

Kate reached into her pocket and handed Miss Pat her birthday money, all six dollars of it. Pat couldn't speak. She kissed Kate on the forehead, put the money in the glove box, and they headed out of town as quickly as they could, leaving Kate at the boatyard entrance bewildered and bleary-eyed.

She turned towards Miss Edna's house, but she had gone inside. Good thing, she thought, she'd probably say something to make me even more sad. She kicked the gravel repeatedly and then turned and headed back into the boatyard. Stepping over the top of Squawk's cage, she perched herself inside the enclosure with the growing duckling.

"So what happened, Squawk?" Squawk, who was always gibberish with duckspeak, was strangely quiet. Instead, the tattered and worn little duck crawled into Kate's lap and nestled in.

"It's O.K., Squawk, you're safe now."

Kate leaned back against the tree and sighed. Exhausted by grief, Kate looked up into the cloudless sky wondering why bad things happen and even with a thousand questions running through her brain, her body became heavy and Kate and Squawk together in their weariness, took a morning doze.

When she awoke, the sun was high above her, and her stomach grumbled. She wiggled her legs to try to stretch them out, and in doing so, Squawk perked up and started talking to Kate. While in her lap, Kate was able to look over the traumatized duck, realizing in her assessment that many of the feathers that were missing she was going to lose with her first molt anyway; her wings were in good shape, which gave Kate great relief. The comfort was soon replaced by dread when she thought of poor Sam. She looked up towards the heavens.

"Jesus, please look out for Sam. He's a good dog, and Miss Pat will be lost without him. Please don't take him yet."

Squawk was strangely silent for the prayer and looked at Kate inquisitively. Kate took a deep breath and gathering strength from nap and prayer, decided to take Squawk down to the river. Once out of her pen and in the grass, she wiggled her tail in happiness. Squawk was very talkative, and let Kate know all about her morning drama. Until now, Kate had always carried her to the river, but today Kate decided she was big enough to walk and encouraged her to follow.

Proudly, Squawk waddled behind Kate's footsteps, eating an occasional bug along the way if they happened upon the path. Once the river was in sight, Squawk ran right to it. Kate was thrilled with her newfound enthusiasm for the green waters as she dabbled along the sandy edge drinking river water. Together the pair talked about all kinds of things. Kate pointed out the oyster shells to Squawk amongst the river pebbles.

"Now these," she preached, "will cut your feet pretty good, be careful of the sharp edges."

Squawk replied with a run at the water. A motorboat wave came in and tossed her about, but she didn't retreat. Kate smiled at Squawk's bravado. The child and the duck played together as quiet winds cooled them from the steady warmth of an unfettered sun in a cloudless sky. Time was irrelevant.

Hearing a truck behind her, Kate turned to see Pat and Mr. Russell pull into the boatyard. "Come on, Squawk, let's go see Sam."

The pair walked across the road and into Pat's yard. By now, Pat was already sitting on the porch, expecting Kate's visit. As Kate approached, she became acutely aware that Pat was alone on the porch swing, and her steps slowed down dramatically as she digested the scene. Pat motioned for her to sit next to her, and she obliged with a lump in her throat that grew larger with each passing second.

Pat began, "Doc Steve is keeping him for a a few days while he heals. The fox got his back legs good."

Kate looked upon her wearied face. Her eyes were sunken and almost black with grief; this she could not only see but feel. She could feel Pat's heartache travel through her veins. Kate turned her head away and sat silently next to her, feeling she would almost burst with pain. Pat grabbed her hand in comfort and let out a troubled sigh. Their combined grief was interrupted by Squawk looking up at them from the yard and bellowing out the loudest noise she had ever made.

One by one, the men from the boatyard came by to let Pat know they were sorry to hear about Sam's run-in with the fox. Saul was the first.

"Miss Pat," he said, removing his hat and bowing his head, "I heard what went on here last night, and I want you to know I'll be praying for Sam."

Pat flushed with pride for the respect Saul had. "Praying is all we can do, Saul, thank you."

Next came one-eyed Charlie. He, too, removed his work hat. "Miss Pat, Sam's a strong dog; I just know he'll pull through."

Pat welled up and covered her mouth as if to suppress a wail. All she could do was shake her head yes. One by one, they came, and their words comforted Pat, and by the time the last man left, she felt like she could breathe again. Kate's hand was sweaty from holding Pat's, and she gingerly broke the connection. Miss Pat hugged her and thanked her for sitting with her on the porch.

Kate wasn't sure what to do next. She wanted to stay with Pat, but she also wanted to escape the heavy weight that hung over the boatyard and pressed down upon her. Miss Pat got up off the bench, offering for them to go inside for a cold drink. Kate was quite thirsty and guzzled her first glass of cold water. Pat poured her another and the two glasses refreshed them both.

"I'm just too sick to eat," said Pat. "Would you like something?"

Kate shook her head no as she, too, was a bit queasy.

Looking for an excuse to leave all this emotion behind, she said, "I think I should go home and check in with Mother."

"Of course," said Pat.

Kate exited and swooped up Squawk from the yard, placing her in the pen.

"I'll be back tomorrow, Squawk."

She began to feel uplifted the further she walked from the scene of the crime. She thought about the men and how she had never seen a grown man cry, as Edison never did. She thought that men didn't cry, only boys, so she was in awe when most of the yard men seemed to choke back tears when they spoke to Pat. The bike ride home refreshed her somewhat and also reminded her that it was a holiday as she witnessed neighbors and friends bustling about their yards and hanging red, white, and blue decorations.

Even Mr. Paul was hanging a small flag on his fence post. Slowing her bike to a stop, she welcomed a visit with him, as distraction was a kind of medicine that suppressed all the pain she had just experienced.

"Hiya Kate," he said quite happily.

"I see you're getting ready for the holiday."

"Oh yes, the Fourth was my Anna's favorite. I'm hanging the flag for her."

Kate smiled. "That's awful sweet of you; are you going to watch the fireworks tonight?" "Oh yes, Miss Kate, I never miss that."

"We always go to my cousin's house," Kate offered to extend the conversation.

"Yes, the ones that live down past Mr. Russell's boatyard?" Kate smiled and nodded.

She looked beyond him, saw his garden looking troubled and he commented as such,"I'm trying to keep it going, but I'm fighting those weeds about every day."

Kate sympathized. "It's like weeds are always there, no matter what."

"Yes," he replied, "I am always at war with the weeds."

They both laughed as Kate mounted her bike.

"Well, you have a good holiday, Mr. Paul."

"Thank you," he said warmly as Kate headed home.

$$\text{⚓ ⚓ ⚓}$$

As the townspeople said goodbye to June and flipped their paper calendars to July, the air became electrified. The town, where forbearance was practiced 364 days a year, pragmatically prepared for the day that self-control became less evident. The mere word "July" was enough to set anyone into a patriotic frenzy.

Some who never drank sipped the suds once a year. Maryland

flags that hung proudly off of screened porches were replaced with the Stars and Stripes. Some were the current flag with all 50 stars and 13 stripes; others were colonial style with the thirteen colonies in a circle of stars, or embellished with the number 76.

The Gadsden Flag, a yellow rattlesnake with the words "Don't Tread on Me," was also on display. Its inception by a brigadier general in the Continental Army had been sparked by Benjamin Franklin himself in his independent mindset leading up to the Revolutionary War. This flag was flown by a few history enthusiasts whose galvanized independent hearts bled red, white, blue, and yellow. The Pine Tree flag also floated off of porches in the gentle July breeze with the slogan "An Appeal To Heaven," another colonial flag design before the red, white, and blue was even conceived. The bicycle shop had begun selling historical flags over the last few years, and as a multitude of colorful fabrics lined the front yards, it felt inherently celebratory.

Lawnmowers let out a low hum that permeated the soundscape of the town. Walking down the main thoroughfare, ladies and children could be found weeding flower beds, sweeping the brick sidewalks, and painting fences bright white in anticipation of celebrating the privilege of independence. Many of the town men had served in World War I, World War 2, the Korean War, and/or Vietnam, and lives had been lost in those battles, of which Walton, Mary's father, was one.

Those who were not called up to serve became part of the effort, working long days in the fields just outside of town or at the boatyards. In the case of Mr. Russell's boatyard, for WW2, they helped construct small infantry craft for the Navy. As such, the townspeople understood sacrifice at the deepest level, whether it be for their country or to put food on the table for family. Hard labor never deterred them from their duties as providers for their families or as patriotic citizens.

Such was the case with the newly constructed Customs House

that had been centered atop the only hill in town, looking down at the wharf. The village ladies had baked tirelessly for many years to raise funds for its construction, and with a goal of having it completed by the bicentennial, it was. Today and tomorrow, it would be open to the public and the dedicated docents in their hand-sewn Colonial garb would be telling stories of the past interwoven with antiquities on display inside. A few teenage girls dressed in colonial attire walked the streets selling sparklers, poppers, and postcards.

With all the preparations to distract her, and the mood in town quite uplifting, Kate's despair dissipated as she pedaled for home. When she arrived, she was immediately handed a broom to sweep the front porch and sidewalk. But Mary saw something in Kate's eyes that gave her hesitation—and she took the broom back. Even though her mood had been uplifted by the wind in her face as she left the boatyard behind, the morning's anguish was reflected in her eyes, and Mary saw and felt it.

"What's happened?"

Kate walked into the back porch and flopped on one of the wicker chairs cupping her hands over her face as the events, so fresh and raw, instantly came rushing back. Laying out the details of the morning she choked on her own words. Jammy appeared in the doorway just as the events were laid bare and soaked the story in. When Kate had finished, without a whisper, her mother and grandmother wrapped their arms around her, and the lump in her throat vanished when they both kissed her on the forehead.

"Let us know what happens with Sam," Mary said. "We will pray for him and Pat and Mr. Russell."

These words and gestures had such a calming effect upon Kate that a wobbly smile appeared on her face and she felt somewhat renewed. The confidence her mother and grandmother had in their faith settled her instantly.

"I will," she answered, reaching for the broom, still in her mother's hand, and headed out front to sweep.

Mary and Jammy had been busy preparing for the crab feast. Everyone had been looking forward to it. Edison was especially anticipating the gathering and was known to sit for hours, just picking. One time, Kate counted 16 crabs he picked and ate in one sitting. Earlier, the ladies had taken a short ride just out of town in the Blue Goose to pick up a dozen ears of sweet corn. When Johnny came in from cutting the grass, the corn was thrust upon him, and he turned right around and headed out back to shuck it. Mary finished up the potato salad while Jammy made a double batch of biscuits. Edison picked two very large red tomatoes in the morning, the first of the season, and when Kate returned with the broom, she was told to slice the tomatoes nicely and put them on a plate. The crab cooker was brought in from the shed, and Mary added the vinegar to the water in the steamer pan. The black enameled coated pot with white speckles was set on the stove to boil, with the J.O. Spice ready to thickly coat the blue crabs before they turned red with steam.

Once finished with the tomatoes, Kate was sent with vase in hand to Jammy's garden to make an arrangement for dinner. There were a few bachelor buttons in bloom and cheery Gladiolus of all colors. The white Shasta daisies grew with tall pride in front of one of Edison's wood piles, which caused a fuss with Edison, but Mary would not let him cut them back until after they had bloomed. Picking a large, deep red Gladioli for the center, she surrounded it with white daisies and sprinkled the blue bachelor buttons about until the vase was quite full. She remembered her moon and stars dinner less than a week ago and how stunning the flowers were, so Kate mimicked Jammy's template but used different flower types and colors. The red, white, and blue were noticed right away by Johnny, who complimented her on it.

It seemed all was in order, except Lowell had not arrived with the fresh crabs yet, which put the Seth family in a stall pattern. Everyone walked around waiting for his arrival: Jammy fidgeted and fussed with the table settings. Mary had time to clean all the dishes, add parsley to the potato salad, and a little more sugar and vinegar to the coleslaw.

With the six o'clock church bells imminent, Mary began to pace, which was brought to attention by Kate.

"Why do you doubt Cousin Lowell?" Kate wondered out loud.

Mary took a seat on the porch. "Kate, alcohol gets ahold of people and sometimes that's all they can think about, and until they decide to stop drinking, there is nothing anyone can do for them."

"Is that why you are frustrated with Mr. Paul?" Kate asked.

"Yes, Kate, absolutely yes."

With that statement, Kate stood up from her chair and saw Lowell through the screen door at the back gate, trying to open it with a full bushel in his hands. Johnny, who was out back playing with River ran over to help. The fever of anticipation broke.

Mary yelled for the whole house to hear, "Lowell is here with the crabs!"

With the steamer hot and ready, Lowell held the bushel basket up high above the opening as Mary used very wide steel tongs to direct them squarely into the pot. Kate stood at the edge of the counter watching the crabs fall in twos and threes at a time, until it was three quarters full. Lowell then laid the rest of the bushel on the floor with the wooden lid placed on top, held down with wire.

The rustling of the crabs in the pot was the sound of pure fury. They danced about slapping the side of the pot, trying to escape their fate. Kate hadn't paid too much attention to this noise before, but now she concentrated on it. It hit her like a revelation: the crabs were being steamed alive and soon they would be dead and they would be eaten. This was the first time Kate had ever felt sorry for the blue crab. Until now, it was a creature all children feared, and those who had been pinched remembered well the strength and pain of a Chesapeake Bay blue crab claw—small but mighty.

With the stove knob turned on high, the water below the catch bubbled and spewed steam from its sides and filled the kitchen with a combination of smells that permeated every corner and leaked their way into the adjoining rooms. The vinegar, spice, and fresh crab combination drifted with the west wind that blew straight through the open house out into the backyard and made Edison appear in the door of his shed looking towards the kitchen. He lit a cigarette as he leaned his right shoulder against the peeling paint of the door frame. Sucking the tobacco in deeply, he exhaled with a smile.

Sally appeared at the back fence with Anna and Justin fighting over who could open the gate latch. Anna won and was the first to run up the brick walk to find Kate. Edison laughed as Justin walked behind slowly in defeat.

Stealing a moment with only Edison, Sally asked him straight on, "How's Lowell doing, really?"

Edison took another long drag on his beloved vice, and as the smoke mingled with his words, he said, "Sally, I can't say he's reformed and all cause the bottle holds tremendous power, but he's trying hard."

Sally smiled. That was all she needed to hear to continue to have hope. Buoyed by Edison's answer, her heart beat faster, and her legs felt lighter.

Lowell had gone up to shower, and Anna, Justin, Johnny, and Kate had gone out front to look for River, so the adult women had the kitchen to themselves. Mary turned away from the sink when Sally appeared on the threshold between the porch and kitchen.

"Smells good," Sally commented.

"Yes, I must say, Sally," Mary gestured, "that this is a fine, fat bushel of number ones Lowell has caught. He would've fetched quite a price at the docks for these."

Jammy cut to the chase. "Has he been helping with the bills?"

Sally nodded yes, and just as she was about to speak, Lowell's feet hit the top step, and the women changed course.

"So I hear it's going to be a clear night for the fireworks?" Sally said as Lowell made his way down.

"I did hear that," replied Mary.

Lowell piped in when his foot hit the bottom step. "Should be a good night." He went straight to Sally and grabbed both her hands. Jammy and Mary turned in unison to watch.

"Will you come to the fireworks with us?" he asked.

"Yes, I'd like that," she said, with a quivering in her voice that Lowell picked up on.

"I promise no drinking tonight." His assurance brought comfort.

Jammy lifted the lid on the crab pot and peeked inside.

"Red as a chimney brick," she said.

Lowell grabbed the top of the boiling hot pan with two pot holders and carried it out to the table that had been thickly lined with old newspapers and jockeyed the pot to lay them out in a line on the center of the table. The steam made his head turn away. He brought the empty pot back to the stove, laid it on top of the steam pan, and with a flick of his wrist, ripped the thin wooden top off of the remaining bushel and walked over to the stove to pour them in. Sally stood opposite of him, watching. His focus shifted to her, and as it did, the last two crabs missed the pot and fell onto the kitchen floor, mad as hell, pinchers drawn for battle.

"Crabs loose!" Sally yelled, and as if that was some kind of summoning spell, all the children ran into the kitchen, anxious for the hunt.

The adults stepped into the doorways, blocking any escape from the kitchen. Johnny quickly jammed a sneaker on his right foot. Justin found the first crab tucked into the corner next to the chest freezer. Johnny went in with his shooed foot, laces flinging about, placed it on top of the crab without crushing it, reached behind the back fin and grabbed it firmly with his right hand, released it from his foot, and raised it up in the air as a prize. Jammy lifted the lid off the steamer, and in it went.

The adults clapped for Johnny and Justin: Anna and Kate sought the same praise. They, too, had cornered one in the pantry under a shelf. Both in bare feet, Kate grabbed a heavy rag and folded it to

place on the crab. It was thick and wide enough to cover its face and claws. She reached behind and grabbed its back fin with confidence and emerged from the pantry, raising her prize high in a sign of victory. The clapping, so satisfying, made her wish there was another escapee.

With the second and final round of crabs in the steamer, the shucked corn went into another boiling pot. The heat of the kitchen drove many out to the porch onto the wicker chairs, and conversation about tomorrow's parade filled the time. As tradition was, the fireworks were held on the third of July and on the fourth, the town had its yearly parade. Floats from civic groups and a few classic cars were a close second to the real show, which was the volunteer fire department equipment. Everyone in town had raised money for it, the ladies' auxiliary being the ring leaders. The fire department was a source of town pride, and as sure as drought in August, the new ladder engine would be washed, shined, and waxed for its debut in the parade tomorrow.

Edison entered the porch and, bypassing everyone, headed straight for the pile of steamed crabs already laid out.

"I'm getting a head start," he said as he sat down at the newspaper-strewn table, pulled out his pocket knife, and began to pick.

"He's got the right idea," said Lowell. "Only about two hours before we go to Cousin Ephraim's house, we better get started."

With the two men seated, Mary interjected a holiday prayer. Once heads bowed and hands held, she began: "Lord, thank you for our freedoms, our families, and food from the fertile ground that fills our plates. We remember on days like today that we are blessed, and we give thanks for your hand in all that is possible. Amen."

"Amen!"

Kate liked crabs but didn't have much patience for picking; as such, she grabbed all the odd claws and cracked them. Some grabbed a basket plate and dished up potato salad, corn on the cob, garden tomatoes, and biscuits, opting to eat the side dishes before they picked. Justin sat next to his father watching him pick and trying to do the same. Lowell made sure he knew to cut out the devils' fingers and not eat them. Everyone knew the lungs would make you sick. Miss Lucille, Tansy's grandmother, had accidentally eaten one a few years ago and was laid up in bed for a week.

Dinner was jovial, with everyone in good spirits and the talking and picking went on for hours until Mary reminded them all that Cousin Ephraim would be looking forward to their company. Clean up was a group effort and then, they walked out the back gate towards Cousin Ephraim's house, minus Jammy. She always stayed home on fireworks night to sit with River, who was scared of the loud noises.

Kate had sparklers in hand, and Johnny, unbeknownst to everyone, had firecrackers in his pocket. Cousin Ephraim lived by the water's edge on what used to be an island but had been connected to the mainland by tons and tons of shucked oyster shells. Past the boatyard of Mr. Russell, the island, only eight acres in size, had in a past life supported a prolific orchard and seafood packing house.

One of many packing houses in town, the business employed many women pickers, mostly the women whose men were out catching crabs or dredging oysters. The land was now repurposed as a marina with slips for rent. A few apricot trees remained, compromised by time and neglect. The fruits they bore were small and diseased. The trees' arms, weakened by illness, stretched out wearily as if they were asking for help. So few fruits were viable for jam that they lay in rot underneath their canopy, feasted on by small animals, and swarmed by scavenger wasps.

Opposite the small grove is where Ephraim's house faced the water and had most likely the best view of the harbor in the whole town. Standing on the dock facing west, one could see the ferry route, the yacht club, all the houses facing the cove, the long sandy beach where Kate took Squawk, and the stone ramparts under the river walk that protected the shoreline. Many sailors anchored during the holiday in the cove, filling it with boats of all rigs and sizes. The beach where Kate took Squawk was now filled with spectators shoulder to shoulder, waiting to see the fireworks display. Children played in the river, and some brought canoes to paddle around in.

Cousin Ephraim was an accomplished man. He had served in the Navy and since retired as a Captain. His wife, cousin Penelope, was one of the nicest people Kate had ever met. She had a fondness for Kate, and as such, Kate knew that she could find a cold root beer just for her hidden in the back of Penelope's refrigerator whenever she and her mother would visit. On this occasion, a metal tub of all kinds of sodas, including root beer, had been set out in the yard on ice for all the cousins. Kate never got soda at home, so she planned on drinking two.

Dusk descended upon the river quickly, and when Cousin Penelope pulled out the ice cream sandwiches, the evening reached a new volume of excitement. Kate's young cousins swirled around the yard, playing frisbee with one hand and eating drippy ice cream sandwiches with the other. The youngest ran wild with bubble wands, creating a swarm of bubbles as thick as fog.

As the darkness bore down, Kate went looking for Edison to help light her sparklers. Mid conversation, he saw Kate coming and handed her his lighter. She paused before she took it.

"You're old enough to light your own sparklers," he said, then continued his discussion.

Kate took the lighter and headed out to the dock to light them. As she rounded the corner of the house, a large "bang! bang! bang!" went off and scared everyone frozen until they realized Johnny had set off firecrackers. The pause that followed was long and made Johnny's mouth dry as sand. The trance was broken with laughter from Edison. Once everyone heard him laugh, they also laughed, and Johnny, who was not expecting there to be such a strenuous pause, could breathe again.

Young cousins followed Kate to the docks and she handed out sparklers. As dusk fell across the river, it glistened angelically under a cloudless moonlit sky, glimmers reflecting off the surface of the placid water. The sparklers reflected, too, like little shooting comets as they were waved in tandem like swords.

A warning shot was fired off the barge anchored off the yacht club. The fireworks were imminent, and everyone found a lawn chair and settled in. Bang! The first of many fireworks in the evening panoramic burst upwards. As each firework burned out, a rounded black cloud blew eastward, filling the eastern sky with a series of dots. Horns blazed and spectators shouted. Noise and revelry bubbled up and spilled over, and Kate could feel the happiness and pride of all those souls that filled the shoreline elbow to elbow. The ruckus grew as fireworks flared and drinks were raised, toasting to freedom and love of country.

Entranced as she was at the beginning of the sky show, while others shouted for more, Kate's senses unraveled like a thick ribbon inside of her. She feverishly looked for a quiet space but found

none. Vibrations flooded and gnawed at her core making her heart thump and her head wobble so that she felt she must flee for a cure.

Overwhelmed by the warmth of joy flowing across the land and sea, it ensnared her as a thick fog smothering her in a strange kind of panic. She turned her eyes to the sparkling river water below her dangling feet for some relief, but the dock no longer felt comfortable. In fact, it felt unbearable. She had become unmoored. The noise hurt her ears, and lights stung her eyes. Halfway through the show, senses overloaded, she left the dock behind and walked out to the front steps of Ephraim's house and sat down, staring at the broken orchard across the road.

With the commotion at her back, she felt a confusing relief. Her flight from such a happy occasion did not go unnoticed and a few minutes after Kate felt like she could breathe again, Mary appeared and sat beside her without a sound. The comforting silence amid the backdrop was settling. Mary's delayed first words brought an elevated connection between mother and daughter.

"It's too much, isn't it?" Mary asked.

After a long pause all Kate felt she needed to say was, simply, "Yes."

"Me too," replied Mary.

The broken orchard in the muted evening took on a new life, one of dark, ominous features. The arms of the trees cried out like decrepit old men. If wisdom was to be lost in old age, it would be here amongst these diseased trees, whose offspring rotted beneath feeble branches, screaming desertion in their own silent decay. But Kate, knowing the orchard in the day, was not afraid and instead mused at the strange features highlighted by the flashes in the night sky.

Breaking the short silence between them, Kate pointed and said to Mary, "See the old peg-leg pirate in the tree on the left?"

"Oh yes!" Mary smiled, joining the game and pointing to her own fictional figure. "See the hunched-over old woman with a cane in the middle tree?"

After some squinted study, Kate agreed with a giggle.

The noise heightened, indicating that the fireworks finale was on. Mary stood up and offered her hand to Kate. Hand in hand they rounded the corner of the house to see the final folly. Kate took a deep breath and realized her panic was gone.

Joining the others unnoticed, the two generations clapped together an applause for the show. Relatives said their goodbyes and gave thank-you hugs to cousins Ephraim and Penelope and began the walk home through bustling streets filled with hollers, firecrackers, and drunken mischief.

Kate surmised when she was a whole year younger, that perhaps she hadn't noticed the drunken patriots as she did now that she was eleven. Inhibitions cast aside, the merriment continued well past the last firecracker with spontaneous singing as joyful as the church choir but not nearly as in tune. Kate smiled at the goofiness of all this unwound revelry until she saw someone in the crowd throwing up in a ditch.

Mary grabbed Kate's hand and bent down and whispered, "Too much liquor."

Grossed out by the scene of gluttony, Kate's smile faded to a more serious focus of just getting home. Her comfy bed and screened windows were waiting. The mosquitos were in buffet mode with all the new blood in town.

Jammy was glad to see the family return home, and so was River. "How was he?" Kate asked.

"He stayed by my side with his tail between his legs, so I just kept petting him and let him know it would all be alright."

River had recovered quickly from his fear as the firecrackers subsided and his tail couldn't have wagged harder when everyone returned. Justin and Anna had come back to the Seth house for an impromptu sleep-over sparked by Mary on the way home. Kate's floor was just big enough for the two worn but soft sleeping bags Mary dug out of the hall closet. None of the three youngest had any energy left for sleepover antics and so as the last cars drove out of town, all three were drifting away to far-off lands with sparkling shorelines, colorful birds, and cloudless skies.

Kate would have drifted right off if not for being startled by the shrill voice of Miss Pearl's daughter, Molly, on a wild midnight bike ride, her hands reaching towards heavenly stars and her lips curved upwards screaming, "wheeeee!!!" Unabashedly unchained, she flew the length of Main and back as free as the bats Kate saw dancing in the moonlight, flittering to and fro like drunken butterflies. Kate smiled and rolled over. Freedom felt good.

⚓ ⚓ ⚓

THE NEXT DAY, KATE AWOKE to yelling, the front street aflame with action. Mr. Jefferson, the locally famous basset hound, unofficial town mascot, and prodigy of the waterfront innkeepers, had escaped and was walking with a brisk proudness down Main Street. Named after one of the crafters of the Declaration of Independence it was only fitting that his namesake be strutting along the main thoroughfare on July 4th with his head held high.

"Mr. Jefferson!" they yelled while his leash dragged on the

asphalt just out of reach. Kate rolled away from the window and, having already forgotten that Anna and Justin had spent the night, was surprised by the empty sleeping bags on the floor next to her. Her senses awakened to the smell of bacon, and she bolted out of bed.

The last one to breakfast, Mary had saved Kate two pieces of bacon and as such was continuously swatting hungry hands away.

"Well, it's about time you woke up!" Mary said with relief. "I'm tired of defending your bacon."

Kate hugged her mother and grabbed a plate, adding the last bit of scrambled eggs in the fry pan to her bacon, then made a stack of buckwheat pancakes and drizzled them with syrup. The way Kate attacked breakfast did not go unnoticed by Jammy.

"The girl is in a growth spurt," she firmly stated, and the adults agreed.

Ignoring the chorus of observers she filled her glass to the top with orange juice, a rare find in the refrigerator.

"Hey, don't drink it all!" said Johnny. "We hardly ever get that!"

As breakfast wound down, everyone scattered to prepare for the parade. Left alone at the table to finish her meal, Kate rather enjoyed the brief quiet. Edison and Johnny left to help polish the fire trucks, Anna and Justin walked home, Mary walked to the park to check on Mildred's hot dog stand for the church, and Jammy was to meet the Colonial Ladies at the Custom's House. Lowell, nowhere to be found, was likely out catching crabs with Mr. Jimmy. Kate, following through on her mother's request at breakfast, took a broom out front to sweep the walk one more time.

She had hardly swept the front step when Tansy appeared at the gate.

"You're back!" Kate exclaimed.

"Mom didn't want to miss the parade and neither did I," said Tansy, as she opened the gate.

"You want to watch with us?" asked Kate.

"Sure do, but my grandmother has already set the lawn chairs out front."

"I need to put ours out front right after sweeping."

"Skip the sweeping, who will know?" taunted Tansy.

"I will know," replied Kate, "besides, if Mom doesn't figure it out, Jammy will. They're like that you know, me and Johnny, we don't get away with much."

"That's true," agreed Tansy, "everyone has eyeballs on their backsides at your house."

Kate sighed and then proceeded to tell Tansy all about Sam and Squawk. Tansy, aghast with the news, wanted to jump on her bike and ride down to the boatyard right away, but the parade was imminent, so the girls decided they would go afterward. Kate finished sweeping and Tansy followed her back to Edison's shed and helped carry the lawn chairs out front. As the last chair was set, Mary appeared with a plate of hot dogs she had bought at the park. Kate grabbed one and stuffed it in her mouth while Tansy looked on longingly.

"There's one for you, too," said Mary, smiling at Tansy.

Without hesitation, Tansy reached for hers and followed Kate's example. At that moment, one by one, from all different angles, everyone returned to the Seth house, grabbed a hotdog and settled into a lawn chair, except for Jammy.

"Where's Jammy?" Kate asked Mary.

"You'll see," was all she replied. Kate did not have time to question her more as the distant sounds of Fife and Drum Corps signaled the start of the Fourth of July parade.

A slow, dramatic musical march ushered a reverent moment of stillness. The first to arrive was the Fife and Drum Corps, and as the red coats approached, hearts swelled with pride, love, and loss.

Kate whispered in Johnny's ear, "Why do they wear red coats? I thought we wore blue?"

Johnny's second favorite thing next to rocketry was war tactics, and he replied quickly in her ear, "So they wouldn't get shot."

Kate looked puzzled by Johnny's answer but was distracted immediately by the music. The white-wigged, black-hatted men's

Revolutionary War uniforms were made of a fine, bright red wool, the jacket opening trimmed in blue with shiny metal buttons. The ivory white vest underneath showed in the open triangle the coats formed and matched their pants and white gloves. Rope tension snare drums beat in perfect unison with fifes to the tune of "The Roast Beef of Old England," so nimbly, the music danced in and out of the townspeople's ears like jaunty water sprites.

A few floats from civic organizations followed the Fife and Drum, and behind them were the fire trucks from neighboring towns. When the bright yellow mammoths of their town came into view, the townspeople cheered loudly with pride and the trucks responded with many horns and its volunteer firemen waving to the crowd.

Next were the fancy and classic cars, sparkling with the sun shining off their perfectly waxed paint. An electric blue 1963 Corvette split window was followed by a customized black 1932 Ford Coupe with the top and hood removed, white-walled tires, and the exhaust hugging the sides. Johnny and Edison stood up when they saw this car, clapping and cheering for it. This was followed by a exquisitely detailed deep red 1937 4 door 7 passenger Packard with bright chrome accouterments, accented by an elegant swan hood ornament with wings reaching to the sky. Johnny and Edison remained standing and looked upon the Packard awestruck, pointing. Kate liked the loud 1957 black Chevy with flames down the sides that followed and clapped excitedly for it. Its unmufflered engine reminded her of the workboats leaving the docks in the early morning hours.

These beauties were followed by a cream-colored 1970 Cadillac DeVille convertible with Miss Fire Prevention dressed in white holding a bouquet of red roses, smiling and waving at the crowd. After the excitement of the fine cars, Edison and Johnny flopped down in their lawn chairs and let out a sigh.

The local high school marching band followed, playing "Stars and Stripes Forever" by John Philip Sousa. The band was, in turn, followed by Mr. Bill, a local farmer driving his 1934 Johnny Popper proudly with his pet rooster, "Hammy," in his lap. Its tricycle front end and John Deere green were respectfully applauded by the townsfolk; its popcorn sound was music to the working town's ears. In a wonderful surprise to the crowd, he hitched a wagon to the back and sitting on hay bales were the Colonial Ladies, dressed in their historical garb, waving.

Jammy looked towards the family and winked at Kate, who, realizing it was Jammy jumped up pointing.

"There's Jammy!" she exclaimed exuberantly.

Just then, the ladies unleashed handfuls of candy to the unsuspecting crowd leaving the children to scatter wildly, chasing Mary Janes, Tootsie Rolls, Atomic Fire Balls, Sweetarts and lollipops.

The Colonial Ladies were followed by five decorated horses walking a parade gait and adorned in western-style saddles with silver trimmings. The hooves were sleeved with sequins and the riders wore red, white, and blue western outfits with white hats. The horses' tails had red, white, and blue ribbons. Jefferson, pulling his owners by a leash, was a proper finale, his head held high and tail wagging with a hubris that only a hound of top brass distinction would display.

Unofficially participating was an exuberant Beezy, wildly dancing a jig behind the stately bassett hound. Emotions amuck, his limbs both robotic and free-spirited, cast a spastic display of joy bordering on the insane, was curtailed by Chief Duncan at the grandstand by shoving him in the phone booth to tranquil him. Five minutes was all it took for Beezy to settle, and when he showed some restraint, Duncan pushed open the doors of the booth, and he stepped out untethered and calmed to a modicum of decorum similar to the nature of a sobered drunk.

Kate cupped her t-shirt front upwards and its bag-like appearance overflowed with sugar as she, Anna, Justin, and Tansy traded with each other so as to favor their own pockets with the candies they liked best. In years past, the children would have lingered long after the parade, discussing the best parts, but Kate and Tansy were drawn away immediately on important business with Miss Pat, Sam, and of course, Squawk.

Meeting at the back gate, pockets laden with treats and charm pops sticking out of their mouths like cigarettes, they took off on their bikes like bandits on the run. Round the corner they raced side by side. Kate was ahead at first, but Tansy, fueled with sugar, began to pull ahead right around Edison's garden. She kept a lead but began to lose ground as they passed the Country Club, which was curiously empty. Tansy took the inside turn nearly clipping Miss Clara's prized rosebushes. Kate gasped when she saw how close Tansy leaned into the gorgeous pink bushes, but when she saw Tansy unscathed, she pedaled as hard as she could, focusing only on the next corner, where she would have the inside track.

Tansy was fully focused like Kate and at the corner they were traveling so fast that they took the turn so wide they ended up plowing their front tires into the beach and wiping out in the sand just across from the boatyard entrance. Sand sprayed up in the air like a broken faucet and rained down upon them. Quietly, they looked each other up and down and since no one appeared hurt, they both began to cackle like crows.

"You crazy young-uns!" yelled Miss Edna. "You're lucky a car wasn't coming round the corner!"

Kate pushed herself up on her elbows, "Sorry, Miss Edna."

Edna waved her hand at them and yelled, "Oh pshaw, Kate!" Then she turned around and walked inside, her screen door slamming behind her.

Cheeks flushed with their spirited ride, they pulled themselves up, brushed themselves off, and pushed their bikes across the street to the boatyard. Squawk saw them approaching her pen and started flapping her wings. This, being the first time they had ever seen Squawk do this, excited them.

"She's too small to fly," announced Tansy in a confused tone.

"Sure is," agreed Kate. "But maybe she's starting to practice…"

They shrugged their shoulders and Tansy reached in the pen and placed Squawk next to them on the grass. At Pat's house the screen was cracked and the door was open. Kate knocked and yelled, "Miss Pat? Miss Pat?" but there was no answer, so they turned around to look at the boatyard and it was empty.

"Duh," Kate slapped her forehead. "It's a holiday; everyone has the day off!"

Miss Pat and Mr. Russell were probably visiting uptown and at the park afterwards, which was the town custom.

While they were assessing the situation, Squawk was headed straight for the river.

"Wait for us!" yelled Tansy when she saw her on the move.

The girls ran after the duck and played crossing guard for her as traffic had resumed and many who had come from outside town were going home. The girls held up their hands as Squawk marched across with an air of importance. The motorists who saw this laughed at the show and waved at the duckling, cheering her confidence and her babysitters' swift actions.

They played with Squawk for a long time with one eye on Mr. Russell's boatyard, waiting for him and Miss Pat to return, but they didn't. So, after many hours of river fun, they walked Squawk back up to her cage and said goodbye. She nestled into a grassy patch and tucked her bill under her wing for a nap. Riding home was the opposite of their arrival. They pedaled with a leisure that barely kept their bikes upright, as such a sauntering drunk would have passed them side by side. As they approached the Country Club they heard boisterous laughing and toasting amongst the men, shouting, "I'll drink to that!"

As they rounded the corner, they saw an unusually large number of men gathered.

"Happy Fourth, girls!" a crowd of them yelled as they raised their cans and bottles high in the air, then lowered their chins to guzzle their affliction with great enthusiasm. It was courage tonic for the din. Kate and Tansy waved, smiled, and pedaled faster.

Edison was in his garden weeding. The girls saw him and stopped by, curious to see if there were any ripe melons.

"Not yet, girls, and there won't be 'til near 'bout August."

Their disappointment was tempered by eating a few sweet, juicy cherry tomatoes. When they left the garden, they looked across to Mr. Paul's, and it appeared as if he wasn't home.

"Probably at the Country Club," Kate said.

"I didn't see him," offered Tansy, "but there were an awful lot of men there."

Kate stopped at her gate and Tansy pedaled a little farther to hers. They waved, and each, in withdrawal from their sugar high, went into their houses and flopped. Tansy in her grandmother's porch hammock, and Kate on the front porch glider.

Mary yelled, "Jobs for dinner!"

It stirred Kate out of an impending slumber. She sat up and crawled through the porch window towards the kitchen. Jammy had returned and had changed out of her colonial attire. Kate ran to her and gave her a hug.

"I was so surprised to see you on Mr. Bill's wagon!" Kate said with a smile.

"I wanted to surprise you!" she replied.

"Well, you did!" giggled Kate.

Edison appeared in the doorway. "Miss Katherine is always full of surprises, aren't you?" he said with a sly look.

"Whatever do you mean, Edison?" replied Jammy.

Edison chuckled, "Don't tell me you had nothing to do with those cars?"

Jammy smiled ever so slightly. "Why Edison, whatever gave you that idea? I did nothing of the sort!"

Edison pried further. "Some of those cars belong to people you know, I'd say - especially the Packard. That belongs to the Judge."

Miss Katherine never admitted anything, but Kate saw her wink at Edison.

Chapter XI

— Rum Cake Folly —

With the Fourth of July just past, summer settled in like a lulla-by. Its rhythm was as soothing as that of a comfortable worn cotton t-shirt that Kate slid into every morning. This morning, after a swig of iced tea, a thick slice of zucchini bread, and a juicy plum, Kate met Tansy at the back gate with the boatyard in mind. They were confident they would see Miss Pat today with the men back at work.

The back gate was a busy place this morning. Johnny and Edison had been up with the sun and were finishing the last of the repairs on the Lapstrake. The old Johnson shaft was currently submerged in a trashcan filled with water. On the water's surface lay a thin layer of gas that shimmered pink, greenish-blue and yellow in the morning light. Smoke plumes twirled upward with the wind, leaving a lingering smell strong enough to make everyone push their noses up. Attempts to start the old engine were numerous, and Kate and Tansy stood back as Johnny turned the key one more time. Edison intently scrutinized the exposed engine, its cover cast aside on the lawn, as if his continual inspection would spontaneously cause it to start.

"She's flooded now, Johnny!" he said loudly, his voice softening as the racket stopped. "Give it 15 minutes and we'll try her again." he said as he pulled out a cigarette and lit it, adding his habit to the lingering smog.

Kate, no stranger to the workings of an engine, asked what Edison and Johnny scoffed at as obvious.

"Did you drain the carburetor and get fresh gas in case there was water in the fuel?" "Pshaw, Kate," Johnny said, waving his hand at her as if to dismiss the whole conversation. "That's the first thing we did!"

Kate, feeling frustration in the air, signaled to Tansy to head out, leaving the fussy men behind. They waved to Mr. Paul, who was with some boatyard workers picking out metal pieces. They yelled "hello" to the blind couple, and glanced at an empty morning Country Club as they rounded the corner to see Miss Pat.

Kickstands down they walked towards her office and to their delight saw Sam sitting in front of the doorway wagging his tail. His chin was lightly raised and as everyone went by, he soaked up the love and a whole lotta pets, smiles, and waves from the men. He was the star of the boatyard this morning and he was loving it.

The girls ran to Sam, both hugging him, smiling, and looking in at Miss Pat, who sat in her office chair beaming. "He's okay!!" the girls said in unison.

Pat got up out of her seat and came out to join the girls. She walked past them about 10 feet, turned around, and called for Sam. She kneeled down and clapped her hands, motioning for Sam to come to her, but he sat there wagging his tail and bowing his head low as if he really wanted to go to Pat, but for some reason, he was hesitant. That's when Kate noticed the bandages on both his hind legs. Kate's heart sank so fast she thought she would cough it up on the ground. Tansy looked like she would cry. Sam, who loved Miss Pat dearly, stood up slowly and hobbled gingerly towards her. Kate suddenly sat her butt on the gravel and watched the animal in obvious pain walk to Pat. He looked so vulnerable that both girls were scared to pale silence.

"Sam has been through a lot, girls, and he has to practice walking a little bit every day. I know it looks painful, but the veterinarian said to let him walk a little each day, and his legs will improve."

Their faces lightened and Kate responded with relief in her voice. "So he can walk?"

"Yes, but not much at first. He has medicine and all of us to help him. I'm certain he will be up and about soon."

Tansy ran to Pat and hugged her and then Sam.

"Girls, will you walk him back to my yard for me? The crushed oyster shells in the boatyard are hard for him right now. I figure he can rest on the grass in the yard, and I'll check him at lunch."

The girls obliged and could not help but mother Sam and help him cross to the yard as best they could. When they reached the yard, they grabbed a blanket off the porch for him and he laid right on it.

"Squawk!" yelled the duckling. They pulled her out of her cage and set her on the grass to look for bugs. Lounging on the grass, belly down and feet up in the air, they told Sam stories of the holiday and watched Squawk gobble three grasshoppers in a blink.

"His legs look pretty bandaged up," said Tansy.

"That old fox did him dirty," replied Kate with a scowl.

Squawk, satisfied with her snack, waddled over and nestled in right next to Sam on the blanket.

"Aww," the girls said in unison.

Squawk cozied herself in as if to sleep, and so did Sam.

"They love each other," said Kate.

"They really do," agreed Tansy.

They slipped away to tell Miss Pat, and when they did, she walked over to have a look-see. "Just leave them be," Pat said quietly. "I have one phone call to make, and then I can sit in the yard for a while until they wake up. I have some knitting to do; I'll swing on the porch."

Pat was so pleased with the animals, she didn't think twice about stepping away from boatyard work for a few hours to keep them company.

The girls walked to their bikes. "Let's head to the ferry," said Tansy. They peddled slowly along the macadam road just above the rocky shoreline and pointed to the boats in the harbor.

"I like that blue sailboat anchored over there," pointed Kate.

"Ooh, nice one," said Tansy, replying with her own preference, pointing at the two-masted green boat anchored not 20 yards away from the blue one.

"That's a nice one, too," said Kate. "A bunch of boats have left since the holiday. Let's go to Sunset Beach and see how many are headed out the river."

The girls peddled onward, past the ferry, and straight onto Sunset Lane. Aged willows flanked the narrow tunnel path as they glided beneath the flowing foliage and it enveloped them. There was something very soothing about riding down the lane. At the end of the road stood a small beach frequented by friends and families during the day and lovers by night. The river from this side looked empty of vessels, and to their delight Kate and Tansy discovered Mary and Miss Lucille sitting on the beach talking. Miss Lucille sat on her woven straw mat in her blue and purple patterned bathing suit, and Mary in her low chair wearing a bright yellow suit with green leaves and white flowers with a short bathing skirt. Having so much to talk about, they didn't notice the girls until they were near about upon them.

"Oh, girls! What are you up to?" asked Miss Lucille, turning towards them.

"Nothin," replied Kate.

"It's never nothin' nothin' always implies somethin'," smiled Miss Lucille, showing the gap in her teeth.

Mary sized them up. "I think these girls might be wanting to swim, Miss Lucille..."

"Well, then they should get at it, clothes and all," she dared the girls.

Kate and Tansy, laughing, ran straight into the river.

"They best enjoy it before the nettles take over," said Mary, turning towards Lucille.

Lucille agreed with a nod, stood up, stretched, and headed into the river herself.

"You gonna swim to the pole? asked Tansy, standing waist-deep.

"You know it girls, want to join?"

Kate got nervous. "Miss Lucille, that's real far."

"Pshaw, Kate," Lucille said while waving her hand. "I was only kidding!"

The pole set just off the yacht club's finger pier next to a very large sign anchored to the bottom by two large pilings that read: "Slow. You Are Responsible For Your Wake." The pole marked the channel and had a weathered reflective red triangle atop with the number 2 on it, although one could hardly make out the number as the trailing sticks from an osprey nest hung down to partially cover it.

Kate turned to Tansy, "You know Johnny says it's nearly 40 feet deep at that pole."

Tansy suddenly looked worried as distance was the only thing on her mind, depth was a new concept.

"Be careful, Gram!" she yelled.

"She's swum it a million times; you know that, Tansy?"

"Yeah..." replied Tansy, still ripe with concern.

"Come on, let's walk out to the drop-off."

That broke Tansy's spell and the girls walked until the ground disappeared from under them. The edge marked the boundary set by the elders long ago for the children who swam on Sunset Beach. It marked where the channel had dug a deep hole, and the water moved faster, especially on a flood tide.

"That's quite far enough!" yelled Mary.

"We know!"

The girls swam back a few yards and stood up, the river water up to their chins. Kate turned and looked towards Miss Lucille and pointed, "See, she's halfway there!"

Tansy's fears faded as she was distracted by something underfoot.

"I got somethin,'" she said as she wiggled her feet around and then dove down to grab it. Treasure in hand, she popped up with a triangular piece of pottery covered in river mud. A quick wipe revealed a blue willow pattern the size of a silver dollar.

"Oh, that's a good one!" exclaimed Kate. She held it up high so Mary would see.

"Pottery fishing! Looks like a keeper!" Mary yelled back from her low chair.

Pleased with the find, they swam in to the beach to wash it thoroughly and showed Mary up close. Mary flipped it over, looking for any kind of symbol.

"No symbol on this one," she said. "But what beautiful colors!"

Kate suggested they make it the centerpiece of a river pipe, and Tansy agreed. This was the best beach in town for making rivers; its slow descent to the river itself led to tiny pools hidden in and about the smoothed rocks on the south side. Large oyster shells made for hand shovels as they set about creating an elaborate maze of pipes and rivulets that rose and fell with the tiny waves that lapped upon the shore. The pottery was used as a floodgate, and they opened and shut it as the water ebbed and flowed. Their creation wound around the rocks like a snake, its head a tiny tidal pool in a crevice of algae-covered rocks banked upon the bulkhead that delineated between Sunset Beach and the Old Inn on the adjoining property.

Their river system was near completion when Miss Lucille returned from her swim, arising out from the water like a sea goddess.

"You did it again, Gram!" Tansy said with pride.

Slightly winded and worn, Miss Lucille smiled, dried herself off with a towel, and plopped onto her grass mat. The rustle of her canvas bag tore the girls away from their project, and they appeared instantly at the foot of the ladies' encampment.

"I suppose you're here for the Cheez-its and not the company?" Miss Lucille laughed as she poured a handful of the snack into each girl's cupped hand. Mary handed them her thermos of water. All means and methods of eating manners cast aside, crumbs fell upon their bare feet like sand from the sky.

"No wonder they are ravenous," said Mary, looking at her wrist-watch. "It's near about 12:30." Looking at the damp-clothed pair she stated, "Go on home to our house and fix yourselves a sandwich, you two."

The girls, spent from the morning's activities, thought it a good idea. The idea grew in stature when a wave broke on the shore, their river flooded, stream banks collapsed, and the pottery gate was nearly swept away with the receding waters. Tansy ran quickly towards the destruction and retrieved her prized pottery, tucking it safely into her pocket.

"These jeans get tight when they dry," she said, yanking and picking at them.

"Yeah," said Kate, "Cut offs always do that," as she swung one leg over her bike and turned the wheel to Sunset Lane. Tansy followed behind, the wind at her back, drying her clothes and cooling her skin as the willows bowed before and fluttered after them. The smell of Miss Lucille's freshly lit cigarette chased them at first and then faded upward as they peddled home.

The Lapstrake was no longer at the back fence, which gave Kate hope it was running again. Edison's truck was also gone, so they assumed no one was home when they entered the back screened porch while Kate told the harrowing story of the night Johnny went missing. Her tale was cut short by the faint smell of liquor and sounds coming from the front parlor. Quieting down, they looked at each other and cautiously tip-toed into the dining room. Kate soon recognized Jammy's voice, and her concern instantly faded as they approached the noise from the parlor. They poked their heads around the corner to discover four impeccably dressed ladies in floral print dresses sitting around a fine creamy lace-covered card table playing bridge.

A walnut lazy bartender tray on a hinged stand anchored a corner close to them, supporting the vice of the afternoon. Kate wiped the sweat off her forehead as she watched linen cocktail napkins soak up beads of water running down the sides of rocks glasses, filled halfway with ice, and a smooth scotch fit for queens. The fine liquor stood singly next to the silver ice bucket and forked tongs that lay beside it. Kate's eyes moved from side to side, watching the reflection of tiny silver bowls dance upon the walls of the parlor as the sun shone against them from the bay window. Filled with mints and nuts, Kate and Tansy tiptoed in for a handful of the elegant snacks.

The finery about the room accentuated the ladies' own elegance and amended their competitive spirit with a civility that was regal enough to assume they were of English descent. No one noticed Kate and Tansy softly scurry in, their bare feet stealthy on the oriental rug. However, when they reached for the nuts, the game was up. Kate looked over at Jammy, who glared at her. Kate learned long ago that bridge cohorts were more serious than the fisherman at the wharf reeling one in, and it was best to say little polite sentences and then leave them to the game.

"Hello, Jammy," Kate said softly.

All the white-haired ladies turned towards the girls, and a whiff of mingled perfumes wafted in their direction, covering their dirty river clothes in Chanel no. 5, Shalimar, Yves Saint Laurent, and Estée Lauder, making them feel somehow fresher.

"Cards, girls," she replied.

"I hope you win," answered Kate softly as she and Tansy quietly backed away and removed themselves to the kitchen.

As they approached the kitchen, Kate realized the liquor smell as she entered the house was actually in the kitchen and not from Jammy's card party. She eyed the veneered mahogany buffet and in the corner she saw the culprit: a moist rum cake certainly brought by Mrs. Crossett, one of Jammy's bridge ladies. She breathed in deeply the rich rum vapors and walked straight to it.

"What kind of cake is that?" asked Tansy.

Kate took another deep breath, exhaling long and slow.

"Mrs. Crossett's rum cake," she said. "The most delicious cake in the whole wide world."

Tansy stood wide-eyed, moving her head back and forth between Kate and the cake. As she did, her hand reached towards the curiosity, and she swiped a finger full of the sauce stuck to the bottom of the cake plate. When the sweet, buttery Jamaican rum hit her lips, her eyes widened further, her smile resembled a Cheshire Cat, and she adamantly agreed with Kate.

"You're right, best cake ever."

Kate's empty stomach and the sweet smell of dark rum spun within her an inner conflict.

"Let's have some," said Tansy before Kate could wrap herself around the choices before her.

"Maybe," said Kate, as she leaned in over and scrutinized the insides left open by the first slices enjoyed earlier. Its crumb was moist, with a marbled darkness towards the top of it where the buttered rum was poured upon it from the top down and it seeped through the small pecan pieces that covered it. The rum, not soaked into the cake, pooled around the edges like a buttery moat.

"If we're going to have some," said Kate, being aware of the fallout, "we should have something with it, like lunch stuff."

They turned and looked around the kitchen, perusing the countertops, hoping to spy just the right item to feel like they were in some way balancing the crime they were about to commit. "Bananas and old biscuits, all I see is bananas and old biscuits," said Tansy.

Kate tore herself away from the buffet and opened the door of the fridge.

"There's ham," said Kate as she grabbed the tinfoil-covered shank in one hand and a stick of butter in the other.

They each had a biscuit with ham and butter and once satisfied that they had eaten something "lunchy" they sliced two slim pieces of the rum cake so that maybe they wouldn't be missed. The rum immediately stained their paper napkins with its pungently prideful drippings.

"Mrs. Crossett doesn't mess around," said Tansy. "It's completely saturated!"

"And so good," Kate said while stuffing her mouth with the forbidden morsel.

"Maybe we'll dream of pirates tonight," she said.

In Kate's mind, she thought that they would have headed out to the porch with their ladylike slices, but instead, they were gobbled voraciously right at the buffet. They stared at the cake, longing for more.

"We could just take one more sliver," said Kate. "Maybe they won't notice."

"Agreed," said Tansy as she picked up the cake knife and cut a considerable slice, placing it on Kate's saturated napkin.

"Tansy, it's way too big; they will notice!"

"Too late," she said as she cut a very generous piece for herself, gouging the cake.

Now they had done it and they decided to leave the yard with contraband in hand before they were discovered.

With one hand carefully holding the moist, sweet, sticky cake and the other holding crab nets, they walked two streets behind to Miss Ginny's boatyard.

"It's supposed to be 'flood tide," said Kate. "Cousin Lowell was talking about it."

"Oh, then we should catch some good stuff," said Tansy, smiling while drips of sugary rum wet her lips and dripped onto her shirt. They walked with their nets over their shoulders smiling with a prideful stride towards the largest ditches in town as if they knew some secret that no one else did.

By the time they reached the ditches, both girls had lined their bellies with courage. With napkins tucked away in pockets and a crab net for balancing, they challenged each other to ditch jumping. The ditches, filled with river water, were easily five feet wide and three feet deep. Tansy pushed for Kate to go first, and she did without hesitation, falling just past the edge of the muddy bank, knees cutting into the tall grass.

Tansy, being slightly smaller, took a deep breath and, using the crab net like a pole vaulter, launched herself across the ditch and landed on top of Kate, crab net flying into the air and then falling and sinking to the bottom of the ditch. Giggles overwhelmed them as fast as a summer squall hits, and they rolled on the grass, thrashed their legs, and hugged their bellies til they choked on their own spit and sat up, dizzied and red-faced from it all.

They breathed deeply, and the twinge of alcohol left in their mouths made their breath feel cool coming in and hot on the exhale. After gazing at the ditch for an unusual amount of time, they leaned forward on dirty knees with butts up in the air and watched the bottom mud scuttle down around the crab net, partially covering it.

"Here you go," said Kate, handing her the remaining net.

Tansy stood up over the ditch to fish it out with Kate's net when she stopped and turned to Kate with her index finger over her mouth. Kate leaned forward to see a small mud turtle swimming along the far side of the ditch. Tansy got on her haunches to get a better view, and her afternoon shadow scared the little turtle. It sped up and went into the culvert nearby that fed the river.

"Aw man," said Kate. "We'll have to jump back across if we want to sneak up on anything."

This time, Tansy got a running start, and when they had both successfully made it across, Tansy fished out the crab net with the one they had left. Silently, they walked along the edge of the road. With the racket and rumble from Miss Ginny's boatyard behind them, it wouldn't have mattered if they yelled, but it felt more like hunting to stalk quietly. With slow yet rhythmic steps they walked the line between the ditch's edge and the shining oyster shell road on their left. A doubler appeared, and Kate snatched it up with quick hands and silent skill.

"I'm going to save the peeler for fishing."

She proclaimed her intent as she laid the net down on the hot road; the crabs separated and raised claws for battle. Without shoes or a rag, she had another trick. She lifted the net and shook it until the crabs were dizzy and then laid it back on the road. Tansy used the bottom of her pole to flick the male back into the ditch, and Kate lifted the net with the peeler still in it.

"… and that's how it's done," said Kate, with pride.

Tansy thumped on her chest with her free fist, and again the girls took to laughing uncontrollably. Tansy, with her foot closer to the bank than she thought, started to slide in, trying to catch herself; she ended up doing a split, her butt landing on the muddy edge. This was too much for Kate, and she jumped across to the other side just so she could roll around on the grass and laugh with true abandon.

Tansy's foot sunk deep into the mucky, dark bottom mud, and she turned and leaned both hands onto the grassy side bank. Kate sat up weak from laughter and extended her hand to Tansy, who pulled herself out, crawled up onto the grass, and lay next to Kate, breathing and laughing loudly.

"You're dripping in mess," said Kate, still giggling. Tansy flung her muddy leg at Kate in a kicking motion; a dime-size blob landed on Kate's forehead and she wiped it off with her forearm. Clothes and skin covered in smelly river mud, Tansy announced she was going home to spray off with a hose. Kate watched as she got up and ran right across Miss Ginny's empty lot to her back gate. Not wanting to give up the hunt, Kate stayed behind with both nets, and planned to keep at it.

She carefully crept along the edges of the ditch bank looking for crabs and turtles but spied nothing but schools of minnows turning and swirling as if playing a game of tag. When she reached the end of the street, she placed her empty net down on the grassy side of the ditch and the other she folded artfully over upon itself as to trap the peeler and then lowered it into the water to keep it cool. She left her nets and headed to the public dock where the family kept the Lapstrake. There were many municipal docks in town, each one with its own peculiarities. This was the smallest of them all, and only five boats tied up here, each with their own pulley systems and two pilings.

Kate wandered down a small decline to see if the family boat was there. If it was, that meant it was repaired and ready to be back out on the water soon with Johnny and his friends. The only boat without a pulley system was an old wooden workboat tied up on the right side of the shallow dock. It had a worn and worried look about it as if it knew it would drown any day now, whether it be from the water seeping through the rotten wood in the transom or a heavy rain. The narrow, Hooper's Island dovetail workboat with raggedy unpainted trim had reached a point of no return. Cracked glass in the wheelhouse and the seagulls circling above its display of rotten eels left in the sun for too long made it look like a lost cause. Kate wondered who owned such a derelict boat.

She wandered out to the end of the dock and was delighted to see the Lapstrake tied up. She hoped that she would be invited out with Johnny again soon. It looked beautiful, all varnished and paint-ed; its windshield glistened in the sun. The creek sparkled under a strong sun and as she gazed out past the Lapstrake, she noticed the boatyard between Miss Ginny's and Mr. Russell's was bustling with activity. The men were stepping a wooden mizzen mast and strong voices carried clearly across the water.

"Ok, men, walk her up."

Several large yard workers groaned and growled under the strain.

"Boys, walk her down, we'll get the crane." Kate heard the fore-man yell.

Mesmerized by the activity, Kate didn't notice she was no lon-ger alone on the dock. But, something inside of her began to stir, her neck felt a cool sensation upon it as an unusual summer chill shot down her back. Feeling suddenly uneasy, she haltingly turned around to find a boy standing in the dilapidated workboat staring at her. He had red hair, hollow eyes, and an expressionless face. All she could think about was getting off the dock, but to do that, she would have to walk right by him. She put her head down and walked straight past him with an assured pace, which she maintained up the tiny hill and straight to the crab nets she had left behind.

Thinking she was way past him paying attention to her, she glanced over her shoulder and caught his continual cold stare. She picked up her nets and headed home quickly. Kate had never had anyone stare so coldly at her before, and it bothered her. When she saw Tansy at her gate, all cleaned up, Kate said she was headed home.

"Just as well," said Tansy. "Gram wants me to help her with something in the kitchen. Did you catch anything else?"

"Nope, just the peeler," Kate replied as she continued to walk home.

"See ya later," said Tansy.

Kate waved.

Upon returning home, she noticed Mary's bike was there, and River was happy to see her. Once inside her gate, she felt safer and sat down in the grass to hug River. She stayed with River for a long while, just sitting and contemplating her experience. "Well, now I know what he looks like," she said to herself.

Mary opened the back screen door and walked out to check on the laundry. Seeing Kate so attached to River interested her enough to come and sit with both Kate and the dog.

"What's going on?" Mary asked.

Kate was silent and felt like crying but really didn't want to. She thought herself so brave until now when she realized she wasn't brave at all.

"Hmm…" said Mary. "What has happened?" Kate, with cracking voice, laid out the story before Mary.

"Hmm…," said Mary one more time followed by a pause. "Kate, I'm proud of you."

"Why?" asked Kate.

"Because you listened to me and came right home. Your actions tell me that you trust my advice."

Kate perked up a bit. "Well, I never thought of it that way, it's just, he's unsettling."

"I know, and that is why you stay away," said Mary. "Now, if we're both being so honest with each other, what happened to the rum cake?"

Kate's stomach rolled and pitched again, just like it had on the dock earlier.

"Tansy and I ate some."

"Some?? Some?? It's more than half gone! We will discuss this at dinner. You're an absolute mess, and you smell like rum and river mud. Go and clean up, and then you can help me with dinner."

Kate picked herself up and trod up the stairs with heavy feet. She put her hands in her pockets and found her sticky rum cake napkin had spread its residue all over the inside of her pockets. She threw the napkin in the corner trashcan and took her clothes off for a shower. Even she could admit she smelled pretty bad, and Kate wasn't very discerning about such things. She'd go for weeks unbathed if allowed, but church every Sunday forced a bath at a minimum of once a week, and Mary and Jammy would never let it go quite that long.

Kate dried herself off from her shower, expecting to feel better, but she didn't. The Tuffin boy's stare was fixed in her mind in such a way that she couldn't forget it. There was a cruelness in his eyes that Kate had never seen in anyone before and it bothered her as she dressed. She thought about what her mother told her about the boy being beaten. She thought it not fair that he never had a chance to be good. His eyes showed a disturbing fate that Kate could neither rationalize nor put into words; just thinking about it made her tingly again as it had on the dock. "Kate, jobs!" yelled Mary from downstairs.

Kate folded up any further thoughts of the red-haired boy like a map and tucked it away as she headed for the back steps. Something inside her shook on the way down the flight that made her go over to her mother and hug her. Mary hugged her back and then put her to work.

"Jammy's taking a nap, so you will need to make the biscuits."

Kate nodded as she watched and helped Jammy make them so many times that rote memory took over. Kate mixed, rolled, cut, and placed the biscuits on a greased aluminum sheet pan for the oven. Then Mary handed her a broom. When finished sweeping, Kate set the table and fed the dog. She was dropping ice in the sun tea when Jammy arrived at the bottom of the steps, looking fresh and hungry. Mary glared at her mother, and Kate stepped back confused by the angry energy of the moment.

"Sleep it off?" Mary struck first.

"I hardly call one scotch with my bridge ladies cause for sleeping it off!" Jammy fired back.

"...drinking in the house, mother? That's a terrible example for Lowell." Mary volleyed.

"Lowell is a grown man; I do not need to set an example for him in my own house!" Jammy raised her voice.

Mary huffed, opened the oven door, put the biscuits inside, slammed it, and turned to the sink to do dishes. A frighteningly quiet pause followed.

"You are right, Mother," Mary said with her back turned. "I am perhaps too staunch." "You are a good Methodist," said Jammy. Mary turned around, and their eyes locked. They both smiled and considered the matter settled.

Kate got nervous; if Mary was this cross with her own mother, how cross would she be with her for eating all the rum cake? Family arrived from different directions for dinner. Johnny came through the front door, and Lowell and Edison arrived in unison at the back screen door just as the bells struck six. Everyone stood in the kitchen and looked to Mary who guzzled an iced tea and then stared at the floor, trying to calm down.

"What's burning?" asked Johnny.

"My biscuits are burning!" yelled Kate, reaching for the door.

Black smoke sputtered out but dissipated quickly and she was relieved to see her biscuits were fine; the smoke was merely from the remnants of an exploded baked potato that had fallen on the bottom burner. Mary, sounding exhausted, said, "Dish up."

As they gathered hands for grace, Jammy volunteered. "Lord, forgive us for the mistakes we make; we are all sinners. With your guidance, we strive to be the best we can be, but fear we fall short and remain at your mercy." She looked at Mary and winked. "We humbly thank you for the food you have set before us, and we will use it to nourish us as we serve you."

Mary let out a sigh. Dinner conversation was slim until Lowell began to share his work day with Mr. Jimmy.

"We got started early today after missing part of yesterday for the parade." He continued, "We more than made up for it; crabs were on and we caught 20 bushel."

"My word, that's a haul!" said Jammy.

"Impressive," said Edison.

Lowell beamed. When plates were empty, Kate thought she had escaped a rum cake inquisition, but she was wrong.

"I'd like to offer dessert," said Mary, "but Kate and Tansy took it upon themselves to eat over half of Mrs. Crossett's rum cake."

"Half the cake!?!" said Johnny. "I'll bet you were liquored up!"

Jammy, looking surprised, turned to Kate. "Hot on the exhale, I'm sure," she said, staring her down.

Johnny continued his fun, "Dizzy as a goose were you?"

"Did you lose your rudder or find your way home?" asked Jammy.

Kate's face was more red than it had been after a day in the July sun.

"I knew how to get home from the ditches," she said in defense, and then, in deference, she bowed her head onto the table and wrapped her forearms over her.

"I'm sorry," she said, sniffling.

"O.K. Everyone, let's remember it's only cake. They couldn't of had more than a snuff," said Edison, thinking the family had taken it too far.

Jammy also saw a line had been crossed and said, "Most of the rum is cooked off except for the shots poured over it. I suspect she was not as drunk as a wheelbarrow but, instead, a bit giddy with the sauce."

Mary reminded the family, "We all have sailor's blood in our genes, and we must be thoughtful of that."

"Amen, then it's settled," said Edison, obviously wanting to move on. Mary then brought in the remainder of the cake, and all had small slivers of what was left, minus Kate and Lowell. Not to be thought fragile, Kate stood up and cleared the plates, and proceeded to do the dishes, with redemption in mind. She received some pats on the back for her efforts on working off her giddy afternoon at the ditches.

When she had dried the last plate, Jammy screamed from the front parlor, and Johnny was the first to arrive.

"What's the matter?" he quizzed.

She pointed at the corner of the room where a bat clung to the wall.

"Get the crab nets, bat in the house!" Johnny yelled.

Kate, knowing where she had left them ran out back. The peeler was still tangled in one in the grass and she thought it dead until she saw the bubbles foaming from its mouth. She grinned and grabbed both nets. She ran straight to the sink and dumped the peeler, who raised its claws in anger, and then took the nets into the front parlor. The family had gathered to look at the bat and come up with a plan.

"O.K.," said Edison, "the last time this happened, we destroyed one of the wooden model ships so let's be more measured."

Since Edison was the tallest, he reached up, but with the ceilings being twelve feet tall, all he could do was bump it with the edge of the net. Startled, it flew out of the parlor towards the dining room. Johnny grabbed Edison's net and Kate the other. Round and round the dining room table they chased the night creature. Swinging their nets in all directions and nearly taking out the center light fixture, Johnny captured it and folded the net over it so it wouldn't escape. Everyone cheered and then gravitated toward the creature for a first-hand look.

It had a reddish hue to its fur and wasn't the typical black color one would expect for a bat.

"That's an Eastern Red Bat," said Lowell, "we have them in our yard too. They roost in the trees and rummage in the leaves. I think they eat lots of mosquitos."

That was all anyone had to hear to treat it with care and let it go.

"Anything that eats mosquitos must be good," Kate surmised.

Careful not to let it escape, Johnny walked the bat outside to the yard and everyone stood back in interest when he opened the net. The bat flew away towards the east.

Kate watched it until it was out of her view, then announced, "I have a peeler if anyone wants to go fishing."

"You'll need that tomorrow," said Mary. "Cousin John called today and has invited you to go fishing with him."

Kate's heart skipped a beat. She loved fishing with Cousin John. Starting at the age of eight, Kate went perch fishing many times with Cousin John (who was more like an uncle) on his boat. He and his wife lived a quiet life by the water's fringe and Kate was very fond of them both.

⚓ ⚓ ⚓

THE NEXT DAY, ON A lazy and warm summer afternoon, Edison dropped Kate off at their home and Cousin John and Kate headed down to his rustic landing constructed of wide pine planks.

"Did you bring a peeler?" he asked, seeing a paper bag in her hand.

"Yes, right here, I caught it yesterday," she said proudly, while holding the bag up to show him.

Arriving at the landing, Kate stepped forward to feel the warmth of the dock boards under her feet. Tied to a piling was a small white wooden rowboat with a rusty red waterline trimmed in gray. An understated yet alluring craft at no more than fourteen feet in length, it was small but seaworthy. Fishing rods and bait and tackle in hand, they climbed aboard barefoot, and Cousin John rowed across the river to the shoreline where the locust and wild choke cherry trees anchored their trunks on the bank, and willows hung low over the river's edge. This quiet spot dappled with sunshine streaks, where the water bugs danced, and dragonflies flitted about, is where the white perch felt at home. This is where they cast their lines for dinner. Unbeknownst to her, this summer ritual with cousin John fed Kate's soul.

When they had caught their fill, Cousin John decided it was time for Kate to learn to row. She had paddled in a boat plenty of times, but never had she rowed, and she felt up to the challenge. He gave her very little instruction and watched as she circled about back and forth sometimes headed up the river, sometimes across, but not in a straight line. After fifteen minutes, he gave her a few pointers, and soon they were pointed in the right direction. By the time they had returned to the dock and tied up, Kate was exhausted from the lesson but nonetheless enjoyed her afternoon.

When Edison picked her up, she was tired and hungry. "Good catch," said Edison, when she showed him a bucket full of white perch.

"I think there's eight," she said, trying to look at the ones on the bottom.

"You can cook them for dinner."

Kate groaned. She was hot and thirsty and worn from her rowing lesson. With the windows down, the quiet ride home renewed her; the breeze on her face felt good, and with a freshened spirit, she carried the bucket into the kitchen and began to clean the fish.

Chapter XII

— Ladies' Day —

The middle of July burned onward, its breezes as dauntless as the heat. Unrelenting, steady southwesterly winds brought joy to the sailors and relief to the laborers on land and on the water. This balance of wind and heat was a welcome one, as often enough, summer heat brought upon nothing but laziness.

Kate noticed that on the hottest of days, men lingered longer uptown, the women cooked less, and a general malaise overtook the town. Porch sitters like Jammy sat fanning themselves, holding a sturdy straw-weaved heart-shaped fan with one hand and sluggishly waving at passers-by with the other. Truman and Miss Mabel leaned on counters, and discussions outside were short and held under the nearest shade tree. However, this July day when Kate woke up, she wasn't sweating; the wind had tempered the heat enough to make it bearable.

Kate had begun to sleep in later. A faint, sharp metal noise accentuated her shipyard adventure dreams until the clanging won out and punctured it. She awoke knowing the river was howling. The clanging of the halyards against the metal masts of the larger vessels at Miss Ginny's boatyard made known the velocity of the winds better than an anemometer, and the clangor ensured a steady minimum of 20 knots. She threw on a soft, worn cotton t-shirt and headed downstairs.

It was 9:30 in the morning, and Jammy and Mary were sitting in wicker chairs on the porch, waiting for her. Kate saw them sipping iced tea in their finery when she left the bottom step behind. River ran over to greet her and she knelt down on the floor and pet him all over while turning towards the porch and the two nicely dressed matriarchs.

"Look at that Mary," said Jammy, "our girl is finally up."

Kate wondered what they were up to. She turned her eyes to one and then the other and saw sparkles in their cheerful eyes.

She quizzed them. "Okay, what do you two have planned?"

"She's on to us, Mother," said Mary, and Jammy laughed.

"Kate," Jammy answered. "We are going to have a Ladies' Day today."

Kate smiled. She immediately remembered all the fun on 'ladies day' they had last summer. She looked down at her old stained t-shirt.

She looked up and proclaimed, "I'm going to have to change my clothes, aren't I?"

"Most certainly," Mary agreed.

"A sundress and flip-flops will do." Jammy added, "and a brush through your hair."

Kate turned to change her clothes and Mary said, "Wait! There is some hot buttered hominy on the stove for you."

"And plums," added Jammy.

Kate turned to the stove and set about dishing up breakfast.

"Where are we going first?" she asked with a mouth full of hominy.

Jammy replied, "To Miss Hattie's shop."

Kate felt what could only be described as a 'thrill' traveling through her blood. Anxious to start the day, she gobbled up breakfast and flew upstairs to get dressed. She had two sundresses that hung from her clothes pole. One was bright yellow with cheery flowers stitched along a green hemline; the other was sky blue and bore finely stitched edges that trimmed the entire dress in a thick purple pattern. Kate liked them both but favored the yellow as she knew Mother had cut and sewn it and Jammy had stitched the garden that grew all the way around it.

With no pockets in the dress, Kate grabbed her coin purse and flip-flopped down the front stairs so loudly it competed with Mary and Jammy's conversation on the front porch. When she peered out the front door, they rose up to meet her, and the three generations of ladies went out the front gate and headed up the bumpy brick sidewalk to Miss Hattie's shop.

The bricks felt different with flip-flops on. The old tree roots below pushed bricks upwards to create a sharp, uneven path, and were easily tripped upon. Even the soberest of citizens might appear under the veil of brew while navigating the walk. Kate needed to adjust to her flops. She hadn't worn them much this summer, and it showed each time she lunged forward, caught up by a brick edge.

Only a short town block away, they could see up ahead that Miss Hattie was just setting up shop. She hung an old pair of linen pants off the rungs of her shed roof next to an old cast iron frying pan. These items were merely decoration or perhaps a sign to let townsfolk know she was open for business, as they had been hanging off the rungs for decades. The frying pan had rust on it, and the black linen pants had been bleached so much from the sun that they showed a dulled brown.

The Seth ladies crossed the street hand in hand and stopped just short of the open French doors to look in the window.

"She has some new Grasshopper shoes," said Jammy.

They were a favorite of hers for casual wear about town.

Kate noticed the dollhouse living room furniture displayed with two dolls sitting on a velvet-lined sofa. It reminded her of one of the sofas in the front parlor, and she pointed it out to Jammy.

"Oh yes," Jammy agreed, "that would make a nice addition to the dollhouse, wouldn't it?"

Mary was already inside. Jammy and Kate heard the bell above the door signal her entrance. One might think no one was tending store, but when the bell rang, Miss Hattie would appear from some obscure corner of her shop as if she had secret doors hidden within the merchandise-strewn walls.

"Hello, Miss Hattie," Mary smiled.

"What brings all three of you out today?" Miss Hattie asked, smiling back.

"Well, Miss Hattie, it just so happens that I need some notecards today; I do have some correspondence to catch up on."

"Don't we all!" Miss Hattie giggled. "Well, you know where the stationary is."

Mary sauntered back down one of the cluttered aisles past the bathing suits to select her cards.

"Miss Katherine, I have the latest Grasshopper shoes in, and I ordered a pair in your size," Hattie said, greeting Jammy and Kate.

"Miss Hattie, you have read my mind; how on earth did you know I was coming to see you today?"

"Well, Miss Katherine, see, I had an inkling. Miss Charlotte told me that River has made off with one of your shoes again and taken it clear under the house."

"Yes!" laughed Jammy. "He steals one every summer, the little rascal!"

Miss Hattie handed her a box in her size to try on. Kate gazed at a tall, indented bookcase of dollhouse furniture; it was filled with miniatures from ceiling to floor. There were so many interesting things to look at: a miniature grandfather clock, a piano, oriental rugs of varying shapes and sizes, a corner cabinet, a whole bathroom set made of blue porcelain, and the red velvet Victorian couch. She wandered over to watch Jammy try on her shoes.

"Perfect fit as always, Hattie."

Right behind Jammy were spools and spools of different colored ribbons: sky blue, chartreuse green, baby girl pink, Easter egg yellow, snowflake white, shiny taffeta silver, and a red fuzzy velvet the color of a Santa Claus suit. If you bought a gift, Miss Hattie would wrap it beautifully. Kate thought about telling Jammy to have her wrap the shoes up like a gift even though they weren't, just so she could have the ribbon, but she knew better.

Mary appeared from the aisle behind them.

"I'll take these two boxes of note cards," she said, putting them on the counter. "They should last me a while."

Hattie rang up her total with an old adding machine as Mary laid her money on the worn wooden counter. Then Miss Hattie put the note cards in a bag and creased it just so.

Jammy then put her shoes on the counter and paused,

"Miss Hattie, I believe you have a beautiful red velvet couch among your miniatures that would brighten up the living room in my dollhouse."

Kate twinkled her eyes.

"Why, yes I do," she said cheerfully. She turned around and pulled a small box out of the gray-painted alcove behind her. She put it into a bag with the shoebox and creased it just so. The adding machine made its charming plinkity plink, and after paying her bill, Jammy, Kate, and Mary left the shop and headed home. Kate reached for Jammy's hand and held it all the way back to the house.

"How come Miss Hattie calls you Miss Katherine, but everyone else in town calls you Jammy?" Kate questioned.

"Miss Hattie's husband went to school with me when I was Miss Katherine."

The answer satisfied Kate, and once inside the Seth house, Jammy reached into her bag and handed Kate the miniature sofa.

"I think you'll find the perfect spot for this," she said.

Kate took the box and ran upstairs to Jammy's room to rearrange the dollhouse. She shuffled furniture to and fro, moved the dolls around, and adjusted the little rugs. She must have spent more time than she realized when she heard Mary calling.

"We are off to the Customs House!"

Kate ran down the steps and as they walked out the front gate, Kate noticed that Jammy had changed into her new shoes. They looked just right with her sundress. Kate was better at navigating the brick sidewalk this time and only tripped once before they arrived at the waterfront.

Jammy had told her the Custom House story so many times she thought she knew it by heart but each time she heard it she learned something new and interesting. Jammy had a way of telling a story that made history play a movie in her head.

As they approached, Kate noticed a bustle of ladies dressed in colonial costumes escorting tourists into the little house, handing out pamphlets and discussing town history on the grassy hill.

"Why is this hill taller than any other in town, Jammy?"

"This hill is special; below it was once a storehouse for the town lamplighter."

Kate's eyes widened. "You mean there is a whole secret room underneath, and what's a lamplighter?"

Jammy replied, "Before electricity, to light the streets there were oil lamps and each night the town lamplighter would light them. His oil was stored in the room underneath but it has since been filled in with dirt."

Kate looked disappointed the secret room no longer existed.

Auntie Tessie turned towards the Seth women and smiled when she saw them.

"Wonderful!" Tessie reached out to hug Kate. "I'm so glad you all came by. Jammy, take a look inside and see what you think."

The house was tiny, so they had to wait until the room was empty before the three ladies could enter.

"I love your pretty sundress," said a lady from their church.

"Thank you," Kate said with her best manners.

As she looked around, it seemed she knew almost everyone there, except of course for the "out-of-towners." Miss Mildred, Lizzie's mother, made a point of coming over to say hello. When Kate first saw her, she became nervous and grabbed Mary's hand. However, she noticed that everyone was being so nice to each other that perhaps the late-night incident involving Johnny and Lizzie had been forgotten.

When it was their turn, they stepped up the brick steps and entered one by one. The small house contained a desk, a chair and a fireplace. Kate was so curious about the spyglass on the desk that she reached for it first.

"That telescope belonged to your great-grandfather times three, Kate; he used it on his sailing ships."

Kate was tickled and pointed the spyglass out the window at the river to have a look.

"This is way cool," she said with excitement while she focused in on the ferry. "I can see Captain Will so close up!"

After an extended review of the spyglass she put it back down on the desk next to an open logbook that was also her great-grand-father's times three. It was a captain's log of one of his four vessels. The handwriting was so fine and elegant she had a very hard time reading it. Another book on the desk was a log of all the ships that had landed there during colonial times and paid taxes.

Hanging on the side wall was a list of ships to visit the port and a picture of the ship, *Intregrity*, that belonged to a very stern-look-ing man with a pointed nose. His picture hung over the fireplace, scowling at all who entered. With his stern look and black coat, Kate wondered if she wanted to be related to this ancestor. She turned back to the spyglass for another look, and after a quick turn, Jammy announced that they should leave and let the tourists in. Stepping outside, they said some goodbyes and headed to the town museum.

The museum was run by a dear friend of Jammy's; the two la-dies often having lunch together wherein they discussed local his-tory. After one scotch Jammy often offered up another family piece to loan the fledgling museum. As such, each room had several fam-ily artifacts relevant to town history.

The museum was housed in the town hall. Miss Elizabeth greet-ed the Seth women with an excited cheerfulness, and the tour began. The first and best thing in the museum's collection was a log canoe in the center of the room. Carved from three logs, it was a gorgeous ves-sel, and Kate marveled at its lines and design. She found it alluring and had to be coaxed away from it when the tour moved forward.

There were silver and nautical items, old pottery and crocks, swords and guns, powder horns, and carved decoys. There were portraits of men of distinction, military uniforms, maps, and aerial views of the town. One room was a blacksmith shop with old tools and an anvil for shaping hot iron. Old pictures of churches also hung on the walls, and a replica of the old Methodist church made by a great uncle sat in an odd-shaped corner near a window so the light could shine through the tiny stained glass windows.

While all of it was fascinating to Kate, she spent much of her time studying the antique maps that hung on the wall. She loved everything about them—the compass rose, the muted colors—and she wondered how the map makers figured it all out. One map in particular captured her attention as it was drawn with ink on an animal skin. A sloop sailed below it, and she recognized the waterlines.

"Is this our town?" she asked.

"Why yes, it is. This map is very old," said Miss Elizabeth.

Kate was struck with awe, as she thought it one of the most interesting things she had ever seen. Outside, the noontime Methodist church bells began to ring and Jammy announced they must return home for lunch. After pleasantries, Kate followed Jammy and Mary out the door and they headed home. Kate wondered why they were in such a hurry.

"Johnny is making us lunch," Mary told Kate. "After all, it is Ladies' Day."

Once inside the door, Kate kicked off her flops and ran to the kitchen. As she was told, Johnny was diligently working on plating a meal for the ladies. He scooped some chicken salad out of a bowl and placed it on a piece of fresh lettuce. Next to the chicken was a biscuit, a deviled egg, and fruit salad in a small glass cup.

"Kate," her mother called from the dining room, "go wash up and come sit with us."

After washing her hands, she sat down on one of Jammy's elegant needlepoint chair covers and sat on her hands to keep herself from touching the shiny silver setting. A bouquet made of black-eyed Susans and white gladioli sat in the center, and next to it a silver butter dish, a small crystal bowl filled with fig jam, and a silver salt and pepper set.

"The rain from the squall last week really brought on the flowers," said Jammy while casually reaching over and adjusting them in the vase.

Johnny arrived from the kitchen holding two plates.

"Matriarchs first," he said while placing plates in front of Jammy and Mary. He then skipped back to the kitchen and returned with Kate's plate. Hers had more chicken salad than Jammy's and Mary's, as Johnny had noticed she had been extra hungry this summer. Kate lifted her fork and was glared at by her mothers. She placed it back where it belonged and folded her hands to pray.

"Dear Lord," Mary began, "thank you for this beautiful day you have made and for the time spent with family. We are grateful for all the paths you create for us to walk. Thank you for this delicious meal and the cook who prepared it. Amen."

"Amen," the three said in unison, followed by a loud "Amen!" that escaped from the kitchen.

Kate placed her napkin in her lap. It was a thing of beauty. Fine linen, edged with a hand-stitched garden, not unlike the garden that circled Kate's yellow sundress.

"Jammy, did you stitch these napkins?"

"Why yes, I did."

"They are very pretty," said Kate.

Jammy smiled and picked up her fork, and with all napkins lining the ladies' laps, they began to enjoy the meal set before them. Kate said very little while Jammy and Mary talked about the events of the morning. She was very hungry and didn't even look up from her plate until she was halfway finished. She eyed Johnny peeking around the kitchen corner, and when she saw him, he quickly disappeared.

"I think our cook would like some feedback, ladies," said Mary.

"Johnny!" Jammy called.

He arrived with an iced tea pitcher in hand and refilled their glasses.

"Johnny," said Mary, "this chicken salad is excellent."

"Yes," said Jammy, "and the fruit is very fresh and sweet."

Mary and Jammy then looked poignantly at Kate, letting her know it was her turn to compliment the cook.

"Johnny, I like the biscuits," she said, making Jammy, Mary, and Johnny very pleased.

When the ladies finished, Johnny cleared their plates and Kate was told to change into shorts and a t-shirt for their next adventure.

All three ladies headed out the back door to the bikes while Johnny cleaned the kitchen. They rode briskly through town, waving at people they knew. They rode by the park that was filled with many blankets. Wind blew from the river through the park and cooled the three ladies.

"Quite breezy today!" Mary yelled to the others as she steadied the handlebars.

Keeping up the pace, they headed out of town to a long stretch of road and turned down Cemetery Lane.

Kate had been to the cemetery many times before, but just like the places they had already visited that day, she had a feeling she would learn something new. Many found the cemetery to be a scary and foreboding place, but the Seth women didn't feel bothered by it in any way. They felt at ease there. The quietness, the green grass, willows, sycamores, locusts, and persimmons that clung to the banks anchored the land and created a retreat for the mind. It was a place of tribute.

Into the afternoon, the wind continued to blow the heat away and cool the sweat off the brows of the peninsula inhabitants. Arriving at the wrought iron gate marking the graveyard, wet with perspiration, the wind cooled them as they pedaled down the lane.

The gate was always left open, most likely because no one knew where the key was nor cared about looking for it. There was, after all, nothing to steal in a cemetery except time away from the rest of the world.

Once entering, the long lane laid before them was flanked on each side by aging cedars and, where the river met the land, phragmites and cattails. At the end of the lane, the land opened up to a widely expansive acreage of meadowland. Two stately holly trees propagated by one of the town ladies long ago greeted them at what was the second entrance. The first stones they saw were of the oldest inhabitants, and those that were wealthy enough to afford a marker.

Across the way lay a noticeable empty space amongst a field of stones. God only knows the number of souls buried without a tombstone, and many years ago the keepers of the cemetery dedicated the area by naming it "Strangers Row." Still, there was no marker, but many knew this area was set aside for the unknown that drowned off a skipjack or simply had no money for a grave.

Their bikes slowed just past "Strangers Row" and stopped right in front of the family plot. Kate knew the spot well and wandered over.

"Tell me about Poppy," she said, looking at Mary.

"He was very well-liked in the town, very friendly, and respected, not because he had money but because he was smart about business and also kind. His hobby was to grow poppies for the flower shop, that is how he got his nickname."

Kate smiled. It made her feel warm inside thinking of her great-grandfather tending to his poppies and treating people well. Mary pointed to some stones to the left of the family graves.

"These stones belong to your great-grandmother's family."

She walked over and put her hand on the largest one.

"This is your great-grandfather times three. He was the Captain of four ships in his lifetime. He was born in England and sailed his ships all over the world bringing back citrus fruits, coffee, and linens to America."

"You mean the one with the spyglass?" interjected Kate.

"That's the one!" Mary replied. She then pointed to a much smaller stone. "This is your great-grandmother's little sister, Nora, who died when she was three. She and I have the same birthday."

Kate felt instantly sad. "What did she die of?"

"I don't know for sure," said Mary, "...but I believe it was typhoid fever."

"What's that?"

"It's an illness caused by contaminated food and or water," Mary explained. "Our food and water is much safer than it used to be."

Mary then walked behind the family plot to a set of much older brittle white marble stones that were surrounded by boxwoods.

"Here's some more of your family," she said, touching a stone of a man named "Issac."

Kate looked at the dates on the stone and did some math in her head.

"He only lived to be 27?"

"Yes, he drowned."

Kate again felt a wave of sadness flow through her.

"Do you remember the model of the Methodist church we saw at the museum today?" Kate thought back on the day, "Yes!"

"Well, he made that," replied Mary.

"Issac did?"

"Yes," replied Mary.

Kate touched the stone. Although it felt cold, internally a warmness filled her, knowing a little more about the man that lay beneath it. Sensing Kate's stamina for sad tales was waning, Mary started walking towards the shoreline, and Kate followed quickly behind, leaving Jammy some quiet time to weed around Walton's stone.

She looked up and down the shoreline from the gangplank that extended from the top of the bank out to an old, dilapidated Skipjack. High tide made the periwinkles happy while resting on the tippy tops of the stones as the cool river water lapped over them. The blue clay bank was strewn with so many interesting objects: oyster shells, broken sea glass smoothed from years of river washing, driftwood, pebbles, and crab sheds.

Mary stood on the deck of the old lady. Abandoned many years ago, the skipjack "Evelyn" barely looked like a vessel at all. Once fit enough to ride the winds and haul the catch, she, like so many other skipjacks, had succumbed to the lashings of the very river she once tamed.

"De-masted and left for dead," Mary said while standing midships.

"It's a shame about it all, the whole business."

"What business?"

"The oyster business, Kate, it was boom and bust, and this old Skipjack was a casualty." Kate wandered the deck carefully, noting the rot and rust. Its anchor chain dangled off the bow to starboard. Its rudder had rusted off its gudgeons, fallen, and lay in the river mud, rotting away.

"What happened to the anchor?" asked Kate.

"No need for one when you run the boat ashore to die; they took it and used it on another boat for sure. Don't know why they left the chain; that can be reused too. They usually stripped almost all the metal off of an old boat to use on another," Mary explained.

Kate thought about it. "So the anchor from this boat is most likely being used on another?"

"Probably."

While the beam of the old boat was still sturdy enough to stand on, the bow and transom were so rotten they dared not go too forward or aft. Kate peeked through the cracked window of the Captain's cabin. It was mostly empty except for some old beer cans floating around inside it.

Before they turned to leave, Mary pointed out an old piling in Cemetery Cove.

"See that piling, Kate?" Kate nodded. "Well, your cousins spent the night in their boat tied to that during a hurricane, which they figured was the safest place to be."

"Was it?" Kate asked.

"Turned out it was, their house got flooded."

"Which cousins?" Kate asked.

"Cousin Jack and Betsy, the ones that live in the rancher at the other end of town near the laboratory. They have that dog Tag that everyone loves so much."

"Oh yeah," said Kate. "I know who you mean. Mom, how do you keep track of all the cousins?"

"Well, that's a funny thing, Kate. There are cousins spelled with a "s" and there are couzins spelled with a "z." The cousin spelled with an "s" in the middle is a blood relation and the one spelled with a "z" in the middle is a friend as close as family, but not related. It is hard to keep it straight. In the end, we are all couzins with a z, do you follow?"

"I think so; we're all family, just some of us are related by blood?"

"Yes."

Jammy had finished weeding around the family stones and stood at the foot of the gangplank. "Anything interesting out there?"

"Nah," said Kate, "it's rotting away."

"It is sad to watch it go. Someday the gangplank won't be there, and the skipjack will just be a memory," said Jammy.

Kate couldn't imagine it gone, and the water and waves continuing on like it had never been there in the first place. It was difficult to think that far ahead so she shrugged her shoulders and followed Mary as she stepped off the gangplank and onto the grassy land. The three ladies walked a little farther along the bank until they came to a grove of blackberries.

"This is one of the things that I hope never changes!" Kate said with enthusiasm as she picked away at the ripe, shiny blackberries.

"They are delicious," remarked Mary.

Jammy was too busy feasting to say anything but smiled and plucked the berries from their thorny branches one by one. They ate and ate until Kate felt almost sick.

"I guess we should stop," said Mary, "and leave some for the birds."

"So true," agreed Jammy, and they headed for their bikes.

The ride home for Kate was a contemplative one. The cemetery was many things, life and death, but it also brought her comfort knowing the stories of her ancestors. She pedaled hard while against the wind, and as she exerted herself she could feel a thirst well up inside and her mouth go dry. Once home, they parked their bikes and headed inside to the kitchen for a tall glass of iced tea, where they were greeted by Edison.

"I was wondering where you ladies got off to," he said smiling. "Beings it's Ladies' Day, I'd like to treat you to dinner from Leo's Place."

Mary's face had a stunned look to it. Jammy was speechless and Kate began to dance.

Mary broke the silence, "Oh! That would be wonderful, Edison!" she exclaimed as she gave him a hug.

"Yes, Edison, what a kind gesture," Jammy added.

Kate began frantically looking through the kitchen drawers for the menu.

"Found it!" She thrust the menu skyward with unchecked emotion as if the world had been put on its haunches for this singular pivotal event.

The Seth house ate out from a restaurant no more than twice a year, and so the women, who did almost all the cooking, were ecstatic. Something in the air akin to electricity flowed through all three ladies, and a long, intense discussion ensued over what they should order.

"Crab cakes? Stuffed Shrimp? Fried chicken?"

They discussed options fervently among themselves while hunched over the menu.

"How about all three?" interjected Edison.

Jammy asked Edison if he had lost his mind while Mary and Kate stood staring at him with mouths open.

"I'm serious," he said. "Let's get some of each, and we will share."

He didn't have to repeat himself, and the ladies quickly moved on to the side dishes, to which they reached their decision much more quickly.

"Coleslaw and french fries."

To which Edison added, "Corn muffins?"

"Yes!" they replied in unison.

Johnny, who had just returned home from a bike ride, arrived upon this scene of unhinged excess and had watched from the kitchen doorway without anyone noticing. He added, "Iced tea; we have to have the iced tea."

All four heads turned towards him and nodded. The sweet iced tea that flowed from the restaurant was perhaps its most famous item on the menu. The crushed ice it swam in made it a cool nectar of sorts. It wasn't too sweet, but hit that spot on your tongue that made you want to guzzle it down and immediately ask for more.

Up until now, Kate had been distracted from her intense thirst that had struck her on the bike ride home. She went to the sink and drew a large glass of water from the faucet and guzzled it down. Meanwhile, Mary had picked up the phone to call in the order. She dialed four numbers and was connected.

With the order called in, the ladies, who every other day of the year would normally be making dinner preparations, suddenly had extra time. Kate and Jammy settled in for a gin rummy lesson, and Mary went upstairs to read. Johnny and Edison went outside to work on some projects until it was time to pick up the meal. Kate's stomach began to grumble and roll the closer it got to dinner time.

All she could think about was the fried chicken, which was her favorite, but she also liked everything they ordered.

When the six o'clock bells were imminent, Jammy and Kate put their cards away and set the table. Mary came down the steps at the same time Johnny and Edison walked in the back screen door with dinner. The feast was taken out of the paper bags and placed in the center of the table. Jammy got a basket for the corn muffins and a pitcher for the gallon of iced tea. Kate handed out the napkins, and everyone helped themselves to whatever they liked.

An early silence spoke an epistle to the meal. They ate with zeal and were so happy sharing their day's adventures with Johnny and Edison that the ladies never noticed that Lowell did not join them. But Edison did.

Chapter XIII

— July's Quill —

The moon began its timely surrender to the light of day, melting like butter and blending in with the bright and creamy arrival of daylight. The stinging eyes of whom the sun's first flashes would awaken begot the day in a sweat; a precursor to July's final wrath. But the watermen took it in stride as they did every summer.

The heat ran amok, filling every corner of the screened porches, the crevices and crannies of shaded pantries, the north-facing bedrooms and every bit of grassy ground under the canopy of the willows. The humidity infiltrated so thoroughly that no respite nor reprieve could be found anywhere, as it suffocated the town until not even the coldest of ice teas could stir workers on. The days carried on as warm as steamed pudding and smothered the town with an insufferable lethargy that could only be relieved by ice cream and the joy of watching children run through sprinklers. The dog days of summer had arrived, and so had Edison's ambrosia cantaloupes.

Cantaloupes weren't the only thing ripe in Edison's garden. Late July would bring a flood of tomatoes, more squash, cucumbers, wax beans, honeydews, blackberries, patty pans, and eggplants. But the cantaloupes by far were held above all else like a scepter, and Edison could be seen any morning in late July and early August holding a ripe golden fleshed melon up to the sun as if he was offering it to the gods.

Today, Edison was up with the sun and woke Kate up too.

"It's time, Miss Kate, I need your help in the garden."

Kate wiped the dry crust from her eyes, dressed quickly and as she sat at the table eating, the sting of the eastern sun slit her eyes like a jagged oyster shell, rough and painful.

"Eat up," Edison said, as he opened the back screened door. "I want to get some melons picked before the heat gets worse."

Kate sat in front of a cold bowl of cereal, one hand holding a spoon, and the other her sleepy head. She didn't care for getting up this early, but it was one of the few times in the year that Edison had her up at dawn. His excitement was akin to a child's on Christmas Day, and she dared not interrupt his good feelings. She finished her cereal and put her bowl in the sink. Remembering the cutting glares of the morning sun, she grabbed her baseball cap and some sunglasses and walked out to Edison's shed, waving hello to Herman the frog on the way. Edison saw her coming and grabbed his wheelbarrow. Kate opened the gate for him and they were on their way to his garden to harvest melons.

"I've been looking," he said while they walked, "and I think there may be at least a dozen or more ripe for today."

Kate, still groggy, muttered a faint "uh-huh."

The cicadas were so loud that Edison didn't hear her and repeated himself.

"Uh-huh," she said with more oomph. The birds were just as noisy as the cicada, but at least their songs were unique; the cicada drone the same old tune.

Mr. Tawes was not yet at his post, so they slipped by, and upon arrival, Kate grabbed the long shiny aluminum pole that lived right next to the compost pile. Edison called it "the melon detector." They took turns using the pole, pulling the leaves away from the fruits to find the ripe melons. It looked like they had about 13 ambrosia, three honey dews, and one sugar baby watermelon to pick. The Crenshaw melons were green and needed more time on the vine. They started on the southern side near the compost pile.

Edison used the pole to make a path for Kate. Some steps were on the stump posts that rose just above the foliage, and other steps had to be taken on the ground, staying clear of the sensitive vines. Kate learned at a young age that an injured vine could not give water to a melon that thirsted for it.

Once she had steadied herself, she reached down, and for the ambrosias, if the fruit was easily plucked from the vine and it was a golden color, it was ripe. Once picked, she would lob the 5-pound fruits towards Edison who would catch them as if they were china dolls and place them gingerly in his wheelbarrow. The honeydews and watermelons needed a knife to cut them from the vines and when Kate reached their patch, Edison threw her his pocket knife, and she sliced the vines and again tossed the melons carefully to her father. This was the third year he let her toss. Johnny used to help, but now that she was eleven, the whole job fell on her to pick and toss.

Midway through picking, Edison commented, "Kate, ever thought about softball pitching? You've got a great underhand arm."

Kate grinned half-heartedly. When the last ripe melon was picked, they took mental notes on what was going to ripen next.

"Two days from now we will have more for sure," Edison said, while lighting a cigarette. Meanwhile, Kate had already hopped two stumps over to feast on the shiny blackberries that covered the west fence. Edison looked the Steuben grapes over and lightly squeezed to test them.

"Looks like the grapes will be ready in about a week or so."

Kate nodded, swallowed her blackberries, and jumped back to the center path by hopping on the exposed trunks to see the grapes for herself. She popped one in her mouth and grimaced.

"They're so tart!"

"That's 'cause they're not ripe yet."

"Well," Kate said, "they're not a favorite of mine when they are ripe anyway."

"That's why your mother makes them into jam and Mr. Paul makes them into wine."

"I didn't know Mr. Paul made wine; I thought it was just beer," Kate said.

"Nope, he makes them both and drinks them both," Edison chuckled. "Come on, Kate, it's getting hot."

They saw Mr. Paul across the street and waved. Edison went right over to his fence, and Mr. Paul met him and took the fruit from Edison with a big smile.

"Thank you, Edison, is this the first?"

"Sure is!" he answered proudly. "By the way," he said, looking backwards as they moved on, "those grapes will be ready next week!"

Mr. Paul smiled from ear to ear.

Feeling sweaty, Kate noticed the locusts were louder, the sun was higher, and it felt like everything had a fever. Kate was glad she didn't have to push the wheelbarrow, overflowing with melons. Edison left them under a tree in the shade just outside the gate, and if history repeated, he was going inside to get a nice shirt and begin his complimentary melon journey throughout the neighborhood. This ritual was Edison's holiday, perhaps his happiest day of the year.

Kate flopped in a wicker chair on the outside porch and wiped the beaded water from her brow with dirty hands. Mary came outside and sat next to her.

"How many?"

"I think 17 all together," Kate said, while slumping in her chair and looking uneasy.

Mary looked at Kate oddly.

"Kate, are you feeling alright?"

"I guess?" Kate said, with little confidence. Sitting up, the world started to turn faster than she liked, and Mary put the back of her hand on Kate's forehead.

"Hmmm… I think you've got a fever."

She left and returned with a thermometer. Kate's world began to stretch out around her as if it were made of silly putty. The backyard expanded to an undisclosed eternity, and her head felt as heavy as an anchor on her shoulders.

"101, yep, it's your annual summer fever," said Mary. "Best you have a cool glass of water and take a nap."

Mary didn't have to coax Kate to bed; she knew the routine by heart. Every summer she got a fever for a day or two or swimmers' ear. She was glad it was the fever, as they disappeared much more quickly than the swimmers' ear. Johnny had his own summer maladies; he would either come down with a wicked case of poison ivy or thrush.

After downing a glass of cool water, she stumbled upstairs. Passing by Jammy's room, she saw her grandmother engrossed in a missive or perhaps poetry. Either way, she was too involved in getting her thoughts on paper to notice Kate slink by. Too tired to even stop and tell Jammy she had a fever, she flopped on her bed and closed her eyes. She didn't like the distorted view of her room and hoped sleep would come quickly, and it did.

MEANWHILE, EDISON BEGAN HIS SUMMER pilgrimage to give everyone he knew a sweet ambrosia cantaloupe. He picked through his pile and removed any that might have a crack or small hole created by a hungry cricket and brought them into the house for the family to eat; he only delivered perfect specimens. With his wheelbarrow full of prizes, he went to see cousin Sally first. Laying the handles of his wheelbarrow down in front of her house, he was immediately greeted by Sally, heading out her front door to her job uptown at the grocery store. "Oh, thank you, Edison," she said, smiling as she took the melon from him and laid it on the porch chair next to her.

"How are you and Lowell getting along?" inquired Edison.

"He's trying, I know that," said Sally, "… he even joined us for dinner last night and did the dishes."

Edison's eyes flashed a bright blue with surprise. "Well, we pray he stays on the right path."

"Me too," said Sally, "and I can't thank you enough for letting him stay at your place until he sorts himself out."

"That's what family does," Edison replied. "Where's Justin and Anna?"

"My mother is watching them for the summer while I work."

With his investigation complete, Edison turned to leave.

"Do you think he is off the bottle?" Sally asked.

"Can't say for sure, time will tell," said Edison, as he picked up his wheelbarrow and headed next door to see Miss Ginny.

Tansy came to visit and was disappointed that Kate had gone to bed, so she went on her way to check on Squawk alone. Mid-afternoon, Mary went up to check on Kate and Mother as well, as she had not seen her all day. She poked her head in the door and saw Jammy intently focused on her writing. From the past, Mary knew this to be a sign, as if somehow Jammy knew luck and misfortune had seasons and the weather was changing.

"Mother, what's on your mind?"

"Something's afoot," was all she said as she waved Mary away.

Mary left her to her craft and poked her head into Kate's room. Kate had awoken a few moments earlier with a dry mouth. "Come have some rice and cool water," Mary said. Kate sat up, woozy but willing to quench her thirst. She pulled herself up and steadied her gait.

Downstairs, Mary had made a small bowl of buttered rice and a piece of toast for Kate. She drank the water down first and Mary got her a second cup. The salted rice tasted so good to Kate along with the buttered toast. Following her small meal, she was sent upstairs again with water in hand and told to lie down and read a comic book. This time she stopped at Jammy's door.

"Did you know I have a fever?"

"Yes," said Jammy clearly involved in her manuscript. She turned to Kate, "You'll be alright in a day or two, Kate, you can count on that."

She then turned back to her writing, and Kate lay back down with "Casper the Friendly Ghost" and read for a while until the weight of her eyelids overwhelmed her and she fell back into the deepest of slumbers.

⚓ ⚓ ⚓

THE FIRE SIREN HOLLERED ON and off with a ceaseless urgency that would have made drowned sailors swim again. Kate awoke, jumped out of bed, and walked the upstairs hall, finding no one in their rooms. Johnny's and Jammy's rooms were empty. Down three steps to mother and father's empty room made her want to knock on Cousin Lowell's door, but there was no need. His door, too, hung open, and his room was vacant, but a glow emanated from his bedside window, so Kate took a few steps towards the light. Once in full view of the window, the light was so strong it made her eyes squint at first. She took a step back and then was drawn forward again as she saw with horror Miss Ginny's boatyard aflame.

Sparks were so high they devoured the darkness of the night

sky. Bright coals supplanted its base. The whole town was aglow, suffused in the angry color of a hungry fire feeding on wooden boats. Hurrying down the steps and striking the screen door with speed and vigor, she ran towards the backs of her family leaning against the fence. Her pace slowed as she counted only two figures; three were missing.

The heat instantly flushed her face as she screamed above the whistles, "Mom!"

Mary turned around as Kate worked the gate latch. "Kate! Miss Ginny's boatyard!"

Kate ran to her mother's arms, and Mary's nightshirt shielded her from the madness, if only for a breath.

"Where's Johnny, and Father, and Cousin Lowell?" She yelled to her mother through the abrasive noises.

Mary yelled back, "They've gone to help with the fire; there's not enough firemen, everyone is helping, they've called other towns to come help."

The longer they stood there digesting the scene, the hotter Kate felt, and not just on the outside. There was a burning inside of her, a gnawing in her stomach, a pain in her throat, and a sting in her heart.

"Mom, where's Miss Ginny?"

"She's safe at home, Kate. She's in her house. She cannot watch. Pastor George is with her now."

"Is anyone hurt?" Kate yelled.

"I don't know, all we can do is look to the heavens and pray."

Jammy was already looking up at the night sky in prayer—it had a much higher ceiling than the house.

Another fire engine arrived from the closest town and dropped its hoses into the river with water pumps churning. Plumes of green river water rose above and through the flames in all directions. Trucks on the south side and north side of the boat shed were joined by a tanker that pulled onto Miss Ginny's empty lot at the corner, driving into the middle of it, squaring its sides with the fire. Burly men with bunker gear hauled a long hose to the inferno, aiming it at the hungry fire. Once the sheer number of hoses had overwhelmed the blaze, it receded to its embers quickly as if scolded by the river.

The sky was hinting at dawn when the fire was considered out. As the flames shrank under the river water tossed at it, hundreds of residents, one by one, confident the danger was controlled, returned to their homes. Few went back to bed. The fire company ladies' auxiliary had started preparing food in the middle of the night to feed the men when they returned to the firehouse. Many auxiliary members were also members of the Methodist ladies' circle, Mary and Jammy included.

Mr. Truman opened his store up early and Miss Ginny bought him out of bread and potatoes, which he sold to her at cost. The eggs he gave freely, as they came from a farm owned by one of the volunteer firemen. By the time the boat house was nothing but a steamy pile of gnarled wreckage, the sun had come up and the men headed to the firehouse for a breakfast to satisfy the hungriest of embattled firemen. Scrambled eggs, French toast, home fries, buttered grits, two donated hams, and a half dozen of Edison's juicy sliced melons made for a thankful breakfast.

Pastor George led a grace and prayer for two of the men who had succumbed to smoke inhalation but had been treated readily by the ambulance crew and were able to enjoy the breakfast the ladies had prepared.

The quiet of a raw hunger was only interrupted by the clanging of coffee cups as the auxiliary ladies kept the mugs full. Satiated bellies were followed by a lengthy discussion by the boatyard foreman and fireman as to how the fire started, and no one knew for sure, although there were some wild theories to keep the town buzzing for weeks until the Fire Marshal finished his investigation.

What they did know from Mr. Charley, who called the fire in, was that the fire started quietly. As he recounted to the men, little

Tommy, who lived behind him, ran into his house at the edge of dark in a state of worry about what he had seen from his bedroom window while his parents were out on a walk. Little Tommy, who was only six, knew Mr. Charley to be a fireman, and Tommy would later be recognized by the town officially at a town meeting, making his parents justifiably proud of his reporting the flames he saw.

Whether Kate's fever had burned itself out or the emotional toll from the fire had knocked it out of her, it felt gone. She had joined the women at the firehouse in the early morning hours and was set to the task of washing and peeling potatoes. Tansy joined the ladies, too, and was given the job of cracking eggs into a very large bucket. While they worked, Tansy reported that she had checked on Squawk and that her full feathers were almost in, and she was definitely a girl according to Miss Pat. This came as no surprise to either of them, as Kate had been emphatic from the first time she saw the little duckling that it was female.

"We went to the beach and there were other ducks there," Tansy began her story. "I thought she might leave with them when they swam off, but she stayed with me."

"Did the other ducks like her?" Kate asked.

"They didn't dislike her, but they also didn't pay much attention, and Squawk kept her distance."

Kate, while glad Squawk hadn't left yet, expressed concern about her future. "What if she doesn't go with the other ducks soon?"

Tansy countered, "Then I guess she'll be our pet duck forever."

When the breakfast was over, the girls dried the dishes along with some of the other children in town who had also come with a parent to help.

"You are our future," announced one of the older ladies to the young pack as they were nearly finished up.

"Yes," Miss Tessie chimed in. "Someday you all will be in charge of such occasions." She smiled and winked at Kate.

Kate had never thought of herself as a grown-up or even pondered what that might be like, and for now, she liked not being in charge of "such occasions."

Miss Lucille invited the girls back to her house when the work was done. "I have something I think you two will enjoy," she said with a smile. They left their bikes by the back fence and ignored the croquet set calling to them. On Miss Lucille's back porch lay her fat white cat sleeping in her indoor hammock.

Tansy commented, "Jack, you sleep too much!"

The cat slit his eyes and rolled over. Miss Lucille had set out goose feathers on her porch table and some small whittling knives.

"Have a seat, girls, I am going to show you how to make a quill."

Intrigued by the craft presented to them, they took their seats and watched intently while Miss Lucille took one of the knives and cut the pointy end of the feather into a triangular shape. Then, she slit the end ever so carefully down the middle. The girls followed her example, and soon Miss Lucille was demonstrating how to dip the quill into the ink and write on linen paper. She made it look easy. Throughout the afternoon, they created all kinds of fun designs and elegant-looking words. As they sat immersed in their new found art, Kate could not help but be distracted by the smell of burnt wood in the air. By late afternoon, Tansy kicked "Fat Jack" out of the hammock and jumped in it herself, tired from an extremely early morning.

Kate headed home, also feeling drained and walked her bike, waving at Miss Charlotte, who was out in her yard doing some light gardening.

"Quite a day for the town, wouldn't you say, Miss Kate?"

"For sure," answered Kate, while covering up a big yawn.

"My cats haven't come out from under the house since the whistle blew…"

Kate perked up and offered to help coax them out.

"You would be a doll if they come," Miss Charlotte said happily.

Kate found herself on her knees in the same spot after the squall a few weeks ago, calling for the cats. "Everham! Maisy!"

Their eyes darted back and forth in the same fashion as before. Kate stood up and brushed her knees off.

"They are saying no again like last time."

She turned her back to the house to tell Miss Charlotte the cats didn't want to come out and noticed Miss Charlotte begin to giggle. Kate looked down to see the cats weaving in and out of her legs and meowing.

"They like you, Kate, you got them out, thank you!"

Kate smiled, "Sure thing, Miss Charlotte." She skipped to her bike, walked it to her gate, and took it inside the fence. Mary came out the back door and called for her. Kate bounced up the sidewalk and around the pond, her energy renewed by her successful extraction of the cats.

She entered the kitchen to see Mary in quite a rush.

"I am so glad to see you, Kate. I am late to my ladies' circle at the church. We're meeting later than usual because of the breakfast for the firemen this morning."

Kate was poised for a job. Mary pointed to a cooked chicken that had been recently pulled from the oven. She handed Kate two pot holders.

"Can you please run this to Mr. Paul? It's cooled down some, but take these oven mitts." Kate took the protection and grabbed the chicken. Mary opened the back door and followed her to the gate, opening that as well.

"If you don't see him in the yard, just go to the back door and call to him."

"Okay," replied Kate, as she headed up the street, roasted chicken in hand.

The chicken didn't seem so heavy when she left the house but the closer she got to Mr. Paul's, the heavier it got. Thankfully, his fence was open, as usual, swinging in a breeze that had just piped up. She didn't see him in the yard, so she headed for the screened door, it also ajar. Standing in the porch she yelled through the second screen door into the house for him.

"Mr. Paul? Mr. Paul?"

There was no answer, only the onset of an uneasiness Kate had never felt before. Her head began to spin, and instantaneously she felt an absolute darkness emanating from inside the house; it felt as if it would swallow her whole.

"Mr. Paul!" she yelled, straining her voice.

Both the air and the chicken were excruciatingly heavy and quite warm, yet she began to shiver. Anxious to put the chicken down, she pushed through the screen door to lay the chicken on his stove, as its weight had become unbearable. Her eyes pulled away from the stove to the dirty countertop, and her sight followed a black mold that covered the kitchen walls and looked as if it had started on the floor and traveled to the ceiling in fingerlike paths. Struck in an instant that she should not be there and missing the stove entirely, the chicken fell from her hands and splattered all over the dirt floor, covering her foot in hot, fatty broth.

Kate screamed and bolted out both doors to the lawn, where she wiped her feet in the grass to get the hot liquid off her. She ran to the ditch and plunged her foot into the dirty, murky water to cool it. She pulled her foot out, and despite it glowing red, she ran as fast as she could home with a lump in her throat and uncontrollable tears dropping precipitously from her blue eyes onto the hot street she ran on.

She got to the gate and Edison, who had heard a wildness coming his way, was shocked to see it was Kate. Johnny too was stunned at what he saw on his sister's face.

"What happened?" they asked in unison, solely focused on Kate.

Kate started heaving as though she would throw up.

"Johnny, get her some water!" Edison barked at him.

Johnny returned with a glass, and she drank the water down,

spitting and sputtering the last of it out and falling on the cold mill-stone precipice of the gate. She pointed up the street. Edison and Johnny surmised something dreadful must have happened.

"Something up the street?" asked Johnny.

Kate shook her head yes. Edison barked at Johnny again, "Go call Chief Duncan! By the time he gets here, we will hopefully have figured this out."

Johnny ran off to the house again, and Edison focused on Kate.

"Did someone hurt you? Cause I'll kill the bastard myself, bare handed."

Kate shook her head no.

"Okay, good. Then what did you see?"

Kate began rocking back and forth and shaking her head no. Edison backed off, hoping she would calm down enough by the time Duncan arrived. She began to shiver and Edison yelled to Johnny to bring a blanket.

By this time, Miss Charlotte had heard the commotion and sprinted to the Seth's backyard. She stood near the back gate, watching.

"Kate," she said softly, "What has happened?"

Edison turned towards Miss Charlotte with fiery eyes, but they softenend when Kate reached her hand out to Miss Charlotte, and she walked cautiously closer. Edison calmed his expression, and the two of them stood together watching Kate suffer under the strain of recent events. Johnny put a blanket over her shoulders and stood back with the other two. Kate's breathing slowed, and just as Duncan showed up, she said, "Something is wrong at Mr. Paul's house."

Miss Charlotte came and sat next to her and put her arms around her while Duncan, Edison, and Johnny ran up the street.

Standing outside the house, Duncan called, "Mr. Paul?"

No answer. Duncan told the Seth men to wait outside while he went cautiously inside, his hand on his gun. There was a stillness in the house, an emptiness that gave him the shivers.

He shook it off and called again, "Mr. Paul!"

Duncan stepped over the chicken, but he didn't smell chicken. Instead, he smelled the ugliness of nothingness and he knew what that smell meant. Sadness befell him as he stood on the threshold to the living room and put his gun back in its holster. Mr. Paul lay dead in an armchair with an empty liquor bottle on the floor at his swollen feet.

⚓ ⚓ ⚓

MISS CHARLOTTE HAD HER ARMS around Kate's back as she sat on the cold millstone, shivering and crying. Her sobs had calmed to quiet tears when Jammy and Mary returned from the church meeting. They both came out the back door, and as if on broomsticks, they sailed smoothly through the backyard at quite a clip. Mary put her hand on Charlotte in thanks.

Jammy hugged Kate and then sat across from her and looked into her wet, troubled eyes.

"What happened?" she asked softly.

Kate repeated what she had said to the men. "Something is wrong at Mr. Paul's house." "Did anybody hurt you?"

"No."

"What did you see?"

Kate cleared her throat and wiped her eyes. "I didn't see anything. It was so cold and dark and empty in his house; I'm not sure what it was…." She paused. "….Mr. Paul wasn't there, I know that."

The three women stood silent, looking at Kate and thinking about what she had said. Miss Charlotte commented that Edison and Johnny were headed their way, and soon they all knew what was wrong at Mr. Paul's house. Kate had felt death, and it scared her.

Dinner was quiet; everyone ate sparingly, picking at their plates carefully with their forks, and Kate sat with an ice pack on her foot. When Aunt Tessie had learned of Kate's fever, she had sent her mini Jello molds with marshmallows, and that lifted everyone's spirits; Jello from Tessie had a way of doing that. Exhausted from the long day, Edison and Mary didn't take their walk, Johnny cancelled his date, and Kate headed upstairs to lie down. She passed by Jammy's room, and again she was sharply focused on her writing, but paused.

"Kate, come here."

Kate walked over, and Jammy gave her a hug.

"Don't be too afraid. Death is a natural end to our worldly life. Paul is with Anna now." Kate hadn't thought about how happy Paul would be in Heaven, and it lifted her spirits tremendously.

"Thanks, Jammy, I never thought of it that way. I'll bet she made him brownies."

Jammy smiled. "You sensed Mr. Paul was no longer in his house because he was already in Heaven."

Kate smiled again. She loved Jammy so much that she hugged her twice. She got ready for bed and pulled down the covers. A poem lay on her pillow from Jammy. With a rush, it reminded her of how the long day began.

Sailmaker's Tears

Sail unstuffed from duffle dry
Wetted with salty spray, briny to the nose,
Raised daily to the sky.

Shield to the wind, its capture divine
I draw you in and hold you close
Our tethered frolic, sails the line.

Away from the water, fire swallowed you whole
With no time to cry,
Flames in the sky.

No more windwards,
Tacks nor beams,
Sails fly upwards in a dream.

⚓ ⚓ ⚓

THE DAY FOLLOWING THE FIRE, the town was abuzz with current events. Miss Ginny, grateful the firemen had contained the fire to just one of the boatyard sheds, set about to personally thank each and every fireman. If she didn't catch them at the firehouse, she proceeded to knock on their doors to express her thanks. After a town incident, it was common for its inhabitants to bring donation checks to the firehouse treasurer. It was so predictable that it became customary, and although a donation of any size was as equally appreciated as the next, those that didn't contribute were only those that didn't have a penny to spare. Their financial condition was in no way discussed, disclosed, or looked down upon. The families with less were the ones that often gave their time to the town churches and firehouse.

After a few days of relative tranquility, the town residents dusted themselves off and dressed in their finest summer attire for Mr. Paul's send-off. Kate had been to many funerals before; it seemed there was always somebody in town they knew that was sent home to be with the Lord. She found such events stressful, terribly sad and they made her weary. The Seth family walked up the street and arrived to find everyone waiting outside the church and visiting.

While also Methodist, Mr. Paul attended a different church in town than the Seths. At Mr. Paul's church, the ladies wore colorful clothes, and the choir was loud and lively. Kate liked all the vibrant, bright hats that stood atop the ladies' heads, making the women easy to spot.

Mary quickly spotted Miss Thelma, her childhood friend, who wore a butter yellow hat with wide brims.

"Mary! I am so glad you came," she said extending her arm for a sideways hug amongst the tight crowd.

"I wouldn't miss it; I have been praying for Paul for so long now."

The conversation faded into the background when Kate caught sight of Kimmy at the same time she caught a glimpse of Kate. They ran into each other's arms, laughing and then fell on the ground in their dresses. Kate looked up and saw Jammy glaring at her.

She turned to her friend, "We probably shouldn't roll around in dresses."

Kimmy giggled. "My grandma looks really mad at me, too."

She waved to her grandma across the lawn. Her seething look could have spontaneously set the dry grass to flame. They got up and dusted themselves off just as the minister appeared in the doorway.

"Let us all proceed into the church to celebrate the life of our friend Paul."

The outside gathering, one by one, entered the church and found seating. The benches were just like the benches in Kate's church, and she sat down sliding on the deep brown varnished wood until she was in the middle of the row next to Kimmy. Kate looked about the church. She hadn't visited it in a while but it was just as she remembered. She looked up to see the numbers for the hymn book on the wall next to the pulpit just like in her church.

Reverend Green wore a long white robe with a braided rope around his waist and a creamy-colored stole around his neck with hand-sewn light green needlepoint crosses; he looked very dignified. The windows behind him were a shimmery light purple and Kate wondered if she was tall enough to see right through them if truths would be waiting on the other side. Their clairvoyant color made the windows look like entrances to heaven above.

"We will begin with a hymn," the minister announced, and Kate and Kimmy quickly thumbed through the pages of the red-bound hymnal so they could sing along. The organist played an opening wordless verse as the choir stood up.

"Amazing Grace" started out with a slow and strong solo by a large jolly looking woman who, Kate could tell, sang with a depth of emotion she had not seen since last visiting this church. One by one, choir members joined in and eventually, the congregation, until the hymn was so strong, so alive and deeply heartfelt, soulful and spiritual, that Kate thought the windows might shatter.

Pastor Green's voice had a soothing quality, and a calmness filled the church after the boisterousness of the opening hymn.

He raised his hands to Heaven, "Eternal God, we praise you for the great company of all those who have finished their course in faith and now rest from their labor. We praise you for Paul, whom you have graciously received into your presence. We feel joy for he is now reunited with his loving wife Anna. As a community, we know how much Paul has suffered after the loss of his beloved Anna, and we are thankful they now rest together in the joy of your eternal home in Heaven. Let us pray together, Psalm 23."

A sermon followed, and Kate drifted off to think about other things as she usually did for sermons, but this time she was brought back to attention by a member of the congregation standing up and passionately yelling, "Amen!" Another jumped up, yelling "Yes, Lord!" Kate looked around, and everyone was nodding their heads yes and at full attention. She wondered what the minister had said to have elicited such an exuberant response. Just then, Tansy, Anna, and Justin slid along the bench, and soon the youthful group sat side by side.

Tansy whispered in Kate's ear, "Sorry we're late, what did we miss?"

Kate whispered back, "I'm not sure, but I think it was very important!"

Kate observed faces in the crowd, all intent on what the minister would preach next, and while she was very fond of Pastor George,

Reverend Green seemed to have powers that Pastor George did not. It was the intense focus of the crowd that intrigued her. She turned to look at Kimmy, and her eyes were fixated on the pulpit as if Kate wasn't even there. If their grandmothers were worried about their behavior in church, they need worry no longer as Kimmy's attention was arrow-like and undeterred even when Kate nudged her with her shoulder. In the end, "The Old Rugged Cross" was sung.

At the conclusion of the service, Kate felt some relief, as this send-off was more joyous and less somber than in her church. There was a level of acceptance and contentment amongst the crowd that made her far more at ease, almost comfortable with the death of Mr. Paul. While waiting in line to exit the church and shake hands with the minister, she looked at the funeral card. The front had a pastel colored picture of Mr. Paul's church, and inside were his birth and death dates and Psalm 23. Kate did the math in her head; he was 84 when he died.

Her thoughts drifted to a visit she had in the kitchen when Miss Anna was alive. Back then, the kitchen was much cleaner and always smelled like brownies. She conjured up an image in her head of how she remembered Miss Anna. She had a pleasant face and a bright smile. The last time Kate saw her, she and Mr. Paul were sitting side by side in their lawn chairs, waving at passersby. The memory was fleeting at best, but still a pleasant one.

Traditionally, after shaking the ministers hand, all were invited to a luncheon put on by the church ladies, but the Seth family, after shaking hands with Mr. Paul's church family, gave their condolences and then, with carefully chosen words spoken by Jammy, politely skipped the luncheon to head to the annual family reunion that was held on a waterfront farm just outside of town. The Seth family saw many relatives frequently about town, but the reunion was a chance to convene together all at once, and for those who had moved away, a reason to come home and a chance to reconnect.

⚓ ⚓ ⚓

WHEN THE BLUE GOOSE STATION wagon arrived with the Seth family, Johnny and Kate bolted to the volleyball net where cousins had already begun a game. Kate saw cousin Amy and ran over and gave her a hug.

"I haven't seen you all summer," they said in unison and then laughed at their timing. Anna and Justin came running up from the parking lot.

"Mother and Father are both here," Anna boasted to the girl cousins.

Kate's eyes veered towards the parking lot where she saw Sally and Lowell getting out of a car together.

"That's cool," Kate said, smiling, and soon the group of them were absorbed into the volleyball game.

The older and taller cousins stood up against the net with the smaller kin in back. Johnny was the server for the other team.

"Here we go!" he said as he launched one hard and fast over the net aimed at Kate.

She bumped it while simultaneously saying, "You did that on purpose!"

Johnny belly laughed with cousin Frank. While the younger members of the clan sent friendly fire back and forth across the net, the adults set up lawn chairs and tables, laid out a potluck lunch in the garage, put newspaper down at the crab picking table, signed the guest register, and greeted one another throughout it all.

Cousin Tessie brought her apple cake, which was reported in whispers among the youngest as it was a favorite and didn't last long on the dessert table. Cousin Betsy, who was quite crafty, had made a tree with each branch representing a line of the clan and set it upon a stand. The adults push-pinned the leaves onto the tree with great discussion over which branch they were on and how they got there. Soon, the president of the reunion called for games and conversations to quiet as everyone turned towards the hostess, Miss Miriam, for grace. Everyone who wore a hat removed it and bowed their heads.

"Lord, we thank you for the opportunity to come together as a family. We thank you for this beautiful day and the sun that shines upon our faces. Our blessings are too numerous to list, but as we think of them quietly, we know they are possible through your guidance and everlasting love. We bless not only the ones who have made the journey here today, but also those who could not make it. Lastly, we ask for your wisdom and guidance to be showered upon our youth, whom we cherish with all our hearts. We pray that you lead them in positive directions and shine the light for them when darkness befalls them. We thank you for the food you have enabled us to share with each other, and we bless it in thy name so we may use it in thy service. Amen."

"Amen!"

The children ran to the buffet first, and many paid a visit to the dessert table next and tucked a small piece of Tessie's apple cake amongst their lunch so as not miss out on it later. Kate looked forward to the dishes that graced the buffet table, and she filled her plate with fried chicken, deviled eggs, sweet buttery corn on the cob, sliced garden tomatoes and cucumbers, cold watermelon chunks and Miss Hattie's onion sandwiches.

After lunch, the children were called to the far end of the yard, next to the concord grapevine, and games entertained them while adults held a business meeting. A favortie activity for the young cousins was a hunt for bubble gum in a small grove of stretching pines on the other side of the property. For this, they ran around the house and across a field to the pines. No one had buckets, so T-shirts were stretched to form cloth baskets when pockets were full. After all the candy had been found, a water balloon toss commenced. Anna and Kate teamed up, and Kate's melon-tossing experience was paying off. Anna was very good at tossing as well, but in the end, she dropped one, much to the delight of the winning team of Justin and Johnny. They each received a silver dollar.

Next, the children convened in the garage for the annual parade of cousins. This was Miss Miriam's absolute favorite part of the day, and as she was the host, whether the children enjoyed being a part of the spectacle or not, they were obliged to participate. An old cardboard box filled with maracas, kazoos, tambourines, recorders, a drum, and noisemakers was invaded by many small hands, and once a patriotic song was chosen, there was a line-up that started with an American Flag holder, followed by a horn blower to begin the musical interlude.

Cousin May, who was 18 and had a heart of gold, was in charge of the parade, and she took it very seriously, scolding those who had broken rank by visiting the dessert table for some cookies. Once lined up, she placed Uncle Sam top hats on everyone and went out to the business meeting to let the adults know the patriotic show was on the ready.

Soon, the garage door was opened, and May signaled the flag holder to fly it proudly and for the horn blower to announce the beginning of the song. The cousins then marched out to the lawn and weaved their way in and out of the crowd singing "America the Beautiful." Kate found it amusing that they chose that song, as nothing she heard during the march was beautiful. However, Miss Miriam's eyes teared, which was beautiful enough for the whole clan.

The children then joined the meeting where a bible verse was read, and then many prizes were given out for such categories as: the youngest present, the oldest present, the longest married, and the cousin who traveled the farthest to be there. Tiny cousin Matthew was too young at age 6 months to accept his silver dollar, so his mother did it on his behalf, promising to save it for him. The last prize was for who came closest to guessing the number of hard candies in a large glass Mason jar. Kate was pretty confident she would win, as she had in the past, but cousin Amy took the prize, being one closer to the true number than Kate. She turned to Kate and handed her a handful of the butterscotches. Tickled by the gesture, Kate hugged her.

When the meeting had ended, the children could not get to Miss Miriam's pool fast enough, which was especially inviting now that the nettles had flooded the river. Cousin Carl was the lucky one to jump in first, and for the rest of the afternoon, Marco Polo and sharks and minnows wore everyone out. After long goodbyes, Kate laid her towel on the hot back seat of the Blue Goose. It had been sitting in the sun, and even with the windows down, the dark blue vinyl seat was so hot it could burn your legs.

Johnny and Kate picked some choke cherries off the grandfather-sized trees that surrounded the driveway and ate them quietly on the way home, spitting the large seeds out the window. It was dinner time when the Seth family arrived home so worn and weary that words took effort. Mary made small sandwiches, and they ate them on the front porch while watching the sun fall closer to the trees.

Overcome by exhaustion, Kate stared out her bedroom window at the little luminaries flitting about. She had noticed more and more lightning bugs as summer progressed, and this small swarm of flickering lights swirling about entranced her until her eyes were overcome with weariness. An evening breeze blew in the window and across her uncovered legs. It felt good on her sunburned skin.

Chapter XIV

— Figs, Flags, and Phonebooks —

Mary and her houseboat friend, Dovie, sang along with Tanya Tucker's "Delta Dawn" on the radio as loud as they could, snapping their fingers along to the song as the baby blue station wagon tested its V8 on the way out of town. Kate sat in the back seat surrounded by phonebooks as tall as the ceiling of the wagon and flanking her on all sides except the forward view of the second sopranos in the front seat.

Kate was still reviewing the circumstances in which she ended up in the car hidden by thick, yellow books. She couldn't recall how she had agreed to be a part of these middle-aged ladies' adventure. A few miles out of town, the car turned right down Sailors Hideaway, a thin, pothole-filled dirt road. With each bump, a phone book would slide off the top of the pile, hit her in the head, or land in her lap until she was buried a dozen books deep. Mary and Dovie paid her no mind until they stopped at an old farmhouse and turned around to look at their cargo.

"Where'd she go, Mary?" Dovie said, unruffled.

Mary laughed whilst reaching down and pinching one of Kate's toes. "I guess we'll have to dig her out!"

They pulled the books off her until a smile was revealed. "I guess we'll have to deliver the first few until you are free," said Mary, as Dovie ran one book up to a very old house.

"Your great-grandfather times three, the one with the four ships, built this house," said Mary.

Kate perked up. "Can we see it?"

"No, doesn't belong to our family anymore. It was sold 50 years ago. Besides it looks like no one is home."

Dovie jumped back into the car and they drove to the next house, which Kate recognized right away.

"Hey, that's Cousin John's house!"

"Sure is, looks like his car is gone. He must of driven into town."

Dovie left the phone book wedged between the screen and door. It was the same for the next house, and then they drove back out to the main road. The pattern continued for the next few roads until Kate could wiggle out. She crawled through the gap in the two front seats, and the books were rearranged so that she could sit directly behind Dovie, open the door, and run books up to front doors. At first, Kate was entertained by this activity, but as the day pushed on, she found herself looking back at all the books they still had to deliver. The cargo only covered the back of the wagon now, and each time a book was taken off a stack, one slid in to fill its place.

One thing Kate enjoyed was having a better idea in her head of where everyone lived, at least the people she knew, which turned out to be many more people than she realized. The phonebook crew stopped for a break at cousin Jack and Betsy's house for a glass of water and Kate enjoyed playing with Tag, a mutt with a bit of hound dog and retriever, which made him an excellent hunting dog. He was very keen, and Kate played hide and seek with him by hiding his ball in the boxwoods. Each time, he readily found it with his nose.

Towards the end of the deliveries, they pulled up at a wreck of a house. A worn looking woman in a housecoat sat on the side steps seemingly uninterested in her visitors. This time, Mary told Kate to stay in the car. Kate quickly came to some conclusions about the inhabitants when she saw trash in the yard and a hole in the side of the house the size of a chair. The windows were down in the car and Kate could hear Mary's conversation.

"I can help you with your situation here. I know people who can hide you and your boy and keep you safe," she said as she handed her a phonebook.

The battered lady shook her head no and turned away from Mary, signaling an end to the conversation. But Mary followed up, "If you change your mind, you know where to find me."

Mary got back in the car and let out a sigh. "I'll be back again another time when I know it's safe and he's not there."

Dovie nodded in agreement. Kate, while processing what she saw, kept quiet in the back seat with new-found fondness and respect for her mother. The ladies finished the job and dropped off Miss Dovie at her houseboat just before the six 'clock church bells. When Kate and Mary finally rolled out of an empty Blue Goose in front of the Seth house, all Kate could smell was baked ham.

The smell coming out of the kitchen was an intoxicating mix of warm peaches, savory ham, onions, and something cheesy. Jammy had been cooking all afternoon. Dinner was served immediately, and as the church bells chimed, all six of them were placing napkins in their laps. Kate dished herself up a large spoonful of zucchini, tomatoes, and onions that Jammy had sautéed together. It was one of Kate's favorites. It filled half her plate, leaving little room for the baked ham, mac and cheese, and skillet cornbread. She complimented her grandmother, and the cook remarked that soon she would be making stewed tomatoes. Kate's heart fell out onto the floor. Stewed tomatoes meant only one thing: the end of summer was closing in.

"Now Kate, don't be too depressed, we still have to get through fig season!"

Fig season! How could she forget!? "How are they looking, mother?"

"I'd say not long now."

Lowell was quiet for the meal, but when Jammy brought out her peach pie, he sliced the silence as he sliced the pie.

"I've been talking with Sally."

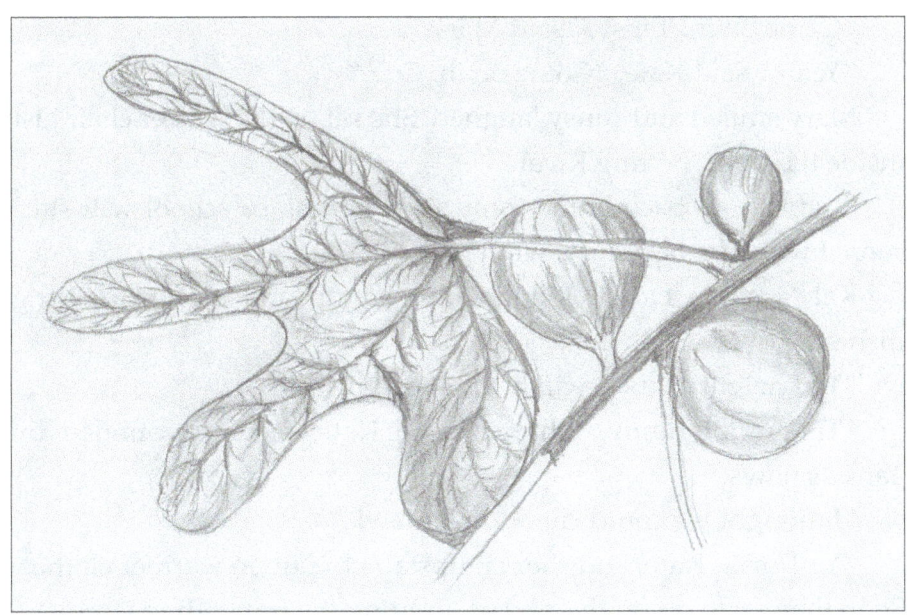

The announcement was followed by a long pause. Kate looked at her plate, Mary occupied herself with handing out a second set of napkins, and Johnny kicked Kate under the table. Only Jammy and Edison looked him in the eye at first. Mary eventually gave him her attention.

"We're getting along good now, and if she'll have me back, I'd like to go home. So what I'm saying is thank you, and I hope I'll be going home soon."

Edison stood up, extended his hand, and Lowell matched his move.

"Your family will be happy to have you back." Everyone nodded and smiled. The proclamation was a relief to everyone and the warm pie was enjoyed. Laughter ensued as Kate told her version of the events of the afternoon.

"They buried you under phonebooks?" Johnny chuckled.

"Only for a little while," Mary said, smiling at Kate.

"Well, yeah, it was kinda fun."

Tansy appeared at the back door, in jeans and long sleeves. "It's chilly out," she said.

"Come on in, Tansy," said Mary.

"Yeah," said Kate, "Come on in, Cuz."

Mary smiled and Tansy laughed. She sat on the wicker chair just inside the door, petting River.

"I got to go back home tomorrow, and since school will start soon, I won't be back for a while."

Kate's smile faded. Johnny jumped up and started clearing dishes.

"The neighborhood will be quieter," he said.

"That's not funny, Johnny!" said Kate, feeling wounded by Tansy's news.

"I thought we could check on Squawk."

"Yes!" said Kate, and she ran upstairs to put on warmer clothes. Soon they were off on their bikes, fighting the impending sunset.

They sailed down the street but paused at Mr. Paul's to look at his house. Without saying a word, they picked up speed and raced to the boatyard. Mr. Russell and Miss Pat were enjoying dinner when they saw them walk by their side window.

Pat yelled through the screen. "She flew a circle around the house and landed on the roof."

Both Kate and Tansy's eyes widened, and they walked up to Miss Pat's window screen. Their fingers grabbed the sill, and on their tippy toes, they peered inside.

"Really?" they said in unison.

"Really, she did." Mr. Russell added, "Won't be long now."

Sam, hearing the girls, yipped from inside.

The girls, with a mix of enthusiasm and dread, rushed to Squawk's pen to make sure she was still there. When they came into view, Squawk gave them a loud greeting. Kate reached in, careful not to bend any of her newly acquired feathers, and put her on the grass.

"I hear you've been flying?!" Tansy asked Squawk.

But Squawk paid her no mind and started walking briskly

towards the beach. The girls followed, and seeing the town ducks, they knew why she headed straight there. When she saw the river, she waddled faster. When the town ducks saw her coming they backed away slightly, but not to the point that they were rude, just cautious of the the new girl in town.

Tansy commented, "I hope they warm up to her."

"Me too," Kate agreed.

The two girls stood back and watched the interaction between the town ducks and the newcomer. Squawk's pace slowed as she got closer to the flock, and she gave them a wide berth. She waddled to the river shore to take a drink. There was some discussion amongst the flock, and Kate and Tansy desperately wanted to know what they were saying, but they didn't speak "duck."

"I wish we knew what they thought," said Tansy.

"I think they are making some decisions about her," Kate replied.

One by one, the ducks settled down, and Squawk inched closer to them, keeping her head low. A few ducks in the flock didn't seem to mind and let her approach slowly. Kate and Tansy sat down several yards away to watch the interaction, but as soon as they got comfortable, the ducks one by one headed out to the river. Squawk stayed behind, watched, and then, with great exuberance, she let out a loud "Squawk!" and came running to Kate and Tansy, jumping into Tansy's lap.

"She's sticking around to say good-bye to you," Kate said with confidence. Tansy looked as if she would cry, but held it in. The sky was losing its glow as the sun headed down below the trees.

"We better get going," Tansy said sadly, and Kate agreed.

They walked to Miss Pat's yard, and Squawk followed behind them at a brisk pace, wanting to keep up. Once back in her pen, the girls waved goodbye. Tansy, knowing it was her last visit, stared at Squawk and turned to Kate, bleary-eyed.

"I'd like to have a few words alone," Tansy said.

Kate went up to the back porch of Pat's house and sat on her swing.

The clanging from the kitchen had stopped, and as if on cue, Miss Pat came out along with Sam, who liked to be at Pat's feet during mealtime. The duo sat next to Kate.

"She's saying goodbye?"

"Yep," was all Kate could get out.

She, like Tansy, was choked for words at the moment.

Kate reached out to pet Sam and noticed his bandages had been removed. She pet him all over and looked at Pat.

"Is he better?"

"Much!"

This swung Kate and Tansy's emotions from sadness to joy instantly. Sam ran to Tansy, and she took a turn petting him all over. Both girls, seemingly awash with mixed emotions, made for an unnerving quiet. Pat filled the silence.

"Y'all have been really good help with raising Squawk and looking out for Sam this summer."

Tansy heard the compliment as she headed to the porch steps. "Thanks, Miss Pat, I'm going to miss them. I go back home tomorrow."

"Oh dear," said Miss Pat, "I will surely miss your visits!"

"Me too," whispered Tansy while lowering her head.

Miss Pat jumped up and gave Tansy a hug. "I'm sure Kate will write and tell you all about Squawk's adventures."

Kate and Tansy perked up.

"Yeah," said Kate, "I'll write and tell you about her."

Tansy smiled and then Miss Pat told them to skedaddle home as it was almost dark and she didn't want Miss Lucille or Miss Mary to worry. Tansy gave Miss Pat a hug one more time and the girls raced home.

⚓ ⚓ ⚓

KATE WOKE ABRUPTLY THE NEXT morning to a cacophony of birds in the neighborhood trees. The ruckus made her look at her squeaky fan. It seemed as though every noise was louder than usual, forcing her out of bed. On any other day, she might complain to herself about the early morning disturbance. However, wanting to make sure she said goodbye to Tansy before she left, Kate threw on yesterday's clothes and followed the smell of home fries to the kitchen. "Up in time to say goodbye to Tansy, are we?" asked Mary.

"Yes," answered Kate reluctantly, as if saying it made it more real. Kate ate her home fries and onions quickly, washing them down with a glass of sun tea and ran out the front door to catch Tansy before she left. She was met halfway by Tansy in bright yellow pajamas.

"What are you doing in your pjs?" laughed Kate.

"I packed all my clothes up and forgot to leave some out for today. Gram thinks it's funny and I should wear them home."

Kate's uncontrollable belly laugh was broken by Tansy's mother arriving in her tiny little foreign car named after a bug. Once she parked and set foot on the uneven brick sidewalk, Tansy ran to her and gave her a big hug.

Kate watched the interaction, and suddenly she wasn't sad about Tansy leaving when she saw how much she had missed her mother.

"And what are you still doing in your pajamas?" Tansy's mother asked while smiling and waving at Kate.

Hand in hand, they walked up Gram's steps, leaving Kate watching from the sidewalk. Tansy paused before they went inside and ran back to give Kate a hug goodbye.

"Write me!" she yelled as she ran back to her mother and went inside.

Fraught with mixed emotions, August played with Kate in its own cruel way. One day, she was flying down the highway delivering phone books and laughing, and the next she was saying goodbye to her best summer friend. Kate found August to be a torturous month.

She went back to her house, opened the screen door, and stepped into the front hall to hear Jammy calling to her from the front parlor. Kate poked her head around the corner to see her sitting on the floor amidst a panorama of old newspapers covering the rug and on top of them, the brass fireplace fender and Georgian-style trivet. Her collection of rags piled next to the bottle of brass cleaner told Kate all she needed to know: that it was definitely August.

"I'm doing my August shining," Jammy stated.

"I see that," said Kate. "Why do you always clean the brass and silver in August?"

"Just seems like the right time to do it, what with the changing of the seasons imminent. Plus, I can open all the windows to help with the smell of these cleaners!"

Kate waved her hand in front of her nose. "They do smell bad," she agreed.

"How's that duck of yours?" Jammy asked.

Kate perked up. "She's really grown up. I expect she'll want to join the other ducks soon." "Oh yes," Jammy agreed. "It is that time of year. How do you feel about that?"

"I dunno," Kate looked down at the floor. "I expect when she leaves, I'll be both happy and sad."

Jammy replied, "A lot of what happens in August is happy and sad." Kate nodded her head yes and headed to the kitchen, as she was still thirsty from breakfast.

She entered the kitchen and found her mother on the phone.

"It's time to buy sugar and lemons," she told the person on the other end.

Kate knew then the figs were almost ripe. These clues played out in the first half of August, and as they did, Kate could feel the excitement well up in Mary day by day. Kate poured the rest of last night's iced tea into a tall glass, just as Mary hung up the phone.

"Won't be long now, Kate. I expect we'll be making preserves in less than a week."

Daily reports leading up to the harvest of figs had officially begun. Many other folks in town also canned figs or made preserves in what was a cultural event as customary as, perhaps, canning peaches, making homemade oyster stew, or having a crab feast.

There were so many fig bushes in town that they were too prolific to count. In her head, Kate could think of seven large bushes just on their back street alone. The fig bush she was most acquainted with grew behind Edison's shed facing east. It benefited from the morning sun, afternoon shade, and the residual heat from its proximity to the shed. As such, it was very happy where it lived, and harvests were abundant. No one knew how old the fig bush was, but Mary suspected that Poppy planted it when he and his new bride moved in, making it at least 75 years old. Prideful tales of fig bushes in town that were over 100 years old were the subject of much debate uptown in the month of August.

Kate decided to check on Squawk and rode her bike slower, without Tansy at her side. She stopped at Mr. Paul's house on her way to the boatyard. She leaned her bike so that she had one foot on the ground and both eyes on his ragtag house. She sighed. A gentle breeze blew the gate open as if to invite her in. Edison appeared by her side.

Kate broke the silence, "What will happen to his house?"

"I'm not sure. Paul and Anna had no children," replied Edison.

"He may have stolen my vegetables, but I miss the son of a gun."

"I miss him, too," said Kate. Edison patted her on the back and crossed the street to his garden. Kate put her foot on the pedals and rode to the boatyard.

Squawk was very excited to see her and let her know with a very loud greeting. Kate lifted her out of her pen, and the duck waddled behind her all the way to the river shore. The beach was empty, and Kate stepped into the river carefully, looking for nettles. Once she was knee deep, Squawk followed, and before she knew it, the two of them, girl and duck, were swimming together. Kate loved to see Squawk glide on top of the water effortlessly and watch beads of river water roll off her back when Kate splashed.

"You are made for water much better than I am," she told Squawk. In response, Squawk took a drink from the river.

"I guess the nettles don't bother you, do they?" This time, Squawk answered by flapping her wings.

A voice came from the shoreline, and Kate turned her head.

"You hungry?" asked Miss Pat with Sam by her side. Kate swam to shore without answering the question. She was always hungry these days and welcomed the invitation. She walked out of the river and wiped the water off her arms and legs with her hands.

"I wish I had brought a towel," she said.

"Oh, you'll dry quick enough in this heat! Yesterday was chilly, but summer is back!" exclaimed Miss Pat, while wiping her brow.

All Squawk had to do was wiggle her feathers and the water disappeared. The four of them walked across the road and up to Miss Pat's porch.

"I'm taking a lunch break," she said, "will you have some with me?"

"Oh yes," Kate said enthusiastically. They left Sam and Squawk on the porch and went into her kitchen. The smell of freshly baked blueberry muffins filled the air.

"You've been baking!" Kate said, grinning with delight.

"I have. I told Mr. Russell that I was taking the morning off. I just didn't feel like working this morning. It must be this August heat."

Kate was relieved to hear she wasn't the only one struggling with the last month of summer.

Miss Pat pulled out a container of cottage cheese, and the two of them headed to the dining room table with bowls of it and fresh muffins. Pat handed Kate a towel to sit on. The windows were open, so there was a pleasant cross breeze that cooled the room somewhat, but the humidity remained. They bowed their heads in prayer, and then Kate shoved a muffin in her mouth, making almost half of it disappear instantly.

"My word!" exclaimed Miss Pat, as she handed her another muffin.

"You must be growing!"

"That's what everyone says," replied Kate, with her mouth full.

Miss Pat and Kate talked well past lunchtime about so many subjects, but mainly they reminisced about the summer's escapades with Squawk. They had both become quite attached to her and lamented she had to grow up and eventually leave them, because that's what wild things do. Miss Pat gasped when she caught a glimpse of the wall clock.

"Two o'clock!?! It can't be! Mr. Russell will not be pleased!"

She handed Kate a small bag of muffins for the family as she rushed out the door. As Pat quickly headed to her office, Kate didn't feel quite as much urgency to move on with her afternoon, so she sat down on the edge of Miss Pat's porch with her bag of muffins. Sam at her side, smelling the paper bag, and Squawk hunting the yard for bugs, Kate sat for a long time staring at the grass and feeling full from lunch, but empty inside. After a while, she picked up Squawk and put her back in the pen, and put Sam back in the house. Miss Pat was still pampering him a bit, and Kate could tell that he loved it.

The ride home was slow, she didn't even speed up when she passed the Country Club. Maybe it was the humidity, maybe it was Mr. Paul's recent death, but the few men who sat in lawn chairs seemed subdued. Kate, mulling over so many things in her mind, barely noticed them, and they barely noticed her. She pedaled past the blind couple's house, and they were not on the stoop as usual.

"Probably inside out of the sun," she said out loud to herself. "I hope they have a fan." The brackish breeze on her face soothed her sunburn. She breathed in deeply as she passed Mr. Paul's house and exhaled as she turned left, coasting down the street until she was at the Seth's back fence. Kate remained preoccupied through several rounds of gin rummy with Jammy, and her distance continued through dinner.

"My, you are quiet, Miss Kate," Jammy stated to the entire dinner table.

"How's Squawk?" asked Johnny.

"She's good," was all she said before jumping up and clearing the plates.

She helped with the dishes and was on her way upstairs when she heard Mr. Brown's voice coming from the front of the house. Jammy was already sitting on the glider when Kate poked her head out the window.

"Well, hey there, little lady," said Mr. Brown cheerfully.

Kate smiled, waved, and sat down next to Jammy.

"I suppose you might like a story?" He turned his attention towards Kate.

"Oh yes, sir!"

Jammy smiled. Mr. Brown had broken the spell that had entranced Kate for the last few hours.

"With you sitting right next to your grandmother, I think maybe I'll tell you about my grandparents. My grandfather was short in stature, but tall in ingenuity, and could fix almost anything. He and his wife, my grandmother, had three children, one of them being my mother. He was a very hard worker. He never drove a car, and rode his bicycle most everywhere."

"What did he do?" Kate interjected.

"He worked as a farmer growing sweet potatoes and also worked at a nearby canning factory. Saturdays he worked at the horse track on the other side of town, and he drove his tractor to that job. The tractor had a flywheel on the side to start it. Once started, it would pop, pop, pop along down the road. I always liked the sound of his tractor. Of course, on Sundays we all went to church, and after church we went to more church."

"More church?" Kate questioned.

"Sundays were busy," he explained.

"On Sunday afternoons, my mother would take all of us," he paused. "There were seven of us.

Kate gasped, "That's a lot of siblings!"

Mr. Brown continued, "...after church, mother would take all of us to see my grandparents who lived out in the country, not far from here. Near their house was a Methodist Church camp that we all went to after we had Sunday supper. But, before Sunday supper, we had to go down to the spring and gather water for my grandparents for the week. They had no indoor plumbing, so we took metal milk cans with us and filled them up and carted them back in a wooden wheelbarrow."

Kate's eye's widened.

"This time of year, it took us longer to collect the water because we would visit a blackberry patch on the way back to their house."

He belly laughed as if he were a schoolboy again.

"There was a smokehouse out back that my grandfather built himself, and that is where he smoked hogs. His country ham was the best."

"Really salty?" Kate asked.

"Oh yes, very salty."

"Mmmm...," said Kate, as she kicked out her legs straight with excitement.

"He loved to eat fatty meat and drink very strong, dark tea." Mr. Brown paused as if to reflect upon his grandfather. "He lived to be 90, which is old today, but very, very old back then!" he said, smiling and flashing his perfectly white teeth.

"When we got back from getting the spring water, my grandmother's rolls that rose all night long would be coming out of the oven. They were like little pillows of heaven."

He got really excited and then exclaimed, "I haven't told you about the turn cake! Sometimes she made biscuits. The biscuit dough would be rolled out and put in a cake pan. When it was done, she would turn it out hot onto the wooden table and then slather it with butter and jam and little slices of country ham."

"Oh," Kate remarked, "That sounds delicious!"

"Nothing like it!" he grinned.

"After Sunday supper, we would go to camp and hear more preaching. It was held in a clearing in the woods, and people came from all over. I had enough churching by the afternoon and would sneak off with the other kids and play in the woods. After everyone had been saved, we would go back to my grandparents' house and talk 'til near about nine at night. Everyone always had lots to say."

"That is a wonderful story!" interjected Jammy.

"Yes," agreed Kate.

"Next time I'll tell you how we got milk across the river in the middle of winter—and, I warn you, it's a rugged tale."

Kate yawned and sank lower into the slider cushion.

"I'd say you look ready for bed," said Jammy.

Kate's eyelids desperately wanted to close, but she tried to keep them open on her way up the stairs.

⚓ ⚓ ⚓

THE FOLLOWING DAY AND FOR the next week or so, Kate overheard more clues about the figs. Mother had taken to giving a daily report about them and each day as she laid out the weather, size, firmness, and color of the figs. A wellspring of enthusiasm flavored her words in sweet preserves. When the ripening was imminent, Cousin Christy, whose real name was Christopher, would change his morning walking routine and would walk past the fig bush in the early mornings.

Mary spotted him and ran out back exclaiming, "Christy is eating my figs!"

Cousin Christy was caught many a morning in August reaching

over the fence, pulling a springy fig branch down to his level to feel and see if the figs were ripe. Once ripened, he would have one fresh fig every morning for breakfast on his daily walk. Although Mary and Cousin Christy quibbled back and forth about the little fruits—it was an August routine Mary wouldn't have missed. Days he didn't come by were much quieter, and despite their playfully aggressive banter, she always came back in the house smiling as Christy walked up the street eating a fresh fig.

⚓ ⚓ ⚓

ONE HOT AUGUST FRIDAY, WHILE Kate was eating a late lunch with Jammy on the porch, they heard a loud bang that reverberated all over town, resonating against the wooden sides of the houses and shaking the fences. It startled them both, and then, Jammy smiled.

"Boats are coming!"

Kate knew what that meant and they got on their bikes and rode towards Sunset Lane. The wind from the southwest at 10 to 12 knots pushed a sticky August humidity onto land. As they sailed down Sunset Lane on their bikes, the weeping willows opened a path for them to the river. They parked their bikes with everyone else's, which made for a large clump of color and chrome under a shady willow. A crowd had already gathered and was cheering, jeering, hollering, and waving to the captains and crew. Not only was Sunset Beach full, but the yacht club beach, was too, and it stretched four times as long as Sunset Beach. The breeze billowed the spinnaker sails to fullness and packed the river with colorful giant balloon-like pillows so much that it obstructed the view of the opposite shoreline.

"Who took first?" Jammy asked Miss Charlotte, who was the first person they saw.

"Shotgun Mary," she said, giggling.

"Oh, that's a fast one!" Jammy said with excitement.

"Yes, almost always in the front of the fleet!" Charlotte replied.

The crowd was rambunctious and the adults yelled clever comments to their favorite skippers while the younger set played on the beach. Seaweed lay rotting in the sun like a steaming compost pile. On any other day those who cheered would have turned their bikes around for the stink of it all, but today no one paid it much attention.

"Smells like wet dog," commented Kate, while holding her nose.

Jammy shrugged her nose in silent agreement.

The finish line was between the channel marker Miss Lucille swam to and where the river took a bend at the corner of the yacht club property. Only the first boat in this fleet got the dignity of a gun, while the others crossed the line to the wail of a horn, which sounded like a sick cow, making everyone hoot and cackle. The revelry of the regatta had begun.

Once all the boats were tied up, the August air filled with live bluegrass music, beer taps began to flow, and abundant cigarette smoke lingered aloft until the prevailing winds carried it away.

⚓ ⚓ ⚓

THE NEXT DAY, JAMMY AND Kate picnicked at the park, with Jammy filling up her elegant picnic basket as a surprise. The basket was small enough to hang elegantly off Jammy's petite forearm, and she carried it like a stylish lady would, with ease and purpose. The outside featured a hand-painted scene of a country town complete with horses, meadows, hills, and farmhouses. The edges were trimmed in a wide green silky ribbon, its inside lined with a picnic-style navy blue gingham fabric.

When they arrived at the park in the late morning, it had already begun to fill with spectators. The colorful picnic blankets covered the grass so as to make a patchwork quilt of sorts on the cool, shaded floor under the trees. True to tradition, the locals had gathered at the locust near the river bank, and as they approached, Kate and Jammy were welcomed by cousins and couzins. The only difference from earlier in the summer was that no one was swimming. The sea nettles were just too thick.

Kate tried to carry the picnic blanket on her forearm as elegantly as Jammy had carried the picnic basket. By the time they reached the park, she had thrown it over her shoulder to leave her hands free in case she saw any toads. On the blanket next to them sat Miss Pearl and her youngest daughter, Molly.

"Good Morning, ladies," they said, welcoming them to sit and chat.

"Where is Miss Mary?" asked Molly.

"Oh, she'll be along shortly. She had to go to the church this morning to practice some new music for tomorrow's service."

Pearl and Molly smiled. "We thought it might be her filling the park with organ music!"

Out on the water, boats of all sizes flitted back and forth like busy bees. The river, peppered with white sails, mixed in with a few colorful ones, was, as Miss Pearl stated, "pretty as a postcard." Both Jammy and Kate agreed.

While everyone was transfixed on the action on the water, Kate lifted the hinged end of Jammy's basket to peek inside. It was filled to the top with tinfoil-wrapped goodies and she smelled fresh zucchini bread.

"Might you wait for your mother to arrive before you start eating?" Mary startled Kate from behind.

Everyone turned to greet Mary, and Kate slowly put the lid down. A gun fired, which turned everyone's attention back to the river. The noise came from a small anchored yacht just off the shore and was accompanied by a white shape being raised on a halyard. Kate focused on the yacht the sailboats seemed to be drawn to. It had a variety of flags all over it. One was blue with an anchor and the letters R.C. Another had what looked like a shooting star, and yet another was red, white, and blue. All of these sat atop a small mast, and an orange flag seemed to be all by itself, at eye level for those on the boat.

Dovie, Bridget, and Carolyn appeared just then and were greeted with open arms by the cousins and couzins.

"Join us!" they exclaimed excitedly.

"The race is about to begin," said Jammy with enthusiasm.

Kate wondered how she knew and turned to Carolyn.

"What are all those flags for?"

Carolyn, who had been teaching children to sail at the yacht club all summer, laid out in great detail what each flag meant, and Kate became instantly fascinated. Another gun sounded, and the shape that had been taken down just prior was replaced by a blue shape.

"That means five minutes til the start," said Carolyn, explaining it all to Kate.

"Why aren't you sailing in the race?" Kate asked curiously.

"I was going to, but my sail ripped this morning, so we took it to Mr. Downey; it should be repaired by tomorrow," she replied with disappointment in her voice.

"Mr. Downey had a lot of business," Dovie said, as Miss Margy's "bundle" rambunctiously ran and flopped on all the blankets.

Their mother, quite exasperated and trying to keep up, yelled, "Manners!"

The boys apologized to the other mothers and straightened their blankets up for them. "My goodness!" she exclaimed, and the mothers commiserated with her about the boundless energy of her brood. They were distracted by a "Bang!" Every head turned west towards the water. Kate noticed that now there was a red shape flying and a pack of sails sailing parallel to each other.

Carolyn piped up above the chatter, "That's the start!"

Even though Kate didn't fully understand what was happening on the river, she found it terribly exciting. The horns, shapes, and guns continued as the children found their way into picnic baskets. Mary opened the red and black checkered thermos she brought, and

Jammy pulled out three glasses and filled them with cold iced tea. Out of Jammy's basket came old-fashioned ham salad sandwiches with pickles, deviled eggs, zucchini bread, sliced sugared peaches that had been sprinkled with lemon juice, Maryland beaten biscuits, fig preserves, and three fancy embroidered linens for napkins. They all watched and pointed as boats tacked back and forth, rounded marks, and they cheered when boats crossed the finish line.

⚓ ⚓ ⚓

THE FOLLOWING DAY, THE RACES continued and so did the revelry until late Sunday afternoon, when all of a sudden the town became still.

All the boats that had packed the harbor and the sailors that had inundated the town, sailed out of the river. Kate and Johnny rode their bikes to the park to watch them leave. As they stood on the bank under the locust tree they saw white sails flitting zigzag, zigzag back and forth. Kate turned to Johnny who had taken sailing class a few years back.

"Why don't they have the colorful sails up?"

"That's because they are tacking out of the river."

"What does that mean?" she asked, confused.

"They only put the colorful sails up when the wind is aft."

Kate looked at the water and the trees, and the wind was indeed at their bows.

"Oh," was all she said while she thought long and hard about it. She broke the silence by asking Johnny if he thought it sad to see them go.

"Oh yeah," said Johnny, "that's money out the river. I made really good tips at the restaurant this weekend."

Kate laughed, and the two of them went over to the swings. "I can't believe I'll be a senior this year," Johnny said out of the blue.

"You will?" replied Kate, somewhat regretful she had not really kept track.

"Yeah, and then I'm going to college. Mom and Dad said they'd take me to visit some this fall."

"Which ones do you want to see?"

"Well I guess one's in Maryland, so I can come home on weekends and earn some money. I've got enough saved to buy a car. Dad is taking me to look at one this week."

Kate smiled, "Will you give me a ride in it?"

"Well, yeah, of course."

They had swung rather high, and with a matching motion, they flew off the swings and instantly looked at the other when they landed to see who had flown the farthest.

"Ha!" exclaimed Johnny.

"How come you always win?" questioned Kate.

Johnny simply replied, "Physics."

WHEN THEY RETURNED TO THE house, Mary was in a dither. Ripe figs filled colanders and covered the countertop. River was at her heels, and she scooted him away.

"Johnny, would you put him outside? He's in the way."

"Mother! The figs are ripe!" exclaimed Kate.

"And there are still more to pick," Mary said, while handing her a bowl.

"I left some on the low branches for you."

Kate took the bowl out back, and River, sensing all the excitement, followed her out to the fig tree nestled behind Edison's shed. She got down on her knees and, crawling through the wild purple violet leaves that had long since finished blooming, she began to pluck the ripe fruits from the branches. Each fruit dispelled a milky white liquid as she severed them by peeling them back in the opposite direction they grew. She heard voices approaching, but trapped by the bush and her back against the fence, she couldn't stand up to see who it was.

"Did you hear? Molly is dating an out-of-towner." spoke one voice.

"Does Pearl know?" replied the other.

"I should think so!"

Kate wormed her body around to peek through the fence slats. All she could see was two sets of feet walking away and she didn't recognize them with their backs turned.

"When they date someone in town, at least you know about the family."

"So true," replied the other, as their voices faded.

Kate felt for sure that she had stumbled upon some salacious gossip, and scooting herself out from under the low-hanging branches, ran in to tell Mary. She burst through the door as Mary and Johnny turned from peeling figs at the sink to see what Kate was so excited about.

"Molly is dating an out-of-towner!" Mary looked at Kate calmly.

"Yes, I know."

"Oh," Kate said, rather deflated.

Mary continued, "Pearl told me the other day. It's hard when you don't know the family."

"That's what they said!"

"Who?" Mary replied.

"People walking by. I couldn't see who they were, trapped under the fig bush."

"Hmmm…" replied Mary, "well, news does get around this town quickly."

"Quickly is an understatement," said Johnny, never turning his back nor wavering from his job at the sink.

In the rush to get the hot news to her mother, Kate had not been very careful exiting from under the fig, and some of the milky white fig juice had gotten on her arm. It began to itch.

"Come wash it off," said Mary, knowing how itchy fig milk could be.

Even after she had toweled herself off, her forearm was still itchy. She returned to the fig tree scratching intermittently but finished the job, anxious to wash off her arm again.

Johnny had peeled five pounds of figs when Mary reminded him, "Watch out for wasps and rotten ones, they will ruin the whole batch."

"I already know that," he fussed back at his mother.

Mary paused, turned towards him, and they locked eyes just long enough to make Johnny squirm. Mary had just finished measuring the sugar and sliced lemons for the first five pound batch when someone knocked on the front door.

"Kate, go see who it is. I can't leave the kitchen, I just put the figs on."

Kate walked to the front door and squinted to see who it was.

"It's Josephine!" Kate yelled.

"Invite her in," Mary yelled back.

Kate opened the door and with a big smile conveyed her pleasure to see her.

"Hello, Miss Josephine."

"Well, hello, Miss Kate. It's August, can you guess why I'm here?"

Kate burst out with giggles as they arrived at the kitchen entrance. Mary leaned away from the stove to give Josephine a side hug, one hand still stretched to the pot.

"I'm here to catch up on Miss Kate's year, and we might eat ice cream." She winked at Mary and Johnny.

"Of course! Of course! But I'm warning you, she might want two scoops this year." Josephine looked Kate up and down and replied, "You do look taller than last year, two scoops it is!"

Josephine and Kate, hand in hand, walked out the front door and up to Truman's store. Once they had left, Johnny turned to Mary. "I know I am too old for it now, but why has Josephine always taken us for ice cream every August?"

Mary paused and then said, "Your great-grandfather, Poppy,

used to manage the oyster shucking house across the river. At that time, not everyone was treated fairly. But Miss Josephine's mother said your Poppy was very kind and fair to her. Josephine, to show her gratitude for the thoughtfulness he showed her mother, took you when you were younger, and now Kate for ice cream."

Johnny marinated in those words for a while.

"Huh," he said, "Poppy must have been some boss to have someone repay him like that after he's been buried so long."

Mary beamed and looked at the ceiling. "I love you, Poppy!"

Chapter XV

— Taking Flight —

The end of August brought on a wet cold dew in the mornings, which when stepped on by Kate's bare feet, sent a chill up her back. She shivered and thought of the impending fall and it made time spin faster.

The far shore moaned a low, distant preemptive emergence of winter wheat seeds pushing up the soil and the sound crawled across the river, slinked up the western bank, weaved its way swiftly through the waterside houses and climbed right up into Kate's ears. And while she knew it wasn't quite time yet, the delicate sound was a warning of the cool season drifting ever so precariously close to the shores.

The subtle winds that brought the ancient consciousness to Kate's ears, carried with it memories of a time before the machines, when weathered men and worn women, dirty from the fields, dutiful to the harvest pressed on with a desperate fatigue thrust upon them by the season at hand.

Corn would be harvested soon, followed by the planting of winter wheat seeds. Soon the watermen would be changing their rigs from trot lining to hand tonging or netting. Soon she would watch the garden sadly recoil and wilt away until all that remained were the heartiest of tomatoes and peppers; and even those would succumb to the first frost. Soon the leaves on the trees would color and fall and although she knew the trees were merely going to sleep, it saddened her and there was nothing she could do to stop it. Soon, it seemed, was a foreboding word stealing away the warm season she cherished.

This was the trickiest time of year, with the water still warm from hot summer sun. It was hard for Kate to navigate the shift. Somehow the farmers knew when it was time to gather the fields, the watermen knew when to re-fit the workboats, and Edison knew when to pick the last of the beans for canning. But for Kate, the seasonal change was hard to handle at her young age and the uncertainty of it all unnerved her. She was relieved she was a kid and all she had to be concerned with was finding her shoes and socks. In short order, summer would shrivel under a weakening sun and one night in a cooling September she would yield with a quiet sadness and reach for a thin blanket in the middle of the night.

But September wasn't now. She still had a week to run barefoot through the grass, ride her bike for hours about town, splash in the brackish river with Squawk and stay late on the front porch visiting with Mr. Brown.

Kate felt no one else could hear it, the consciousness of the field workers from years, decades, centuries before, except maybe Mother and Jammy. Too struck with it all to ask them, she swallowed the sounds whole, which in turn, made her tummy ache. The day the distant sounds shook her, she felt very alone so she wandered the yard, visiting Herman, playing with River, listening to Edison work with his tools and watching busy squirrels steal away the last of the figs.

Kate's somber mood was interrupted by Mary poking her head out the back door.

"Kate, Tessie called to say she needs your help in the orchard."

Bolstered by the invitation, Kate ran straight away out the back gate with her bike, and by the time Edison asked her what her hurry was all about, she was already at break speed. She heard him faintly and bemoaned the question.

"What's my hurry? What's my hurry, he asks? Summer is almost over and Tessie needs my help. That's what I would tell him," she said out loud.

⚓ ⚓ ⚓

"IT'S NEAR 'BOUT HURRICANE SEASON," Tessie said while they picked the last of the peach crop.

"Hurricane Hazel near 'bout did us in," she began, as she told Kate about the hurricane of 1954.

Kate was captivated by the tale of the far wharf washing away, pausing the ferry service for some time, and the town being cut off from the mainland at the causeway by the flood tide. The story was a lengthy one and they had peeled, sliced and sugared all the peaches they picked during Tessie's soliloquy. The giant canner began to boil as they filled the last of her quart jars with the sugared peaches. Steam filled Aunty's kitchen when she lifted the lid and pulled up the basket with a pair of tongs.

"It's a lot of work now," commented Tessie, "but we'll be happy we did this when the cold sets in. There's nothing like a local peach in the dregs of winter."

Kate agreed and happily handed her the readied jars one by one until the basket was full. Tessie then lowered the basket into the boiling water and set her timer. A few sweet peaches were left over and they each grabbed a fork and promptly ate them, wiping the juice from their chins with paper towels as they enjoyed the last precious slices.

While the hot canner boiled, Tess and Kate shared stories of the summer as if to review the season. They gave it high marks for all the beauty and bounty observed and adventures taken. Kate looked to the corner of the kitchen where a very old, large heavy glass canister sat, handle up. She knew what was in the container but went over and unscrewed the lid to view the contents with fresh eyes. She held up a cookie cutter shaped like Santa's boot.

"This one is my favorite," she said, smiling at Tessie.

The timer dinged and Tessie grabbed her pot holder and

removed the lid. A billow of steam burst upward crawling across the ceiling and then following the walls down to the cabinets. Kate laid a clean thick towel down on the counter and one by one her aunt pulled the jars out with a special tool Kate had only ever seen her use while canning.

"What do you call that thing?" Kate asked.

"A jar lifter," she replied. "The rubber ends keep the jars from slipping, and the rubber on my end keeps my hands from getting burned.

"It's a cool invention," Kate marveled. "I wonder who invented it?"

"I wish I knew," replied Tessie.

The quart jars looked so beautiful sitting on the towel.

"We mustn't disturb them until they are cool, which will be many hours from now. Tell your mother I will drop some by later." She hugged Kate and thanked her for helping as they walked to the door.

Kate jumped on her bike and rode down to the boatyard to see Squawk. Parking her bike as usual, she rounded the corner to Miss Pat's house and her heart bled when she saw that Squawk's cage was empty. "Squawk!" came a loud outburst from the roof and Kate looked up to see Squawk staring down at her. When Kate eyed the duck her heart filled with joy and sadness all at once. She knew this was it, that Squawk was leaving and her eyes welled up with salty river tears and her throat swelled like it had been stung by a nettle.

To her shock, the duck swooped down and landed at her feet. "Oh Squawk!" Kate cried as she flopped down next to her. Squawk turned her head cock eyed as if to watch Kate's emotional pain and take it all in. Kate sat up on her knees and looked her squarely in the eye and pulled herself together.

"I don't know why I am so sad, Squawk, I should be happy for you."

The duck flapped her feathers as if to tell Kate it was time to go. She wiped her tears with the back of her hand and wished her all the luck on the world. Squawk belted out one last burst of duck speak and flew back up to the roof. Kate stood up and waved good bye as Squawk spread her wings and took flight. Circling the house, she buzzed by Kate like a jet and then disappeared over the house towards the river.

Feeling very glum, Kate wandered to Pat's shack and peeked around the corner of the door. Miss Pat looked up from her desk as Kate laid bare the sad departure all the while choking down her grief. Miss Pat stood up walked over and gave her a hug.

"I'm so sorry you didn't get to say goodbye, Miss Pat."

"Oh but I did!"

"You did?"

"Oh yes, this morning she greeted me from her vantage on the roof and then swooped down to see me one last time. Kate, she was waiting for you. She had already said her good-byes to me."

Kate perked up, "Really?"

"Yes, really!"

With this revelation, Kate felt lighter and her tears dried up.

"Wild is as wild does," said Miss Pat, just before her phone started ringing.

"You okay if I get that?"

Kate smiled and nodded and turning to leave, grabbed one last hug from Miss Pat. Running to her bike, she was now on a new mission. She must tell Tansy.

After arriving home, the watercolor set that Miss Lucille gave her was put to the test with Kate diving into a watercolor painting of Squawk flying over Miss Pat's house towards the northeast. She painted the sky just as she had seen it, peppered with silky thin cirrus clouds feathering the robin's egg sky well above Squawk. Once finished, it was set in the sun that shone through the porch screens and made one of the small tables between the wicker chairs very warm. It was then that she breathed in deeply and in doing so caught the vapors of an old familiar smell, stewed tomatoes, signaling the true end of summer.

She ran back to her bike, jumped on and went to the ferry dock. She had just missed Captain Will and he waved to her as the ferry gained momentum. Walking through the cattails on water's edge to the left of the ferry, she picked up an oyster shell from a sandy patch and skipped it across the water, counting the number of times it touched the water's surface.

"Three." She said to herself. "I'll stay until I hit ten." Over and over she skipped shells until finally she found an oyster shell with not much cup at all. The flat shell grazed the river at least a dozen times as if it was walking on it.

Satisfied, she hopped back on her bike and still not ready to return to the smell of stewed tomatoes, she rode all over town. She peddled out to where Miss Dovie kept her houseboat and to where Mr. Jimmy shed his crabs. She buzzed by the lab, over to the Little League ball field, and then all the way to the cemetery where she waved at the ancestors grave stones. She stopped only once, to see if there were any blackberries left, but alas, there were none. It felt good to feel the wind in her face, and to breathe deeply as she peddled to her next destination. She turned down Miss Margie's street then rode on Shell Street with the ditches on her left and past the charred remains of Miss Ginny's boat shed on her right. She noticed the yard workers were almost finished cleaning up the debris from the fire.

Thirst called her home and she arrived to Mary on the phone. "Have you tasted the figs this year? Phenomenal. Of course I will bring you a jar! Talk later," she said as she hung up the phone. Kate's back was turned to her as she drank a cup of water.

"I saw your watercolor drying in the sun."

Kate froze. During her bike ride she had almost forgotten about Squawk and now, with Mary's comment, the sadness of her departure flooded her veins. She slumped and braced herself on the sink, holding back tears as best she could. Mary, reading her body language, came over and hugged her from behind.

"Wild is as wild does." she said.

Kate turned around, surprised. "That's what Miss Pat said when Squawk left."

"Well, it's an old saying around here. I'm surprised you haven't heard it before."

"Maybe I have," Kate replied, "but didn't pay attention, til now."

"Could be," said Mary. "This summer, you seem to be paying attention to many things you didn't when you were younger."

Kate paused and thought about Mary's words. "Maybe that's why my summer has felt like a roller coaster."

Mary agreed, "For sure, you are waking up to the world."

This was so helpful to Kate in that the world seemed more joyful, more painful, more colorful, and more haphazard than it ever had in summers before. She saw everything with bold eyes and an open heart - laid out and ready to be wounded. Mary looked at Kate and smiled, but Kate could tell it was fake.

"Why are you pretending to be happy?" Kate asked. Mary, taken back, paused.

"You think and feel like Jammy and I do, and it is a gift and a curse."

Immediately, Kate understood what Mary meant. "It's hard to live with," Kate said, looking down at her feet. Mary gave her another hug, this time from the front, and whispered in her ear, "I know."

Kate's heart fluttered and in that moment she knew she wasn't alone and would never be alone with her worrisome blessings. Years later, when Jammy and Mary were gone, she would look to the ceiling to ask for their counsel and she knew, even if they didn't answer every question, they were close by helping in ways she may not know or understand because Kate wasn't an angel yet.

For the remainder of August, fig cake was eaten for dessert and fig preserves and biscuits were eaten for breakfast everyday, and

without fail Johnny and Kate would fight over the lemon. One slice went in each jar of preserves and if you were lucky there were two. Candied, sweet and tart, they were worth fighting for. Mary would hand out fig preserves to cousins and couzins, but first, she gave one to Mr. Brown, who was beyond delighted with his gift. Days got shorter and mornings were wetter as dew laid out a thin fragile apron upon the clover, a net trying to capture the last of the lawn's vibrant green.

September arrived by setting evening skies aflame and the first geese to arrive stirred a fall frenzy, their honking sounds warning of the seasonal shift. Although there was much heartache as summer began to wither, Kate thought there nothing more captivating on earth than the flying triangles in the sky the geese made as they headed south.

The last summer dinner before school started, Edison settled upon the idea that Kate should take sailing lessons next summer. That night in bed, the curiosity of it burned in her head as she looked upon the night sky, overcast and dull. The sunset had burned out all color, leaving it dark and murky with a fuzzy muted dull moon trying to break through the frontal cloud cover. She thought back to the earliest part of the summer when Jammy told her the story of the gypsies and how they had no anchors in their life.

Kate thought differently than Jammy. What if anchors just weigh us down? What if we drag our anchors behind us our whole life? Conversely, she thought it lovely to have home and family as her anchor. Perhaps some anchors were good and some were not. Mr. Paul had been anchored to the bottle, which was not a good anchor at all, she concluded. She then thought back to when she set the anchor on Mr. Brown's Jon boat the day they caught a bucket of hard heads. A yawn overcame her and she rolled over in bed thinking fondly of Mr. Brown and how wise he was… soon, Mr. Brown's fishing boat morphed into a pirate ship. Kate and the other ruffian crew were strong and fast and the giant ship sailed through the water as swift as a dragonfly. The wind blew steady and strong behind them as they entered a rocky edged harbor under full, colorful sails. The harbor was filled with sailboats of all colors and sizes.

The captain yelled, "Head to wind!" as he spun the wheel to starboard with his right hand while swishing a sip of sweet buttery rum from his left.

When the boat turned up into the wind and sails slapped a luff, he roared, "Lower ye sails ya dirty swabs!"

While spitting on his own shoe a piece of chew tobacco, he looked towards Kate who stood on the bow. She could see absolutely everything, the men working the sails, the boats in the harbor, the blue sky above and the green river below.

"Kate, ready the anchor and hold her steady, drop her on my mark," he bellowed.

Kate untied the thick, cleated wet rope and held tight to it, bracing against the chock. She stretched her neck to look over the rail on the starboard side to make sure it was free. The anchor swung back and forth, back and forth.

Author's Afterword

Simply put, I wrote this book because I love the Eastern Shore. It is because of this love that the Eastern Shore I knew as a child thrives vividly in my recollections. The passage of time is steadfast, and as I get farther and farther removed from my childhood, I realize that unbeknownst to me, as a child, I was watching the sun set on a culture that would not survive the near future. As time marched on, native inhabitants watched their way of living that had anchored them for generations, fade away.

Native Oxfordians were some of the brightest, hardest-working people I have ever known. The town was replete with a quiet intelligence that never postured. The community sent many of its youth off to college and thoughtfully apprenticed those who stayed to work the water or boatyards under the guidance of wise master boatbuilders and seasoned watermen.

For centuries the boatyards have produced everything from the working skipjack, to Navy Ships, to sleek wooden racing vessels molded to perfection by master craftsmen who know how to bend wood and varnish it the color of a luscious, smooth bourbon.

The watermen were and still are a hardworking, hearty bunch that make one of the toughest jobs in the world look easy. These working men were very keen and had an encyclopedic knowledge of their surroundings, including nuanced absorbed information not written in books but carved into their minds and felt within their bodies by studious, tireless, keen observations of weather, wildlife, and water at work in the microcosm they called home. Nature's beauty and fury taught them patience, persistence, and pragmatism. The hardworking watermen of today honor our Eastern Shore heritage by continuing to provide fresh seafood direct from the Chesapeake Bay and its tributaries.

In 1952, a newly built Chesapeake Bay Bridge connected the Western Shore of Maryland with the Eastern Shore. In doing so, the traditional Eastern Shore culture would become exposed to the wider world, and vice versa. Little by little, native people began to leave town, especially when watermen saw a rapid decline in their catch in the 1980s. As locals began to leave, new people trickled in. Many came to escape the city. Others were inexplicably drawn to the water town by its inherent charm, alluring southern feel, and slower pace of life.

As the decades progressed, the scale tipped towards a more worldly influx. The minimum amount of that special something required to maintain a cohesive interconnected community became fragmented, and an inverse property was at work; what the town gained in stature, it lost equally in old Eastern Shore culture.

Around the same time, communication and information were experiencing a revolution. While technology advanced, many social customs would fade away. Learning from grandparents, scholars, books, nature, and extended family was challenged by YouTube and social media. A communication system is of no value unless there is a critical mass of users. As such, old customs of face-to-face discussion were replaced with hitting send. This societal shift away from human interactions and towards the blue light was not unique to this community. This is just one of many small hamlets where the communication and information revolution would challenge the viability of cultures all over the world.

I find it next to impossible to explain in one word what these changes meant for the future of the town and its generational water culture, but the Welsh have a word for what the locals were and are experiencing: Hireath.

Hireath is a combination of longing and grief for a lost or

specific time and place. It is also the ability to hold tight the love of that time period and to also accept that you cannot go back. The Mora Temporis, or 'time delay', Jammy speaks of in Chapter 7, was very real. Looking back, the town was in a suspension in time in the 1970s. It was in its own and final nexus.

The "golden hour" is the time between light and dark when the sun has just crossed the horizon and light is projected upwards lessening its intensity. It is a surreal, magical time, but it is fleeting. In its golden hour, generational inhabitants became connected by an unexplainable bond—a bond that continues today.

In a world where change seems to be the only constant, many find themselves yearning for something that gives them a sense of belonging, a sense of place. This is what Oxford gave me as a child. Human beings yearn for this, which is perhaps why so many people have a fondness for towns similar to Oxford.

In my lifespan, the way of centuries has faded in a few short decades until only a handful of natives remain. I cherish my time with them and write to preserve what once was.

Acknowledgements

We never reach our goals in life alone. Along the way, friends, family and sometimes strangers help us in ways we don't even recognize until our goals are reached. Keeping this in mind, I would like to express my gratitude to those who encouraged and helped me while writing this novel.

Foremost, my family was a huge help. My husband Brian listened and critiqued as I read countless paragraphs from the novel to him. He edited too. My daughter, Hannah, also helped edit the very first draft. My son, William, developed the website and son, Joshua, created my bookmark. Finally, I am blessed that my daughter, Natalie, keeps a close eye on the family home, the setting of this book.

Jennifer Latham was my executive editor and put countless hours and used up many red pens to keep me in line. I cannot thank her enough. Additional editors and listeners include: Lisa Harrington, Pucky Lippincott, Barbara Cross, Judith Reveal, Casey Cep and Kathryn Schulz.

My illustrators were a delight to work with, and I thank them all:

Patti Hopkins for the gorgeous oil painting of the Oxford Strand. Shelby Clendaniel for creatively capturing that nostalgic feeling with his pencil sketches. And, Peter Hanks who graciously allowed me to use his box turtle watercolor.

For those who helped me and perhaps had no idea they inspired me, I would like to thank Betsy Thompson Willey, longtime resident of Oxford. Susan Benson, Nancy Howard, and Rusty and Debbie McKay and their gifts of history from the Benson house, including trusting me with the care of Sara Benson's journals. They have given me much joy. Your kindness and generosity embodies the spirit of old Oxford.

Recipes

R ecipes from the book are nothing fancy, just old fashioned good food. That being said, some 50 years later, my how food has changed! My family has multiple allergies and intolerances so I used substitutions for some of the recipes and they turned out well. For example, I used King Arthurs Measure for Measure Gluten Free flour in place of wheat flour. I used almond milk in place of cow's milk. I used a butter substitute or oil in place of butter.

There are no recipes for the deviled eggs or fried chicken because there is none. They were just made. The biscuit recipe was also not written down, but I have included a similar one.

— Savories —

Ham Salad

1 # from cooked butt or shank, small dice

2 T minced celery	2 T minced scallion
1 T pickle relish	½ cup mayo
⅓ cup sour cream	⅛ tsp black pepper or to taste
½ tsp dried dill	

Mix all ingredients together. Serves 4-6 ppl. Good for tea sandwiches if diced very small.

Pan-Fried River Fish (spot, perch, croaker, rock)

Dredge fillets in a mixture of equal parts flour and cornmeal. Season to taste with salt, pepper and Old Bay. Pan fry in light oil, turning halfway through cooking.

Old Fashioned Potato Salad with Cooked Dressing

2 qts. cooked potatoes cut in pieces and cooled
½ sweet onion, diced small
¼ red onion, diced fine
2 ribs celery, diced small
¾ of a green bell pepper, chopped small
Celery seed (important) to taste
Salt & pepper to taste

Place all in a large bowl and mix. Refrigerate.

Cooked Dressing

2 eggs (beaten)   2 cups sugar
1 cup white vinegar   1 cup water
3 T prepared mustard   2 T cornstarch

Combine all dressing ingredients, whisk together and bring to a boil, stirring often.

Cool and use about ½ of the dressing on the potato salad. The remainder will keep in the refrigerator for a week or so and can be used on coleslaw too. When combining dressing and potato salad ingredients, everything should be cold.

Coleslaw

½ large cabbage or one small, cut in small pieces

2 carrots, shredded

1 TBS sugar

⅔ cup mayonnaise

2 TBS apple cider vinegar

⅔ cup sour cream

½ tsp each salt and pepper

Mix all ingredients together well. Add more sour cream, mayonnaise or seasoning as needed. Put into refrigerator. Serves about 6-8.

Biscuits

2½ cups flour

½ stick of butter or ¼ cup shortening

Dash of salt

1 TBS baking powder

1 cup milk

Combine flour and baking powder. Cut in butter or shortening until it is in very small pieces. Make a well and pour milk in. Stir until just combined - do not over mix. Roll out on floured surface about 3/4 inch thick. Cut with biscuit cutter and place on greased or parchment lined cookie sheet. Bake at 400 degrees for about 15 minutes or until done.

Sweet Cornbread

1 cup cornmeal

1 cup flour

6 TBS sugar

1 egg

4 tsp baking powder

½ tsp salt

1 cup buttermilk

1/4 cup vegetable oil

Mix dry ingredients in a medium bowl and then form a well in the middle. Separately beat the buttermilk, egg and oil together and then pour into the well and mix ingredients. Mix thoroughly but do not over mix. Pour into greased 9x9 greased Pyrex pan, or greased muffin cups. Bake at 375 degrees for about 20 minutes for the pan. About 15 minutes for muffins.

Toothpick should come out clean. Can also be baked in 9" cast iron skillet; check at 15 minutes.

Buckwheat Pancakes

1 cup buckwheat flour	½ cup flour
1 TBS sugar	¾ tsp baking soda
½ tsp salt	1¼ cups milk
2 TBS lemon juice or vinegar	4 TBS melted butter
1 tsp vanilla extract	1 egg

Combine dry ingredients. Make a well in the middle and add the wet ingredients. Mix until combined. Unused batter can be refrigerated and used the next day.

Jammy's Stewed Tomatoes

2 lb garden tomatoes, cut in chunks	½ stick butter
¼ cup flour	½ tsp salt
¼ tsp pepper	¼ tsp allspice
1 TBS sugar	

Melt the butter until it begins to turn brown. Add tomatoes, and stir. Sprinkle the flour, allspice, salt, pepper and sugar on top and stir in. Cook at medium until thickened and cooked through. Stir often. Should be done in about 15 minutes or until the consistency you like. Can be made a day ahead. Serve warm or cold. Makes about 4 cups. Serves 6ish.

— Sweets —

Zucchini Bread

1 cup sunflower or canola oil	3 cups shredded zucchini
3 cups flour	1 TBS baking soda
1 TBS cinnamon	¼ tsp baking powder
Pinch of salt	3 eggs
2 cups sugar	1 TBS vanilla

Preheat oven to 350 degrees. Combine oil and zucchini. Mix dry ingredients. Beat eggs with sugar until light. Add vanilla. Mix egg mixture with zucchini mixture and then add flour mixture a little at a time. Beat well after adding. Bake in preheated oven.

Bundt pan - 1 hour

2 loaf pans - 50-55 minutes

3 -1.lb. coffee cans - 50-55 minutes

Church Supper Baked Pineapple

¼ lb butter or margarine	½ cup sugar
Pinch salt	4 eggs
15 oz can crushed pineapple, drained	
5 slices of bread broken into small pieces	

Cream butter; add sugar and salt and mix. Add eggs one at a time, then pineapple, then bread. Place in greased casserole dish. Bake at 350 degrees for 45 minutes or until done.

Blueberry Pie

Pastry for 9 inch pie   ¾ cup sugar
½ cup all purpose flour   ½ tsp cinnamon (optional)
6 cups fresh blueberries   1 TBS lemon juice
Cinnamon & sugar mix (¼ cup sugar to 2 tsp cinnamon)

Heat oven to 425 degrees. Prepare pastry. Mix sugar, flour, and cinnamon in large bowl. Stir in blueberries and lemon juice. Put into pastry lined pie plate. Place top crust, seal and flute adding a slit in the middle and prick with a fork for steam to escape. Brush finished top crust with cold water and lightly sprinkle some cinnamon sugar mix (there should be some left over). Bake for about 35-45 minutes or until blueberries start bubbling up through the crust. Cool on wire rack. Refrigerate any leftovers.

Peach Pie

Pastry for a 9-inch, 2-crust pie   ⅔ cup sugar
⅓ cup all purpose flour   ¼ tsp ground cinnamon
6 cups sliced peaches (6-8 medium)   1 tsp lemon juice
Cinnamon & sugar mix (¼ cup sugar to 2 tsp cinnamon)

Heat oven to 425 degrees. Prepare pastry. Mix sugar, flour, and cinnamon in a large bowl. Stir in peaches and lemon juice. Put into pastry lined pie plate. Place top crust, seal and flute adding a slit in the middle and prick with a fork for steam to escape. Brush finished top crust with cold water and lightly sprinkle some cinnamon sugar mix (there should be some left over). Bake for about 40-45 minutes or until peaches start bubbling up through the crust. Cool on wire rack. Refrigerate any leftovers.

Chess Pie

8" pastry pie crust	3 eggs
1 cup sugar	2 TBS yellow corn meal
1 TBS apple cider vinegar	½ cup melted butter
1 TBS vanilla	

Preheat oven to 425 degrees. Place prepared pie crust in the oven for about 8-10 minutes or until it is just beginning to turn light brown. Take out of oven. Reduce heat to 350 degrees and prepare filling. Whisk together all 3 eggs well and then mix rest of the ingredients, adding melted butter last. Do not over mix. Pour into pie crust shell and bake at 350 degrees for about 35 to 40 minutes. The pie is done when the filling is set and there is a thin brown crust over top. Serve warm. Rich, buttery deliciousness.

Tessie's Apple Cake

5 TBS sugar	3 tsp cinnamon
4 or 5 apples (Granny Smith work well)	
2 cups sugar	1 cup canola oil
4 eggs	2½ tsp vanilla
¼ cup orange juice	3 cups flour
3 tsp baking powder	

Preheat oven to 350 degrees. Grease tube pan. Mix 5 TBS of sugar with 3 tsp. cinnamon and set aside. Peel and very thinly slice apples and set aside. Mix 2 cups of sugar with oil. Add eggs, one at a time, then vanilla and orange juice and mix. Layer: batter, apples, cinnamon & sugar. Repeat layers 2 more times. Bake for 1 hour 20 minutes. Check with toothpick to make sure insides are done.

Mrs. Crossett's Famous Rum Cake

1 package yellow cake mix	1 small box instant vanilla pudding
4 eggs	½ cup cold water
½ cup Crisco oil	½ cup dark rum
1 cup of chopped pecans	

Preheat oven to 325 degrees. Grease a Bundt pan. Put nuts in the bottom of the pan. Mix all other ingredients until well combined. Pour cake mixture over nuts and bake at 325 for 50 min. Let cool a little and then turn out onto a plate. Cool completely.

Glaze

¼ lb. butter	¼ cup cold water
1 cup confectioner's sugar	½ cup dark rum

Melt butter; add water and sugar and bring to a boil. Stir vigorously for 5 minutes. Remove from heat and pour in the rum. After cake cools, make holes in the top of cake and drizzle glaze into the holes and over top of cake gradually until all the glaze is used up. Tastes best if made a day or two ahead so the flavors can marinate.

Ida May's Fig Preserves

1 to 1 ratio of peeled whole figs to sugar
Do not make any less than 4 pounds of figs at once
        (8 pounds total ingredients in the pot)

For every 4 pounds of figs, slice and add two fresh lemons. Add just enough water in the bottom of the pan so it doesn't burn in the beginning (no more than ½ cup). Cook at low heat stirring often until the figs cook down and the mixture begins to thicken. May take about 4 hours or so. Spoon into jars and process if canning. It can be kept in the refrigerator for several weeks.

Fig Cake with Candied Lemons

1 cup sugar	2 cups flour
1 tsp baking soda	1 tsp salt
1 tsp ground cinnamon	1 tsp allspice
½ tsp ground cloves	1 tsp ground nutmeg
1 cup sunflower oil	1 cup milk
3 eggs	1 cup fig preserves
2 tsp lemon extract	1 cup coarse chopped walnuts

Preheat oven to 325 degrees. Combine dry ingredients, add oil and beat. Add eggs and beat one minute. Add milk and lemon extract. Stir in preserves and walnuts. Bake in greased Bundt pan for about an hour. Cool, then slice and serve with candied lemons.

Candied Lemons

1 cup sugar
1 cup water
2 TBS lemon juice
2-3 whole lemons, cut thinly

In large fry pan, combine sugar, water, and lemon juice and cook on low heat, until combined. Increase to medium heat and bring to a boil, then reduce to simmer and add the sliced lemons. Cook for 15 minutes, turning a few times. Place on wire rack to thoroughly dry. May store in refrigerator for up to 2 weeks.

Lemon Sauce

1 TBS cornstarch dissolved in small amount of water
½ cup sugar   1 cup boiling water
1 TBS butter   Lemon zest from ½ lemon
¼ cup lemon juice

Combine and bring to a boil. Stir constantly until sauce thickens.